Praise for *The Perfect Assassin*

"*The Perfect Assassin* is one of those rare books that manages to be both thrilling and tender. It's full of rooftop fights, frightening magic, and nonstop excitement and mystery, while at the same time it's a thought-provoking exploration of what it means to be a monster and the power of love and forgiveness. I absolutely loved it from start to finish!"

—Sarah Beth Durst, award-winning author
of the Queens of Renthia series

"K. A. Doore has crafted a thrilling and poignant tale on the costs of loyalty. In the city of Ghadid, ideas of justice and family battle and braid themselves around each other in action-packed fashion. Part murder mystery, part family saga, part coming-of-age chronicle, *The Perfect Assassin* intrigues and excites in equal measure."

—Tochi Onyebuchi,
author of *Beasts Made of Night*

"In a high-flung desert city, a reluctant assassin's choices threaten his family's way of life, those he loves, and, worst of all, the spirits of the dead. Amastan Basbowen's options are all dangerous, but he must move forward. The ensuing intrigue forms the core of a highly exciting adventure."

—Fran Wilde, Hugo- and Nebula-nominated,
Andre Norton Award–winning author of *Updraft*

"Set in a world of believable richness, *The Perfect Assassin* combines a suspenseful plot with a memorable cast of characters, and an assassin protagonist who is compelled to make hard choices."　　　　—Ilana C. Myer, author of
Last Song Before Night and *Fire Dance*

BY K. A. DOORE

The Perfect Assassin

The Impossible Contract

The Unconquered City (forthcoming)

THE
PERFECT
ASSASSIN

K. A. DOORE

TOR®
fantasy

A TOM DOHERTY ASSOCIATES BOOK
NEW YORK

This is a work of fiction. All of the characters, organizations, and events portrayed in this novel are either products of the author's imagination or are used fictitiously.

THE PERFECT ASSASSIN

A Tor Book
Published by Tom Doherty Associates
120 Broadway
New York, NY 10271

www.tor-forge.com

Tor® is a registered trademark of Macmillan Publishing Group, LLC.

ISBN 978-1-250-20855-2

Our books may be purchased in bulk for promotional, educational, or business use. Please contact your local bookseller or the Macmillan Corporate and Premium Sales Department at 1-800-221-7945, extension 5442, or by email at MacmillanSpecialMarkets@macmillan.com.

First Edition: March 2019
First Mass Market Edition: May 2020

Printed in the United States of America

0 9 8 7 6 5 4 3 2 1

To Hazel, for arriving at exactly the right moment and being my rock in this hurricane

1

The wind tore at Amastan's wrap, trying to slide warm fingers beneath the fabric and unravel the knots. It tasted of heat and dust, the only products of the sands that stretched endless before him. His tagel kept the worst of the sand from getting into his mouth and between his teeth, but he still had to squint to see through the onslaught.

If he turned and wove back between the buildings, the wind would taper and calm. But here on the edge of the city—on the edge of the platform—there was nothing between him and the sky and the sands several hundred feet below.

The sun had set and night fell fast. Straight east, the first stars began to appear. In another hour, the moon would rise and fill the void that the sun had left, but until then Amastan would have only the light the stars gave him.

It would have to be enough.

"The unshakeable Amastan isn't *scared,* is he?" taunted Dihya.

His eldest cousin stood to one side, her thick, muscular arms crossed. When he glanced her way, Dihya flashed him a smile that was all teeth. Amastan didn't reward her with a response.

Silently, he reviewed for the fifth—okay, sixth—time the assortment of tools he'd brought. Rope, chain, knives, gloves, water, shoes. He touched the charm that hung between his collarbones. Its leather was soft and bulged with the usual herbs for protection. But for this journey, the charm maker had added a scrap of vellum inked with words that would protect him from jaan. At least, the charm maker had insisted it would. Amastan hadn't exactly had a chance to test it in the city.

Fear tightened his chest at the thought of jaan. He pushed the fear away, breathing deep and focusing on the steps he'd take to complete this one, final test. A dizzyingly long drop and a short sprint across the sands was all that stood between him and becoming an assassin. While deceptively simple, Tamella had built this test around his weaknesses: strength, stamina, and a willingness to be flexible.

He couldn't help but wonder if, on top of all that, Tamella had known about his fear of jaan. Nothing got past his teacher, but then again, that specific fear had never come up during their years of training. He knew. He'd been careful about that.

The wild jaan below were little more than stories. Jaan were as rare as storms. He had nothing to fear but the time limit and, if he failed, Tamella's disappointment. He wouldn't run up against either with the right mindset and planning. He could do this. He *would* do this.

"Why're you stalling?" asked Azulay, almost shouting as he overcompensated for the wind.

"Stop pestering him," said Menna. She bounced up and down on her toes, betraying her own impatience.

Dihya, Azulay, and Menna had trained with him almost daily for the last five years. The four of them were this generation's candidates, handpicked by Tamella to carry on the family's secret, bloody tradition. In the beginning, the only thing they'd had in common was a very loose relation by blood and the family name they could claim if they wanted. Now, they shared calluses and scars, hopes and dreams, fears and nightmares. Now, they were cousins.

The other three had already completed their tests, each tailored to their particular weaknesses. Amastan had watched each of them pass with increasing trepidation. Tamella had promised that one of them would fail. And now here he was, the only cousin that remained.

"I just want him to go already," whined Azulay. "I could be sleeping instead of standing out here, getting sand in my teeth."

"Sleeping? Really?" Dihya's voice was heavy with skepticism. "Don't you mean losing baats gambling with the caravanners?"

"No. I mean sleeping." Azulay paused, then added, "There aren't any caravans at the end of season and you know it."

"They'll return in a few weeks with the rains, don't worry," said Dihya. "Now, can't you enjoy watching your cousin sweat a simple climb with us? It's not often you get to see 'Stan nervous."

"I'm not nervous."

Amastan immediately regretted rising to the bait. Dihya laughed at him and his cheeks and ears warmed with the rush of embarrassment. Thankfully, his tagel hid any sign of his awkwardness from his cousins. He could've worn his tagel low tonight, since he was among family, but he'd chosen to wear it high, above his nose but just below his eyes to protect against the blowing sand.

"I'm sure Tamella was joking when she said one of us would fail," said Menna.

This time, Azulay laughed, high and sharp. "Have you *ever* heard the Serpent joke?"

"Shut up, Az'," said Menna. "I'm trying to give him some confidence."

Amastan closed his eyes, ignoring them both. He took a deep breath, then cast away all of his doubts and focused on the task at hand. It was simple, really.

First: he had to get down to the sands.

A metal cable hung above his head and plunged from the edge of the platform into the thickening darkness. Somewhere below, its other end was affixed to a large pole dug deep into the sands. During the day, a carriage descended on that wire to pick up anyone waiting below. Now, at night, the carriage was locked in place at his back.

He wouldn't be unlocking it; Tamella had made it clear that he couldn't take a carriage down. One would be waiting for him on the sands beneath the next neighborhood, but it was up to him to find a way to it in the allotted time.

Amastan adjusted his tagel and wrap, testing the knots and pulling the fabric taut. Then he uncoiled his rope with a flick of his wrist. He wound the rope around his waist twice, looping it through his belt each time, before pulling a length of chain from the bag at his feet. Fabric wove through the links on both ends and covered the metal in cloth. He tied the rope to one end of the chain, then stood on his toes and tossed the chain over the cable. He caught it and tied off the other end.

With both hands overhead to keep the chain from slipping down the cable, he paused to reassess his preparations. Had he forgotten anything? He had two sheathed blades at his waist and a smaller knife strapped to his bicep. Charm pouch. Full water skin. Wrap and tagel were knotted tight. He even had a fire striker and tinder. Just in case.

He had everything he needed and time was falling fast. Yet he hesitated. Why?

Sometimes, said his sister Thiyya in the back of his head, *you don't even know when you've been possessed by a jaani.*

Thiyya had liked to frighten him with tales about jaan and madness when he was young. In Ghadid, the jaan were little more than words whispered late at night to scare children, yet Amastan had never been able to shake his fear of them. Now dread squeezed his throat as he faced the reality that he would have to walk on the very sands where the jaan weren't just stories. Jaan that struck travelers mute and made it impossible to find any path. Jaan that entered minds and drove men mad. Jaan that made you forget who you were.

"Right," said Amastan, pushing away his fear with that one word.

And with that, he took one, two, three steps to the edge of the platform and—before he could think—a fourth step onto nothing.

Amastan dropped. Someone gasped. Not him: he was holding his breath to keep from screaming. Down, down, with just enough time to panic—then a jolt as the cable caught his weight and now he was truly falling, flying forward into dizzying darkness. The screech of metal chain on metal cable was almost as loud as the wind wailing in his ears. Despite his care, his wrap caught and flapped in the rush.

The chain warmed, then turned hot, the metal burning his hands even through the cloth he'd wrapped around it. He glanced back once to see the pale glow of the platform reeling away like a horrible dream. The friction between the chain and the wire spit up a trail of sparks that dazzled his eyes and soon hid the platform's glow.

It was much easier to face forward, his knees curled up to reduce drag. If he tucked his chin in, just so, then he avoided the worst of the wind. Still, his eyes watered and smarted as he sped down, down, down toward the smear of darkness below.

Soon he burned all over, from his abdomen to his shoulders to his hands. He tightened his grip on the chain despite the pain of forming blisters. Just another moment, then another—

Suddenly, the ground was more than a blur. He could make out the lines and ridges the wind had sculpted in the sand. Amastan could see where the cable terminated at a long metal pole that grew from the ground like a miniature pylon. A pole he'd run smack into if he didn't do something, *fast*.

He twisted the chain around the wire until its screech was louder than the wind. He slowed down, but not enough. The pole was coming at him like an angry camel. He pulled harder and the chain burned as hot as fire. All he wanted was to let go, but now he'd slowed from a panicked gallop to an ambling run.

The pole was a dozen yards away, a dozen feet—finally Amastan let go and dropped the remaining short distance to the sand. The rope around his waist caught and stopped him from falling face-first. The chain kept sliding until it hit the pole with a loud *clang* that was swallowed by the emptiness all around him.

Fingers shaking, Amastan undid the rope's knots and unwound it from his waist. He coiled it tight and slipped it through his belt. He fished the chain out of the sand and held it by its tattered cloth, the metal still too hot to touch. Then he swore under his breath and dropped the chain, letting the sand claim it. The links at its center were all but melted through. Another few seconds and it would've snapped.

He pushed the thought away. Another few seconds would've seen him swimming through sand. It was nothing to worry about.

Amastan turned in place, scanning every inch of his surroundings. Sand, sand, and more sand. But when he looked closer, there was more than just sand. Small rocks were scattered across the landscape, clustered close to the pole. The persistent wind had shaped the sand into patterns and ridges. Farther away the sand rose and fell in bumps and bubbles like the surface of rising bread.

Farther still, a wide swath of darkness cut through the sand and sky and rose impossibly straight and impossibly far: a pylon. A circular platform capped the pylon, a faint glow delineating its edges against the night sky. More pylons broke the ground and the sky to the west, spreading north and south in a gradual curve that hugged the Wastes. There were easily hundreds of them, each holding up its own circular platform and life.

Ghadid. The city looked so distant and empty from beneath. Amastan realized how bizarre it must appear to the iluk who spent their entire lives down here. He wished he could see it during the day.

The wind picked up, whispering and reminding him that time was falling. He counted the pylons nearby, placing them on his mental map of Ghadid. He needed to go to the next neighborhood to find the carriage, which meant he needed to head for the—one, three, five—*seventh* pylon away. He could just barely discern its hulking shadow in the darkness. He would have to run to make it in time.

He unslung the sand shoes on his back. They'd cost more baats than they were worth, but that was the price he'd had to pay, wanting an iluk item when no iluk were around. The leather straps were already perfectly set for his bare feet. He had the shoes on and tightened within seconds.

The sand felt more like firm ground. He took a few steps, then jogged a few more. The sand was slippery and deceptive, but if he put his foot down just *so,* he wouldn't lose his balance. Good.

A dim, silvery glow hulked on the horizon: the moon threatening its arrival. He had until the moon had fully risen to make it to the carriage. Twenty, thirty minutes, maybe. Enough time to traverse the same distance up above, in the city. Down on the sands, with no buildings or bridges between him and his destination, it should take even less time.

So why did he feel so nervous?

He ran. He stumbled a few times before finally finding his stride. The shoes were wider than camel feet and helped spread his weight out across the sands and keep him from sinking. But the extra width was tricky to walk with, let alone run. He fixed his gaze on the direction he needed to go and didn't think about how open and empty his surroundings were. The sands extended forever on all sides, leaving him nowhere to shelter or to hide. He was exposed. Alone.

Except.

Except he didn't *feel* alone. The back of his neck prickled as if someone, somewhere was watching him. But that was impossible. No one could see him from the city and no one else would be down here this late in the season, when all the wells were dry.

No one sane, anyway.

Just the wind, he told himself.

Jaan ride the wind, whispered his sister late at night as the wind whistled through the cracks of their home. The candles had flickered and spat, sending shadows skittering across Thiyya's grim smile.

He glanced back. He couldn't help it. But there was nothing except sand, dark and starlit. The night had already swallowed the cable he'd come down on and its metal pole, but he couldn't yet see his destination. He felt displaced. The pylons moved past at an indeterminable and unstoppable rate, as if they were the giant sajaam of old. The only noises were the *shh-shh-shh* of his footfalls, the wet rasp of his breath beneath his tagel, and the wind.

Where *was* the cable? He stared hard ahead, willing the darkness to reveal a hint of metal. He counted the pylons, matching them to the map of Ghadid again. The city he knew so well, he could navigate its rooftops blindfolded. But down here—

He wasn't lost. That was impossible. He'd headed straight north, which should have brought him within spitting distance of the next cable. That is, as long as he'd kept running straight. And he had . . . hadn't he?

The fear he'd been suppressing flared, threatened to overwhelm him. For a moment, he knew he was lost. He'd never find the carriage in time. Tamella would leave him stranded down here until morning and by then he'd be driven mad by a jaani. His mind, his memories, his self—everything would be gone.

Or—he told himself forcefully, shoving his fear back down—*I'll find the carriage and everything will be fine.*

There—a glint in the darkness, a line cutting through the air. The next cable. Relief flooded him and only then did he realize how terrified he'd been. He was going to be fine. He was going to complete this test. Soon he'd be back platform-side, surrounded by his cousins, safe from jaan. He would laugh at his fears. Tamella would congratulate him. And he would never have to come down to the sands again.

Except . . .

Where was the carriage? He'd traced the cable down to its pole, but the pole was empty. In another minute, he reached the pole and stopped. He touched it, reassuring himself that this was real. The pole was still warm with the day's heat. But there was no carriage.

He followed the cable back up with his gaze. He could see the platform, the warm glow of torchlight spilling over its edge, but no movement; nothing approaching. He turned, checked the horizon. The moon had peaked over the edge, but he still had time before it fully rose.

He wasn't too late. So where was it?

Amastan checked the sand around the pole for marks, but there were only his own prints. If *he* wasn't late, was Tamella?

He swallowed, his throat scratchy and dry. He shifted from foot to foot and took a swig of water. The wind picked up. His water skin slipped in his sweaty palms and almost fell. He caught it and rehooked it to his belt with trembling fingers.

Focus . . . focus . . . he needed to focus on his next steps. The carriage would come down. He would be off the sands, soon. He just needed to wait and be patient. Unlike Menna, he was patient. He could wait forever.

The wind swirled around him like a hot breath, hissing in his ears. His heart pounded fast as if he were still running, even as he stood and waited. That feeling of being watched returned.

You can't see a jaani coming, said his sister.

The moon cast off the horizon and rose like a dream into the sky. Its thin light spilled across the sands, casting a million tiny shadows and throwing the pylons into stark relief. Amastan could see better now, almost as well as at midday. That only made everything worse.

He could see the wind swirling across the sand. He could see the dunes in the far distance, a blurred threat. He could see things that he knew weren't there, figures in the corner of his eye that were only shadows when he turned. And he could see that the cable was still empty, that no carriage was on its way.

Dread knotted and weighed down his stomach. Despite the prickly heat, he felt a chill. He realized, then, that the carriage wasn't coming. Of course it wasn't. Tamella was testing his weaknesses, not his strengths. He'd prepared for exactly what she'd told him to prepare for, but the test was more than that. If he was patient, he would fail.

Would that be so bad? Tamella expected one of them to fail and it might as well be him. After all, he was the one who'd begun to wonder whether or not he could really be an assassin. It'd all been fun when it was theoretical: a set of skills to master, a family legacy to uphold. But as the day of his final test approached, the reality of his new profession set in. Doubt had spread its smoky tendrils through him as the question he'd brushed aside so easily in the beginning returned like a wild jaani whispering in his ear:

Could he kill?

Something hissed, angry and sudden. Amastan whipped around, a knife already in his hand. But there was nothing, no one, for as far as he could see. His heart thudded, heavy as a rock. The hiss came again, but this time he realized it was only the wind rushing across the sand. The emptiness was getting to him.

Never mind failing. He had to get off the sands. The carriage wasn't coming, wouldn't come, and there was only one other way up.

He took the sand shoes off first and left them next to the pole. He used his knife to cut a notch in the bottom of his wrap, then tore off a long strip. He cut the strip in two and wound one piece between his fingers and across his palm. He tied a knot just below his wrist. He balled his hand into a fist, adjusted the fit, then did the same to his other hand.

With his hands protected, he unwound the rope from his belt. Like before, he looped it twice around his waist and tossed one end over the cable. This time, he twisted a loose knot around the cable before tying the rope off at his belt. He tested the knot. It slid up the cable until he put his weight on it, then it tightened and held. Good.

He squatted deep, then leapt high, grabbing the cable at chest level. With a heave and a swing, he hooked one leg over it. He hung sideways for a breath, then he swung the other leg over. He swayed upside down from the cable while he tested his weight and strength. Then he made the mistake of sighting along the cable at the distance he must climb. It was so far.

Too far.

The words were so low he almost thought they were his own. The wind had picked up, its hiss become a whistle become a low moan. Amastan hummed a prayer, then focused on the cable right before his eyes. Hand over hand, foot by foot—that was his plan.

He began climbing.

The cable was taut enough that it didn't swing, but it bounced just a little each time he moved. He held tight with one hand and reached as high as he could with the other. He followed his hand with his body, pushing off the cable with his legs while he pulled with his arm. Then he slid the knot the half foot or so he'd climbed before repeating the whole process.

Too far, said thoughts that were not his.

Jaan talk in your voice, said his sister, eyes alight with candle glow.

Was his charm hotter than before? The wind louder? For a moment, all Amastan could do was hold on, paralyzed by his fear. But he had to move, had to get away. So he kept climbing.

The first few minutes were easy. His arms were strong and he made it several feet before taking a break. He looped his arms around the cable and hung for a moment, his muscles burning.

Too far, said the jaani. But this time Amastan ignored it.

The next few minutes were more difficult. His muscles kept burning, even when he rested. Minutes blurred into hours and days and became endless and Amastan refused to think about anything but the next movement. Slip the knot forward, stretch, grab, pull. Ignore the sharp pinch and the growing fatigue in his shoulders. Repeat. Repeat. Repeat.

He only made the mistake of gauging the remaining distance once. While he could see the platform's edge, it was still miles and miles away. For a moment, his stomach plummeted. He wondered what was so bad about letting go and falling. Everything hurt, everything burned, and he couldn't possibly go any farther. But this time, there was no voice in his head.

This realization gave him a burst of energy. He brought his gaze back to the cable and slipped the knot farther along. Stretch. Grab. Pull.

When he finally crossed the platform's edge, he didn't notice. His outstretched hand touched cooling metal and he started out of his trance. He looked up to see a carriage in his way. Then he looked down.

He hung above the platform, having crossed over the edge several feet ago. He stared at the solid ground so tantalizingly close, but his arms and legs were too stiff to move. He'd have to hang here until morning, when the watchmen would find him and unhook his limbs.

"Congratulations, Amastan," said a voice from the darkness. "You've passed. Now stop being ridiculous and come down from there."

2

The voice cut through Amastan's exhaustion. He opened eyes he didn't remember closing and blinked away sand. The speaker stood near his feet, their back to the moon.

"Just drop. It's only a few feet."

Amastan slowly unhooked one leg, then the other. Once his ankle passed the cable, his lower body dropped and his bare feet hit solid ground. Wonderful, G-d blessed, solid ground. He kept one hand on the cable to steady himself as he swayed. When he was confident that he wouldn't topple over and off the edge of the platform, he looked at the speaker: Tamella Basbowen, the Serpent of Ghadid, the most dangerous person on or off the sands. His teacher.

Tamella was a half inch shorter and equally lithe. Her muscles were smooth cords that shifted beneath her skin when she moved, her strength apparent in the way she held herself, loose but ready. She wore a dark brown wrap that matched her skin. Her hair had been woven into three thick braids and twisted into a knot at the base of her neck. Silver streaks ran through her otherwise black hair and claws crinkled at the edges of her sand-brown eyes.

Grinning, Tamella stuck out her hand. Three large brass rings studded her fingers. Amastan knew what was in those rings—poisons to make you sick or stop a heart—but took her hand anyway.

He'd expected to feel excitement when he passed his test, or at least relief. But all he felt was exhausted and sore.

"Now what, ma?" he asked, hoping the answer included a pillow and bed.

Tamella's grin faltered, but didn't fade. "Right. What next? Well—I have one last lesson for the four of you."

That didn't sound like bed. "Tomorrow?" asked Amastan hopefully.

Tamella shook her head, her grin finally fading. "Now. It may be the most important lesson of your training, and you need to understand it, even if . . ." She trailed off, her gaze sliding away. "Well, I'll get to that, too." She turned and snapped her fingers at him. "Come. The others are already there, waiting for us."

"Where?"

But Tamella didn't answer and Amastan hadn't expected her to. She took off at a fast walk, her long stride forcing Amastan into a jog to keep up. Then she rounded a corner and by the time Amastan reached it, she'd disappeared.

He didn't bother following the narrow alley any farther. He knelt and ran his palms along the stones, picking up the fine sand accumulated there. He straightened and rubbed his hands together to clean off any oil or sweat. He gave the wall a cursory glance, picking out divots and pockets in the well-worn and sun-bleached bricks.

Then he began to climb.

His arms and shoulders protested, but the sharp soreness soon gave way to a dull ache. It was only a few seconds' climb to the roof. Tamella hadn't waited; she was already halfway to the next rooftop and lengthening her stride into a run. Her movements were smooth and effortless, graceful as a cat. Trying to match her now made Amastan feel every imperfection and misstep.

Tamella slipped ahead. She leaped from rooftop to rooftop with ease, finding the narrowest space between them without any hesitation or thought. She knew Ghadid's roofs better than anyone alive and she could be on the opposite side of the city in half the time it would take even Menna, the fastest of his cousins.

Amastan had to slow down to make the jumps and occasionally resorted to finding a board to cross. Tamella pulled even farther ahead, became little more than a silhouette against the dark sky.

Thankfully, she didn't lead him too far. After crossing several platforms, Tamella disappeared over the side of a roof instead of leaping across. Amastan clambered down to the ground below and found himself in a small courtyard, a squat building across the way. Dread dropped like a rock into the pit of his stomach as he realized exactly where they were.

Tamella had brought him to a crypt.

"No," said Amastan.

But Tamella wasn't close enough to hear. She'd already crossed the courtyard, heading for the crypt. Lamps burned bright on either side of the thick metal door, their orange glass bathing the area around them in a warm, inviting glow. Charms hung all around the door, simple lengths of beads that glittered in the torchlight as well as intricate stringworks. Beneath one of the lamps, a pot brimmed with baats—more than enough to provide a large family with water for several comfortable years. Mourners left behind what they could to pay for the water the marab used.

As he neared, he could make out the intricate carvings in the metal: a network of powerful symbols and words to keep what was inside, inside. He might not have the fear of G-d that his father had tried so hard to instill in him, but he had a healthy fear of the dead. He'd only had reason once to go into a crypt and he never wanted to repeat that experience. Yet here he was, weighing his discomfort and fear against Tamella's displeasure.

One of which easily won out.

Tamella had already gone inside. He eased the door

open with his toe and followed. The door closed behind him, cutting off the torchlight. But he'd seen the railing at the room's center and he knew where he had to go.

Amastan caught the railing with his outstretched hand. He slid his palm along its warm, worn wood until his foot caught on empty space: the top of the stairs. By then his eyes had adjusted to the light that poked around the door's edges and he could tell the difference between the dark room and the true darkness into which he was about to descend.

He took a deep breath. He'd faced the sands alone, where jaan ran wild. He could face a simple crypt, where the jaan were at least quieted. He kept one hand on the smooth stone wall and quested for each step with his toes. Slowly, methodically, in total darkness, he descended.

After the stairs' first turn, the darkness thinned. He could pick out the lines of each step and the uniform gray of the wall under his hand, which had transitioned from stone to metal. After the second turn, the stairs abruptly ended in a door. Light from beneath let him find the handle. It gave under his hand, dispelling any lingering hope that he was in the wrong place, that Tamella was only playing with him and had slipped out a side door.

The marab would never have left this door unlocked.

The door opened onto a curved room filled with syrup-thick light, as stale as the air itself, which was heavily spiced with cinnamon and anise. But beneath the spices was something cloying and rank. Sconces lined the inner wall, each full of oil and flickering flames. Charms hung from the sconces, the nearest one twisting slowly this way and that in a phantom breeze, its beads of colored glass winking and flashing. A shelf, filled with an assortment of scrolls, curved with the wall. A spectrum of darkening browns and yellows told the varied ages of the scrolls. Overall, the room was inviting.

As long as he didn't look at the outer wall.

"'Stan!"

Menna waved him over. She stood with Dihya, Azulay, and Tamella near the inner wall and a couple of woven baskets. One basket was overflowing with vellum sheets, an ink-stained cloth draped over its side: the tools of the marab's trade.

"Good," said Tamella, catching Amastan with her glance and drawing him in. "I thought for a moment I'd lost you." She gave the others a wide, tooth-filled smile. "First, congratulate your cousin. Amastan successfully completed his trial."

Menna grinned and threw her arms around Amastan, squeezing him tight. "Thank G-d!"

"You mean, all of us passed?" asked Dihya, surprised. "I thought you said one of us would fail."

Tamella spread her hands. "Someone usually does."

Azulay thumped Amastan on the back as soon as Menna let him go. "Good on you."

Amastan tried to smile, but he couldn't find the excitement he knew he should be feeling. Now that he'd had a chance to shake out his stiff muscles and pick up a second wind, he couldn't blame his exhaustion for this numbness. He'd been training for this day for so many years, ever since Tamella had appeared in his room one night and explained the family business.

He'd been barely fourteen. His father had been pressing him for years to pick up glasswork like his father had, and his father before him. But Amastan had chosen to apprentice under the historian Barag instead. His father's disappointment had hung heavy over the house and their relationship. Then Tamella had slid in through his window, silent as a shadow. She'd been watching Amastan for years. Every member of the extensive Basbowen family, however far-flung, learned from a young age how to defend themselves.

Amastan hadn't been exceptionally good at defense, but Tamella had been impressed by his precision. The rest of her decision, she'd later explained, was based on pure instinct. She'd told him she'd never been wrong. He'd trusted her.

At the time, becoming an assassin had seemed both exciting and intangible. He'd wanted to learn everything. He knew all there was to know about how to fire glass, but how to fight, how to climb, how to hide, how to conceal, how to poison—he knew nothing. When he'd learned how to kill, he'd been fascinated. A person could die in so many ways. Life was surprisingly fragile.

Amastan had understood that someday he'd have to put everything he'd learned into practice, but *someday* was so far away. Then Tamella had set their trials and someday was no longer a vague, distant point. That's when Amastan had begun to doubt. And doubt had turned to worry. Could he do it? When the time came, could he take a life?

Someday had become today. And now as Azulay thumped his back and Dihya squeezed his hand, Amastan had his answer: he couldn't. Standing here in this room full of the dead was too much for him. Jaan terrified him. All he wanted was to return to his scrolls, safe and free of blood. Maybe he would end up failing after all.

Tamella clapped her hands, drawing their attention back to her. "You might be wondering why I brought you to a crypt."

"I just thought you liked the ambiance, ma," said Azulay.

Tamella flicked a knife into her palm and pointed its tip at Azulay. "Don't cheek me. Not tonight. I cannot stress the importance of this lesson enough. I've brought you here because this'll be the closest you ever get to a jaani in our fair city. That is, unless you thoroughly fuck up. And if you do, not even G-d will help you."

The others exchanged a glance. Amastan kept his gaze fixed on Tamella, not willing to look beyond her. Not yet.

"This is just as important as learning how to hold a knife or climb walls," continued Tamella. "More so. Which is why I'm telling you now, so you can't forget it. No matter how terrible our marks' crimes were, no matter how much they deserved G-d's embrace, no matter your own personal feelings, we must respect death. Honoring the mark's jaani is just as important as planning and executing a contract."

Tamella stepped to the side and gestured at the wall behind her, the outer wall. The wall Amastan had been trying to ignore since he'd entered the crypt.

Dark holes had been cut into the solid metal, continuous rows stacked four high. Tombs. Most held a body, tightly wrapped in gray cloth which had been stained with ink and dust. The bodies were laid feetfirst so that their cloth-covered heads were easily available for the marab. With their heads set at each tomb's mouth, they looked like rows upon rows of inverted eyes.

"Each week," said Tamella, "the marab quiet the jaan of all these bodies. Each body will lie here for seven years until their jaani can be ushered across. Menna can explain the particulars, I'm sure. But what I want—need—to impress upon you is how important the marab's job is. If they miss a jaani, if they miss a single week, then the jaani will go wild. And I'm sure you've all heard stories about the jaan that hunt the sands."

Amastan swallowed, remembering his time on the sands only hours earlier in vivid detail. He didn't need the reminder.

"The marab are the reason why there're jaan on the sands but not in Ghadid," continued Tamella. "A person who dies on the sands, dies alone, with no one around to quiet their jaani. That jaani becomes lost and confused, adrift on the sands. All it wants is what it once had: a warm body to keep it safe. Any warm body will do, especially water-hungry travelers and those foolish enough to cross the sands without protection charms. But here, we have marab to ensure that never happens. And as assassins, we must do our part to make sure it never will."

Tamella held up a finger. "The number one rule in our family—aside from not getting caught and not spilling our secrets—is that we must make certain the body will be found before its jaani can run wild. We aren't murderers."

"How long does it take to go wild?" asked Azulay.

Tamella gestured to Menna. "Our resident apprentice marabi should know the answer to that."

Menna looked at first startled, then pleased. "Five to six hours," said Menna. "It can vary, depending on the person's age and temperament and the time of year, so the rule we follow is no more than three hours, to play it safe."

Dihya frowned. "That shouldn't be hard."

"Exactly," said Tamella. "It's not. But care should be taken that the body is found. Most of our wealthier, older marks have someone to check in on them once a night. They're not a problem. The others—it all comes down to timing and place. This is why a cousin has never shoved a mark off a platform and called it done. We are instruments of G-d and we must act that way." She spread her hands. "Any questions?"

"What if we mess up?" asked Azulay. "What if no one finds the body in time?"

"Oh, that's simple." Tamella smiled. "I'll kill you."

Silence met her avowal. After a heartbeat, Azulay laughed, but it was strained, a noise to fill the void.

"They're just jaan—" he began.

Tamella's smile sharpened with teeth. "And that's where

you're wrong. They're not *just* jaan. The stories you've heard are always about the jaan on the sands and in the Wastes. The anonymous dead whose names have been lost in storms. But these jaan are your neighbors: your charm makers, your gear workers, your watchmen, your stormsayers, your family, your *cousins*. They were people once, alive and whole, and they deserve our respect. G-d created us and gave us each a piece of G-d, if you listen to the marab. We are nothing without G-d, as we are nothing without our jaani. And a jaani unquieted is lost and cannot return to G-d."

"All right," said Azulay. "We get it, ma. We won't hide any bodies."

Tamella stalked toward the tombs. She gestured with her knife. "Azulay. Come here."

Dihya let out a low whistle while Menna tried to hide a snort behind her fist. Amastan could only watch, feeling sick. Azulay sighed and shuffled to Tamella. When he was within a few feet, she grabbed him by the shoulder and pulled him close, her fingers digging deep into his wrap. She pointed at the tomb in front of them, its occupant's shroud more white than gray. Fresher. New.

"This body has been here for three weeks," said Tamella, using the tip of her blade to underline the date on the plaque. "It's been six days since the last quieting ceremony. The marab will return tomorrow. Would you feel comfortable spending the night alone in here? Well . . . I guess it wouldn't be *alone*."

Amastan swallowed, Tamella's threat working even though it wasn't directed at him. Fear prickled his scalp as he tried—and failed—not to imagine being surrounded by so many jaan for an entire night. *Don't you dare antagonize her, Az'*, willed Amastan. If they had to spend the night in this crypt because Azulay couldn't hold his tongue, then he might just cut it out for him.

"Menna—what would happen if, for some inexplicable reason, the marab weren't able to get in here tomorrow morning?" asked Tamella, sweet as a date.

"They would get in." Menna's eyes darted from Tamella to the door and panic spiked her voice higher. "They'd have to get in."

"And if they couldn't?"

"The jaan would begin to untether themselves by the end of the day," said Menna.

"And if someone was trapped in here with them?"

Menna licked her lips, glancing from Azulay's wide eyes to Tamella's sickly sweet smile. "The jaan would possess them. The burden of having two jaan would drive them mad or—or just kill them."

"Have you ever seen this happen?"

"No."

"Why not?"

Menna spread her hands. "Because we make sure it doesn't happen."

"Right." Tamella turned back to Azulay. "So I ask again: do you want to spend the night?"

"Of course not, ma," said Azulay, his voice shaky.

"Then maybe you can begin to understand why it's so important we don't let a jaani loose in Ghadid." Tamella let go of Azulay and pushed him away. "Am I understood?"

"Yes, ma," answered Amastan and his cousins in unison.

"Good." Tamella folded her arms behind her back and assessed them, her lips pressed tight into a thin, grim line. "Now. I have one last thing to tell you. Normally after this lesson, I would wish you luck and turn you loose, trusting that Kaseem would find each of you as needed. But Kaseem won't be visiting, at least not anytime soon." Tamella closed her eyes. "I'd foolishly assumed I wouldn't have to give this talk. That the drum chiefs would've come to their senses by now. But, here we are. Here *you* are." She opened her eyes. "There are no contracts."

The single sentence fell on the room like a thrown stone and it took a moment for them to understand. Azulay gasped, Dihya took a step back, and Menna tilted her head and said, "What?"

But Amastan let out a breath. Could he be so lucky . . . ? No contracts meant no work. No work meant no killing. Assassins only took the lives they were contracted and paid for. Beyond that was murder.

Tamella continued. "There haven't been for some time. Not since . . . well, you don't need a history lesson. Let's just say the drum chiefs placed a ban that should've been lifted by now." She sighed her annoyance. "But the ban *will* be lifted. If not for your generation, then the next. Which is why it's still important that you work on your skills and even more important that you pass them on. What we do is necessary. The drum chiefs will remember that. Someday."

Someday. Not today. Amastan breathed deep, once, twice. His lips twitched up with a smile that he tried to keep hidden beneath his tagel while his cousins grumbled in dismay.

Tamella held up a hand and the grumbling subsided. "I know you're all disappointed that there're no contracts now that you're ready. You might be wondering what the point of all of this was, all the training, the tests, the rules, if you'd never get to *apply* your skills. Why bother, right?"

She paused and waited. They nodded, one by one, Azulay last.

"We're not here for us," she continued. "We're here for Ghadid. As long as Ghadid needs us, we'll keep training new assassins. The contracts are relatively recent in the history of our family. We've persisted through worse. But one thing has stayed constant: Ghadid will always need us. So this may be your last official lesson, but I want you to keep practicing. Keep honing your skills. If not for yourselves, then for the next generation. Ghadid will need us again. And we'll be ready."

3

The words on the vellum blurred and smeared. Amastan set his pen down and dug the heels of his palms into his eyes, willing them to work. But when he tried to focus on the scroll again, the lines ran together as if he'd dropped the vellum in a bowl of water. It was useless. He set the scroll aside.

"Long night?"

Amastan looked up. Barag peered at him across his own pile of scrolls. Three ink bowls sat precariously close to his elbow, but he didn't appear to notice. His unassuming brown wrap was tied loose and he wore his colorless tagel low, just barely hiding the bottom of a wide, flat nose.

Behind him, shelves upon shelves overflowed with tightly wound scrolls. A dozen chests were stacked three high along the far wall, filled with even more scrolls. These, though, were older scrolls or originals of the ones they'd copied and filled the shelves with. A basket held stacks of vellum and parchment, another bundles of string, and a third had neatly stacked jars of ink.

All of it was densely packed and threatening to overflow into the rest of the living area. Yet in the years Amastan had worked with Barag, their tools had stayed on this side of an invisible line. The other side was open and welcoming, the floor swept clean of dust and sand, the pillows fresh if stained. A fire was almost always crackling in the hearth, the kettle full of water and ready for tea.

At least, that was the case for most of the year. As season's end approached, the fire was usually little more than coals and the kettle often empty. Even Barag, who received most of his work from the drum chiefs, was running low on baats.

"I hear congratulations are in order," continued Barag, his voice warm and as light as risen dough. "Although, of course, I know nothing about anything. Especially not what you and my wife were doing last night." He chuckled as if he'd made a joke.

"It doesn't change anything," said Amastan, not sure if he was trying to reassure himself or Barag. "There's no work."

Barag pointed his pen at Amastan, his fingers black with ink. "Don't give up hope. Tamella doesn't waste her time."

Amastan shrugged and leaned back in his chair, grimacing as his stiff muscles protested. "It's okay. I'm relieved, actually. I don't think I could do it."

Barag set his pen down. He looked at Amastan as if he were a barely legible scroll. "Why did you accept, then?"

Amastan fidgeted, unable to meet Barag's gaze. "You know how hard it is to tell Tamella no."

"It's an important skill," said Barag. "She, more than anyone I've known, needs to be told no occasionally."

"It doesn't matter now."

"Oh, but it does." Barag's eyes glittered with amusement. "You trained with her for five years and you only started to doubt now? I . . . *doubt* that."

Amastan shifted uncomfortably. "I wanted to be something more. More than a glassworker. Becoming an assassin would've upheld a tradition spanning centuries."

"So would glasswork," pointed out Barag.

"Yes, but *anybody* can be a glassworker," said Amastan. "It's just heating sand and trying not to burn yourself.

Not everyone gets chosen to become a cousin. Tamella said I'd be good at it, because I never overlooked details. I thought that training would make it easier to do the, well, hard part. The other cousins all looked forward to getting their first contracts, but I . . ." He frowned. "I never did."

"If you wanted to, you wouldn't be the first to leave the family," said Barag carefully.

· Amastan turned the possibility over for a moment. He'd considered leaving many times, but it had never felt right to him. "No. No, I don't want to leave."

Barag steepled his fingers. "And why not?"

"I can still teach the next generation. Or—or something. But I don't want to leave. It's my responsibility."

"Hmm." Barag considered him for a long moment, then pushed himself back in his chair. "You want to uphold a tradition? Then I have a proposition for you. What do you say to taking on a special project of mine? I promise it'll be more fun than transcribing decades-old Circle decisions and cleaning up messy merchants' script."

Some of Amastan's exhaustion flaked away. "Oh?"

"Yes," said Barag. "Get here nice and early tomorrow and I'll start you on a new project. It's been my personal little secret for years, but the drum chiefs would never pay for it, so I haven't given it the time and attention it deserves."

"What is it?"

Barag smiled mysteriously, but he could only hold on to his mystique for so long. "The history of the Basbowen family," he said with no small amount of pride.

The door slammed open before Amastan could pry further. They both jumped at the *bang,* but Amastan also stood, his hand going to his belt. The evening sun poured into the room, backlighting a tall, thick figure. Amastan blinked rapidly against the glare, but already the figure was inside, the door shut. By the time Amastan's vision had cleared, the figure had split in two. The taller one was Usem, Tamella's brother, his high-worn tagel a dusty blue. The smaller was tagel-less—a young girl. Her features were smooth with youth, her skin a glowing dark amber, and she had her mother's sand-brown eyes: Thana.

"Usem," said Barag, rising from his chair just as Amastan relaxed.

Usem raised his hand and Barag sank back down. "Don't let me interrupt, sa. I'm just escorting the young ma home from her lesson."

"If you want to stay for tea, Tamella will be back soon," said Barag.

Amastan wiped his pen clean and capped his ink, then began rolling up the scroll he'd been working on. Thana's return meant the end of his day. Even though her mother was the Serpent, Thana often trained with her uncle. Being the Serpent's daughter had its drawbacks, one of which was that she couldn't risk being associated with her own mother. So Thana spent most of her days with Usem, and her uncle and his wife stood in for her parents at public events. He finished cleaning up his desk and turned to grab his water skin. He nearly jumped out of his own skin when he found Thana standing at his elbow, silent as the stars.

"What do you *do* all day?" she asked. She brushed her fingers across his stacked scrolls, upsetting the one on top. It rolled across the desk and over the edge, but Amastan caught it before it hit the floor. He gently placed it back on top.

"Nothing nearly as fun as what you and your cousins get up to, I'm sure," said Amastan.

"Thanks, but I can't stay," Usem said. "Give my sister my fond regards. And tell her she should be proud of her daughter. The only other person I've ever seen throw a knife that precisely was Tam'."

"I'll pass it along," said Barag, but he sounded weary.

Thana stared intently at Amastan. "Is it true?"

"What?"

"You're an"—she dropped her voice to a whisper—"*assassin*?"

"As of last night," admitted Amastan. He stood and hooked his water skin to his belt, then ran down his mental checklist to make certain he wasn't leaving anything behind or out of place.

Thana stared at him in wonder. "What's it like?"

Amastan shrugged, uncomfortable. It wasn't up to him to tell her about the contract ban. "Not much different than before. You'll see for yourself someday."

"Yeah," said Thana. She reined in her wonder and marshaled her features into a grave mask. "I will."

With that she turned and headed for the stairs. Amastan watched her go as he straightened his wrap and knotted his tagel higher. She couldn't be more than twelve seasons old, yet Usem was already teaching her to throw knives. Most cousins weren't selected for their training until they hit puberty. Of course, there was no question about whether the Serpent's daughter would follow in her footsteps.

Amastan raised his hand to Barag. "I'll see you tomorrow, sa."

"Remember: nice and early," said Barag.

Amastan opened the door to a blast of heat and a sinking sun. He ducked his head against the light and blinked away the glare. When he could see again, he stepped into the hot evening on light feet, feeling the searing heat even through his sandals. Things really weren't that bad. He'd passed his test, but he didn't have to take a contract, perhaps ever. And now Barag was trusting him with a special project. Not just any project: the history of the Basbowen family.

He knew a little about their history, about their place in Ghadid. He knew the family's assassins had played a role in keeping the city safe, from threats both within and without. But Tamella had never been keen on particulars.

She preferred application, and she believed that history couldn't be applied.

Amastan drifted through the streets, which swelled with merchants and errand-kids as the worst of the day's heat dissipated. Home was a neighborhood and two bridges away, but he barely remembered crossing them. He was still in his own thoughts when he shoved the door open with his sore shoulder. The pain jerked him back to the present and he paused in the doorway as noise briefly overwhelmed him.

The acidic warmth of fresh-brewed tea washed over him. A cluster of women sat around the hearth. They'd gathered all the pillows in the room into a heap, stripping the rest of the room bare. His entrance cut their chatter short and half a dozen heads turned toward him. Amastan froze beneath their collective stare.

Then he caught himself and waved, stepping inside. Here were his sisters, an aunt or two, and a collection of close family. Cousins, but related by blood instead of knowledge: the safe kind. Once or twice a week, they got together to share chores and gossip. His youngest sister, Guraya, threaded beads for a charm. His first cousin, Tatrit, wove a wedding scarf. His second cousin, Kura, poured water for tea. And Menna, his cousin by profession instead of blood—

Menna smiled sickly sweet at him and plunged a needle into the heart of a tagel.

"The boys are on the second floor, if you want to join them," said Tatrit, her round face soft and earnest.

"Or you could take a cup and join us." Menna playfully punched Tatrit's arm. "We're celebrating an engagement."

Tatrit dipped her chin and averted her eyes, but she couldn't cover the reddened tips of her pale ears. That explained the wedding scarf. He took a moment to look again at the circle of women. This time, he noticed that his older sister, Thiyya, held a bowl of water in her lap.

A blue glow wrapped gently around Menna's exposed knee. Even as Amastan watched, the bloody scrape that stretched from her knee down her shin closed over with new, pale skin.

Thiyya was a healer, one of the few professions in Ghadid that one was born into instead of trained. Healing required more than a knowledge of herbs and stitches. A healer used water to speed the body's natural healing processes, to replenish blood and close wounds, to heal what would normally kill.

But there was never enough water for all who needed it, and Thiyya shouldn't have been wasting water on mere scratches that would heal on their own. None of the women said anything about Thiyya's egregious use, so Amastan didn't, either. She was still in training and probably needed the practice.

The blue glow released and Thiyya took a deep breath. She passed the bowl to an aunt, who added the remaining water to the kettle. Thiyya sat back and pushed her braids out of her face. As he always did when he saw his sister, Amastan counted the colorful salas that wove through those braids. Every life a healer saved was represented by a piece of cloth or string that they wove into their hair. Since Thiyya was still training, she only had a few. Amastan counted no new ones.

Menna slid her wrap back over her knee and squeezed Thiyya's hand. Menna's expression was soft in a way that Amastan rarely saw. Thiyya was the real reason why Menna had started coming by Amastan's house so often. Menna had made the mistake of looking for Amastan at home once and struck up a conversation with Thiyya. There'd been no turning back. Now Menna treated Amastan like a brother: a younger, annoying, naïve brother.

Guraya piped up. "Are you going to join us or just keep standing there?"

Amastan cleared his throat. "I'll pass on the tea, but

I hope you enjoy yourselves." Then, just to Tatrit, "Congratulations."

His gaze slipped over Menna as he turned for the stairs, and she caught it with a wink. Amastan returned the signal with the smallest of nods. He ascended the stairs slowly, savoring their cool wood against his feet. He passed the second-floor landing, briefly registering the sound of male voices nearby, and kept going. His room was on the third, the only closed door in a line of open ones. Most of his close family slept up here. He shared the house with his father, two aunts, an uncle, and his two sisters. An occasional cousin came and went, but otherwise there were enough of them to fill the house and give it breath.

He slipped into his room and closed the door with a sigh. He only had eyes for his bed, a comforting mess of thin blankets under the window. But that would have to wait.

He turned to the corner next to the door. "You're fast."

Menna stepped out of the shadows, a smirk firmly in place. "You're slow. Now we're gonna have to push it." She started toward the window.

"Wait—where are we going?"

"Practice," said Menna without turning. "We gotta stay sharp somehow."

"Why? There's nothing to stay sharp *for*."

Menna paused next to the window, one hand on the sill. "The drum chiefs could lift the ban at any time. We have to be ready. That means we keep practicing, keep our knives sharp."

When Amastan still hesitated, Menna huffed and turned back around. "What is it, 'Stan?"

Amastan swallowed. "Aren't you—you're not even a little relieved?"

"Relieved?" Menna frowned. "Why? Disappointed, yes. Upset—maybe. Okay, yes. G-d, why wouldn't I be? I've only wanted to be an assassin my entire *life,* 'Stan. I was going to be more than just another marabi. I was going to be special. Shards, I *am* special. I will be more than this." She pushed out a breath as if trying to push away the topic and abruptly turned back to the window.

"Come on."

She threw open the window and climbed out. She stood on the ledge outside and for a moment, all Amastan saw were her shins—one with sleek new skin—and bare feet. Then she disappeared from view as she climbed. Amastan redid one of the knots in his wrap a little higher before following. He caught up to her on the roof.

Menna scanned the roofline. "Where are they?"

"What—they're meeting here?" An edge of panic shot through him. "We should never practice near where one of us lives."

"You worry too much, 'Stan. Of course we're not going to *practice* here. Ho—Dihya!" Menna waved her arms at one of the rooftops.

A head popped up in response, then a body rolled over and stood. Dihya dropped a board between the two roofs and came across, her ax balanced on one shoulder. She was all grins.

"Took you long enough," said Dihya. "I've been waiting there for an hour, at least."

"Wasting your time," said Menna, still turning.

A thump and a grunt was their only warning. Metal *shnnged* against stone and a machete trembled, blade buried in the rooftop at the center of the three. Amastan turned to find Azulay sauntering toward them. Menna sighed and yanked the machete free. She hooked it onto her belt.

"Hey, that's mine," said Azulay as he reached them.

"Is it?" Menna widened her eyes. "Oh, I'm so sorry. I thought it just grew here."

Azulay shifted from foot to foot, but when Menna

didn't move to hand over his machete, he held out his hand. "You gonna give it back or what?"

"Nah." Menna put her palm on its hilt. "I've always wanted a machete."

"Oh come on, don't make me fight you," said Azulay.

Menna grinned. "Try it and see."

"Is this what you meant by practice?" asked Dihya, one eyebrow raised and her thick arms crossed. "Bickering?"

"What's even the point," grumbled Azulay. "There aren't any contracts. I can't believe she lied to us all that time."

"She didn't lie," pointed out Dihya. "She just didn't . . . tell the truth."

Azulay snorted. "Right. And now what? I was going to live off the copious contract money for the rest of my life. Now I have to earn baats?"

"No, now you have to actually get *good* at gambling," said Menna.

"*You* can laugh," said Azulay. "You're already trained as a marabi. *You*," he pointed at Dihya, "got your family's metal work. And 'Stan here writes scrolls all day, even if I can't understand what use that is." He spread his hands. "I've got nothing."

"You better marry rich, then," said Menna.

"I just—I wish she'd told us sooner, is all."

Menna stepped forward and clapped him on the back. "I'm sure Dihya would take you as an apprentice if you just asked her, Az'."

Azulay rolled his eyes and shook his head and then ducked his shoulder to slip his machete free. Or at least he tried to. Menna's hand caught his wrist before he could draw the machete from her belt.

"Let's pair off tonight," said Menna, her gaze locked on Azulay and her fingers tight around his wrist. "We'll spar. Dihya and Amastan, me and Azulay." She showed all of her teeth in a wide grin. "Winner gets Az's machete."

"Hey!" protested Azulay.

"I'm not sure this is what Tamella meant when she told us to practice," said Amastan. "We should be honing other skills, not fighting each other. A mark won't fight like us."

But Menna ignored him and spun away, Azulay's machete held before her. She waved it at him, taunting. "Come on!"

Amastan didn't have a chance to object further. Dihya barreled into him, using her weight to throw him down and pin him to the roof. She smirked, one hand on either side of his head, a knee in his stomach. Her breath smelled like cloves and stale meat.

"You're the one who always wants to be prepared for everything," said Dihya. "Maybe someday you'll need to fight us. Better be prepared to lose."

Amastan drew up his knees and kicked. His foot met Dihya's stomach, hard as stone. But Dihya let out an *oof* of breath and then Amastan was sliding out from under her, rolling to his feet, and running. He couldn't match Dihya for strength, not for long, but he *could* match her for stamina. Let her try to catch him.

The four of them spread across the rooftops, chasing each other over the city as they sparred. After fighting both Dihya and Azulay, and managing to pin both, Amastan faced off against Menna. She eyed him from across the roof, one hand holding Dihya's ax and the other holding Azulay's machete. Amastan spread his empty hands. Menna grinned and barreled headlong at him.

Amastan waited until the last moment, then he stepped neatly out of the way, bringing his hand up as Menna passed and chopping with his fingers across the side of her neck. Menna took two, then four more steps before stumbling and falling. The weapons fell from her fingers, clattering to the stones as she threw her hands out to catch herself. She shook her head, disoriented. Amastan advanced.

But before he could attack, Menna stood and whistled a shrill note that cracked across the roof and halted the other two in their tracks.

"That's enough for tonight," she announced.

Amastan blinked and checked the sky. The stars spelled midnight, which meant they'd been sparring for several hours. All at once, exhaustion crashed into him like a heavy cart. He couldn't wait to get home. A quick glance around told him that he was still several neighborhoods away, though.

"We'll practice again in two nights' time," said Menna. She held out the weapons she'd taken. Dihya and Azulay snatched them back. "Next time, 'Stan gets to pick what we practice."

"No stringwork," said Azulay.

Amastan scowled. Dihya waved with her ax, then swung over the edge of the roof and out of sight. Out of the four of them, she preferred to take the streets instead of the rooftops.

"Maybe it won't be so bad without contracts if we can keep practicing." Azulay shrugged. "Too bad about the baats, though."

Without waiting for a response, he sauntered away, humming an iluk drinking song to himself. Menna wiped her face, but only ended up smearing some of the dirt and sweat around. She met Amastan's gaze with a smile.

"Come on," she said. "I'll race you."

"I'm not really—"

But Menna was already off running. He watched her go, darting like a mouse to the edge of the roof. Without any hesitation, she jumped, sailing across the space between the roofs and landing soundlessly on the other side. She whirled and gestured to him to hurry up. Aware of each and every aching muscle, Amastan followed at a much slower pace.

He paused at the edge of the roof, not quite ready or willing to jump. Maybe he should follow Dihya's lead and climb down to the streets, let Menna go ahead. He scanned the roof he was standing on, looking for anything that'd make his way easier. At first, he didn't notice the sandal.

When he registered it, he'd already walked past it and was reaching for a wooden board leaning against the side of the glasshouse. He paused, almost didn't turn back, but curiosity got the best of him. Someone must have left their sandal behind by accident. He and his cousins weren't the only ones who used the rooftops.

The sandal peeked out from between two large crates, its leather so new it was still uncracked from use. A fine layer of sand dusted its top, at least several days' worth. A fact that wouldn't normally have sent alarm surging through Amastan.

Except the sandal was still attached to its wearer.

4

An icy chill spilled through Amastan. The wind had picked up, warm across the sweat now prickling the back of his neck. He inched forward, following the sandal and its foot to a leg, then the leg to a spill of malachite-green cloth.

Menna's voice cracked through the air. "Stop dawdling."

Amastan jumped, but he couldn't tear his gaze away from the cloth. Its brightness fixed him in place, but also kept the certainty—and fear—away for another precious moment. *Sand deceives,* he told himself. But he knew in his gut that he was right, that this sandal and its foot and its leg and its cloth had lain here for too long, undisturbed. Unattended. Unquieted.

Five to six hours, Menna had said. It must have been days.

He hastily backed away.

"Amastan!"

Menna's voice was too close. A heartbeat later, she slammed into him. No, not slammed—shoved. Menna had shoved him hard with both hands. Now she looked up at him with no small amount of concern.

"Shards, 'Stan—*speak* to me!"

But Amastan couldn't speak, not yet. Even with his head turned and eyes averted, all he could see was the body.

Days . . . that much sand only accumulated after several days, but it could have been longer. So much longer.

Hours . . . the time it took for a jaani to become wild. And clearly a marabi hadn't been here in that time.

Seconds . . . a jaani could possess you in a heartbeat.

The iluk say you never even notice, said his sister's voice. How long had he shared the same roof? How long before he'd even noticed the body? Long enough? It might be too late for him. Was that a whisper in his ear?

"Amastan."

He jolted back to awareness. Menna stood right in front of him, her usual calm fractured with worry. She'd grabbed his sleeve and he hadn't even noticed.

"What. Is. Going. *On*?"

Amastan opened his mouth and then closed it again, deeply embarrassed. He knew how to kill a person a hundred different ways and yet here he was, afraid of a corpse. In all likelihood, the jaani was long gone, blown away and out of the city by the wind, off to torment some poor, lost iluk on the sands. He had nothing to fear. If only he could convince himself of that.

Thankfully, shame was stronger than fear. He cleared his throat. Pointed. "I found a body."

Menna let go of his sleeve. "Why didn't you just say?"

She didn't wait for his answer. She found the foot first, like he had, and followed it up to the body. Amastan didn't move—couldn't—but listened as she examined the corpse. Was that the wind picking up, scraping between the alleys, or the rising wrath of an angry jaani? He touched the charm at his neck, but it was no warmer than his skin.

Just a body, he told himself. He slowly unstuck his feet from the ground and moved closer. Menna had found a stick and was poking the body with it. Now she knelt and drew some of the brilliantly dyed fabric back from a hand. Rings glittered, simple unassuming loops of metal: wedding bands. Four.

Menna jerked back as if bitten. She glanced at Amastan, his own panic reflecting in her eyes.

Only two types of people in Ghadid had more than one wife. Rarely, someone in the lower class could afford two, but the luxury and status of three or more was reserved for the most successful merchants—and the twelve drum chiefs. Taking the rich fabric and the like-new sandals into account, that meant they'd stumbled onto the corpse of a drum chief.

Worse yet, now that Amastan was actually looking instead of panicking, he noticed the blood. It had pooled around the drum chief in a broad circle that encompassed both him and Menna. Amastan stepped back, but the blood had long since dried to black. The drum chief's wrap was stained from the waist down, but was otherwise clean. He'd died too quickly to fight.

"Fuck," said Menna with an impressive amount of calm. She added a few more choice words, then said, "That's Drum Chief Yanniq. Of the Aeser neighborhood."

Aeser was a neighborhood two east and south, and one of the several entry points for iluk and their caravans. Amastan had stood on the edge of that neighborhood with his cousins just last night. He'd probably crossed it while they'd sparred.

So what was Yanniq doing *here,* in the Seraf neighborhood? And why had he been shoved between two crates on a disused rooftop? Whoever had killed him hadn't wanted him found, at least not right away. If they'd wanted the body to disappear entirely, all they would've needed to do was toss the body over the edge of a platform to the sands. Which meant—had the killer *wanted* his jaani to run wild?

The death had been clean and fast. It had happened on

the rooftop. The killer had led Yanniq here first, or followed him. That meant planning. This wasn't a killing committed in a moment of rage or passion, soon regretted. This was worse.

This was murder.

"We should go," said Menna.

"We can't just leave him here."

"Oh, yes we can. I'm not about to get caught near a drum chief's body and tried for killing someone I didn't. Come on."

Menna didn't wait. She hurried to the roof's edge and swung down. Amastan heard her land on the street below a second later. He followed, surprised by his own reluctance. He knew, logically, that being near the body didn't decrease the chance of the jaani being close by. Yet right now, that was the only place he knew for sure the jaani *wasn't*.

For now.

Amastan followed Menna over the roof's edge. She started off and away again, but this time he grabbed her sleeve before she could get too far.

"We need to tell someone."

Menna shook him off, but stayed. "Not our problem."

"It's not," agreed Amastan. "But the marab need to know there's a wild jaani loose."

"*I'm* not telling them," protested Menna. "If the jaani is still here, I'm sure someone else will find it and let us know. People tell us all the time that their kettles or their dogs or their whatever are possessed by jaan. And—and the jaani probably isn't in the city anymore. No need to start a panic."

"But the body—the drum chiefs should know."

"Then you go tell them. Or you tell a watchman. You know the first thing they're going to ask you is what you were doing on that roof. You want to be the one they suspect? 'Cause that's how you get to be."

"Not a watchman." Amastan bit his lip, running through all the possibilities and discarding them one by one. He quickly realized there was only one person they could tell. "Tamella."

Menna blinked several times, frowned, then broke into a grin. "Well, yeah. She knows the drum chiefs. She could tell them herself." Her grin shifted, settled, and faded. "I just don't see how it's our problem."

"It's the right thing to do," said Amastan. Not only that, but the sooner the body was gone from the rooftop, the sooner he'd feel at ease. He didn't like the idea of forgetting the body was there and running across it again. Not that he could possibly forget.

Menna rolled her eyes. "Fine. I'll go with you. You know, so she doesn't think you're possessed and stick a knife through your eye."

They took the streets this time instead of the roofs. They were only two platforms away, and even with the night's bustle filling the streets, it didn't take them long. The evening's lingering glow was long gone, leaving them with torchlight and the promise of a moon. Tamella's door looked different at night, its faded red now a dusted gray.

The door cracked open after he knocked. "Are you just that excited about work?" asked Barag.

"I need to speak to Tamella," said Amastan.

"Oh." Barag sighed. "Of course you do. Well *one* of these days, you'll come around near midnight looking for *me,* I'm sure. Come in, come in."

He ushered them inside. The room was quiet and empty, save where Tamella stood next to a table. Her daughter sat with her hands folded in front of her, her face turned upward in patient expectation. Tamella held a blade, turning it this way and that as she examined it. More knives lined the table in front of Thana, a honing stone next to her elbow.

Tamella set the knife down with a heavy *thunk*. "You're not applying an even pressure to each side of the blade. These all need to be re-sharpened."

For the briefest moment, Thana's shoulders slumped and her carefully neutral expression collapsed in on itself. But in the next heartbeat, she was composed and as cool as stone. She stood, collecting the knives with her head bowed, then headed for the stairs.

"Song of my heart," said Barag. "You have visitors."

Tamella brushed off her hands, folded her arms, and leveled an expectant gaze on them.

"We found a body," said Amastan.

Tamella raised an eyebrow. "And you came to me . . . ?"

"It's Yanniq."

Surprise flitted across her features like a spring cloud, there and gone in the same instant. Her mouth worked around a curse, but she never spit it out. Instead, she ordered, "Tell."

With a swallow, Amastan said, "I found him on a rooftop. His body was hidden near a glasshouse. I couldn't tell exactly how long he'd been dead, but it's been a few days at least. The fabric of his wrap wasn't sun damaged, so it can't have been more than a week. But there's a dusting of sand across his body, so more than just a day or two. It looks like he lost a lot of blood, and I'd guess the cause of death—"

"—is not for you to determine." Tamella cut him off. She waved her hand dismissively. "Leave that to the healers."

"But we can't bring him to the healers," said Menna. "He's *dead*."

"Any healer worth their water can tell you how he died," said Tamella. "You just have to find one who won't ask why you want to know."

"Regardless of *how* he died," continued Amastan, "we need to let the other drum chiefs know."

"Is that why you came to me?" Tamella crossed her arms. "You think I have some sort of secret line to the drum chiefs?"

Amastan shrugged. "We couldn't go to the watchmen."

"Well," said Tamella. "You're right. Finding a dead drum chief would be suspicious, no matter who found him. And being an assassin only complicates things. We can't give them any reason to suspect us." She closed her eyes, sighed, then opened them again. "I guess I *am* the right person for this."

Amastan shifted uncomfortably, one final question remaining. "The person who killed him . . . that wouldn't have been a cousin, right?"

"Did nothing I told you yesterday get through?" snapped Tamella. "No. That wasn't the work of our family. No assassin would disrespect the dead like that. And if I'm wrong, I will personally write the contract on them. No—this isn't any of our business. Let's leave it where it belongs: in the drum chiefs' hands."

5

A steady drumbeat pulled Amastan out of deep sleep. At first, he confused it with the sound of his own pulse in his ears, but the mismatch soon became obvious. He opened his eyes to a room full of morning sun that was warm but not yet hot. Then the beat took on a sense of urgency and he rolled out of bed.

He finished winding his wrap and knotting his tagel as he hurried for the stairs. He nearly collided with his uncle at the top, who was doing his own version of getting dressed, and together they joined the growing group in the living area below.

"Amastan, Uncle—there you are," said Thiyya. "We're just about to go out. The call has been beating for the last ten minutes." Thiyya peered at Amastan. "G-d, Brother. You look like you've been listening to jaan all night."

Amastan ignored her jab. "Do you know why there's a calling?"

Guraya bounced on her toes. "Maybe to announce a celebration?"

One of Amastan's aunts laughed and another shook her head. Their husbands were already at the door, along with his father.

"It's the end of season, 'Raya," said Thiyya gently. "There's not enough water for a celebration."

The drumbeat slowed to a single, heavy beat on each second. An aunt cried, "We're going to be late!" and hurried for the door. The rest of the family followed. Amastan came last, a knot of worry in his stomach.

Outside, the drift of the crowd swept them along across the platform and over a bridge to the center of the Seraf neighborhood. The crowd grew denser until they slowed and stopped altogether, just on the edge of the platform's center. Amastan rocked onto the tips of his sandals to see better. He could just make out a figure standing on the central dais, beating a large drum.

Thiyya squeezed through the cracks in the crowd, there and gone in the heartbeat it took for someone to shift their weight. Amastan followed, leaving the rest of his family behind. As they drew closer to the dais, he could make out more of what was up there. The figure was a slave, his head shorn clean, his features tagel-less, and his otherwise dull wrap embroidered with blue geometric designs that marked which household he belonged to.

He pounded a large drum with twin sticks. Not just any drum, though. Thick red needlework circled its top and bottom, the mark of the drum chief's office. Drum Chief Hennu, to be exact, who stood wearing a wrap as blue as the sky only a few feet away. A handful of slaves and other, free members of her household accompanied her. At her side stood a watchman, who surveyed the crowd with a hand on the hilt of his sword.

Thiyya stopped within arm's reach of the dais, head tilted back to take in its occupants. Amastan stood at her elbow. This close, the drumbeat thrummed through his bones, rattling his thoughts. Then, with a quick flourish, the slave stopped drumming.

The ensuing silence was thunderous. Amastan could hear the breeze whispering over the rooftops. Someone coughed. A baby fussed. Someone else sneezed. A sandal scuffed stone.

Drum Chief Hennu raised her hand. Gold dangled from her wrists and ears and cascaded down her throat, catching and glaring in the harsh noon light, some of it for show and some of it for station. Rings glittered on her fingers; she wore almost as many as Tamella. She surveyed the crowd. Then she took the drum from her slave and raised it overhead with both hands so that all could see and affirm her right to speak. She set it down between her feet.

"Citizens!" she called, her voice smoky rough. "Greetings and G-d bless. You have answered my call; now stay and listen. We gather here today under this harsh sun to pay our respects to Drum Chief Yanniq, recently deceased. I ask for a moment of prayer in his name, that G-d may ease his journey and rest his jaani."

A murmur pulsed through the crowd, but it was quickly silenced when Hennu clasped her hands to her chest and bowed her head. Together, the crowd rumbled a breathy prayer. Amastan touched his charm, a shiver of panic in his own words. He knew Tamella must have told the drum chiefs, but he hadn't expected them to make Yanniq's death public so soon.

When the crowd faded back into silence, Hennu lifted her head and continued. "Unfortunately, I haven't called you today just to mourn the deceased. I've called you because Drum Chief Yanniq was murdered."

The crowd grumbled with confusion and alarm. Amastan resisted the urge to glance around, instead keeping his gaze trained on Hennu as she rode out the response.

When the grumbles had gone on long enough, Hennu lifted her hand and quiet fell heavy as a rock. "Now more than ever we must come together as a neighborhood, as a city, and as a people. I stand here before you because we're still searching for the one responsible for Yanniq's death. We will, of course, find them. No sin goes unpunished under G-d's watchful eye. But we'll need your help and assistance. Anyone with information about the murder will come forward. Anyone we suspect might have information about the murder who doesn't come forward will be detained. I promise you, we won't rest until the guilty one has been found, tried, and punished." Her eyes narrowed. "Our city does not tolerate murderers."

The drum chief swept her hand across the crowd, letting it come to a stop with her fingers pointed toward the watchmen's office. "The watchmen will make their rounds and ask questions as they see fit. Please give them your full compliance. Do not be alarmed. If you're innocent, you have nothing to fear. That is all. I thank you for your attention."

Drum Chief Hennu placed her fist over her heart and the slave took up the drum. He beat out a slower, staccato rhythm to release the calling. The crowd stirred to life and began to disperse. Thiyya headed back toward the bridges, but Amastan lingered. The crowd jostled him as it moved past. The Drum Chief stood as still as a statue on the dais, watching the crowd like a bird of prey.

To avoid standing out, Amastan started walking. But he didn't head home. Instead, he turned down a side street which dumped him onto a bridge and brought him to the next platform. Two platforms farther and he stood outside a faded red door, his stomach knotted with fresh worry.

"You're early," said Barag when Amastan stepped inside.

Amastan closed the door gently behind him. "You said to arrive early. I came from the calling. Didn't you go?"

Barag waved a hand dismissively. "I don't have time for that. If it was really important, they'd send someone. Come here." As Amastan approached, Barag gently patted the pile of scrolls in front of him. "These are some of the source materials I've been able to gather or put together myself over the years. Take a look."

Amastan picked up a scroll at random. He unrolled it, scanned its contents, and frowned. "This is nonsense."

Barag peered at him over his glasses. "Not just any nonsense."

Amastan reread the first few words in a long list, but they were no words he knew. He scanned the rest of the scroll and quickly noticed a pattern. "They're names." He looked up. "Is this code?"

The corners of Barag's eyes crinkled with a smile. "Yes."

Amastan puzzled over the list for another moment, then held out his open palm. Barag dropped a piece of thin charcoal into it. Amastan made a few marks, then said, "Basbowen—they all share that name. Are they family?"

Barag leaned back and took off his glasses. "How did you figure that out?"

"There're a few other names repeated on here and knowing what letters are most common in names along with which names themselves are most common . . ." Amastan trailed off with a shrug. "It's simple substitution."

"You think you can make a better code?" asked Barag.

Amastan drummed his fingers on the table. "With a little time, yes."

"Good." Barag nodded. "Then that will be your second task. Your first task is to transcribe these scrolls out of code. It'll be easier to put together a history when you can read the texts. I should warn you, not all the codes are the same, nor as straightforward as that one. The family has always kept its records in code, but they're disjointed and chaotic, with whole decades simply missing." Barag gestured at the scroll. "What you're holding is one of the very first records: a list of the original members of Ghadid's militia."

"Militia?" Amastan set the piece of charcoal down. "When did we have a militia? When did we *need* a militia?"

"The sands were much higher once," said Barag. "Our city has not always been so safe. In those days, all it took was a ladder or a really tall camel to reach a platform. We were constantly threatened by raiders and bandits."

Amastan tried to picture the sands so close that a ladder could reach them, but it was just too absurd. He shook his head. "How?"

"Sands shift," answered Barag.

"But hundreds of feet worth of sand?"

"Yes. Even from year to year, you can mark the movement of the sands as they slip up and down the pylons. Imagine what could happen over the course of several centuries. Someday, the sands will return and we won't be so invincible. We'll need the militia again when that happens. Back in those days, Ghadid was regularly beset by bandits, guul, and even the other cities in the Crescent." He smoothed out another scroll with his palm. "So the drum chiefs called for a militia."

"But what does that have to do with the family?"

"It was the beginning." Barag opened his hand, palm up. "The family's method has changed over the centuries, but they've always protected Ghadid." His hand hovered over the pile of scrolls. "Most of these I've translated once already, but there are a few I only deciphered enough to figure out what they contained. You'll need to match the original to my translation and then check for any errors. If you can come up with a better code to translate the whole of them back into, that would be wonderful. Otherwise, I just need a lot of help bringing all these pieces together into a semi-recognizable whole. So"—he held out his open hand—"what do you think? Does it sound like something you could do?"

"Absolutely. The translations shouldn't be too difficult, unless you're hiding something from me, and you've taught me more than enough to begin piecing together a history. But . . ." Amastan paused, chewed his lip. "Why me? I know I'm your apprentice, but this seems more like a project for, well, family. What about your daughter?"

"Thana?" Barag chuckled humorlessly. "She'll follow in her mother's steps someday. She won't have time to preserve our history." He shook his head. "No—her mother is the Serpent of Ghadid. Even without contracts, she has a lot to live up to. It's best if I teach another cousin instead."

Amastan looked at the pile of scrolls and thought about all the work they represented. His fingers itched for a pen to get started. He'd once thought he knew about the family, but now there were clearly many pieces he didn't know the first thing about. For one, he hadn't known that the family business had started as a militia. What else had Tamella glossed over?

"How did we go from a militia to, well, this?" asked Amastan. "I'm sure I'll find it in there," he gestured at the scrolls, "but it would help to have some kind of context."

"It was a very special kind of militia," said Barag. He patted the table. "Come—sit. You're right—you need a framework to start."

Amastan dragged over his chair, all but thrumming with excitement. He folded his hands in his lap to stop himself from drumming his fingers on the table.

"From the very beginning," said Barag, "the militia was never intended to fight like a traditional army. Out on the sands, the iluk bandits had the advantage. But in Ghadid, the iluk could be overwhelmed by fighters who knew the city better than them. The militia members learned to work in small teams and they taught themselves how to fight with whatever was at hand. They learned how to hide in plain sight and they learned how to use poisons. Sound familiar?"

When Amastan nodded, Barag continued. "Over the centuries, as the sands shifted and Ghadid rose higher, the militia lost its purpose. When the raids stopped altogether, the militia was forgotten. But one family continued the tradition of training each of their generations. Unfortunately, their trainees weren't satisfied in merely keeping up a tradition; they wanted to use their hard-earned skills. It became known that if you whispered a word in the right ear, your problem could be solved."

"That's when we became assassins," said Amastan.

Barag shook his head. "Not quite. More like thugs for hire. Then, of course, the worst happened—the drum chiefs started using the family against other citizens, claiming it was for their own good. But a thief here and an adulterer there became a merchant who'd spoken out or a charm maker who'd slighted a drum chief."

"Why did the family go along with that? Wouldn't they have noticed?" asked Amastan.

"Oh, they did. And some resisted. But this was long before there were any rules in place. And, remember, each cousin had been trained to kill—and that's what they wanted to do. If you teach a man how to make a fire, you can't be surprised when he lights tinder." Barag picked up his long-forgotten cup of tea, swirled it, took a sip, and made a face. He set it back down. "When one drum chief tried to use the family to kill the other drum chiefs, the family came together for the first time and refused. They drove out the traitor, then met with the remaining drum chiefs to agree on some rules."

Barag held up a hand and began ticking off fingers. "First, a contract must be drawn up, both to establish a record of the request and to force hotheaded individuals to calm down. Second, there must be payment for each contract, enough to be prohibitive, but not impossible. Third, a crime must have been committed against G-d. And fourth, it should be better for the people and the city if the accused doesn't have a public trial."

"But we don't have anything to do with the drum chiefs now," said Amastan.

"We distanced ourselves," said Barag. "After the near-coup, the family decided that they would serve all of Ghadid and not just the drum chiefs. They feared that the drum chiefs would either make them into executioners or decide they were too much of a threat. It was in their best interest to fade out of memory. The family's business became a rumor. It was still known that a whisper in the right ear could bring justice when nothing else would, but they were no longer thugs for hire. They were assassins. Common knowledge became rumor became myth."

". . . Until?" prompted Amastan.

The corners of Barag's eyes crinkled with a wide smile. "Until my wife."

The door slammed open, startling them both. Three watchmen poured into the room and fanned out. Barag jumped to his feet, his hand going to an empty waist. Amastan stood more slowly, careful not to reach for any of his knives.

The head watchman, his status designated by the blue rope around his waist and a bright gold sash, announced, "Tamella of the Basbowen family. Is she in?"

"No—" began Barag.

"Yes."

All heads turned toward the stairs, where Tamella stood, smoothing out her wrap. She flashed a smile that was all teeth, cold and predatory. "How can I help you, sai?"

"You've been summoned by the drum chiefs. We're here to escort you to their Circle."

Tamella didn't even blink. She gestured to the door. "Well then, sai, lead the way."

But the watchman didn't budge. "I was also instructed to ask if anyone else saw the body."

Amastan stiffened, but Tamella only shrugged. "Just me."

The head watchman nodded and one of the others opened the door for Tamella. She paused on the threshold, though, and said, almost offhand, "I'll be back."

6

"She'll be okay," said Barag. But Amastan couldn't tell if he was reassuring Amastan or himself.

Amastan watched the door, as if Tamella might return at any moment and claim it was all a misunderstanding. But he knew better. Her relationship with the drum chiefs had been on shifting sands ever since she'd outed herself to save the city.

Until my wife, Barag had said. Tamella had made a name for herself and the family when she'd stopped a civil war, but at the same time she'd ended her career. Everyone knew about the Serpent of Ghadid, if only through rumors and myth. And an unmasked assassin couldn't be an assassin anymore. She'd been reduced to a story to scare children.

"They've left her alone all this time," continued Barag, still more to himself. "It's only natural they'd want to question her when a drum chief died."

"But there are no contracts. Why would they want to talk to her?" said Amastan. He finally wrenched his gaze away from the door and found Barag watching him thoughtfully. "What?"

"If you're going to learn all of the family's secrets," said Barag, "you might as well learn this one: Tamella has killed outside of a contract."

Amastan stared, felt something inside him shift as the new knowledge took its place. As realization spread through him, he wondered how he'd never made the connection before. He knew that over a decade ago, a handful of merchants had conspired to pitch Ghadid into a civil war and profit off the chaos. He knew Tamella had stopped them. He knew that that single, selfless act had unmasked her and ended her career, even forced her to withdraw from the community to avoid compromising her cousins, her brother, even her own daughter.

He'd assumed Tamella had misstepped somehow in her execution, that she'd revealed herself. But now that he'd learned about the contract ban, he also realized it had to have been more than that. The drum chiefs had punished the entire family. They'd been afraid.

And if Tamella had killed outside of a contract, they'd had every right to be.

"But she didn't kill Yanniq."

"No."

"What will they do to her?"

"Nothing. Probably." Barag pushed a scroll toward Amastan. "Now, stop worrying about my wife and start working on these. We've still got a lot to do today and our clients won't forgive us if we're late, murder or not."

The light through the windows had shifted from brightest white to dusky red to a thin, flickering glow. At some point, Amastan had helped Barag light a few torches. He didn't usually stay this late, but he'd wanted to start on the family's history and to do that he had to finish his other duties first.

Usem had come and gone, dropping off Thana and a basket of still-warm bread. A piece of crust remained at his elbow, already too dry to eat. His eyes hurt from the strain of reading all afternoon and evening, and his fingers cramped from transcribing. He had just finished rerolling the scrolls he'd been working on, and stood, reaching up as high as he could in a back-cracking stretch, when the door banged open. Then Tamella stalked in and he realized that he'd been dawdling for another reason.

Tamella's hands were balled into fists and her jaw clenched and worked. But it was another heartbeat before she could spit out the words she was chewing on.

"They want me to find the killer," she said. "Or they'll condemn us. Publicly."

"*What?*"

Barag shared the single exclamation with Amastan. Barag stood and moved around his worktable, but stopped a few feet from his wife.

"They want me to be their personal *watchman*," she spat. "As if it's *our* fault Yanniq was stupid enough to get himself killed. They think, just because we're assassins, we're responsible for every death. Next they'll want us to quiet his jaani."

"But only a marabi—" began Amastan, immediately regretting his words.

Tamella's gaze fell on him like a thrown stone. "*I know that.*" She turned her whole body toward Barag, shutting Amastan out. "How dare they do this. How dare they threaten us. After everything we've done, *I've* done, for them. By G-d, if it wasn't for me, there wouldn't even *be* drum chiefs anymore. And yet—the *audacity*. I just—I can't—*aargh!*"

Tamella punched the table. Amastan jumped. Barag closed the distance between him and his wife and wrapped his arms around her. For a moment, she remained tense, as if she might fight him. But then her shoulders and chin sagged and her body shook. Amastan looked away, his cheeks and ears too warm. He shouldn't be a witness to this much emotion. To preserve their modesty, Amastan slowly and deliberately made his way toward the door.

"Where do you think you're going?"

He froze, his hand outstretched for the doorknob. Tamella had untangled herself from Barag and now glared at Amastan, her eyes red-rimmed and wet.

"I—to give you privacy."

"No," said Tamella. "You're going to stay and help clean up this mess."

"But I—I'm not involved," protested Amastan.

Tamella's smile was as sharp and deadly as a knife. "You're an assassin. You found the body, Amastan. You are very much involved."

Amastan recognized the futility of arguing with that smile. Still, he couldn't help but protest, "I don't know who did it."

"Neither do I," said Tamella. "You'd better find out, though, and fast. The drum chiefs only gave us until season's end. You're a scholar, right? Then this should fit right in with your other skills."

"Historian," corrected Amastan.

"Glorified records keeper, it doesn't matter. Those sand-cursed drum chiefs aren't giving us a choice. They're just looking for an excuse to blame this murder on *us*. They don't want anyone involved in this who isn't already, because they don't want certain unsavory details getting around. They think people will panic if they know there's a wild jaani on the loose."

"Maybe people *should* panic." Amastan felt a flutter of panic himself. He'd been doing pretty well not thinking about the wild jaani until now.

"That's not up to us," said Tamella. "But the end result is this: I can't bring anyone else in on this, and I can't exactly go around asking pointed questions myself. No one will trust the Serpent. And Barag's out, too. That leaves you, Amastan."

His stomach sank. "And Menna," he added, not because it would help, but because it was true.

"Yeah." Tamella sighed. "Two novices who've never had a contract." She forced a smile. "Well, we work with what we've got. And after we find this killer, I'll personally give the drum chiefs a piece of my mind. Light of my moon," she turned to Barag, "what do we know about Drum Chief Yanniq?"

Barag folded his hands in front of him. "You should remember him, joy of my heart, because he was the only drum chief who *didn't* want to have you executed or exiled."

Tamella waved a hand. "Yes, of course, but that was over a decade ago. I meant: what *else*?"

"Off the end of my tongue, he was close to sixty seasons old, had four wives and six children, and had been a drum chief since his brother died some twenty seasons ago. It was a contentious issue at the time, if I recall correctly. Which I do. The brother had children, but they were too young to lead. Yanniq took up the drum as regent, the assumption being that he'd step aside. But when the eldest came of age, the Aeser neighborhood wanted Yanniq to stay."

"There." Tamella jabbed a finger at Barag. "The brother's kids. One of them killed him. We find them, we're done."

Amastan shook his head. "It's been twenty seasons. Why now? Why would they wait so long? Yanniq was old enough that they could've just waited a few more seasons. Or pushed him down some stairs. Instead, someone bled him out on a rooftop and hid the body. Whoever did that—that's all they wanted. Not a drum."

Barag walked over to one of the shelves. His hand hovered over a section before plucking a thick scroll from its top. He unrolled it and scanned the text before saying, "His family makes most of their money through trade. They were hit particularly hard during the Empire's last caravan embargo. Maybe they never recovered."

"He owes someone money," said Tamella. "They got tired of waiting, confronted him, and it turned bad."

"Why hide the body?" challenged Amastan.

"People are stupid, fearful creatures. They probably panicked."

Amastan pictured the scene, the way the body had been carefully laid out and hidden, the undisturbed, desiccated pool of blood. "It wasn't panic."

"I don't see any evidence that they avoided paying their debts," said Barag, reading a different scroll now. "At least, no one brought their grievance before the drum chiefs' Circle. Yanniq had a few against him recently, but they were small things. People unhappy with the way he decided a dispute, or displeased at his baat allocation, or generally worried about the water rationing."

"Nothing that stands out?" asked Amastan.

Barag shook his head. "Not recently."

"We could be dealing with a madman," said Tamella. "Perhaps they thought Yanniq looked at them wrong."

"Could a madman plan? Someone lured Yanniq up there, or at least knew he would be on the roof," said Amastan.

"A jilted lover? Maybe he was having an affair."

"I don't know," said Amastan, exasperated. "We don't know anything about the man. How're we supposed to find his murderer?"

A slow smile spread across Tamella's lips. "How *would* you learn more about Yanniq?"

Amastan frowned, thrown off by the sudden change in the conversation. It took him another moment to realize what Tamella was asking. Cautiously, he said, "Surveillance? But he's not a mark and he's dead."

"The same principles apply. Watch, wait, learn." Excitement laced her voice. "We need to find where Yanniq was vulnerable. We need to discover his enemies, his routines, his likes, dislikes—everything."

"Treat him like a mark," said Amastan, finally understanding.

"Exactly." Tamella's smile this time was subtler, and yet somehow more terrifying. "This is like a contract, but the hard part is already done—the mark's dead. We just need to work backward to find out who killed him. Congratulations, Amastan—you have your first contract."

7

The leftover date wine splashed into the barrel and across the front of Amastan's wrap. He grumbled under his breath but didn't dare move back lest he spill more. This mixture of undrunk wine and spit, collected from the bottom of each patron's glass, would be used in the glasshouse to keep its scrubby plants alive until season's end. Idir had made it clear as glass that Amastan was worth less than spit.

Amastan left the empty jar next to the barrel and patted ineffectively at the damp spots on his wrap. But there was nothing he could do. They would dry and join the myriad of other stains he'd accumulated over the last three days working in the inn.

"Asaf!" Idir's voice boomed down the narrow corridor. "What's taking you so long? You pissing in the barrel?"

Amastan breathed deep and channeled his frustration into one long breath. Then he wiped his hands off on his wrap—lost cause, that—and headed back to the kitchen.

The innkeeper, Idir, pointed with one thick hand toward the only full table. "Take these bowls over there." As Amastan passed him, Idir slapped his shoulder, making him flinch. "And don't forget the bread this time, Asaf."

"Yes, sa," said Amastan tonelessly.

He set the bowls of rusty red porridge on a tray, then added two circles of flat bread from off the counter. Before

Idir could harass him again, Amastan hurried out of the kitchen and into the well-lit room, which was warm and stuffy with torches and talk. For most of the year, iluk travelers and caravanners clustered in the inn, close and tight, speaking in foreign tongues and wearing foreign fabric. Part-time whores worked the crowd, and the whole room stank of alcohol and exhalations.

But not tonight. With season's end so close, the only travelers in Idir's inn were those who were here for the long term. Outside Ghadid, the wells were dry and grass nonexistent and the air crackled with a dangerous heat. At this time of year, only death-keen and fools crossed the sands.

The inn was relatively quiet, so the table crowded with men drinking and laughing stuck out. Amastan headed toward it with his tray, passing two whores sitting alone, discussing something over a half-empty bowl of porridge. The rough, dull cloth of the men's wraps and their low-knotted tagels showed their low class. One wore no tagel at all, his head shorn clean—a slave. Amastan had discovered that this varying collection of servants and slaves belonged to Drum Chief Yanniq. They spent their free evenings drinking and gambling in Idir's inn, mingling together as if there was no fundamental difference between their classes. It hadn't taken Amastan long to find their favorite haunt; Idir's was the only inn in Yanniq's neighborhood.

Idir's regular server, Sarif, had fallen ill three days earlier—tainted date wine had that effect—and a man named Asaf had arrived at Idir's door, looking for a temporary position. The timing had been fortuitous. Although Asaf was slow and frequently mixed up the patron's requests, he didn't ask for much in payment and Idir couldn't be bothered to find someone more capable, not at this time of year and not when Sarif would be back any day.

Amastan hoped he wouldn't have to work here long. Keeping Sarif sick was proving tricky; the man had already visited the healers once. If he returned, the healers would become suspicious. Amastan was betting that pride—and a lack of baats—would keep Sarif home in bed for another day. Hopefully two.

He just needed Yanniq's servants to let something slip. So far, they'd only talked about their own problems, which wasn't too surprising, but it meant he needed to try a different tactic. Amastan set the porridge and bread on the table, keeping his eyes down. But as he turned to go, he raised his head and caught the gaze of one of the men.

For a moment, Amastan stared into steel-dark eyes. The man's gray tagel was knotted higher than his friends', covering both his nose and his ears. The fingers he curled around his mug were stained black and blue with ink. Amastan had him marked for a scribe and someone who might be useful.

The servant next to the man said something and he blinked. The man gave his head the slightest shake, then said, "I'm sure you're correct as always."

The servant frowned, his gaze flicking toward Amastan. "So you *are* obsessed with the new server. Why don't I call him over and ask his name?"

Amastan pretended not to hear, but he dragged his feet on his way back to the kitchen.

"No!" said the first man with a mixture of horror and surprise. Then he laughed and added, "I'm just—He's so *bad* at this. Where'd Idir find him?"

"The brothels, probably," said the servant.

"*Megar.*"

"I'm going to call him over."

"You wouldn't."

"Watch and learn, little brother." Megar raised his voice. "Hey, you!"

Amastan paused and looked back. Megar was half out of his seat, finger pointed at Amastan. The servant beckoned to him while his friend looked away, clearly mortified. Amastan glanced around, as if Megar could possibly mean anyone else in this empty inn, before returning to the table.

"What's your name, boy?" asked Megar.

"Asaf, sa."

"Come on, take a break." Megar scooted over on the bench. "Sit with us. If the old man harasses you, you can tell him we threatened you."

Amastan took the offered seat. This close, the air reeked of stale breath and cheap wine. Through it, Megar smelled like oil and leather and metal. He wore a drab bronze wrap like the other servants, the black embroidery around its edges marking him as Yanniq's. But silver detail was interwoven with the black: he was a gear worker. If he worked for Yanniq directly, then that meant he was in charge of the pumphouse for this neighborhood—the most important job a servant could possibly have.

But he was still a servant and he wore his tagel low. When Megar smiled, Amastan could see the bridge of his nose crinkling along with the corners of his eyes. The slave shoved a half-empty mug toward Amastan, his own bare features slathered with a smile. Amastan couldn't bring himself to look the slave in the eye, even though the rest of the servants managed to. A man's emotions shouldn't be on display like that, even if a slave's emotions were never their own. It was just crude.

"G-d be with you, sai," said Amastan.

"You work here long?" asked Megar.

"No, sa." Better to stay as close to the truth as possible. "The other server is sick. I'll only be here until he recovers."

"Shame." But Megar sounded pleased. "Well, when

you're done here, you should try for a position with us. Now that you know the right people, you shouldn't have a problem. Then you'd get to work with the best of the best. And by that, I—of course—mean myself."

The steel-eyed servant snorted into his drink, but Megar ignored him.

"And where would that be, sa?"

"The late Yanniq's household," said Megar. "Or what remains of it. Several servants have already left. They think the house'll lose repute, but I'm betting the opposite. And I'm never wrong. Basil ma Yanniq will turn things around. She's fierce and she'll keep the other wives in line. She was already running the household before Yanniq took a lungful of sand."

"You don't know anything about me, sa," said Amastan, perplexed.

"I know you're willing to put up with an old ass like Idir," said Megar. "And my friend here thinks you're pretty."

Amastan ducked his head to hide his embarrassment. The man with the steel-dark eyes and silver tagel next to Megar choked and coughed into his hand. Megar laughed, throaty and deep, and clapped Amastan on the back.

"I never said—" began the other man.

But Amastan wasn't ready to let the conversation change. He was so close. "It might be unlucky," he said quickly. "Working in Yanniq's household."

Megar shot his friend a glance filled with meanings Amastan couldn't parse. Then he leaned back. "Unlucky? Just because the old mule is dead doesn't mean the whole house is cursed."

"But . . . didn't he die in unfortunate circumstances?"

"Oh, somebody offed him, but I wouldn't call that *unfortunate*."

The slave coughed into his hand. "I wouldn't be so free

with your words, sa. If Basil hears you, she'll have your tongue."

"She wouldn't dare," said Megar breezily. "No one else knows how to get the pumps working when those gears freeze up. And what good is a drum chief without water?"

"Do you know who killed him?" pressed Amastan. "I mean, what if they have something against the whole household?"

Megar's friend spoke, his voice almost as cold as his eyes. "No one knows, but the other drum chiefs have sworn to find out."

Sworn to push it off on us, you mean, thought Amastan. Out loud, he said, "Everyone has enemies, though. Surely you know who those were."

Megar lifted the bottom of his tagel and picked his teeth with a fingernail, blackened by dirt and oil. "Bet it was Basil. She probably caught him having an affair."

"Eww," said another servant, who'd been leaning into their conversation. "I don't want to think about that old wrinkled raisin like that."

Megar batted at him. "Then don't!" He turned back to Amastan with an apologetic shrug. "The man's dead. May his jaani rest quiet and whatever. Honestly—and don't tell Basil—I didn't much care for the old mule."

"Why?" asked Amastan.

Megar pressed his mug to his lips, but didn't swallow. "He was just . . . weak. His wives were always talking about how the rest of the drum chiefs walk all over him. He wasn't much of a man. And, I don't know, maybe he was just too old." He set the mug down without taking a drink. "Now is as good a time as any for the household to move on."

"Megar," said the man in the silver tagel with a note of warning.

"What?" Megar leaned back, spreading his hands. "Is

it a crime to speak the truth now? You can't deny that whoever killed him did us all a favor." He raised his mug into the air, his arm unsteady under its weight. "Long live Basil ma Yanniq!"

The table of servants and slaves rumbled in agreement. Megar smiled with smug satisfaction, but his friend shifted uncomfortably.

"You worry too much, Yufit," said Megar, standing. He swayed and splayed a hand on the table to keep from falling. "Here, I'll stop ruining your night and go ruin someone else's." His gaze swept the room before fixing on Amastan. "You remember my offer, Asaf. Come round if you want a job. And don't listen to a word Yufit says about me—it's all lies."

"Sa," said Amastan, not trusting himself with any other words.

But Megar was already staggering away, heading for the two whores.

"G-d, he didn't even pay for his share of the drinks," said Yufit with an aggrieved sigh. "*Again*. Thinks that just 'cause he's a gear worker, he's a gift from G-d. But with his talk, he's only going to get himself into trouble. Word of advice: stay away from him." He settled his elbows on the table. "What did you say your name was?"

"Asaf."

"Yufit. This isn't your neighborhood." It wasn't a question.

"No," admitted Amastan. "But my cousin tipped me off about the opening. She knows Idir." It was true, in its own way. Tamella did know Idir. She'd even helped Amastan select the right poison for the server.

"Is this what you usually do?" asked Yufit.

"No, I just need the extra baats. I'm a scribe—well, historian. What about you?"

Yufit peeked into Megar's abandoned mug, then pushed

it away with a sigh of disgust. "I handle the master's correspondence."

The servant who'd interrupted earlier spoke up. "Don't believe him." He smirked and elbowed Yufit. "He's new. Just got the job last month, and he'll be going right back out on the street once Basil remembers he's being paid to do nothing."

"You don't need to let our friend know all my secrets." Yufit playfully elbowed the man back. "He's not interested in my upcoming idleness."

"Keep your eyes open," said the man with mock concern. "He'll come after your job next."

Yufit gave him a light shove. "Shut up."

The man laughed, then turned away as someone called his name. Yufit smiled at Amastan. "Don't listen to him. I have something else lined up, just don't tell Megar. But if you need something, Megar wasn't lying about Basil having a few spots open. More than a few servants have left since Yanniq died."

Amastan leaned forward, sensing an opportunity. "Why's that?"

Yufit glanced around, then lowered his voice. "Some are saying the house *is* cursed. By jaan."

Amastan's mouth opened, but he couldn't find the words to respond. Thankfully, Idir responded for him.

"Asaf!"

Amastan popped out of his seat as if he'd been kicked. In truth, he'd been anxiously waiting for that summons, having lingered much longer than was appropriate. He gave Yufit an apologetic smile and hurried toward the kitchen with a slight sting of regret.

It seemed like he was finally getting somewhere with the servants. He even had a few leads: Megar, who didn't like Yanniq and seemed to be hiding something; Basil, Yanniq's widow, who might have wanted revenge for something unspecified; and Yufit, who had handled Yanniq's letters and would know with whom Yanniq had been speaking in his last days.

One of them would lead him to the killer. If he handled this right, he could be done with this whole mess in a matter of days.

8

After scrubbing pots with stale oil for over an hour, the alley's faint bite of urine and dung was almost refreshing. Amastan savored the hearth-hot air, his skin prickling with sweat that dried instantly. A salty crust had formed on his brow from the evening's manual labor, which he itched to clean off.

He picked at the salt on his forearm as he headed down the alley toward the street. He was deep within a daydream about wearing a clean wrap and sleeping in his blanket-strewn bed, the window cracked for a stir of breeze, and maybe Barag wouldn't mind if he was a little late in the morning—

"No!"

Amastan stopped. A hot wind brushed his cheek. Had he heard that faint, sharp cry or just imagined it? The noise had come from the other end of the alley, near the edge of the platform. Even if he *had* heard something, that didn't mean it was any of his business. He could ask the first watchman he came across to check on it.

And yet, he wasn't leaving.

The wind had picked up, and now it gusted down the alley, teasing and grasping at the edges of his wrap. It smelled distinctly of gutted candles and charred iron. Somebody grunted, and a shoe scuffed across stone. Heat spread over Amastan's collarbones; his charm was growing warm.

Amastan turned toward the end of the alley, his heart

beating so hard that his chest hurt. Fear stuck thick in his throat like week-old porridge. He hadn't forgotten about the jaani, but he had begun to hope: that the winds had dragged it into the Wastes; that it had already grown weak and harmless; that the marab had found and quieted it; that there really was nothing to fear after all.

Now that hope snapped and folded like a rusted ladder, and his stomach dropped with dread. His skin prickled with a cold, fresh sweat and his feet refused to move—either away or toward. The sensible part of him knew he should walk away. The panicked part of him thought he should run instead.

Someone screamed.

Amastan ran.

But not away—no, *toward*. The wind all but dragged him along, sucking him down the alley to the platform's edge. It didn't matter how terrified he was. He had to help. What if it was him, alone, trapped by a jaani?

The alley's end came into view, a looming square of darkness. But a red haze swirled and smudged the darkness, blurring the platform on the other side of the gap and the man that was backed against the railing. A tagel glinted silver through the haze.

Amastan's charm was now so hot it hurt. He felt blisters forming beneath its heat. *Take it off.* His hand had already lifted the pouch off his neck before he realized the thought wasn't his own.

It hurts, said the jaani.

He let go of the pouch and gritted his teeth against the pain. He was breathing too quickly and becoming light-headed. He tried taking deeper, longer breaths, but it was a fight. As soon as his attention slipped, panic took control again. He stopped at the end of the alley, only a few feet from the jaani and its victim. The man hadn't noticed him. His hands covered his ears and his eyes were squeezed shut, as if that might keep the jaani out.

Amastan hesitated, still a few feet away. He'd never seen a jaani before, hadn't known it was *possible* to see a jaani, but he was more than confident that what tore up the air in front of him and made his charm burn was just that. This close, the jaani's heat was as intense as a roaring fire. The jaani whirled in place, whatever will it had focused on the man. Amastan trembled as he fought the urge, the *need,* to flee.

But he couldn't leave this man to a fate worse than death. Before he could think about it, Amastan leaned forward and pushed his hand through the swirling red.

"Grab my hand!"

The man looked up through spread fingers and Amastan recognized those wide, steel-cold eyes. Yufit. It took the servant a moment to find and focus on Amastan and in that moment, Amastan knew it was too late. The jaani had Yufit, he'd been too slow, he should run—

Run, said the jaani.

Yufit grabbed his hand. Amastan yanked hard, pulling Yufit to his feet and through the jaani's whirling winds. At the last moment, the jaani started to condense, becoming thicker than air, dragging at them. But it couldn't stop their momentum. Yufit fell forward and into Amastan, toppling them both. Amastan caught himself with an outthrown hand, but Yufit had nothing to hold onto except for Amastan. For a heartbeat, their bodies were pressed close, Yufit's steel-dark eyes only inches from Amastan's. Yufit's tagel fluttered with his breath, warm and wet and laced with anise and stale wine.

"Asaf?" gasped Yufit, his voice raw.

The wind shifted. It was no longer blowing down the alley and out, but twisting around them both, hissing and clawing. Angry. Amastan slid his arms beneath Yufit's armpits and hauled him upright. He grabbed Yufit's hand and barked one word.

"Run."

They ran. Yufit easily paced Amastan, even when he fell into an all-out sprint. The wind buffeted them, seeking to draw them back, but then they burst out of the alley's mouth, onto the street, and into a pool of stillness. Yufit began to lag, glancing back, but Amastan tightened his grip and kept running. No way he was stopping. Not yet. Maybe never.

They passed through the center of a platform, garnering a few curious glances from passersby, then flew down the opposite street and across a bridge to the next platform. Here, Yufit tried to slow again, but Amastan's panic wouldn't let him stop. Only a bridge and platform later did Amastan begin to slow, and only then because his legs and lungs burned and there was just one platform left between them and the eastern edge of Ghadid.

Amastan stumbled to a stop outside a pumphouse. He leaned against the squat building's wall as he sucked in breath after breath. Even as he recovered, he kept an eye on the way they'd come, expecting the jaani's whirling red to appear at any moment. Beside him, Yufit wheezed and gasped, sweat shining on his forehead. He looked up as his breathing steadied, and Amastan offered him a shaky smile. Yufit smiled back, equally unsure, then snorted with laughter.

Amastan shared the laugh despite his own bewilderment—or because of it. They'd escaped the jaani, they'd survived, and even though it was still out there somewhere, it wasn't *here,* and that was all that mattered right then.

Yufit straightened. "What a mess we are."

"Are you okay, sa?"

Yufit turned his arms over as if examining them. "You should ask if I'm sane."

Amastan frowned. "Are you sane, sa?"

"Yes," said Yufit, sounding surprised at the answer. "Oh, thank G-d." At Amastan's perplexed look, he explained, "A jaani can't lie. In case you ever run into one. Again."

"That's convenient, sa."

"That is, assuming the Azali who told me that wasn't lying himself." Yufit shrugged. "You can never trust an iluk, except perhaps when it comes to jaan. They're a fact of life down on the sands, after all." He messed with his tagel, which had come loose during their flight.

"What happened?"

Yufit pulled his tagel back over his ears, his gaze unfocused. "I don't know. I was trying to go home when the wind picked up. By the time I realized it was a jaani, it was too late."

Amastan nodded. Silently, he cursed the drum chiefs for their decision to keep the news of a wild jaani secret. How many other innocent people would be attacked? How many wouldn't be rescued in time? "I thought jaan stayed on the sands."

"I thought so, too." Yufit finished knotting his tagel and dropped his hands. "Obviously not."

He finally looked at Amastan, his features fully hidden save for his metal-dark eyes and thin, wiry eyebrows. The skin was smooth around those eyes, young. Yufit couldn't be more than a few seasons older. Amastan found himself wishing he could see behind the tagel and read Yufit's expression. Shame flushed hot across his neck for thinking such thoughts.

"Thank you," said Yufit, his voice softer. "I owe you."

The heat spread to Amastan's ears. "It's nothing, sa."

Yufit took Amastan's hand, his gaze fixing Amastan in place. His hands were warm and smooth save for his fingertips, which were rough. Amastan pictured the ink staining those fingers. Writing would do that.

Yufit was a scribe. Yufit was *Yanniq's* scribe. Amastan mentally shook himself. The hand he held might have written something that would reveal who had killed Yanniq. Out of Yanniq's whole household, his scribe would know about his dealings, his enemies, his business. Perhaps more than even his wives knew.

And here Yufit was, admitting he owed Amastan a debt. Amastan couldn't let this opportunity go to waste.

"You braved a jaani to save a stranger," said Yufit. "It's not *nothing*. Come, drop the 'sa' and at least let me repay you." He reached for a pouch at his waist, one Amastan assumed was full of baats.

In that instant, Amastan saw the future play out. He accepted the money. He saw Yufit again, at the inn, but it was awkward now. The attack hung between them, unspoken and heavy and blocking any potential conversation aside from a greeting and a good-bye. Amastan lost the possibility to get more information from Yufit.

Or—

"All right," he said. "You can buy me tea sometime."

Yufit's fingers froze. He hesitated, clearly thrown off. But then his eyes crinkled with a warm smile. "Okay. I can do that."

"Tomorrow," said Amastan, pushing ahead. "Do you have time in the evening?"

Yufit tilted his head. "I do, but—don't you have to work?"

"Idir said Sarif was feeling better," said Amastan. Idir hadn't, but if Amastan didn't poison Sarif tonight, he might be well enough to work the next day. He'd gotten everything he could out of the servants about Yanniq. He might still be able to talk to Megar on his own, but if he asked any more questions about Yanniq's death in the inn, it would get suspicious, quick. No—this was his best lead. He just had to follow it. "I think tonight was my last night."

"Oh."

"It's okay," said Amastan quickly, pushing past his own discomfort. "Like I said, it was only for the extra baats. So—tea. What time?"

Yufit was silent, his eyes betraying none of the emotions that might be playing beneath his tagel. Amastan bit his lip, hoping his nerves didn't show. Had he pushed too hard? Too fast? But he didn't have time to waste, not while Yanniq's killer was still out there. He only had until season's end, after all.

"Sunset," said Yufit.

Amastan hid his relief with a nod. "Sunset it is."

"We can meet here," continued Yufit. "I live nearby, anyway."

"Okay." All at once, exhaustion crashed over Amastan. Now that he'd secured his lead, all he wanted to do was go home and pretend a jaani hadn't just chased him across the city. The realization that he'd had a brush with a wild jaani—and *survived*—was only now catching up to him. He'd faced a jaani and lived.

The likelihood of surviving a second encounter with a jaani must be vanishingly slim.

"G-d be with you," said Yufit. "And take care, Asaf."

Yufit headed south. Amastan watched him go, the unease in his gut lingering. The jaani was still out there. Why had it attacked Yufit? And if it was Yanniq's jaani, why hadn't it attacked anyone else? Clearly the jaani hadn't been blown out to the sands and the Wastes like they'd assumed, which meant it had been running free in the city for several days now. At least.

Amastan tried to shake off the feeling that he was sending Yufit back into danger. Did Yufit even have a charm? Amastan pictured his neck, the silver tagel covering most of it, his wrap high enough to hide the rest. But even beneath a layer of cloth, Amastan should've been able to spot a lump where Yufit's charm would be. There'd been no lump.

Amastan touched his own charm, which had cooled to skin temperature. If something happened to Yufit . . .

"Hey—wait up!"

Yufit paused in the alleyway and waited for Amastan to catch up. A flicker of annoyance crossed his eyes, but was gone as quickly as it came. Amastan undid the knot of his charm as he approached and slid it from around his neck. He held the small leather pouch out to Yufit.

"Take this," said Amastan. When Yufit began to shake his head and hold up his hands, Amastan pushed the charm into his palm and added, "I have another at home."

Yufit's fingers closed around the pouch. "I've never needed a charm before."

"You've probably never been attacked by a jaani before, either."

"Fair." Yufit smiled and laced the pouch around his neck. "But now I owe you once more."

Tell me who killed Yanniq and we'll be even, thought Amastan. Out loud he said, "I just wanted to make sure you could clear your first debt. If you're possessed by a jaani on your way home, I won't get tea tomorrow."

Yufit's eyes quirked with a half smile. "Well, aren't you practical."

Amastan wasn't sure if he was teasing or not. He didn't care. Yufit had a charm—he would be safe until Amastan saw him again.

"Take care, Yufit," said Amastan.

This time, he forced himself to walk away. He didn't glance back to see if Yufit was watching him go. And now he needed to get home even faster. He felt naked without his charm. But even though he was unprotected, he breathed more easily knowing that at least Yufit would be. Now he just needed answers.

9

If Barag noticed that Amastan was distracted, he graciously didn't say anything. He gave Amastan just enough direction to get started, then left him alone to translate a heap of scrolls.

Slowly, Amastan stopped wondering if Yufit had made it home all right, if the jaani had attacked anyone else, if this season would end sooner than the stormsayers predicted, and focused, instead, on meticulously transcribing the scrolls. It helped that they detailed the excruciatingly dry minutiae of dozens of drum chief Circles during the formation of the militia. Amastan wouldn't have been surprised if the scrolls included what the drum chiefs'd had for breakfast.

The change in light was so gradual Amastan didn't at first notice. One moment, the room was filled with bright afternoon light. The next, Barag was chasing away shadows with torchlight. Amastan blinked dry, scratchy eyes and stretched out his aching fingers. Then he all but jumped from his chair. *Sunset.* It was sunset. How had it gotten so late?

His answer lay in the pile of scrolls filled with his tight, careful script on the table. Amastan hastily rerolled the scrolls he'd been working on and laid them next to the pile in a neat line. Barag glanced over from the shelves where he stood at the top of a ladder, leaning precariously forward on tiptoe.

"See you tomorrow," called Barag.

Amastan waved at his back and hurried for the door, worry stuck in his throat. The door opened before he got there and Amastan almost ran into Usem.

"Careful, little cousin," said Usem, putting his hand on Amastan's arm and steering him to the side. "Keep your eyes open."

Amastan heard a snort from behind Usem. Thana slipped past, flashing Amastan a smile and an open palm. Then she greeted Barag with a tight hug before disappearing up the stairs.

"Tea, Usem?" asked Barag.

Usem turned, stepped out of the doorway, and let go of the door. Amastan didn't wait to hear his response. He slipped outside before the door could shut. He was late. Would Yufit wait for him? He had bet everything on this lead—if he lost Yufit just because he was late . . .

The crowd grew denser as he navigated his way across platforms and neighborhoods to the edge of Ghadid. Now that the sun had fallen and its searing heat subsided, merchants began setting up their stalls and shouting their wares. This late in the season they mostly sold fabric, leather, metal tools, and dried herbs. Amastan paused long enough at a charm maker's stall to exchange a half baat for a new leather pouch, stuffed with herbs and words.

With the soft leather at his neck, the worry tightening his throat loosened.

Yufit was leaning against a wall, his silver tagel and long, slender form giving him away. He stared across the platform's center, arms crossed over his chest. He turned as Amastan approached, straightening and dropping his arms as his eyes warmed with a smile.

"Asaf," said Yufit. "I'm glad you came."

Amastan smiled back. "Sorry I'm late."

Yufit waved away his apology. "No worry. I'm the one in *your* debt, remember?"

"All the more reason I shouldn't squander it," said Amastan. He glanced across the open space to the tea shop and felt a flush of self-consciousness. Like Idir's inn, the tea shop was a place for people to meet. Unlike Idir's inn, the clientele tended older. Through the open doorway, Amastan could see several men clustered together over a board and its pieces, their bare hands as wrinkled and dark as old leather.

When Amastan glanced back at Yufit, the other man was watching him with a smirk. Amastan's ears warmed and he wished he was back in the safety of his own room. It was too late to change his mind now.

"Shall we?" asked Yufit with a lavish gesture toward the shop.

Amastan swallowed, reminded himself that he was doing this to save the family, rolled his shoulders back, and marched across the open space to the tea shop's door, forcing Yufit to hurry after him. A man as wrinkled as his patrons greeted them in a voice that whistled and spat, and an old woman, her eyes nestled in lines, guided them to the back of the room, the farthest from the door and the day's heat.

Without a word, she left them to settle into a pile of cushions. As Yufit grabbed and pulled more cushions over to their area, Amastan glanced around the room. Aside from the lively game going on toward the front, they were the only ones in the shop. Not too surprising, considering how close to the end of season they were. Very few people had the baats left to spend on someone else's tea.

The thought reminded him of his own circumstances, and as Yufit twisted to get one of the cushions *just so*, Amastan brushed his hand across his coin pouch. It was just as light as he'd been expecting, unfortunately. *He* shouldn't be wasting his baats on tea. He'd better make sure it wasn't a waste, then.

The old woman drifted by, leaving two glasses of delicate amber liquid and a jar of sand-brown sugar on the floor between them. Yufit held the jar out to Amastan, who took a scoop and scattered it across the top of his tea. The sugar dissolved in caramel swirls and gratifying eddies. Yufit dumped two spoonfuls into his tea, then settled into his cushions as if they'd been made just for him. He peered at Amastan over the rim of his glass, silent and appraising.

The tea was too hot to drink just yet, but Amastan tried anyway, if only to avoid that intense stare and gather his thoughts. He'd trained in how to read a man's eyes, how to use a knife, how to scale a building, and how to pretend he was a slave or a servant or a merchant. At one point, he'd even learned how to gather information about his mark. But all of that left his mind now, leaving him nothing but cobwebs and dust. How was he supposed to ask about Yanniq without seeming suspicious?

The tea burnt his mouth. Amastan tried not to wince, but Yufit caught him while blowing across his glass. Yufit snorted and his tea rippled.

"I know you're thirsty, but it pays to wait."

Amastan set his glass down. It was safer that way. "Sorry, sa."

"Didn't we agree to drop the sa?"

"Sorry, s—" Amastan barely caught himself and Yufit laughed.

"How old are you, Asaf?"

Amastan frowned. "Nineteen seasons."

"I thought so."

That made Amastan snort. "Unless I'm mistaken, you're only a few seasons older than me."

Yufit raised his eyebrows. "And how do you know that?"

Amastan turned his glass in his hands for a moment before deciding on honesty. "The skin around your eyes is not as sun-worn as Yanniq's other servants. Only the tips of your fingers are calloused. The color of your tagel is only slightly faded and there are just a few stains—I'd expect more if you'd been scribing for longer. The way you carry yourself is effortless, the kind of strength that comes from youth or hard work. And you wear no rings, which means you aren't married and you haven't established yourself."

Yufit blinked several times before he was able to answer. "You've been paying very close attention to me, haven't you? Why?"

Amastan looked at the ground. It needed to be swept; it was sprinkled with sand and dust. "I pay attention to everyone. I've always noticed things like that. The little things, that everyone else thinks are insignificant. They usually are."

"Oh." Yufit sounded disappointed. "And here I thought I was special. Instead it sounds like you are."

"No." Amastan couldn't lift his gaze up, not yet. "I'm not special. It might sound useful, but it's distracting. Sometimes, I don't notice the obvious because I'm too busy noticing all the details."

"Still," said Yufit. "That must be a very useful skill to have as a historian."

"It is," agreed Amastan. Finally he looked up, but Yufit was staring into his tea. Amastan silently chastised himself. He was supposed to be finding more information out about Yanniq, not telling Yufit all about himself. "So, are you?"

"Am I what?"

"Twenty-two seasons old."

Yufit laughed and his eyes softened just a little. "Almost exactly."

"How did you end up working for a drum chief?"

"My mother knows Yanniq. She suggested I ask for a position in his household." Yufit sipped his tea and scrunched his eyes. He leaned forward and dumped more sugar into his glass. "And how did you end up working . . . wherever you do? Who hires historians in this city?"

"Mostly I just make copies and keep records," admitted Amastan. "It's not very exciting."

"But you enjoy it."

Amastan shrugged. "Do you enjoy what you do?"

"No." Yufit smiled. "But it brought in the baats."

"What do you *want* to do?"

Yufit peered into his glass thoughtfully. He took a sip and scrunched his eyes, and then drank half of his tea. "What does anyone *want* to do? I don't know if anyone *wants* to do what they do. We do what we must, and sometimes we might enjoy doing it in the moment, but the moment never lasts. If we all did what we *wanted* to do, we'd be like Megar."

"A well-respected gear worker?"

Yufit snorted. "A lecherous, low-class servant."

"So . . . if you didn't want to work for Yanniq, why were you there?"

Yufit finished his tea and set the empty glass down with a *clink*. Then he leaned forward and nailed Amastan to the spot with his intense gaze. "Let me ask you a question instead: at the end of your night, did you *want* to save a stranger from a jaani?"

Amastan frowned. "Of course. I didn't want the jaani to hurt anyone."

Yufit shook his head, but his eyes never left Amastan. "That's not what I asked. If I asked you what you *wanted* to do after you left Idir's, what would you say?"

"I . . ." started Amastan, then paused as he realized he was reluctant to admit that all he'd wanted to do was go home and sleep and wake up and discover that Yanniq's murder had been little more than an unsettling dream.

Thankfully, Yufit made his own assumptions about Amastan's hesitation. "Exactly. You wouldn't have answered with 'fight a jaani.' But that's what you did. Why?"

"Because if I didn't, you would have been hurt. Possessed. There was no one else around."

"Which makes you a better person than most of Ghadid," said Yufit. "But it also makes my point. You didn't want to. You did what you felt you must. I didn't want to work for Yanniq, but I felt that I must. So I did." He spread his hands as if to say, *as simple as that.* Then his eyes crinkled with a mischievous grin. "When you asked for tea instead of baats—was that a need or a want?"

Amastan's whole face grew hot. He fought the urge to tug his tagel up over his eyes and hide. He needed to stay cool and calm and coy and play this game that he was so terrible at. He'd already fumbled his way into another meeting with Yufit, now he just needed Yufit to trust him enough to talk more about his job and Yanniq.

He didn't like flirting. It made him uncomfortable. His sisters had always teased him for being uninterested in other girls, in other boys, but it should have been the other way around. He'd never understood his sisters' obsessions and crushes. Even when his cousins would talk about the people they were interested in, Amastan hadn't understood. It all seemed a terribly messy ordeal, and to what end? Touching? Kissing? Sex? He didn't want any of that. He had his books and his family and his friends. That was all he needed.

So the irony of his situation wasn't lost on him. Yufit seemed intrigued, if not interested, and if Amastan was going to get any information out of him, he needed to encourage that interest.

He needed to—*shudder*—flirt.

Amastan looked at his hands. "A little of both." He cleared his throat. "And coming here—was it a need or a want?"

Yufit's smile deepened. "A little of both," he echoed.

Amastan swallowed. *Careful,* he reminded himself. "Why wasn't working for Yanniq both? I'd think anybody would want to work for him. He's a drum chief, he has power and money."

"He does. Maybe too much of each. No"—Yufit shook his head—"Yanniq wasn't a good man. He was corrupt and selfish. When he made his decisions for the Circle, he never had the good of Ghadid in mind. He once let murderers walk free and somehow convinced the rest of the drum chiefs to look the other way. Honestly, I'm not surprised he's dead. It was only a matter of time before someone took the law into their own hands." He made a spitting sound. "Ghadid is better off without him."

"If he hadn't died, would you have continued working for him?"

Yufit laughed drily. "Not for long. It's hard to work for someone you don't respect."

Amastan chewed on Yufit's words. *Took the law into their own hands* . . . Tamella hadn't even considered the possibility that a cousin could have killed Yanniq. She might swear that a cousin wouldn't have hidden the body, but Amastan wasn't so sure. Of course, the contract ban was the other problem. A cousin would've had to kill without a contract. One of those conditions could be true, but both were extremely unlikely.

But that didn't mean *impossible*.

Then again, if Yanniq had let criminals walk free, then their victims could be angry enough to take the law into their own hands. That would solve the contract problem. Still, he couldn't dismiss the possibility that a cousin had been involved. Not yet. If his calculations were right, he'd been walking the sands when Yanniq was murdered, which meant he couldn't account for any of his cousins.

He needed to know who these criminals were. That was something he could find himself, somewhere in Barag's collection.

Amastan decided to try a different direction. "Now that Yanniq's dead, do you want to stay there? Or need to? Will ma Yanniq keep you on?"

Yufit let out a breath. "I . . . left today." Amastan waited expectantly. After a moment, Yufit sighed and leaned back, sinking farther into the pillows. "Basil has no need of my services. She has her own scribe. That—and she never liked me much."

"Why's that?"

Yufit shrugged. "Basil never liked anyone Yanniq spent time with. Never mind that I was only with the household for a month. I wasn't there long enough to figure out what was going on between the two of them, but Basil clearly didn't trust her husband."

Amastan turned the possibility that Basil was the killer over in his thoughts. Jealousy could drive someone to act both calculated and cruel. If the killer had been someone Yanniq knew, then that would explain why it appeared that he hadn't fought. Basil could have lured him to the rooftop and killed him without any struggle. Would he have believed that one of his wives was capable of murder?

"I don't want to talk about me, though." Yufit shifted, angling his body toward Amastan along with his eyes. "You're much more fascinating. What is a historian doing working for Idir? And what is a server doing facing a jaani to save a stranger?"

"I'm not interesting, I promise," said Amastan. "I just needed some extra baats. It's end of season and I . . . planned poorly."

Yufit raised an eyebrow. "Gambled one too many times?"

"What? No—"

Yufit put a hand on his arm. "I'm only teasing, Asaf. You need to learn to relax. I don't know much about what historians do, but I'm starting to think it doesn't involve a lot of downtime. Or fun."

Amastan shifted uncomfortably. "I'm relaxed. This is . . . calming."

At that, Yufit laughed. As his mirth receded, he shook his head. "You're stiff as a mule that's seen a serpent. You know, sometimes you can just . . . *be*. Look at the world. Enjoy the moment. We never know how many moments G-d will grant us, after all, and it's always far fewer than we'd expect."

Even though his ears were burning, Amastan smiled. The accusation wasn't unfounded; Menna frequently pointed out that he needed to loosen up. But he didn't have time for fun. Not now. Not yet.

He needed to know who Yanniq's enemies were. He was starting to get an idea. Basil was easily jealous and Yanniq had made some poor decisions in the past. If Megar was anything to go by, then not even his own servants had been loyal. But who else? Who had Yanniq been communicating with in his final weeks, his final days?

"What do you think happened to that jaani?" asked Yufit, interrupting Amastan's thoughts.

"I don't know," admitted Amastan.

Yufit picked up his glass, remembered it was empty, and set it down again with a slight frown. His fingers found his throat instead, where they brushed against a small bump beneath the fabric of his wrap: the charm Amastan had given him last night.

"It must be gone by now." His gaze slid past Amastan, and it sounded as if he was talking more to himself. "Jaan don't stay in Ghadid. The winds will have blown it away or the marab will have quieted it." For a moment, Yufit's calm cracked and Amastan saw a flash of worry in his eyes. Then he collected himself and straightened. "The marab will have quieted it," he repeated, louder and with more certainty.

"I'm sure," said Amastan, even though he knew better. If it was Yanniq's jaani—as he suspected—then it had already persisted in the city longer than it should have. He needed to talk to Menna, ask if the marab were aware of it. Make sure they were. But there was one thing he did know. "It must have been a fluke. There won't be any more jaan."

Yufit's fingers strayed across the charm again. Then he dropped them, his certainty back in full force. His eyes caught Amastan's and he smirked. "If there are—who knows, maybe I'll save *you* next time."

"I hope so," said Amastan, hoping instead that he'd never have to see a jaani again.

"Tell you what." Yufit leaned forward, his elbows perched on his knees. "I've got to leave, but I'll make it up to you next time. You desperately need to learn how to have some fun away from your dusty scrolls and I think I know just the thing. How about it—same time and place tomorrow evening? Except this time, *I* get to pick our destination."

Amastan licked his lips, his mouth suddenly dry and his pulse fluttering erratically. He felt loose and light and utterly terrified. He wanted to say he was busy, but he needed to find out anything else he could about Yanniq. At least, that was the lie he told himself.

"Okay."

10

"A-ma-stan!"

The punctuated syllables of his name came from behind, each one closer than the one before. He was halfway across the bridge when he felt it ripple with another's weight. Before Amastan could fully turn, Menna grabbed his shoulder.

"That's only the third time I called you," she said. She tried to look annoyed but it only lasted a moment before a smile broke through. She let go of his shoulder and patted him on the back. "Are your ears full of sand or is your head full of smoke?"

Amastan shook his head. "I was just . . . preoccupied."

"Head full of sand." Menna nodded, then she set her feet and crossed her arms. "Where were you last night? We had practice, but you never showed."

Amastan vaguely remembered a promise to meet at Dihya's for another round of practice. The jaani yesterday must have driven it completely from his mind. All he'd thought about since then was Yufit and the information the scribe could get him. His head still whirled with thoughts, but now there was more than just information. His conversation with Yufit had gone better than he'd hoped, but it had left Amastan more confused than before.

He had several possible leads now, but scant information. He'd wanted to return to Barag's immediately so that he could look up more details about Yanniq's past decisions, but the evening had passed and the night was growing thicker and he'd been caught by a dozen or so yawns already. His thoughts were growing fuzzy with exhaustion. He needed sleep.

Menna was still waiting patiently and Amastan realized he hadn't answered. Where *had* he been last night? At the inn, and then—had that *only* been last night? And when was the last time he'd seen Menna? Not since they'd found Yanniq's corpse. Menna didn't know about the drum chiefs' demand, didn't know about his current mission, didn't know about the jaani or Yufit or what would happen to the family—to herself—if he failed.

"Oh," he said.

Menna stopped when they reached the next platform and solid ground. "What? That's it? That's your excuse? Just 'oh'?"

"It's . . . a lot," he admitted.

Menna's eyes brightened. "Are you in trouble? Were you too polite with the baker's daughter? Did you keep walking when a watchman told you to stop? Are you selling day-old porridge?"

"I— What?"

"G-d, 'Stan, I'm only teasing. I can't imagine the kind of trouble you'd get yourself into."

"It's Yanniq."

Menna frowned. "But Tamella was going to deal with that."

"She did." Amastan sighed. "The drum chiefs decided to push it off on us. Which means me, because Tamella can't exactly go around asking pointed questions."

"So you *weren't* meeting with one of your many secret lovers last night?"

Amastan's ears instantly burned. He forced himself to meet her eyes. "I was getting information about Yanniq. And then I was attacked by a jaani."

That made Menna pause. "A jaani? Was it . . . ?"

"Yanniq's? Who else?"

Menna closed her eyes and let out a breath through her nose. "That's not possible. The sands should've taken it. Jaan don't stay in Ghadid."

"Well, this one did."

"Shards. If you're right—well, there've been more than a few people claiming they'd seen a jaani. I'd assumed they were just sun-struck, 'cause it's end of season and everyone's been stupid about water. But no, Yanniq's jaani really did decide to stick around. . . ." She opened her eyes and looked at the stars. "Shards. I'll have to let the elders know. We can't leave a jaani loose in the city. Did it"—her gaze dropped and sharpened on Amastan—"are you sane?"

"I am."

"How'd you get away?"

"Ran."

That made Menna snort. "'Course you did." She shook her head. "What about the man himself? You learn any-thing good about Yanniq?"

"Maybe."

Menna rolled her eyes. "I can help. I was there, too, you know."

"Thanks," he said sincerely. "If you can find and quiet Yanniq's jaani, that'll help me concentrate on the drum chiefs' order."

Menna mock-yawned. "Fine. You go fight killers and leave me with the boring bits. It's not like I've got any-thing better to do." She gestured at her wrap.

Amastan frowned, finally taking in Menna's strange attire. She wore her marabi wrap, the pale gray softly glowing in the moonlight. "What are *you* doing here?"

"What does it look like? Working, obviously. An old lady was on her way out and Elder Dessin wanted me there. We did the rites and quieted her jaani. It was the first time I'd done either. I'd kinda hoped it'd be more challenging." Menna turned down an alley. "Come on—are we going home or not? This way'll be faster."

She tightened a few knots in her wrap, then gave the wall a cursory glance before finding her first handhold and beginning her climb. Amastan watched her for a moment, then followed. Suddenly, he didn't want to walk home alone. Not when the jaani was still out there, somewhere.

A few breathless moments later they were both on the roof. Menna dusted off her hands and Amastan glanced around, not sure what he'd expected to find. A smudge of red, an unworn sandal, or a pair of steel-gray eyes. He shook his head to clear his thoughts.

"So who is it?"

Amastan's heart jumped into his throat. But she hadn't been reading his mind, she was only continuing their conversation from a few minutes ago.

"I don't know yet," he said. "But Yanniq let some criminals free during his time in the Circle. It's possible a victim wanted revenge."

"Sounds good to me," said Menna. "I bet you'll have this all cleared up before season ends. At least *you* get to do something fun."

"I wouldn't call it fun, exactly."

Menna pursed her lips. "Of course you wouldn't. You'd rather be sitting in a dusty library surrounded by nothing but scrolls. Some of us actually *wanted* to be assassins, 'Stan."

"So did I," protested Amastan.

"Uh huh. Which is why you were relieved when you found out about the contract ban. You know, you can leave the family, 'Stan. You wouldn't be the first, not by far."

Amastan shrugged. "No, I don't want to leave. I just . . . didn't you ever have doubts? About whether you could kill, when it came down to it?"

"Of course. We all did. We're not murderers," said
Menna. "But that's also part of the excitement, not knowing if you're going to choke or not when it's just you
and the mark. Not knowing whether you're going to get
caught. Not knowing what could go wrong."

"If you plan properly, nothing would go wrong."

"And there you go again, taking all of the fun out of
it." Menna sighed. "But you're missing my point: Tamella
didn't choose us because we'd enjoy killing. She choose
us because we'd be *good* at it. Entirely different things."
She took a deep breath and straightened. "I *will* be good
at it. The ban will be lifted."

"Eventually," said Amastan. "But it's been over a decade, at least."

Something cracked in Menna's expression, but she
looked away. "They'll lift it. They'll have to." But she didn't
sound certain. Without warning, she moved toward the
roof's edge. When she turned back, a grin split her face as
sudden and bright as a spark, burning away whatever had
been there a moment before. "But until then, let's *live*."

"Wait—!"

Menna took off running, laughing as she reached the
edge of the roof. Amastan couldn't help but smile as he
took off after her. Although he had a longer stride and
stronger legs, she was tiny and built for speed. It was easy
for her to propel her small frame across the wide gaps
between rooftops, gaps that forced Amastan to find a
narrower spot or divert to another roof or find one of the
boards the street kids sometimes left behind.

But he kept up. This was all a game to her, always had
been, and for a moment Amastan could see why. The
warm wind against his face, making his eyes water and
his vision blur; the dark sky overhead and the smear of
stones beneath his feet; the constant calculation and re-
calculation of each stride, each direction; the rooftops
and platforms ahead spiraling away into darkness—

Menna disappeared behind a glasshouse on the next roof. Amastan vaulted to the same roof and circled around the glasshouse, but he didn't see her there or on the adjacent roof. He was about to jump across when he heard a short, sharp cry.

He stumbled to a stop just shy of the roof's edge. His throat constricted and his pulse thudded with a surge of fear. Menna had been startled by something. That was all. She was fine.

But he loosed the knife at his belt as he turned and scanned the rooftop he'd just crossed. Moonlight spilled through the glasshouse, casting dark shadows across its floor. Raised beds remained empty but for a few stiff stalks. Outside the glasshouse stood several metal barrels and an abandoned ladder. Amastan didn't see Menna.

He moved toward the glasshouse. Its door was on the other side, and from here he couldn't quite see all the way through. Menna could be hidden by a beam or a shadow or any number of things. She couldn't be dead.

But he didn't hear anything else except the pulse in his ears and the wind as it picked up speed. The wind spun around him now, sudden and tight as it tugged at his wrap. His new charm grew warm, then hot. The wind carried the smell of burnt vellum and over-boiled blood. It wasn't the same as the scent in the alley near Idir's inn, but it was terrifyingly close. Amastan froze halfway toward the glasshouse.

"Menna?" he whispered, not sure why he didn't raise his voice to a shout. No one else was up here. No one else would hear him.

A foot scuffed the roof behind him and he spun, raising his knife. Menna stood inches away, eyes wide. He lowered the knife but didn't re-sheathe it.

"There's a body," she said, voice unnaturally even. "Another."

She pushed past him and walked around the glasshouse. Dread filled Amastan, but he followed. Even though he expected another body, he wasn't ready for what he saw when he arrived at the front. The glasshouse door was shattered, its edges painted with something dark and thick: dried blood. More blood spilled across the stones inside, smears that led to a prone figure facedown in the middle of the glasshouse path. The rows of raised beds had hidden the body from a casual outside glance.

"Who is it?" asked Amastan.

"I don't know," whispered Menna. "But, 'Stan—that fabric—"

Amastan immediately understood. In the harsh light of day, the wrap would have been a damp green, but at night it was barely indistinguishable from the shadows. The wrap was designed that way, so that assassins could complete their contracts unseen. Which unfortunately left no doubt that this was—had been—a cousin. Worse still, one who had reason to slink around at night.

"But there aren't any contracts," said Amastan, more to himself than Menna. He met her gaze. "Right?"

The wind picked up again, circling them before spinning into the glasshouse where it played with the dried leaves and stalks, making them dance. The leather pouch at the hollow of his throat flared with sudden heat. Amastan cried out and grabbed at it, pulling it away from his skin. But he didn't dare take it off. He caught Menna's gaze and saw the same conflict warring there. She hadn't ripped off her charm, but she held it away from her chest by its cord. A wisp of thin smoke curled out of the pouch's neck.

Amastan grabbed Menna's arm, pulling her back and away from the glasshouse door. "We have to get out of here. This isn't like Yanniq—his jaani was already gone. This is too recent, the jaani is *still here*."

But Menna resisted. "We have to see—"

She yanked free and stumbled toward the corpse. When Menna stepped through the broken door, the wind picked up. Amastan hesitated, cold fear sweeping through and immobilizing his limbs. He could only watch as Menna picked her way down the blood-spattered walk and slid to her knees next to the corpse. She pulled at its shoulder, trying to roll it onto its back, but the body was big and she was small and she was only using one hand, her other still holding the charm away from her skin, and now the wind had grown storm-strong, spitting grit and sand and dirt. Menna tucked her chin to her chest to avoid the worst of it.

More than just dirt thickened the air, though. Amastan caught a smear of red and his heart jumped into his throat. At the same moment, Menna snapped out a loud curse, let go of her charm, and grunted as she shoved the corpse with both hands.

Amastan pushed through his fear and the wind to get to her side, where he gritted his teeth and added his strength. Together, they rolled the corpse onto its back. Amastan pulled back the tagel while Menna yanked her charm off her skin. He looked at the dead man's face. He'd seen him once, probably, or twice—family, a cousin, older than him with a graying puff of hair and a closely shorn beard. But no name rose from his memory to match the face.

His charm burned—no, not just burned—*seared*. The pain tore through him and he knew that if he looked, he'd see only a hole where his skin had once been.

Take it off, said a voice he now recognized as a jaani's. *It burns. It brings only pain. Remove it. . . .*

The air had turned red. Amastan hissed through his teeth and stood, pulling Menna with him. She resisted for a moment, her hands at the dead man's waist, then they were both stumbling toward the shattered door. Amastan closed it behind them, as if that would do anything to stop the jaani.

Menna freed herself again, turning and rushing back toward the glasshouse. Amastan lunged for her, but too late. The jaani swirled inside, condensing, forming into a column, one that grew two arms, a head, two legs: the vague shape of a man. One arm, grotesquely long and with too many fingers, reached toward the door and Menna.

Menna raised her hand as if returning a greeting, the smoking charm dangling at the end of her fingers. Amastan's stomach lurched—she'd torn it off. She was mad, the jaani had somehow gotten to her, it was too late. Yet he ran after her anyway.

But Menna didn't go inside to the jaani's waiting grasp. She stopped at the door and jumped, looping the charm's cord around a glass shard jutting from the side of the door's frame. She fell back and into Amastan, letting him wrap his arms around her, as if mere skin and bone could protect her from the jaani, but she didn't take her eyes off the door. At a loss, Amastan held her and hoped that she knew what she was doing.

The jaani's hand touched the door, but there it stopped. The jaani spun tighter and darkness tore through its head, opening a gap that widened into a maw. But it didn't come any closer.

Menna let out a breathy laugh, then squirmed out of his grip. "What're you dawdling for? That's not gonna last. Let's get out of here."

She grabbed his arm and pulled him away from the glasshouse toward the edge of the roof. Amastan glanced back once to make sure the jaani was still trapped. Thick, greasy smoke roiled from Menna's charm and, as he watched, the charm burst into flame. Then he slid over the side of the roof and grabbed its edge. He fell, caught himself on the lip of the roof, then fell again to land with a jarring thud on the street below. A pulse of wind made him glance up, but there was no sign of the jaani pursuing them. Not yet.

This time when Menna tugged on his arm, he resisted. She glared at him and any lingering trace of doubt about her sanity vanished in that moment.

"What're we doing?" he asked, surprised at his own calm. This was the second jaani he'd now faced, after all—and survived. He suppressed a laugh at the thought, knowing it would come out hysterical.

"Getting away," said Menna.

"But we can't just leave an angry jaani trapped on a roof."

"Why not? It hasn't fully untethered. It won't get far enough to harm anyone, not yet, and who else is climbing roofs at this time of night? Any kids who get up here will know better than to get near *that*. There might even still be a chance to quiet it, but I'd need to get some water or ink." Menna bit her lip, glanced up. "By the time I can get some, it'll be too late. Maybe if I were more experienced, maybe if I could find one of the elders . . ." Her gaze fell back on Amastan, annoyance cutting through her regret. "If we'd been there only a few hours earlier, I could've stopped it. Whoever did this . . ."

"It's their fault. Not yours. We'll find them."

"They were messy," said Menna with disgust. "Yanniq didn't put up a fight, but our cousin did."

"You think it's the same killer?"

"Who else, 'Stan? Or do you really want to believe there're two murderers going around Ghadid, hiding bodies?"

Dread filled his stomach, heavy as lead. When he closed his eyes, all he saw was blood-stained glass. So he didn't close them. "But . . . why Yanniq *and* the cousin?"

Menna poked a finger at him. "You're the one in charge

of that question, as you made so clear earlier. *I'm* just here for the jaan." She glanced back up at the roof. "We need to let someone know. We can't let a watchman find him."

"Tamella," said Amastan instantly. "She'll know for sure if he was a cousin." He shook his head. "This isn't supposed to happen."

"No. It isn't," agreed Menna. "But it did."

11

Even though it was late, Amastan knocked on Tamella's dusty red door while Menna impatiently bounced on her toes at his side. It didn't take long before the door opened. Tamella herself stood in the doorway, the hasty knots of her wrap the only sign that she might have been in bed moments before. That, and the irritation that laced her tight lips and furrowed brow.

Then her eyes slid past Menna and found Amastan and that irritation loosened into concern. She gestured them inside without a sound, closing the door and locking it behind them.

Inside was dark and quiet. Even the hearth held only dim embers that gave the room a warm glow. Amastan slipped off his sandals at the door and followed Tamella to the hearth.

"What happened?" asked Tamella.

Menna glanced at Amastan. "We found another body."

Tamella frowned. "Do I need to separate you two?" She leaned against the hearth, arms folded. "Who was it this time? A rich merchant?"

"That's the problem," said Menna. "We didn't recognize him."

"But he's a cousin," added Amastan. "I've seen him before and he was clearly on contract—he was wearing an assassin's wrap."

Any lingering mirth vanished from Tamella's expression. "Are you sure?"

"I know what I saw," said Amastan.

"Take me to the body."

"That's not a good—" began Amastan just as Menna cut in with a sharp, "*No.*"

Tamella's eyebrows lifted incredulously. Amastan doubted that many people had ever told her *no.*

"The body's jaani is trapped along with it in a glasshouse," continued Menna. Then she added apologetically, "It was the best I could do. We'll need an elder if we want to try anything more than that, but I can tell you now that by the time we get back, it'll be too late even for an elder. I'm sorry."

"Don't be," snapped Tamella. She rubbed her face, sighed. "How long before someone can go up there and retrieve the body?"

Menna frowned. "Unless the charm breaks first, a day. Unquieted jaan won't go far from the body before then, and they're usually too strong to do anything about. Too wound up, you see." She flashed a smile, but it held no humor. "I can bring an elder up there late tomorrow."

"You can't take an elder if this was a cousin on contract," said Tamella. "And I don't know any other cousins who are marab." She looked Menna straight in the eyes. "How long?"

Menna chewed her lip. When she spoke, she sounded exhausted. "Another day. The jaani may still be near, but it'll be completely untethered. It won't follow the body."

Tamella nodded, lips pressed tight in a grim line. "We'll need to know who the assassin was before then, to let the family know. But not only that—if he's truly a cousin, then either he was incredibly stupid, or there's someone out there who can best us."

"It's not just that," said Amastan. "His body was hidden

from view in an empty glasshouse at the end of season. If it hadn't been for us, he wouldn't have been found for weeks."

Tamella's intense gaze fixed him in place. "You think the same person who killed Yanniq got him?"

Amastan swallowed, nodded. But Menna spoke up. "It's either that or hiding bodies is the new thing kids're into these days."

"I don't know what Yanniq and a cousin have in common," said Amastan. "I haven't come across any connection."

"It'll help if you know whose body you found." Tamella crossed her arms. "You won't make any progress otherwise. And we'll need to find out whether he actually *was* on a contract or just playing at being an assassin. Because if he was . . ." She shook her head, unwilling to complete her sentence. "There's someone who can tell us both."

Her gaze pinned Amastan. "It's time you pay a visit to Kaseem."

The sun pounded against the back of Amastan's neck as he raised his hand to knock on the wall a third time. Beside him, Menna rocked from her heels to her toes and back again, her impatience infectious. Even though the morning was still young, the heat was already unbearable. The hottest time of the year was in the days right before season's end, so although Amastan was broiling alive, the misery gave him an edge of hope.

Noise bubbled from the doorways on either side. Pans clinked and a kettle whistled and children screamed and laughed and cried while adult voices cajoled and chuckled and murmured. Amastan had been surprised when Tamella's instructions led them to a low-class neighborhood. He'd expected better for the man who procured and provided their contracts. Not a place where the buildings held no spaces between them, where the walls had been constructed and mended with sand, where men wore tagels threadbare and stained with age.

Stringwork hung over most of the doorways, spun into shapes to ward off jaan and curses and bad luck. Kaseem's had been one open doorway among many, the curtain that kept his privacy just as sun-faded and dust-streaked as the next.

That curtain twitched to the side before Amastan could knock. A wiry old man wearing a dark green tagel and matching wrap stood in the doorway, just out of reach of the sun's harsh light. He leaned on a wooden cane, a bulb of amber at its top, and peered at them in weary, if expectant, silence.

Remembering Tamella's instructions, Amastan pressed a closed fist to his chest and inclined his head. "Kaseem, sa. I'm Amastan Basbowen. Tamella sent us."

Kaseem's watery eyes swiveled to Menna, who mirrored Amastan's motions. "Menna. Sa."

"I can't turn away family," said Kaseem, his voice etched with none of the burrs or scratchiness of old age. Instead, his voice was fresh and clear and entirely at odds with his appearance. Amastan looked again, and this time saw the strength in Kaseem's arms and posture and the way he leaned too heavily on his cane. Kaseem was putting on a show.

He used his cane to pull the curtain farther back and stepped out of the way. "I hope neither of you are expecting tea because it's season's end and I don't want to share."

Amastan stepped into the small home, Menna right behind him. He shook his head. "We're just here to talk."

He took in the narrow room with one glance: the cold hearth with the rusting kettle, the small table and two accompanying chairs, the worn and stained rug that barely

covered half the dusty floor. In the shadows at the very
back of the room was a leather cot, a thin sheet hanging
off its end.

The bright light dimmed as Kaseem let the curtain
drop back into place. He secured it on one side so the
curtain wouldn't blow open, then, still leaning heavily on
his cane, limped toward the table and settled into one of
the chairs. That limp, if nothing else, appeared to be real.
He stacked his hands on top of the amber orb and peered
at them for a heartbeat, then gave a curt nod.

"There's an assassin dead on a roof right now, sa," said
Amastan. "We need to know who he was."

Kaseem's expression remained neutral. "What compels
you to assume I would know?"

"He was on contract, sa."

Kaseem gave no reaction. Tamella had warned them
that it might be difficult to extract answers from the old
man. Kaseem's work as the contract purveyor required a
fine, delicate balance. As the public face of the family,
he bore no relation to any Basbowen and kept his own
lineage secret. If someone needed a contract, they'd eventually find a way to him. A network of ears shepherded
along anyone who might have a legitimate case. From
there, Kaseem weeded the cases further.

Only he knew both the makers of the contracts and the
assassins who completed them. The continuance of his
work—and life—required that he maintain confidence on
both sides. A mere whisper that he might have compromised a contact would mean the end of his work—and,
more than likely, his life.

Which was the reason why Amastan and Menna were
here, now, without Tamella. The Serpent of Ghadid
couldn't be seen anywhere near Kaseem.

"Look, sa," said Menna, her impatience flaring. "We
know you're not supposed to say anything, or even admit that there was a contract, but can we just skip that?

A cousin's dead—murdered—and his jaani is wild. We need to know who you selected for the last contract."

"Your family's troubles are of no interest to me," said Kaseem. "Nor are they reason for me to betray my clients' confidence."

"Troubles?" said Menna.

Amastan touched her arm but spoke to Kaseem. "Sa—a cousin is dead. It appeared he was working a contract. I think that should be of interest to you."

"I will handle the reassignment," said Kaseem, but doubt flickered across his eyes. "My duty to your family and the city necessitates the utmost secrecy on my part. To betray that would destroy more than you realize. Delving into knowledge that isn't yours won't bring the dead back to life."

"We're not asking for him back, *sa*," said Menna, her voice as sharp as a blade. "We just want to know whose body we're collecting."

"Surely you can identify your own dead."

Menna stepped closer. "You see this, *sa*?" She plucked at the pale gray fabric of her wrap, so much of it now stained with smoke, dust, and blood. Unlike Amastan, she hadn't bothered to change. "I know what I'm talking about when I say we can't return to the body for at least a full day or more. Whoever killed our cousin hid him in a glasshouse. At the end of season. If not for us, he wouldn't have been found for days. The killer *wanted* the jaani to go wild. So right now we have an angry jaani occupying the same glasshouse and *I* don't want to go in there and identify a body. Do you? Sa?"

Kaseem's eyebrows had slowly risen through Menna's tirade until he looked incredulous. "What you describe is criminal on a whole different level. Have you thought about informing the drum chiefs?"

"They know, sa." Amastan chewed his lip beneath his tagel for a moment. But if anyone could keep a secret, it was Kaseem. "Drum Chief Yanniq was found under similar circumstances."

"How similar?" asked Kaseem, eyes narrowing.

"His body was hidden on a rooftop and his jaani went wild." Amastan closed his eyes for a moment, but he didn't see Yanniq's shriveled corpse. Instead, he saw a whirl of red and a man cowering against a railing. Had that first jaani really been Yanniq's? Or were there more bodies out there, waiting to be found? He took a breath and opened his eyes. "Except with Yanniq, we were several days too late."

Kaseem let out a low whistle, but suspicion clouded his gaze. "You want me to believe that a drum chief was not only murdered, but disrespected, and the other drum chiefs haven't turned the city upside down searching for the culprit?"

"They've kept those particular details quiet," said Amastan. "And they've . . . *asked* us to find his killer. If the person who killed Yanniq also got this assassin, then we need to know who he was. The sooner you tell us, the sooner we'll know if this was a fluke, something related, or . . . worse."

"What could be worse than murder, boy?"

"A pattern of murders," said Menna, catching on.

"I'd assumed that Yanniq's was the only one of its kind," said Amastan. "But what if it's not?"

"You think the killer will strike again," said Kaseem.

"Give me a reason to think otherwise, sa."

Kaseem shifted his cane between his hands, his gaze boring into Amastan. "I owe you no explanation."

"Then the drum chiefs, sa," pressed Amastan. "If this information helps us find Yanniq's killer—"

Kaseem's harsh laugh cut him off. "You think I answer to the drum chiefs?"

"Apparently not," snapped Menna. "Since you've been handing out contracts when they aren't allowed. Sa."

"I won't tolerate such insolence." Kaseem's gaze was sharp. His hands had stopped fidgeting with the cane and now his whole body stiffened. "Leave."

"I only get insolent when someone's being profoundly stubborn, *sa*."

"Menna . . ." warned Amastan.

"Well he *is*!" Menna looked like she wanted to stomp her foot, but somehow she resisted. "A man is *dead*, 'Stan, and worse, I couldn't even save his jaani. Now this trussed-up self-important sand peddler thinks he's above telling us the poor man's name."

"Do you speak to all your elders this way?" asked Kaseem, annoyance warring with amusement.

Menna lifted her chin. "No. Only the ones who deserve it. Sa."

Kaseem laughed again, this time a less harsh sound. Then his cane whipped out, cracking across the back of Menna's knees. She gasped and toppled, her legs giving out from under her. Amastan grabbed her arm to keep her from falling face forward, but she'd already caught herself. She rose shakily to her feet. Kaseem's cane was back beneath his palms as if it had never moved. He was smiling.

"Leave."

Menna hissed through her teeth. "Not until—"

"Maybe you should," interrupted Amastan. "Just . . . wait outside for a minute."

Menna stared at him, hurt mixing with betrayal. Then her nostrils flared and she stomped her foot, lips pressed so hard together that the edges turned white. But she turned and went, ripping open the curtain so hard that Amastan feared she'd tear it down. She didn't. The curtain fell back into place. The sudden thwack of flesh smacking stone made Amastan jump and Kaseem flinch. It sounded suspiciously like a fist hitting the wall. Then— silence.

Kaseem breathed out and some of his strength leached into his breath. He looked older by a decade in the span of a second. His gaze fell to the floor.

"I'm sorry, sa," said Amastan quietly.

Kaseem waved him off. "She's not you. I appreciate her passion, but I didn't get this far by letting anyone talk to me like that." He lifted his gaze. "I can't tell you his name, you understand."

The sinking sensation that Amastan had been fighting off returned. He sighed. "I hoped otherwise, sa."

"Do you really think whoever got him will kill again?"

Amastan chewed his lip, his fingers curling and un-curling at his sides as he reexamined the similarities between the two deaths yet again. "I do."

Kaseem nodded, more to himself than Amastan. Then he reached across the table and picked up a pen. He un-capped a small inkwell, dipped the pen, and wrote on the edge of a scrap of thin papyrus. He ripped off the edge and pushed it toward Amastan before standing up.

"I'm not telling you anything you didn't already know," said Kaseem. "Your impudent friend should've known who he was. She would've remembered on her own."

Amastan stared at the scrap in disbelief, then snatched it off the table.

"Thank you, sa," he said.

"Don't thank me yet." Kaseem settled his hands back on top of his cane. "The drum chiefs aren't known for rewarding good deeds. Remember that."

Amastan ducked his head, the piece of paper clutched to his heart like a treasure. Yet he was afraid to look at it. "G-d be with you, sa."

"Just go."

With another nod, Amastan fled for the door as if Kaseem might change his mind at any moment and de-mand the paper—and the name—back.

Menna waited just outside, her hand outstretched. Amastan passed her the scrap of paper and she looked at it. Then she let out a tiny puff of air, not quite a gasp.

"My father's brother. I mean, my uncle. I should've recognized him. I just—It's been so long since I've seen him. My father's family never wanted much to do with us. But I—I didn't know Emet was an assassin."

"What does he have to do with Yanniq?" asked Amastan.

But Menna was already shaking her head. "Nothing. Nothing at all. I'll ask around, just in case, but—I'm sorry, Amastan." She put the scrap of paper back into his hand. "This only complicates things."

12

Amastan ran his finger across the stacks of scrolls, the circles of vellum rough against his fingertips. The familiar movement he'd repeated a hundred or a thousand times helped ground his jumbled thoughts. Behind him, Barag's pen scratched across vellum, the occasional pause followed by a sigh or a breath or a *shh* of shifting fabric.

In essence, Amastan was in his element. So why did his fingers shake as he searched the shelves and why did his heart pound when his thoughts strayed to last night? But not to the jaani—for once, he didn't think about corpses and madness. In the light of day, the blood-smeared glasshouse seemed so far away. He believed Menna when she'd said the jaani would be trapped in the glasshouse for another day or longer. And neither did his thoughts stray to Emet, a cousin he'd never known.

No. To Yufit.

But why? He barely knew the man. Yufit was only Yanniq's old scribe, a means to an end. Amastan had forced himself to show interest. He'd gotten the information he'd wanted, the beginning of a thread that he hoped wouldn't become as complex as stringwork.

And then Yufit had shown interest back. Amastan hadn't planned for that, didn't quite know how to handle it. Bemusement, curiosity, confusion, dislike—*those* Amastan had planned for. After all, Yufit had all but called him dull and boring. And *yet*.

Now as he tried to focus, he couldn't help but think about his next meeting with Yufit tonight. *Fun,* he'd said. What did that mean to a man like Yufit, who had worked for a drum chief, who had spent many evenings drinking with servants, who had made friends with a man like Megar? Amastan didn't know, but he did know that the nauseating prickling sensation that whirled in his gut whenever he thought about Yufit wasn't *entirely* unpleasant.

He shook himself mentally and forced himself to focus. The evening would come. Meanwhile, he didn't have much time to waste. The killer would kill again.

The scrolls in front of him blurred together. Barag thought Amastan was looking for corroborating texts to help clarify the smudged script on the scroll he was copying. Instead, he was searching for records of past drum chief Circles and their decisions. Who had Yanniq pardoned?

And what could Yanniq have possibly had in common with Emet?

Unfortunately, the scrolls that recorded the decisions made during the drum chiefs' monthly Circles filled an entire shelf. Amastan didn't know where to start, so he picked the ones for the six months prior to Yanniq's death. He started toward his desk, then hesitated. After a moment, he plucked another scroll off a different shelf: the record of deceased. Barag had mentioned he'd added Yanniq to the record earlier, but Amastan hadn't had a chance to look yet. He doubted it would tell him much, but any context could only help.

The decisions ended up being entirely unhelpful. For the past six months, Yanniq had voted with the majority of the other drum chiefs on almost every decision. The ones where he hadn't, he'd abstained. Amastan picked through the decisions one by one. Dull stuff, mostly. Petty trade arguments between merchants, undisputed confirmations of inheritance, marriage blessings, and disagreements between families. The most exciting decision had been about

a husband accused of infidelity. He'd been fined an entire
bo-baat.

Nothing stood out as a possible impetus for murder.

But Amastan did get a better feel for the man Yanniq
had been. He even understood some of Yufit and Megar's
disdain. If the drum chief'd had any opinions at all, he
hadn't voiced them. His decisions came across as weak-
willed and his leadership ineffectual. While the other
drum chiefs fought over resources for their neighborhoods, Yanniq had remained silent.

You can't deny that whoever killed him did us all a favor.
He found himself agreeing with Megar. The Aeser neighborhood was probably better off without Yanniq.

Amastan shook his head and rolled up the last of the
Circle's scrolls. He couldn't think like that. Yanniq might
not have been perfect, but that wasn't a death sentence.
He deserved justice. Not for the first time, he wondered
if Megar could have killed Yanniq. As a gear worker, he
was strong enough. But dislike wasn't enough to motivate
murder—he'd have to find more.

Amastan unrolled the last scroll. Yanniq's entry was
one of the latest ones. A few names came after, but Emet's
wasn't on there. Of course not; his funeral hadn't even
been held yet. One of the entries, though, was for an old
woman who had died peacefully in her own home. That
must have been the woman Menna had mentioned. His
finger traced Barag's familiar script from the bottom of
the scroll upward, until he came to Yanniq's entry.

*Yanniq Feqamen sa Basil, sa Ziri, sa Kura, sa Thama,
Drum Chief of the Aeser Neighborhood*

*Took up the drum from Annat Feqamen, may his jaani
rest with G-d in peace, in the year 345. Ruled with fairness and faith for 21 years . . .*

Amastan started skimming. The drum chief's entry
was by far the longest on the scroll, but that didn't tell
him much. A lot of it was formulaic, the kind of stuff they

had to write about the drum chiefs who weren't reviled or revered for any specific reason. According to the record of deceased, every drum chief had ruled with fairness and faith, no matter how corrupt or immoral they might have been.

He found nothing that could connect Yanniq to Emet or any of the other cousins. Amastan wasn't surprised. He'd hoped, but he'd known better than to expect. Instead, he took wry amusement at how the record listed his cause of death. *Extreme blood loss.* Not wrong, but not quite the truth, either.

Amastan returned the scrolls to the shelves, disappointed at how little he'd found. As he placed the last scroll, the record of the deceased, in its slot, a realization hit. Of course he hadn't found a connection between Emet and Yanniq. He'd been looking in the wrong place. He dropped his hand and turned back toward his desk, toward the heap of scrolls in the basket that constituted Barag's special project.

Emet was an assassin. He had died while on contract. That part of his life wouldn't be in the public records. And neither, perhaps, would whatever connected Yanniq to Emet and possibly to the family.

Amastan was halfway back to his desk when the door opened. Thana split from the hulking shadow at her back, aiming with focused intent for her father. Usem stepped inside, letting the evening light spill into the room.

"Tea?" asked Barag, paper rasping as he began cleaning up his desk.

"Thank you, but no. I want to hit the markets before they get too busy."

Thana wrapped her arms around her father and settled her head on his shoulder. She was easily half a head taller than Barag. For a brief moment, she looked fragile, like the child she was. Barag paused in his task and put his hand on hers. Amastan looked away, focusing instead on the scrolls he wouldn't finish today. He itched to stay anyway, but with Thana's arrival, the library had turned back into a home.

"Tell Tam' that her daughter was exceptional, as usual," said Usem, still hovering by the door. "Let her take a day off tomorrow to visit her cousins or friends. She's earned it. I can send Rema by, if Tam' wants."

"What about you?" asked Barag. "Tam' wants to see you, I'm sure. Why don't you come by and share a meal with us?"

Usem shook his head. "I want to, but I have something I've got to finish up first. But as soon as that's done, I promise I'll be by. I've got a lot to catch Tam' up on."

"Good night, Uncle," said Thana.

Amastan finished cleaning off his desk and headed for the door. Usem held the door open for him and they both stepped out of the stuffy darkness together. Amastan squinted against the glare. The city felt as if it were holding its breath for sunset, the streets swept empty by the heat and the wind. The markets Usem had used as his excuse to turn down Barag's tea wouldn't even be set up yet. Was Usem avoiding his sister? And if so, why?

The door closed, but Usem didn't leave. His presence was like a wall's: immovable, vast, and harmless. But Usem was far from harmless.

"Barag treating you all right?"

"Of course."

Usem grunted. Amastan looked up, trying to read the strip of Usem's face. He wore his tagel higher than usual, so all Amastan could see were his eyes, as pale as his sister's.

"You wear charms, right?"

Amastan touched the lump that lay between his collarbones. "Always."

"Good." Usem scanned the area, but didn't look at Amastan. Then he started walking.

"Wait," said Amastan, catching up and keeping pace with Usem's long stride. "Why'd you ask?"

"Nothing to worry about," said Usem, but he didn't sound confident. "There's just been rumor of a jaani loose in the city. But I'm sure it's just that—rumor. Still, better safe than mad."

A chill wound itself deep in Amastan's gut. "A jaani?"

Usem paused and gave Amastan a smile, but although the edges of his eyes crinkled with the gesture, his eyebrows betrayed his worry. "Like I said, probably just a rumor. I wouldn't worry about it. You know how people get at the end of season. So tense with waiting that they start making things up, seeing stuff. Speaking of—you got enough baats to last you? I know work's been scarce for you younger kids, but you shouldn't have to go thirsty because of mistakes made years ago."

"You knew about the ban," said Amastan. As soon as the words were out, he realized how stupid they sounded. Of course Usem knew about the ban—it must have ended his career as surely as it had Tamella's, along with every other assassin of their generation. Including Emet. "Do you ever resent her for it?"

Usem tilted his head back to look at the sky. "Not Tam', no."

"But the drum chiefs."

"Resent is a strong word," said Usem carefully. "But it's hard to blame any of them. If I'd been in Tam's place, I can't imagine treading a different path. Perhaps I could've been more subtle than her, but subtle might've let the conspiracy—and the warped ideology that fueled it—continue to fester. As for the Circle, well. Tam' broke one contract and then killed without one. They couldn't exactly let that go unpunished, could they." But his tone held a tightness to it that suggested he thought otherwise.

"Tamella broke a contract?"

Usem glanced at him. "She never told you about that, huh?"

"No."

"Shame. It's a good story." Usem checked the sky again. "One that'll have to wait. Ask Barag about it sometime— after all, she broke it for him. Here." He pulled a few coins from his belt, grabbed Amastan's hand, and pressed them into his palm. "And don't try to pay me back, either."

Amastan closed his fingers around the cool baats. "Thank you."

Usem looked away. "Don't hesitate to ask if you need more. I need to go. Take care of yourself, 'Stan. G-d bless."

"G-d bless," echoed Amastan.

They split ways, Usem turning and heading north, deeper into their neighborhood, while Amastan crossed a bridge to the next. The baats felt heavy in his hand, but the story Usem had hinted at hung heavier in his mind. He'd never assumed he knew everything about Tamella, but now he was finding out he knew very little at all. How little did he know about his other cousins? What secrets were they hiding?

And Barag? *After all, she broke it for him.* What was Barag hiding?

Did it even matter? All of this was from over a decade ago, events long past. And it still didn't explain Emet. Usem and Emet would've been the same generation. Amastan paused and glanced back, but Usem was long gone. He'd have to ask Usem about Emet tomorrow.

Usem had been right about one thing, at least. Amastan's water skin was almost empty. His meeting with Yufit was drawing close, but that didn't mean he couldn't stop by a pumphouse on his way and fill his skin. Unlike yesterday, he wasn't going to be late. If anything, he was too early. He didn't want to appear too eager to see Yufit, even if he'd been looking forward to this meeting all day. *Fun,* Yufit had said. But what did that mean?

The day's heat wafted up from the stones and a wisp of breeze accompanied Amastan as he wove through the streets. He passed two pumphouses before he finally stopped at one. Only when he reached for the door did he fully register that he was in Aeser, Yanniq's neighborhood. This just happened to be the closest pumphouse to where he'd be meeting Yufit.

Even though Yanniq's jaani could be anywhere in the city, Amastan touched his charm. Its lack of warmth reassured him. He entered the pumphouse's cool interior and pulled back the hatch at its center, revealing steps winding tightly downward. They led him below the platform's surface to a wide, circular room. Down here, the air tasted of moisture and metal. The pylon sat exposed at the center of the room, its smooth metal dark and matte. A long bench jutted from the wall for the line that often formed after the aquifers refilled. A beggar lay across it, his dirty and faded wrap pulled over his head. A thin, reedy snore echoed around the room and the beggar's hand rose and fell with each breath, fingers pointing toward a bowl holding a few cracked glass baubles.

Like the crypt, the room wrapped around the pylon. Unlike the crypt, the bodies down here were still alive. A faint *glosh* of water came from the pylon, magnified by the emptiness. A basin had been carved into the pylon at waist level and orange rust ate at its edges. More orange and red rust crept up the pipe that hung above the basin.

Amastan slipped one of Usem's baats into a slot at the basin's side. The *glosh* became a *glug* and ancient pistons and mechanisms deep within the pylon were set into motion. Hundreds of feet below, a pump fed water from the aquifer into a pipe, bringing it all the way up inside the pylon to this font. The people who'd built Ghadid had tapped the aquifer that stretched for miles and miles deep beneath the sands. They'd run pipes down to it and built pumps that brought the water up to these basins and fonts, found in each neighborhood. This system of pumps and pipes and gears made it possible for a city as big and diverse as Ghadid to not only survive, but thrive, where life was otherwise impossible.

But while their technology had lasted, their knowledge hadn't. No one knew quite how the pumps worked, just that they did. Gear workers had tinkered with broken pumps until they'd gotten them working again, learning as they went and passing on what they had learned, their secrets almost as well guarded as the family's. But a lot was still unknown and a lot could still go wrong.

Thankfully, it hadn't, at least not in the last few centuries. The pumps remained reliable. A baat inserted meant a pint of water. Above, people traded baats back and forth for other things, other wares, but as the season wore on, they reserved their baats for water. The people continued to trade, they just used their own work and wares in place of baats, but season's end inevitably meant a slump. The markets quieted as people started rationing their baats to make it until the end of season.

When the storms finally broke and the aquifer refilled, the basins released their hoarded baats. It was then the responsibility of each neighborhood's drum chief to distribute those baats as they saw fit. A wise drum chief knew how to dole out their baats to keep their neighborhood healthy, hydrated, and stable, while a foolish drum chief could do a lot of harm.

Even if Drum Chief Yanniq had been ineffectual in the monthly Circles, he must have done a decent job distributing baats. Otherwise he wouldn't have lasted so long as drum chief. But it was possible that something had changed in his last years.

Amastan held his water skin under the pipe as it slowly expanded. When he'd captured the last drop, he tied it shut and returned it to his belt. The skin hung heavy off his belt in a uniquely satisfying way. He paused at the stairs, then stepped back and dropped Usem's other baat into the beggar's bowl. The ring of metal on glass seemed to fill the small room. He was just turning back to the stairs when the sound of footsteps echoed down them. The stairs were too narrow for two, so he waited.

A servant wearing a bronze wrap came down the stairs. Black embroidery coiled around the edges of the wrap, marking him as a part of Yanniq's household. Silver at his sleeves showed that he was a gear worker. Yanniq only had one gear worker.

Megar.

13

Megar didn't appear to recognize Amastan and walked right by. He approached the basin, carrying a leather bag and a small glass lamp. Amastan hesitated at the foot of the stairs. He still had a few minutes before his meeting with Yufit. He might be able to get more information out of Megar, maybe better understand his dislike for Yanniq, and ask a few questions about Yanniq's baat allocations. When else would he have a chance to run into the gear worker?

Megar set down the leather bag he was carrying and rustled through it. When he straightened, he held a long metal screwdriver, its head narrow and sharp. There were at least fifteen different ways to kill someone with that screwdriver. Megar used the tool to pry open a panel at the bottom of the basin. His bag was just out of reach behind him, but tantalizingly close to Amastan.

What other tools did a gear worker use? Could all of them be used as weapons? Amastan itched to grab the bag and see, but waited and watched instead. Dislike of Yanniq might not have been sufficient motivation, but maybe Megar thought he'd been doing the household— and his neighborhood—a service.

Megar undid the knots of his wrap and pulled it down to his waist, exposing a broad expanse of wine-dark skin. Scars littered his chest, short punctures mixed with longer slices. Megar rolled onto his back and slid beneath the basin. He set the lamp on his chest and his arms disappeared inside the pylon. He worked with the ease of proficiency, the muscles in his arms and chest thick cords of rippling movement. He was more than strong enough to take an old man. But was he strong enough to kill an assassin?

Whatever Megar was doing didn't take him long. Without warning, he pushed himself back out of the basin and sat up. He extinguished the lamp's tiny flame, replaced the panel on the basin, then stood and stretched, muscles shifting beneath his taut skin. The screwdriver dangled from his hand as he assessed his work.

When he turned and finally noticed Amastan, he started. Frowned. Blinked. Then he smiled, the expression warm beneath his loose tagel.

"Asaf!"

Amastan swallowed, looking at his hands instead of Megar's uncovered chest. He heard Megar chuckle, followed by the rustle of fabric. When he lifted his gaze, Megar had pulled his wrap back into place. Amastan returned Megar's smile as the gear worker approached, his bag clanking with a dozen more metal tools. Megar raised the screwdriver. Time slowed.

Amastan's hand went to his belt, but before he could draw his dagger, Megar had lowered the screwdriver. Megar paused long enough to put the tool into his bag, then reached for Amastan's hand and patted his back firmly.

"And just where have *you* been?"

Amastan tried to ignore the frantic beating of his heart and shrugged. "Sarif got better, sa. Idir didn't need me anymore."

"To be honest, you didn't seem particularly suited for the job," said Megar. "How about you join me for a drink? I'm done for the day. This was the last pump I had to check for her royalness ma Yanniq. She wants to

be certain they're all one hundred percent working before season's end. Any hitch with allocation will reflect
poorly on her, you know. You can tell me all about what
Yufit's been up to. I've got a few bets to settle."

Megar was already guiding Amastan toward the stairs.
When they stepped out onto the street from the pumphouse, Amastan was surprised—and relieved—to find
that the sun hadn't already set. Time had passed slower
below than above, it seemed. He wasn't late for his meeting with Yufit, not yet.

But if he took up Megar's offer of a drink, he would be.

Megar beckoned him toward Idir's inn. Even though
Amastan knew he should follow Megar, needed to, he
hesitated. Why was this so hard? Logically, it made sense
to keep Yufit waiting if he could get more information out
of Megar. Yet guilt filled him—guilt and something else.
Something he couldn't quite place.

Want or need? Yufit had asked.

Amastan wanted to leave and find Yufit. But he didn't
need to. Yufit would wait. Megar wouldn't.

The inn was thick with stale breath and conversation.
A few eyes cut their way, but none held any interest. A
server wiped down one of the many empty tables. With
another pang of guilt, Amastan recognized Sarif. Thankfully, Sarif had never met Amastan or Asaf, and when he
paused to call out a greeting, it lacked either recognition
or blame.

Some of Yanniq's—*ma* Yanniq's—servants were clustered at a table. The inn seemed even emptier than it
had been a few days before. Megar headed for another
table on the opposite side of the room. Heads turned and
Amastan heard snatches of whispered interest.

Megar patted one side of the table, then swung into the
chair opposite. He leaned on his elbows, his sleeves falling back to reveal his arms, tight with muscle. Where
Yufit was slender, almost angular, Megar was dense and

rounded. His eyes were just as dark, but they lacked Yufit's sharpness. Megar was clearly a product of physical labor, his nails stubby and black with oil. Amastan wondered if they'd ever been stained by blood.

Megar lifted a hand in the air as Sarif passed. "Two glasses, and be quick about it."

When he dropped his hand, Amastan asked, "Why is ma Yanniq worried about allocation?"

Megar shrugged. "Why are any of the drum chiefs worried about it? Depending on how well it goes, her year will either be that much easier or harder. I wouldn't worry—she's been handling allocation since long before Yanniq ate sand."

So Yanniq had been shirking more than just his duties for the Circle. But if Basil ma Yanniq had picked up his slack, then there wouldn't have been any disruptions to the allocation. No anger among his neighborhood, at least not widespread. Perhaps Basil had grown weary of doing all the work of a drum chief without any of the rewards.

Could *she* have dispatched Megar to kill Yanniq? Maybe Megar hadn't been motivated by anger, but loyalty to Basil. He and Basil could have planned the whole thing together, come up with a plausible excuse to bring Yanniq onto a strange rooftop. Letting Yanniq's jaani go wild might not have been an act of rage, but one of contempt.

Sarif dropped off their wine and Megar immediately took a long pull. "I wasn't joking when I told you that you should apply to ma Yanniq. There're a lot of positions open and she's got a steady hand. Besides, with Yufit gone, ma Yanniq needs someone to write letters. A man like you can't do much better than working in a drum chief's house."

Amastan pulled his glass close but didn't drink. "But doesn't ma Yanniq already have someone? I thought that was why she'd fired Yufit."

"Why would she? She was only a wife. Now that she's ma Yanniq, though, she needs one."

Had Yufit lied? No, Amastan doubted that. It was more likely that he'd glossed over the truth. Amastan looked at his hands. "I want to, but what if whoever killed Yanniq isn't done?"

"He wouldn't go after a servant," said Megar with absolute certainty.

"He?"

Megar shrugged. "Well, you don't think a woman could kill a drum chief, do you?"

Amastan thought of Tamella, Menna, and Dihya, each cousin stronger and faster than him. But he didn't say anything. Instead, he saw Megar on a rooftop, blood pooling at his feet.

"It was probably another drum chief," continued Megar, his words spreading out as he took another long drink. "They have special people, you know." He leaned across the table and added in a mock whisper, "Assassins."

The hair on the back of Amastan's neck prickled. He tried to gently redirect the conversation. "Why would a drum chief want Yanniq dead?"

"Dunno." Megar rolled a shrug. "But he didn't get along with most of them, not for a long time. Part of the reason he was so useless. Hard to work together when no one wants to work with you. Had a big fight with them years back. Plus, he's friends with the Serpent."

"The Serpent?" echoed Amastan, even though he knew exactly who Megar meant.

Megar raised a finger, his eyebrows coming together as if in sudden realization. But he overplayed the effect. "Y'know, I wouldn't be surprised if *he* killed Yanniq."

Amastan stared, lost. "Who?"

"The *Serpent*. Pay attention."

"But the Serpent's not—" began Amastan before thinking better of it. He was on shifting ground; how much did the average person know about Tamella?

Thankfully, Megar hadn't noticed. "They used to be buddies, those two. But I bet the Serpent turned on him. I mean, what can you expect from a trained killer? It has to be in his blood."

Amastan bit his tongue to keep from defending Tamella. It was best if no one understood what—and who— the Serpent was. But this line of conversation was going nowhere; Tamella hadn't killed Yanniq. Even if Amastan had reason to doubt her sincerity, she wouldn't have killed Emet, and she certainly wouldn't have left both of their jaan to go wild.

But there was his connection between Yanniq and Emet, plain as a vulture in the sky. Of course, a connection could be drawn between Tamella and any of the drum chiefs. It might be a false lead, but it was the first one he'd had. He'd have to ask Barag about it tomorrow. He had a lot to ask Barag.

Still, he couldn't rid himself of the image of Megar on that rooftop. He had to be involved, somehow. Amastan just needed to find the evidence.

Megar upended his mug into his mouth. He raised the mug overhead to get the attention of Sarif, then thumped it heavy-handed on the table, denting the thin, pressed-wood panel that covered the metal beneath. His hand slid across the wood to find and grab Amastan's mug, which he pulled to himself. Amastan let him, watching with morbid fascination. He wondered if Megar had actually tasted any of the wine he'd just had.

Amastan decided he had enough information for now. Although a drunk Megar might divulge more, Amastan didn't want to risk missing Yufit entirely. He needed to know more about the relationship between Yufit and Megar, and what Yufit believed Megar was capable of. He pushed back from the table and stood.

"Thank you for the drink, sa," he said, even though he hadn't had a drop of it.

Megar's head tilted back and his eyes narrowed. "Where you going? I've got all night—don't you?"

"I have a meeting," admitted Amastan.

Megar's eyes narrowed even further. "Not with that Yufit, is it?" At Amastan's surprise, Megar laughed. Then he leaned farther forward, as if to bridge the distance Amastan had put between them. "Don't look so alarmed. I fix things that're broken and I'm good at what I do. Yufit needs someone; he always tried too hard to be a loner in the household. I'd never seen him look at *anyone* like he looked at you. So, the way I see it is, you owe me. You can't go until you answer some of my questions."

Amastan hesitated. "Like what?"

"Who is Yufit?"

"Don't you know? You worked with him."

"For a month." Megar frowned. "Like I said, he kept to himself. I want to know where Yanniq found him. And"—he leaned farther still, his chair threatening to tip over—"I want to know why he left without saying anything. Tell him he owes me."

"I can ask," said Amastan carefully. He could and would—and he'd also ask if Yufit trusted Megar. If he'd really left without telling Megar, then there had to be a good reason.

Megar suddenly pushed himself up from the table. He swayed precariously but didn't lose his balance. "No, tell you what. I want to ask him myself. Besides, it's getting dark and you shouldn't be walking these streets alone. You never know what could be lurking out there. If the Serpent is back in business, not a one of us is safe."

"I'll be all right, sa," said Amastan. "It's only a few platforms away."

"Then you shouldn't mind me tagging along." Megar

rounded the table. He pulled at his wrap, trying to straighten it out but only yanking it further askew.

Amastan bit his lip, thinking fast. The last thing he wanted was for Megar to tag along and intrude on his meeting. He suddenly saw Megar in the pumphouse, holding the screwdriver up like a weapon. But this time, Yufit was there, crumpled before him. What if Yufit had left because he'd realized Megar had been behind Yanniq's death? And now Megar wanted to find him.

"I just want to see that he's all right," continued Megar. His eyes were glassy with drink, but every word was crisp and clear. As if practiced. "We left off on a misunderstanding, him and I."

On the edge of his awareness, the inn's front door opened and closed. It was an unremarkable event that caught Amastan's attention nonetheless. He glanced over. No one was near the door; someone must have just left. A hot breath of wind swirled around him and although he knew it had just come from outside, the hair on the back of his neck prickled.

"I'm not meeting with Yufit," lied Amastan, backing away. "But if I do—"

Megar was fast. He grabbed Amastan's wrist and pulled him in close. "Yufit smiles like a knife. He's a sharp one. Take care he doesn't cut you."

Amastan breathed deep to reply. The air tasted of pinched candles and burnt iron. His stomach dropped and suddenly, he couldn't remember what he'd been about to say. When had his charm started to feel so warm?

The breeze twisted and played with his wrap. The torches on the walls flickered and guttered. The murmuring of conversation in the inn wavered, paused. In the brief silence, the wind's voice was the loudest, a whistling, incoherent whine. Then the conversation continued, if a bit louder than before.

Amastan pulled himself out of Megar's grasp. Behind Megar's shoulder, the air smudged. Red spread, deepened. Fear froze Amastan's tongue and lips. A jaani? It couldn't be. Not now. Not *here*.

Amastan didn't have time to understand Megar's words. Someone shouted, "*jaani!*" and chaos erupted. Amastan ducked to the side as the servants swarmed past, scrambling for the door. Above their heads, the wind churned and the red condensed into a distinct shape, one he'd seen in a glasshouse only last night. A wavery figure with two long arms and two long legs and two empty spots where eyes should've been. These shifted in the tumultuous air to stare at him.

"Run!" he shouted to Megar, then took his own advice and broke for the door.

Someone had already wrenched it open and people spilled into the street. But a gust of heat and iron caught up to Amastan before he could reach the door, and as the last servant escaped, the door slammed shut.

Amastan spun. He stared into those hollow eyes, mere feet from him now. His charm burned as if it were flame, but he couldn't move. His fear had swallowed him whole, left him as solid and immobile as stone, his mind just as blank. He was back in the glasshouse with Emet's body, but now there was no Menna to stop the jaani.

The jaani blew closer, its red form endlessly shifting like smoke. Drums beat beneath his skin—or was that only his heart? Tendrils swirled around him, wiping out the sight and sound and smell of the inn, so that all Amastan knew was red and wind and sun-forged iron.

"You get away from him!"

A chair broke the hypnotic swirl, cutting the jaani in half. Amastan blinked as the sensation of place and time returned to him. He dropped his hand that had been about to rip off his charm. Meanwhile, the jaani churned faster, bringing itself back together, and turned its sightless eyes on the man wielding a chair like a weapon. Megar.

Amastan had enough time to feel surprise before the jaani struck. But not him—it lashed out at Megar with one of its too-long arms, hitting him square in the chest. Megar let out a startled grunt and crumpled to the ground. The jaani swirled tighter for a moment, its arm hovering over Megar as if it wasn't sure what had just happened.

Amastan swallowed his cry of surprise and fear. Megar was still conscious, blinking owlishly up at the jaani with his tagel half off. Beneath, Megar's dark lips moved soundlessly. He frowned and his chest swelled with a deep breath, but when his mouth opened again, no sound came out. The jaani whirled around him, its legs disappearing as if it were kneeling, enveloping Megar in red. His eyes widened in fear.

Amastan grabbed his charm and yanked. "Hey!"

The jaani swiveled its attention back to him. So did Megar. Amastan lobbed his charm through the jaani's torso to Megar, who caught it. The jaani immediately dispersed, as if blown away by a hard wind. But Amastan's momentary thrill of victory was replaced with panic when the jaani began to coalesce again, this time around him. And now he didn't have any charms.

He took in the room. No one was left but him and Megar. With the thinnest shred of a plan, Amastan hurled himself through the jaani. But not toward the door.

He slid next to Megar and held out his hand. Killer or not, he wasn't about to leave anyone to the mercy of a jaani. Megar grimaced and took it and Amastan hauled him to his feet. Amastan folded Megar's fingers around the charm, then put his own hand on top. He gestured toward the back of the inn. Megar didn't need any further prompting.

They stumbled between the tables and overturned

chairs toward the door in the back that led out onto the alley. The wind tore at their wraps and hissed in their ears, but its grasping fingers slipped off. The air darkened around them, turning red. And between them, the charm began to smoke. Amastan could feel the heat even through Megar's hand. But Megar held on.

Amastan reached the door first and threw it open. Then he was outside, turning, grabbing Megar and pulling him through the door. In the same motion, he yanked the charm from Megar's fingers and slammed the door shut. He slipped the charm around the door's handle, then snatched his hand back. The charm had burned his fingers and now they sang with pain.

The door shuddered and shook, then went still. Thick smoke curled from the charm, its edges turning black. Amastan wasn't sure how long it'd last, and he didn't want to think about what would happen when the charm failed. He needed to find a marabi.

He needed Menna.

Megar was already stumbling down the alley. Amastan passed him, spilling out onto the platform's center. As he took a moment to reorient himself, he thought he heard the creak of a door opening. But the inn's front door was still shut fast.

The center was devoid of other people. The fleeing servants must have scared them away. He hoped that meant the jaani wouldn't hurt anyone, but as he headed north, he couldn't help but wonder why the jaani had come to the inn. Why it had come inside. It had almost seemed as if it were looking for someone.

But that couldn't be possible.

Amastan had just stepped onto the bridge when the breeze picked up, bringing with it the too-familiar smells of burnt metal and gutted flame.

That was his only warning.

Something slammed into him as hard as a camel's kick. He hit the railing at the wrong angle. Heat and wind and hot iron buffeted him, lifting him up. Over. Down.

He fell.

14

Amastan didn't have time for fear, only nerves and instinct. His hands shot out, grabbing for anything they
could catch. The railing slipped from his grasp, but his
fingers hit and snagged on a wooden slat. His fingertips
and nails scraped across rough wood as his hands took
the full weight of his body and his arms felt as if they
might jerk right out of his sockets.

But his arms held and his grip didn't give. Amastan
hung from the bridge by his fingertips, fighting the pain
building in his forearms and the terror building in his
chest. He didn't dare look down.

Let go.

The jaani swirled around him, filling the gap between
the platforms. Its heat and smell seared his nose. Amastan tried to ignore it, but the jaani's red smeared his vision and something tugged at his wrap. His fingers were
beginning to slip. He couldn't hold on much longer.

He tried to pull himself up, but the jaani was pulling
him down with equal strength. Already his arms were beginning to tire, his fingertips slipping by a hair's width. If
he could inch along to the platform, he might be able to
get a better grip.

The jaani whirled tighter, its red deepening. Sound
grew muted, as if Amastan's ears were clogged. He could
feel the jaani trying to find its way in through his nose,
his mouth. Tiny, weak fingers tugged at the skin of his

face, unsure but persistent. He held his breath and tried to scoot along the bridge. His fingers slipped. Suddenly, he was hanging by only one hand.

Let go, whispered the voice again, smooth as smoke.

Amastan closed his eyes. He was going to die. For some reason, the realization filled him with calm instead of panic. And a wry sense of amusement. Of all the ways to go out, he'd never imagined plunging to his death. At least it'd be over quickly.

"Asaf!"

Amastan's eyes shot open, but all he could see was red. He tried to crane his head, but the movement made his fingers slip another precarious quarter inch. His heart raced.

"Grab my hand!"

Fingers shot through the red. Amastan reached up with his free hand. The fingers wrapped around his wrist and pulled. The jaani's hold loosened, slipped. Another hand reached down and grabbed his forearm, helping him up and over. Amastan tumbled onto the bridge. In that moment, he'd never been happier to have his cheek pressed against warm wood.

A hand covered his and Amastan started. He looked up into steel-gray eyes. Then those same hands were helping him stand and the rush of wind brought Amastan back to the moment. He might not be dangling over the sands any longer, but he still had an angry jaani to contend with.

An angry jaani that for some reason was intent on *him.*

Yufit stood close, as if Amastan might fall over at any moment. "Thank you," said Amastan. "Now run."

They ran. Like an angry nightmare, the jaani whirled up and over the bridge. It chased them, still undeterred. Amastan's thoughts, calm and quiet only a few moments ago when he stared death in the face, spun back to life. The jaani was behaving differently this time. When he'd rescued Yufit, all he'd had to do was put some distance between him and its anger. But now—

The jaani had found him in the inn, had gone straight for him. He'd stopped it with the charm, but only for a little while. Somehow, it had found him again. Which meant he could run as far and as fast as he wanted, but the jaani would still be right there. And he couldn't run forever. He needed a destination. He needed a plan.

All he had was a hope.

He ran. Yufit easily kept up. They dodged people and markets, but Amastan was no longer worried that the jaani would attack someone else. And just as he'd expected, it kept its focus on them. On him.

Thankfully, his destination was only a few platforms away. They arrived in the Seraf neighborhood with a few seconds of distance between them and the jaani. Amastan paused for a heartbeat at the platform's center, searching for a familiar door.

There. The door was propped open next to a shuttered storefront. Beyond the door was a staircase. Amastan flew up these stairs, then hesitated on the next landing. He needed a moment to line up the doors in front of him with the windows outside. He'd never come this way before. But he couldn't exactly scale the wall and climb in through the window with Yufit at his side.

He knocked on the third door. He glanced behind him as they waited. He'd bought some time with their full-out run, but not enough. The jaani would catch up to them at any moment. *Them*—Amastan glanced at Yufit, suddenly conscious of his presence. How would he explain—?

Menna threw the door open, eyes wide with worry, and gestured for them to enter. She locked the door behind them and turned to Amastan, her mouth already opening, but he beat her to it.

"Are your doors warded? Your windows?" He scanned the doorframe as he asked, but he didn't see any charms.

Menna scuffed a spot beneath the door with her foot. "Of course. What's wrong"—her eyes cut to Yufit and back again—"friend?"

Yufit looked to Amastan as well, a similar question in his eyes. The window on the opposite side of the small, sparse space rattled. Yufit took a step back and grabbed for Amastan's arm, but his hand fell short and he didn't make a second attempt. Menna glanced at the window, eyebrows creased in a frown. But the worry was leaching away, replaced with confused concern.

"What do you know about angry jaan?" asked Amastan.

"Oh, I swear by all things holy—you brought a jaani? *Here*?"

"You're a marabi," said Amastan. "You must know something. The jaani chased us all the way from the Aeser neighborhood."

"I do know *something*. I know how to quiet a tethered jaani. But what you've brought me is a wild jaani. I've *told* you, I can't quiet a wild jaani." Menna wrung her hands, glancing from the door to the window. "How did you even get the jaani to come here?"

"It followed us."

"Jaan don't *follow*," said Menna, annoyed. "The wind blows them about and they attack whatever's closest."

"But this one did," said Yufit. "Something's different about this one."

"*Sands*." Menna bit her lower lip. The window rattled harder. "A jaani shouldn't have that kind of will. It shouldn't have any will at all."

"The jaan on the sands might not," said Yufit. "But this one's different. It's stronger. I—" he glanced at Amastan, as if for permission. When Amastan nodded, he continued, "I've met it before. In an alley just two nights ago. Asaf saved me. I wonder if that's why it chased him now?"

Menna threw up her hands. "I don't know! I'm not a

jaani expert! I don't have them over for tea and ask them how they've been or what they're thinking."

Amastan had never seen her so rattled before. He tried to keep his voice level and calm, even as his own fear flared. "Please. You know more about jaan than either of us. There must be a way to protect ourselves from it or—or send it away."

"Not quiet it," said Menna, softer now.

"No. You're right, it's too late for that."

"It's . . . maybe . . . but I'd have to ask Elder Dessin, and I don't have time for that." She glanced at the window. "If it's somehow stronger than a normal jaani, then my wards won't keep it out long. I might be able to drive it away, but whatever I do won't stick. It'll come back."

"Even then, that gives us time to find a real solution."

"Hopefully," said Menna grimly. But then a smile tweaked the corner of her lips and she started rolling up her sleeves. "I guess this counts as exciting, huh? Right. Whatever water you two have, I'll need it."

Amastan unhooked his water skin, still full from the pumphouse, and handed it over, but Yufit hesitated. Menna held out her hand.

"What, you'll run into a woman's room but you won't trust her with your water? Typical." Menna opened and closed her hand impatiently. "Asaf brought you here because I'm a marabi. I know what I'm doing."

Yufit reluctantly set his skin in Menna's open hand. She turned and went to a low table pushed against one wall and cleared a space on its cluttered surface. She pulled a glass bowl from the shelf and dumped the contents of both skins into it. The combined water came to within an inch of the bowl's lip.

A loud crack rent the room and Amastan spun, heart hammering. A fine line now stretched from one corner of the window to the other. Red filled the crack like putty and air sputtered into the room.

Menna didn't turn. Her lips moved soundlessly as she leaned over the table and began filling a sheet of vellum with looping letters. When it was full of black ink, she dunked the vellum into the bowl and swished it around. The ink leached into the water, turning it first gray, then black. When Menna pulled the vellum out, the sheet was clean of words.

She passed her hands over the bowl and the rattling stopped, only to start up again a heartbeat later. She frowned, then cast about the room.

"I need a fire," she said, more to the room than to them.

"Do you have oil?" asked Yufit.

Menna nodded, pointed. Yufit let go of Amastan's hand to retrieve a glass jar from the low shelf. Amastan looked around as well, trying to piece together what Yufit was doing. They still needed something for the fire to catch on. Amastan didn't see any balled tinder, but he did see cloth.

When he grabbed the sheet from Menna's bed, she didn't object. When he began ripping it into strips, she winced but still didn't say anything. Instead, she scattered salt beneath the window, then in a circle on the floor. She pointed and Amastan dropped the cloth strips within the circle. Yufit drenched them with oil. Menna rustled through her drawers until she found a striker. She let a spark fall onto the pile.

The oil caught and flared and almost immediately died down, but the cloth kept the fire going. In a few moments, they had a flashing hot fire in the center of Menna's room, oily smoke curling upward and pouring toward the ceiling. Menna pulled her wrap over her mouth and retrieved the bowl of water. She gestured for Yufit to add more oil to the fire, then pointed Amastan toward the window. Amastan stared, disbelieving. Menna gestured again, this time with more emphasis.

Amastan edged toward the window as if it might shatter

at any moment. The closer he got, the stronger the smell of spent candles and hot iron grew. He reached out with one shaking hand for the latch, which rattled and shook along with the rest of the window. Using a single finger, he undid the latch and jumped back. The window slammed open and the glass shattered and fell.

The angry jaani filled the room and brought the wind with it. The fire spun in the center of the room, tight as a rope as it reached for the ceiling. Menna ignored the jaani and the wind and drizzled inky water over the fire. It sputtered with annoyance, sending up great gouts of smoke—and steam.

The first burst of steam hit the jaani and it flinched, its color fading for a moment before flaring back redder than before. Then the next cloud of steam rolled into it and this time the jaani reared back, spreading outward as if it might go around the steam.

Menna dumped the rest of the water onto the fire, which sputtered and went out—but not without first sending a last, great burst of steam through the room.

Amastan's teeth and skull sang in pain. Yufit clutched his head and Menna gritted her teeth. The red was thinning, dispersing, the wind in the room dying down, until all that was left was the three of them, their wraps sticky with steam, and an open window. The pain tapered off, becoming a pounding memory instead.

Menna looked between the two of them as water dripped from the smoke-stained ceiling. "Well. That was fun."

15

Yufit stood at the window, staring out as if the jaani might come back at any moment. Amastan kept a careful distance from the glass, keenly aware of his naked neck. A soft breeze circulated the room and the moisture in the air soon thinned and dissipated completely.

Amastan looked at Menna for what felt like the first time. Her wrap stuck to her skin, streaked with soot and sweat. "What did you do?"

Menna nudged the pile of wet, charred cloth with her toe. "I banished it." She sounded dazed, but when she looked up, her face glowed with excitement. "I *banished* it, 'Sta—Asaf. I've never done that before. I didn't even know it would work. I just threw something together. But look!" She opened her arms to encompass the mess of her room. "I did it! I'm amazing. Dessin's gonna see stars when I tell him."

Her smile could have lit up the night. Amastan couldn't help but feel a little of her excitement. It was a welcome relief after so much panic.

"So . . . it'll be back?" asked Yufit.

Menna's smile faded. "Well, yes. But that gives us time to figure out how to quiet a wild jaani. And not just any wild jaani, I might add. The ones we've been taught how to deal with are weak and thin. This one was not only much, much stronger, but fixated. I don't know why. I need to find out."

"Maybe it just hasn't lost its strength yet," said Yufit, turning away from the window. "Someone must've died and their jaani wasn't quieted in time."

Amastan and Menna shared a glance. She took his lead and didn't mention Yanniq. Yufit couldn't know about the drum chief's unquieted jaani. Instead, she set her bowl back on its shelf, lips pursed in thought.

"I'll talk to the other marab later," said Menna. "In the meantime, the jaani shouldn't come after you for . . . well, *normally* that kind of banishment would take centuries for the jaani to recover from. But this one? I'd say you've got a day, maybe two, tops. Go to Salid's first thing and get yourselves new charms. They won't do much, but they might give you enough time to get away."

Amastan nodded, but he made no move toward the door. Despite Menna's assurances, he was wary of leaving the room. What if she was wrong? What if the jaani was waiting outside for them?

Menna looked between them again, then frowned and shooed them toward the door. "Go! This isn't an inn and the jaani's gone for now. In case you forgot, you're in *my* home and I still have work to do."

"Okay, okay," said Amastan, hands raised in defense as he edged toward the door.

"Are you sure you don't need help cleaning up?" asked Yufit.

Menna glanced over the mess of her room with disdain. Then she rolled her shoulders back and lifted her chin. "I'm fine. It'll help me think. I need to do a lot of that, right now."

Yufit grabbed her hand and held it between his. Menna startled, started to pull away, but then stopped when Yufit said, "Thank you for your help, ma. You saved us. We're in your debt."

Menna laughed, her sand-brown cheeks darkening. Yufit let her hand slip away as he straightened, his eyes still on Menna. Amastan cleared his throat, inexplicably annoyed with the display.

"Come on, Yufit," he said. But he caught Menna's eye before turning and she winked.

He opened the door without waiting to see if Yufit followed. He took the stairs two at a time, suddenly craving to be outside again. The lingering humidity from the fire and water stuck in his throat and he couldn't shake the acrid smell of burnt cloth.

Yufit caught up to him just outside the bakery. His warm hand found Amastan's forearm and his touch sent a cold shock across Amastan's skin. Amastan slowed down and turned.

"I guess now I owe you some tea," said Amastan. "I'm sorry I didn't quite make our meeting."

"I'd begun to worry about you." Yufit's smile was hesitant. "Seems I was right to."

"I was lucky you were there," said Amastan.

"Well . . ." Yufit shifted from one foot to the other. "I don't know how much luck has to do with it. I was on my way back after deciding you'd lost the nerve to see me. I saw the jaani throw you over the side of the bridge. Now *you* owe *me*: an explanation, at the very least, and another chance to show you some fun. Although it looks like you were having enough of that on your own."

"What explanation?"

"*Why* did a jaani shove you over the side of a bridge?"

"It was chasing me," said Amastan.

Yufit crossed his arms and raised his eyebrow. He waited.

Amastan swallowed, casting for a plausible excuse that didn't start with a drink in Idir's inn seated across a table from Megar. If he was going to ask about Megar, he wanted to do so when his questions wouldn't be colored by what had just happened. "It found me on my way over. I was already a few minutes late, and then I had to stop for water. When I came out of the pumphouse, the jaani was there. I ran, but it followed. I don't know how or why, except that it must've remembered me from when I saved you. I thought I could wear it out—or something."

"Instead you fell off a bridge." Yufit clapped his hands together. "Well done."

"It pushed me," said Amastan, his voice quiet. The words started as defense, but ended as realization. The jaani had pulled at his wrap, had shoved Megar. It shouldn't have been able to do either. He tagged that information as something he needed to tell Menna. Menna, who was waiting for him upstairs.

She could wait a little longer.

Yufit stepped closer. "That still doesn't explain why you were over an hour late."

Amastan looked at Yufit's hands instead of his eyes. Most of the ink stains were gone, the skin scrubbed clean. Even his fingernails were pristine. "I lost track of time at work."

The corner of Yufit's eye crinkled with a smirk. "I don't believe you."

Amastan made the mistake of looking into those eyes. He forgot to breathe.

With a sigh, Yufit dropped his gaze, releasing Amastan. "I'll let you keep your secrets, Asaf. It makes you more interesting. Besides, I'd rather not believe you sat with dusty scrolls for an entire hour instead of coming to see me, even if that's the truth of it."

Amastan's stomach dropped. He couldn't risk losing Yufit, not yet. He still needed Yufit. He might suspect Megar, but he needed more than mere suspicions. Yufit could help him find the connections between Basil, Yanniq, Tamella, and Emet. And there might be something else he had missed. Besides, before the jaani had attacked, Megar had been almost *too* eager to talk with Yufit. Amastan should keep an eye on him. For his own safety.

"I did," said Amastan. "I really— There was a deadline. I have to have this project done by season's end. I really did lose track of time. I'm sorry."

"Sadly, I believe you." But Yufit's tone had an edge of amusement to it.

"We can try again. I—I'm curious about what you were going to show me."

"I'll give you another chance," said Yufit, smiling. "But not tonight. It's too late for what I'd had in mind. Tomorrow I'm busy with something else, but—the night after? Will that work for you and your demanding schedule?"

"Yes." Amastan breathed out. "Okay."

Still smiling, Yufit glanced toward the stairs leading up to Menna's. "And by then maybe your friend will have figured out how we can both avoid another run-in with a jaani. We can't keep meeting like this."

Amastan's ears warmed. Some of his embarrassment must have been obvious because Yufit laughed.

"Stay safe, Asaf." Still chuckling, Yufit took off.

Amastan watched him go, sauntering down the street like a man who owned half the city. Yufit had more confidence in his sandals than Amastan had in his entire body. Only when Yufit disappeared around a corner was Amastan able to breathe freely again. It had to be the responsibility of finding Yanniq's killer that made him feel a little breathless and a little nervous around Yufit. That was all.

The glass may have been gone, but Menna had shuttered her window. Amastan perched on the sill outside and knocked politely. Before he could finish knocking, Menna had unlocked the shutters and swung them open. She was dressed in a different wrap, this one clean and a darker gray than her marabi wrap. She'd covered her puff of black hair with a purple cloth and wiped away the smoke and dirt from her face—all of it except for a smudge just below one eye.

"Took you long enough." Menna finished knotting her

belt. "What were you doing? Proclaiming your undying love to each other for all to hear?"

"That's Yanniq's scribe," said Amastan. "Or, was."

Menna paused in her preparations. Then, with complete seriousness, she said, "So he might know who killed Emet."

Amastan nodded.

"Fine. I won't tease." She finished checking her belt and wiped her hands on her wrap. "It's late, but Elder Dessin should still be awake. You're coming with me. This jaani problem is getting out of control and it'll help if you can give Dessin a firsthand account of what happened. Jaan don't *follow*. They just— They don't have the will for it."

"The jaani pushed me," said Amastan.

Menna started for the door, then stopped. She turned completely around and stared at Amastan. "Jaan don't push."

"This one did. It hit someone else who was trying to help me, and it pushed me off a bridge."

"Jaan don't push," she repeated. "They physically can't. They don't have anything to push *with*. Unless . . ." She trailed off and her thoughts crossed her face, clear as light. Amastan wanted to look away, but he couldn't help but watch as first consideration, then realization, then horror contorted her features.

Finally, determination.

"We'll figure this out before anyone else gets hurt." Menna grabbed Amastan's arm and all but yanked him down the stairs. "Elder Dessin will know what's going on. He always knows what's going on."

Elder Dessin hadn't known what was going on, but he'd already been planning on bringing the other elders together to discuss the situation. Even though the jaani had been intent on Amastan instead of hurting anyone else, enough people had seen it in the Aeser neighborhood to start a panic. After announcing that he would speak with the elders, Dessin had shooed them out, claiming that he needed to go back to sleep.

The meeting of the elders should be happening soon. Amastan dipped his pen in ink and wondered if Menna would be there. He'd given her as many details as he could, down to how the jaani had shoved Megar and stolen his voice. He just didn't mention that he knew Megar. Nor what he suspected Megar had done.

It was in the elders' hands now. He had to trust them to know what to do. That was their job, after all. And he had his own job to do.

Amastan scanned over his work from yesterday, but his attention was split. Thinking of Megar reminded him of what Megar had said. He'd mentioned the Serpent, had claimed that she and Yanniq were once more than mere acquaintances, maybe even friends. Amastan could hardly believe it and suspected Megar was inflating rumors, but any connection between Yanniq and the family was worth following up.

He also remembered what Megar hadn't said, his strange obsession with Yufit. If Megar was the killer, maybe Yufit had seen something he shouldn't. He wouldn't have a chance to ask Yufit until tomorrow, though. But two were dead and time was falling. He didn't have time to wait. He'd have to seek what answers he could from the scrolls.

His gaze drifted from the scrolls in front of him to the hearth, where Thana sat alone, practicing stringwork. She bent over a set of leather strands and wove them together, only her fingers moving as she set and tightened the complicated knots. It was unusual for Thana to be home while he and Barag worked. Usem usually picked her up for her lessons before Amastan arrived, but he wouldn't be stopping by today; he'd given Thana the day off.

"Do you remember doing that?"

Amastan looked up to find Barag had materialized in front of his table. The old man carried two cups and a pot of tea. He didn't look like he was harboring any secrets, but Usem had said . . .

"Stringwork?" Amastan picked up his pen and uncapped the ink. "Tamella wouldn't let us do anything else for *weeks*." She'd insisted it was good for their precision. As with everything Tamella had insisted on, she'd been right.

"Here—it looks like you could use this." Barag set a cup in front of Amastan and filled it with steaming tea. "It also looks like you were out all night. Tamella mentioned you've been interviewing Yanniq's old servants."

Amastan gratefully wrapped his hands around the tea even as guilt rose and stuck in his throat. "I haven't got very far." He watched the steam rise from his cup, curling and twisting and spinning like the jaani. He pushed the cup away. "Did she say anything about Emet?"

Barag nodded gravely, his hands curled around the teapot. "A cousin dead. And the healers confirmed he died the same way as Yanniq: a knife wound to the thigh. He never had a chance."

"I'm at a loss," admitted Amastan. He rubbed his forehead, pushing his tagel back. "I don't know what Yanniq and Emet have in common or why someone would want to kill either of them. I have leads, possibilities, but none of it feels right. I'm missing something." He drew a deep breath, met Barag's gaze. *Ask him about it sometime,* Usem had said. "Did Tamella ever break a contract?"

Barag held his gaze a little too long. "Who said that?"

"Usem."

"Of course." Barag huffed in annoyance, then leaned back, considering Amastan. "I don't see what it could have to do with Yanniq or Emet. It's not a secret, not exactly. And you'll find out eventually when you reach that part of the history." He raised a finger. "Don't tell Tam' I told you, all right?"

Amastan nodded.

Barag took a deep breath. "I used to be the drum chiefs' records keeper and occasional poet."

"You were a poet?" asked Amastan, despite himself.

"I'm *still* a poet," corrected Barag. "History is a kind of poetry. It also pays better." He cleared his throat. "When one of the drum chief's records didn't match up, I did some rustling. That's how I discovered a conspiracy between them and several prominent merchants. Naïve fool that I was, I pointed out the discrepancy to the drum chief who had the most to lose. That earned me a contract."

"Wait—a contract? On *you*?"

Barag chuckled darkly. "Yes. And that was only their first mistake. Tamella took the contract, but she realized something was off. What they'd claimed I'd done didn't match with what she saw during her surveillance. Instead of killing me, she saved me. And instead of completing her contract, she took it upon herself to find the conspirators and stop them. So yes, she broke her contract." He smiled and poured himself a cup of tea. "That's how we met."

Amastan sat with that information for a moment. Tamella had broken her contract, but the contract had been unjust. Tamella had killed outside of a contract, but she'd saved the city. The drum chiefs had condemned her, yet Megar spoke as if Yanniq had been her friend. And Amastan had only heard Tamella speak of the Circle with disdain.

"Did Tamella—" began Amastan.

A heavy drumbeat cut off his question, followed on its heels by another. It reverberated through his skull and stilled his tongue. He exchanged a glance with Barag, who appeared equally puzzled. A third drumbeat confirmed what he'd begun to suspect: this was a calling.

Barag rolled his eyes and set his teacup down. He gestured to Thana, but his daughter had already discarded her stringwork and was headed for the door. A cold dread bloomed in Amastan's gut as he followed, the drumbeat dragging them all to the calling.

What was it this time? Drum Chief Hennu had called them last time to announce Yanniq's death. Had another drum chief died? If so, maybe the drum chiefs would finally take responsibility for finding the killer. Amastan didn't dare hope.

The heat was already at an exquisite peak when they stepped out into the too-bright daylight. A haze had settled over the streets, leaching both color and life from the city. All around them, other people hunched and blinked under the onslaught. But just the same, the drumbeat drew them out, brought them one by one and in groups to the center of the neighborhood. Unlike last time, Amastan didn't push his way forward. Barag and Thana stood with him at the edge of the crowd.

Drum Chief Hennu's bright blue wrap was a beacon on the dais. Her gold necklaces and bracelets and earrings shone like tiny suns, too painful to look at. Beside her, the slave pounded on her drum. Behind her, her retinue of servants, slaves, and watchmen stood, straight-backed and attentive. At her other side, a frail old man in a brilliant red wrap stood, leaning heavily on a staff: Elder Dessin.

The slave beat the drum for another minute. Then Drum Chief Hennu sliced the air with her hand and the slave stopped. She picked up the drum and raised it over her head, turning this way and that. The crowd, already quiet, grew still as stone. Hennu set the drum down between her feet and clasped her hands before her.

"Citizens! Greetings and G-d bless." Her voice rang out loud and clear. "You have answered my call; now stay and listen." She paused and glanced at the marabi at her elbow. Elder Dessin nodded. She continued. "First, I bid you: do not panic. We have everything under control. The elders are working on a solution to our problem. I trust them with my life, as should you.

"Rumors have been flying that monsters are loose in our city. You might've heard some of these rumors. I'm here to tell you the truth: there are no monsters in our streets. There is, however, one—possibly two—jaan loose and unquieted. But this is no reason for alarm. As long as you wear your charms and stay in groups, you will be safe."

She paused, riding out the surge of anxious grumbling from the crowd. When it was silent again, Drum Chief Hennu continued. "Aside from wearing your charms, I ask you to be especially vigilant for possible possessions. Ask your neighbor if she is sane. Ask yourself. If you suspect there is a jaani in your area, seek shelter first and alert the watchmen second. The marab will be keeping careful watch over us. Don't be alarmed—even if you are possessed, the marab will be able to help you. All will be fine."

Hennu raised her hands again. "I will call you when the danger is past. In the meantime, remember: stay calm, stay vigilant, and stay sane. That is all. I thank you for your attention."

Drum Chief Hennu dropped her hand to her heart, and her slave took up the drum. He beat out a slower rhythm to release the calling. The crowd woke as if from a dream and broke apart. Amastan started to head back, but Barag didn't move. He stared at the dais with a frown creasing his brow. When he caught Amastan watching, he shook his head.

"Will you take Thana back with you? I have an errand to run. I won't be gone long."

"Sure," said Amastan.

Barag barely seemed to hear him. He glanced around

the emptying area, then looped his fingers through his belt and headed across the platform. Amastan watched him for a moment. Then he met Thana's gaze and offered his hand, but she turned and started back home without waiting for him.

The workspace seemed much quieter and emptier than earlier, even though only Barag was missing. Thana took up her spot next to the hearth and returned to messing with her stringwork, but she seemed distracted. She kept glancing toward the door.

Amastan settled into his seat and looked from the work he still had left to do today to the basket of scrolls that comprised the family's history. The faster he got the one done, the sooner he could turn to the other. With a sigh, he pulled the first scroll toward himself and began painstakingly transcribing it.

The day wore on, but Barag didn't return. Silence buzzed like a fly at Amastan's ear. When the noon bell rang and Barag was still gone, Amastan set his finished work in its own basket and took up Barag's.

Evening settled with a creak and groan of cooling stone. Amastan wiped the ink off his pen and blinked tired eyes. Thana had lit the hearth and left a candle on his desk. He stared at the flickering flame. Barag would be appalled to find any fire source so close to his precious scrolls. Amastan rolled up his scrolls with extra care and cleaned each of his pens, but by the time he'd finished, Barag still hadn't returned.

Come to think of it, he hadn't seen Tamella all day, either.

Thana had finished her stringwork and now sat next to a pile of mended sandals. She looked up as he stood, her expression no less serious than before. Then she returned her attention to the ripped leather and stabbed it with a thick needle.

He stretched and considered the door. He didn't feel

comfortable leaving Thana alone, not when there were jaan on the loose. Not when he didn't know when Barag would return. Thana seemed to sense his hesitation. She scooted over on her bench without looking up. Amastan joined her and they sat in silence together as the hearth crackled and spat. For once, he let himself think about nothing.

The door slammed open. Amastan started and Thana jumped to her feet, a knife in her hand. Then she dropped the knife and it clattered, loud as a drum, to the ground.

Tamella stood in the doorway. She swayed, eyes wide and skin ashen. She stepped inside and the door closed behind her. Blood covered her hands and smeared across her jaw, thick and dark as glasshouse mud. Panic tightened Amastan's throat. Had the jaani possessed her? What could he even do if it had? She was stronger and faster than him. He didn't stand a chance.

"Are you sane?" he asked tentatively, afraid of the answer.

Tamella ignored his question. When she spoke, her words were a bitter accusation.

"He's dead. Usem is dead."

16

When Barag arrived, the madness in Tamella's eyes had vanished. She sat catatonic near the hearth and clutched the cooling cup of tea Thana had brewed for her. Tamella hadn't said anything else since she'd uttered her brother's name. Her silence unnerved Amastan more than her sudden appearance and the blood on her hands.

Upon seeing his wife, Barag said, "Merciful G-d," and hurried to her. He grabbed her hands and, noticing the blood, turned them over. He checked her wrists and forearms next, pushing up the sleeves of her wrap until Tamella yanked her arms free.

"*I'm* fine," she snapped.

Barag looked up from where he knelt on the ground before her. "Where've you been? I was looking all over for you. What happened?"

Amastan quietly swung the kettle back over the hearth. His throat was knotted with shock and guilt. He'd never seen Tamella so shaken before, so raw.

Tamella looked away, unable to meet Barag's eyes. She clutched her arms close and said, "I found him."

Barag winced, as if he'd been hit. He reached for her, but changed his mind at the last moment and let his hands dangle between his knees instead. "Usem."

The cups rattled. Thana stood in front of them, her head tipped forward and her face obscured by braids. She had gone to get a second cup but now it appeared she couldn't move. Her shoulders shook and her hands clenched at her sides and she emitted a small, choked noise.

"Star of my sky," said Barag softly. "Go upstairs. Please."

"Why?" asked Thana, not turning around. "I want to be here for this. I'm old enough. Usem—Usem was *my* uncle."

"That's why you should go upstairs," said Barag. "You don't need to hear this. It will only upset you."

Thana whirled, anger sparking in her wet eyes. In that moment, she looked every bit her mother's daughter. "I'm not a child!"

"Thana." Tamella's voice was quiet, but dangerous. She lifted her head and Thana wilted under her stare. "Go upstairs."

Thana's mouth snapped shut and her defiance left her all at once. She stood for a moment longer, then turned and left. For a few seconds, they all listened as she stomped up the stairs. A heartbeat later, a door slammed.

Amastan held his breath. Would Tamella order him to leave as well? Maybe he should go before she did. This was a home to grief now, and he had no place in it. But he lingered, worry and confusion and a growing, unpleasant knowledge that he knew just what had happened churning in his gut.

Tamella closed her eyes, took a deep breath. When she spoke again, her voice was empty, flat, and more unnerving than any time he'd seen her angry. "He didn't tell me he had a contract."

There shouldn't be any contracts, Menna had said, angry and confused outside the glasshouse. Amastan knew all at once what Tamella would say next. The sick feeling spread from his gut to his chest. He didn't want to stay and listen. But he had to.

"When I couldn't find him anywhere usual, I asked around. His wife mentioned he'd been out a lot the last few days, that he'd been coming home late. She thought he could be having an affair. I knew better. I found Kaseem, asked him—he didn't want to tell me anything, but . . ." She paused and Amastan imagined her unyielding anger wearing through even Kaseem's stubborn streak.

"I found the mark," she continued after a brief silence. "Still alive. I searched the area. It took a while, but I found him."

This time when she paused, the silence stretched for several heartbeats. Neither Amastan nor Barag moved, each watching and waiting as Tamella swallowed air. When she spoke again, her voice was rough.

"There was a room that had been gutted by fire not long ago. The windows were melted ruins, but someone had bothered to cover them with cloth. He'd been dumped inside and hidden beneath a pile of burnt garbage. If I hadn't looked *everywhere,* no one would have found him for days, weeks even. He'd been . . . it'd been too long. I *tried.*" She lifted her hands, the blood on them explaining more than words.

The smears of blood across her knees, her hands, her face revealed every point of contact between Tamella and Usem's body. Amastan could see her kneeling over her brother's corpse, unwilling or unable to believe he was dead. Checking his pulse, then compressing his chest to try to get his heart started again. Shaking him, holding him, her face pressed against his.

Barag grabbed Tamella's hands and held them close. Tamella shuddered, but she didn't break.

"I hid his body well," continued Tamella. "Then I came here." Her head swung around and her gaze found and pierced Amastan. "Are three bodies enough for you, Amastan? Will you be able to find their killer now? Or should we wait for a fourth?"

Amastan didn't know what to say. Tamella was right. He should have found the killer by now. Usem's death was on his hands.

"You can't be sure it was the same killer," said Barag softly.

"I can," snapped Tamella. "A slash to the inner thigh. The body purposefully hidden. That isn't a coincidence. It's a pattern."

"His jaani?" asked Amastan, dreading the answer—but he had to ask.

Tamella looked away, her jaw clenched. "Too long. I'll go back tonight to retrieve the body."

"Oh Tam'." Barag stood and enveloped her in a tight embrace.

Amastan's fingers went to his neck, but the reassuring soft leather of a charm pouch was missing. He let his hand drop, feeling exposed and ill. He wanted to go home and hide under the covers of his bed like he had as a child when the first storms rolled in, shouting thunder and throwing lightning.

He had failed. He had failed Emet. He had failed Tamella. He had failed Usem. He had failed the family.

Yet a piece of his mind continued to churn, picking incessantly at the problem like a vulture at a corpse. There shouldn't have been any contracts. *Pick.* What did Yanniq have to do with *two* dead cousins? *Pick.* How could someone sneak up and overcome an assassin? *Pick.* What was the history between Tamella and Yanniq? *Pick.* How many more contracts were out there? *Pick.*

Amastan felt Tamella's intense gaze on him and looked up from his hands. Barag had disappeared, leaving her sitting alone at the hearth. Sorrow had stripped her down, making her thinner, even weak. Shadows pooled beneath her eyes, and for the first time Amastan truly understood how much older she was.

"Have you made any progress at all?" she asked, her tone holding nothing but bitterness.

Yanniq had pardoned murderers. Yanniq had quarreled with the other drum chiefs. Yanniq had known Tamella.

That was it. That was the extent of his knowledge. Megar seemed like only a faint possibility now. How two dead cousins fit into it all, he couldn't begin to guess.

No—he could. Tamella might be the link, if only he could find out what that link was. But seeing the anger and pain in Tamella's gaze, he knew that asking her now would lead nowhere. She yearned for any reason to lash out and inflict her pain on someone else. He wasn't strong enough to be that person.

No. He would ask her, but not yet.

There shouldn't have been any contracts.

All at once, he knew exactly what he needed to do. History might give him a motive, but he needed more than that: he needed to catch a killer. Two cousins had now died on contract. If he didn't get his nose out of a scroll and act, there *would* be a third.

"I have," lied Amastan. "And I have a plan."

Kaseem looked about as pleased to see Amastan as Amastan was to be there. Dawn had only just cracked, but Kaseem could have been awake for hours. He peered at Amastan wordlessly through the doorway, the curtain pulled aside just far enough for him to see.

"G-d bless, sa," said Amastan.

"You should know when to quit," said Kaseem. "G-d doesn't take kindly to those who ask for more than they're due, and G-d's much more forgiving than I am."

"Usem is dead, sa."

If Amastan hadn't been watching for it, he would have missed the surprise that flitted across Kaseem's eyes. It was gone again in an instant and all that remained was a deep frown.

"I don't know what that has to do with me."

"Hopefully, nothing, sa," said Amastan. "But two cousins have died while they were on a contract and I'm here to make sure there isn't a third."

"Clearly they were not the right men for the task."

Something in Amastan had begun to fray last night and now the first strand snapped. "Did you tell Tamella that, when she came asking about her brother? Would you tell Usem's widow that, clearly, he had not been up for it? Do you tell yourself that at night to help you sleep, instead of accepting any of the responsibility that came with choosing these men? Sa?"

"It's not my fault they failed."

Amastan sucked on his teeth and sent up a silent prayer for patience. "May I come in, sa? To make my case?"

Kaseem's gaze shifted. "Depends. Will you be civil?"

"Have I ever been anything else, sa?"

Kaseem shrugged, considered for a moment, then stepped out of the way. Amastan pushed through the curtain into a room unchanged from the last time he'd been there. Kaseem hobbled over to his chair and settled into it with a sigh. He laid the cane across his knees and leaned back, regarding Amastan.

Amastan closed his eyes, trying to find calm and courage. But the last few days had left him with little of either. He couldn't stop seeing the blood on Tamella's forearms, the stringwork in Thana's hands. He kept his eyes closed, forcing himself to see those images.

"Two cousins were murdered, sa," said Amastan slowly, carefully. "Both of them were working contracts. One, at least, was found near his mark's home. We could assume one was incompetent, but two stretches probability. The more likely scenario is that they were both caught unawares, by someone who knew where they would be, and when."

He opened his eyes to Kaseem's silent frown. Kaseem's fingers were wrapped around his cane, but otherwise he hadn't moved. Amastan knew he walked on thin glass. He wasn't sure he cared.

"According to Tamella, there haven't been any contracts in years. The drum chiefs haven't allowed them. But clearly, they've been allowed again. Can you tell me, sa, when the drum chiefs lifted the ban? Was it recently? Say—two weeks ago?"

Kaseem's silence was enough of an answer. Amastan forged on as another strand inside him snapped.

"The ban is lifted and the very first two cousins who take contracts are killed," said Amastan. "Tell me, sa— has that ever happened before?"

"Of course not," said Kaseem. "And I don't like the way you're going with this."

I don't care, Amastan almost said, but he bit back the words. Another strand, gone. "Can you be certain that these contracts are legitimate?"

Annoyance flashed across the visible strip of Kaseem's face and hardened. "I have been in this business for well over thirty years, child," he said. "And before that, my mother held the dubious honor of this profession. If, during any of that time, I had not acted in the full faith of the drum chiefs and the people, do you think I'd still be here? Not even your cousins are immortal. Some mess up and some are caught. So don't come into my house and insult me." He leaned back in his chair, rolling the cane to his lap. "You are free to leave."

"But neither Usem nor Emet were *caught,*" said Amastan. "This wasn't a contract gone wrong. Someone—the same person—knew where they would be. Someone caught them off guard. And then that same someone arranged things so their bodies wouldn't be found before their jaan went wild."

Kaseem sat forward, eyes narrowing. "What you're implying—"

Snap.

"Someone knew, sa," interrupted Amastan. "What I'm implying is someone *knew*. I can't say how or why, but the killer knew about the contracts. That's the only way they could've surprised a cousin. Two cousins. Because the killer knew exactly where to find them."

"Out."

"I'm not accusing you—"

Kaseem stood, his cane clutched in one hand. "You're not? Have you heard a word you've said? First you implied I don't carefully vet every one of my contracts. Now you're saying I've been so careless that someone else knows about them. I do and I haven't and I don't have to listen to this kind of vile nonsense. *Out*."

"If I leave, someone else will die."

Kaseem whipped his cane around and would have smacked Amastan against the back of the knees. But Amastan was ready for him and had danced out of the way. Kaseem hissed, advancing on him with the cane raised. This time he made to strike from above, but then dropped and swung hard from the side. Amastan caught the cane in his hand, the smack of wood on flesh cracking through the room. His palm sung in pain and he was certain it was bruised, if not broken, but he held tight to the cane and met Kaseem's gaze.

In that moment, Amastan knew what he had to do.

"Give me a contract," he said.

Kaseem tried to tug his cane out of Amastan's grip, but Amastan held tight. Kaseem glared at him over the top of the cane. Amastan matched his glare with what he hoped was calm and resolve. Inside, though, he roared like the wind from the Wastes. Part of him wanted Kaseem to keep resisting, to give him a reason to fight. Then he might be able to lay all the blame for his cousins' deaths on someone else.

But Kaseem didn't give him that satisfaction. He let go of his cane and stepped back. Amastan waited another heartbeat before relaxing. He held the cane out to Kaseem, who snatched it back and used it to settle himself into his chair.

"Why?" asked Kaseem as if their confrontation had never happened.

"Why not?" countered Amastan. "You can't tell me anything about the previous two contracts and I respect that, sa. But if I take a contract, you can tell me about that one. If I'm right, and someone is using these contracts to target cousins, then this is my best shot at catching the killer. If I'm wrong, then I'll complete the contract. You risk nothing, sa."

"You're an untested assassin. That's a huge risk. I hand-select my assassins based on their previous experience. You've never worked a single contract, not even with another cousin. No—it's out of the question."

"Then the next assassin who takes a contract will die," said Amastan. He sighed, suddenly very tired. "I'm not accusing *you* of anything. But if there's a hole in your network, if there's a spy, or even if someone is locating and sending legitimate clients your way—wouldn't you want to know about it? Wouldn't the mere possibility deserve an investigation? Two assassins are dead, sa. There will be more. Please, sa. Look me in the eyes and tell me I'm wrong."

Silence filled the room, thick as porridge for one, two, three heartbeats. Kaseem fixed Amastan with those watery eyes, staring into him with an intensity that nailed him to the spot. Amastan held his breath, some of the roar within him calming, returning him to reason. This was it, he realized. If he hadn't convinced Kaseem by now, nothing would convince him. He still had Yufit, Megar, and his stacks of scrolls, but he knew this was his only shot at finding the killer before someone else died.

Without softening his gaze, Kaseem said, "If I give you a contract, what's your plan?"

Amastan started to sag in relief, but caught himself. "I'll set a trap. Usem and Emet were caught unaware. They shouldn't have been alone. I'll ask Menna to be my partner. One of us will hide while the other is the bait." He shook his head. "They should have had partners. That's how we work, isn't it?"

"These contracts specified that only one assassin would be paid," said Kaseem, his voice strangely hollow. "They were straightforward and simple. They didn't need two."

"That's . . . odd. Sa."

"But not unprecedented. I've seen much stranger. And you must also remember, it's been over a decade since the last contract. A lot has happened. A lot still needs to happen." Kaseem rolled his cane between his fingers. "If you take this contract—and I'm not saying you will—you will need to work alone."

"But then I can't—" began Amastan.

"As far as I know, you are working alone," interrupted Kaseem, leveling his gaze at Amastan. "Understand?"

"Yes, sa."

"You still haven't answered my question," continued Kaseem. "If I give you a contract, what will you do?"

Amastan frowned. "When we catch the killer, we'll turn them over to the drum chiefs for judgment."

"That's not what I meant."

"Who else could judge him, sa?"

Kaseem leaned forward, his gaze intent. "You must fulfill the contract. You can't treat it like a tool that you discard when you're done. This contract is not a means to an end. It's a promise you must keep, whether or not it helps you. Do you understand?"

Amastan swallowed, the roar finally condensing into cold certainty. He understood. He'd understood the moment he'd realized what he needed from Kaseem. He'd thought he'd dodged the inevitable when Tamella told them about the contract ban. He should have known better. He'd trained to be an assassin, after all. Not a watchman. If he'd learned anything at all about the family from Barag and his coded histories, he knew this was exactly what he and his cousins were meant to do: save the city when no one else could.

He just had to do it within the confines of a contract.

He no longer had the luxury of doubt, of wondering if he could kill. He would have to. Because hesitating almost certainly meant another cousin would die. He'd already failed Usem and Emet. He couldn't fail anyone else.

"I do," said Amastan, putting the force of his sincerity behind those two words.

Kaseem met his eyes and held them for a heartbeat, then another. Finally, he nodded, accepting whatever he'd seen there.

"I have a contract," he said. "Flush out the killer and complete this and I'll consider you for future contracts. But if you fail at either, you're done. Failure will unmask you and leave you exposed to revenge. You won't be able to remain in Ghadid, at least not without watching your back for the rest of your days. Personally, I wouldn't recommend it."

Dread filled Amastan. He knew there were other cities along the edge of the Wastes, some like Ghadid and others coexisting with the sand, but he couldn't comprehend living anywhere else. Forced to leave his friends, his family, everything—failure simply wouldn't be an option.

"Do you understand?" asked Kaseem. When Amastan hesitated, he said, "You have another option." His voice grew soft, almost gentle. Fatherly, if Amastan's father had ever been kind. "Walk away. Forget about the killer. Warn your family. Surely whoever this killer targets next will get him instead."

Tempting as it was, Amastan knew it wasn't a real option. If he walked away now, Tamella's unspoken accusation would become judgment. Emet and Usem's deaths had become his responsibility the moment he thought he could play at watchman and find a killer on his own. His naïveté and inaction had cost the lives of two cousins. He should have done this sooner, he should have demanded a contract from Kaseem the last time he stood before him, Emet's name on a slip of paper. He'd hoped to find his answer in the past without shedding a single drop of blood.

But you didn't know.

He should have known.

Amastan met Kaseem's gaze. "I understand, sa. I'll complete the contract."

The slightest of smiles touched Kaseem's eyes. "Good. Let's talk terms."

17

Usem's funeral was held three days later.

The crypt was packed with family, cousins Amastan knew and cousins he recognized and cousins he didn't know. Cousins by blood and cousins through blood. Most wore white and those who didn't have mourning clothes wore their palest colors. Amastan had borrowed a white tagel from his father, who'd decided not to attend. He'd avoided funerals ever since Amastan's mother had died. The tagel itched and smelled faintly of ammonia. He preferred that to the dusty-sweet decay of the crypt.

Even with the curved room of the crypt full of living, breathing people, Amastan still felt a chill on the back of his neck. He was constantly aware of the dark holes of the tombs, no matter what was going on or where he was looking. He'd assumed it would be easier to be in the crypt when he'd already faced wild jaan three times. He'd been wrong.

Out of all the bodies here, Usem's was the only one without a jaani. The marab had confirmed this unpleasant fact after Tamella had retrieved the body. There was no reason for his body to go into the crypts, no reason why the seven years couldn't be skipped and this funeral couldn't be held on the sands. Yet here they were, hemmed in by stone and metal and jaan, putting on a show for a lie.

"Hey."

Amastan started, turned. A marabi had appeared at his elbow, her white wrap lined with novice purple and blue. A white cloth concealed her hair, but Amastan would know those sand-pale eyes anywhere.

A smile twitched up the corner of Menna's lips, but it held no humor. "What a way to have a family reunion."

Amastan tried to smile, but the dread in his stomach twisted the smile into a grimace.

"How're you feeling?" asked Menna.

The question was innocuous, but Amastan knew what she meant. After his meeting with Kaseem, he'd found Menna and asked her to partner with him on the contract. She'd said yes before he could even explain what the contract was.

As the funeral preparations consumed the family, he and Menna had used every free moment to plan. Amastan had gone over every detail, every possibility, every angle for hours and hours. Menna had listened and occasionally chimed in with a thought of her own. There was no room for error. They'd decided to wait until after the funeral. No cousin would act before then.

But tonight they would set their plan in motion.

"Fine," he lied.

Menna squeezed his hand. "We'll get them, 'Stan. This'll be the last funeral."

"I hope so." Amastan didn't know what he'd do if it wasn't.

Menna opened her mouth to say something else, but a drum began to beat, silencing the murmuring voices. Schooling her face into a blank mask, Menna pushed her way through the press of people. The ceremony had begun.

Amastan had only attended one other funeral—his mother's—but that'd been over a decade ago, when he'd been much less aware of the world around him. Certain aspects of the funeral ceremony felt achingly familiar while others were just as alien to him. Close family read aloud from prepared scripts. Elder Dessin explained the importance of quieting the jaani and interring the body.

Then the crypt fell silent and all three marab wrote charms for quieting and peace in large, looping letters on a broad piece of smooth vellum, stretched high for the crowd to see. One marabi cleaned the vellum with a wet sponge and another squeezed the sponge's ink-stained liquid into a glass jar. This liquid they dripped over the corpse, starting at its head and moving toward its feet. Meanwhile they chanted prayers which the crowd echoed in response.

The words of prayer hummed through the crypt, through rock and metal and bone. Amastan felt them and couldn't help but think of the wind on the sands and the words in his ear. The marab's act was all for show; Usem's jaani was long gone.

Finally, the marab and a select few of Usem's close family, Tamella included, lifted the body and slid it into its tomb, where it would remain for seven years. When those years had passed, the marab would hold another, much smaller ceremony down on the sands.

While the marab murmured one last prayer, Amastan scanned the crowd. He doubted Usem's killer would be so bold as to attend his funeral, but he also would've doubted anyone could get the best of Usem. It was hard for Amastan to remember Usem was dead, to remember that the body sliding into the tomb was the same man who'd filled a doorway, who'd given him baats, and who'd made such a serious girl as Thana laugh.

Amastan's scanning gaze fell on Thana. She stood next to Rema, Usem's widow, holding her hand. Thana's expression was blank, her cheeks smudged with dried tears. She couldn't be seen with her mother, not in public. And now even her assumed father was dead.

As if feeling his gaze, Thana turned her empty stare on

him. Amastan looked away immediately, but not before
he felt the accusation in her gaze. No—she'd only noticed
him staring. She couldn't know it was his fault the killer
still walked free. His fault Usem was dead. The only guilt
he saw was his own.

The murmuring stopped and a silence fell over the crypt,
the only sounds those of breathing, shifting cloth, and the
faint gurgling from the pipes within the pylon. Then Elder
Dessin raised his hands and, just like that, the ceremony
was over. One person broke free, then another, then the
whole crowd was moving as one, dragging Amastan up the
stairs and out of the gloom into the late evening's heat.

He broke from the stream of people and turned into an
alley. He crossed to the next street, then turned north until he found a narrow seam between two buildings, hardly
wide enough to be called anything. The walls here were
crumbling, full of soft spots and indentations. He cast
one glance back to make sure no one was watching, then
scaled the wall.

It was hotter on the rooftop than down below. He
sought and found shade next to a large compost barrel. It
stank of putrid-sweet garbage, but Amastan didn't mind;
the rot helped to clear his thoughts. He settled next to the
barrel and waited, watching what might be clouds—or
what might be mirages—bubble and boil and burst on the
horizon.

A sandal scuffed across stone. He didn't turn. A moment later, Menna stepped in front of him, obscuring his
view of the maybe-clouds. She'd traded her funeral whites
for a more subtle beige, a color that made her blend into
the cityscape. The white cloth that had covered her hair
was now tied around her waist, the only reminder that
there'd just been a funeral.

"I could've been the killer." Menna sounded disappointed.

Amastan kept his gaze where the horizon had been,

which just happened to be Menna's knees. "No, you couldn't have been. The killer has only attacked cousins while they were actively pursuing their contracts—at night and near their marks. Our mark is several neighborhoods away and it's still early evening."

"Amastan—are you going to be able to do this?"

"I have to."

"I mean the contract." Menna settled into a squat, forcing him to look her in the eyes. "I can do it, if you want me to."

Amastan didn't have to ask her what she meant. He let the offer hang between them, tantalizingly close. During all their planning, they hadn't answered the question of who'd kill the mark. Depending on how their surveillance unfolded, it could go either way. Amastan hadn't wanted to commit to one, only to have circumstances force them into another. He had a plan for any eventuality.

Any—except for the one where he couldn't kill the mark. Which was why Menna's offer tempted him. It would take away some of the uncertainty. Some of the unknown. Some of the fear.

Could he kill?

But this was his contract, his responsibility. If the opportunity arose, if his hand was ready, he would have to do it.

"I'll be okay," said Amastan.

Menna chewed on her lip, but didn't push it any further. Instead, she sat down next to him, tucking her knees to her chest. "I've been talking to the elders in between all these funeral preparations. They have some ideas about the jaan. The jaan's pattern has been troubling, though. The pushing, the intent, the fixation—they think at least one of them might be turning into a guuli. Which would make my little banishment trick that much more amazing."

Amastan frowned. Guul were demons that preyed on the dead and the dying, picking and choosing body parts to create their own bodies. "But guul only live in the Wastes."

"Guul exist wherever there are jaan with sufficient motivation," said Menna, her words plucked and precise and clearly memorized. "At least, that's what Elder Dessin said. And somebody has given this jaani sufficient motivation." An animated excitement underlined her voice. "Of course, no one knows for sure, because as far as anyone remembers, a guuli has never existed in Ghadid. This would be the first. And no one really understands how they're created. Dessin thinks this jaani has possessed several people already. Being such a new and strong jaani, though, it would've destroyed whoever it possessed before it could get too far. But that just gave it more strength. Dessin said it'll keep trying to possess people until it figures out how to stabilize itself, and then it'll collect body parts like a guuli, because it'll *be* a guuli. We need to stop it before it gets that far."

"If it's already killed people, why haven't we heard about it? Wouldn't the drum chiefs have said something?"

"Not if they were beggars and slaves," said Menna quietly. "People who don't have the baats for charms."

Amastan thought of the beggar asleep in the pumphouse, safe from the day's heat but not from the jaan. The jaani had already been so strong when it'd entered the inn. Had it killed the beggar only moments before?

"But I thought jaan only drove people mad. How do they kill?"

"The body can only sustain one jaani at a time," said Menna. "The jaan on the sands and in the Wastes are thin and weak. They drive you mad. But this jaani—these jaan—they're too strong. They tear the body apart, burn it up from the inside. Much like guul do, when they possess a living person. That's why guul prefer corpses. But this jaani doesn't know any better, and it'll keep trying to regain the body it lost no matter how many it burns through."

"G-d."

"Yeah. The elders are working on a way to quiet them, though. Dessin has a few ideas himself and they're asking *me* for any ideas, too. In the meantime, we just have to stay careful and stay safe."

Menna rummaged around in her pockets. After a moment, she produced a leather cord with five opaque glass beads. She held it out to Amastan, who took it and weighed the glass in his palm. They were heavier than he'd expected and cool to the touch.

"I got that from Salid," said Menna. "He'd been working on something a little stronger for me. It should protect you from any jaan, even these. I have one, too." She pulled down her wrap, exposing her throat and a matching string of beads. "We can't risk any distractions tonight."

Amastan curled his fingers around the beads, but he didn't put them on. "Thank you."

Silence filled the space between them. Below, a mule grumbled as it pulled a cart laden with leather and brightly colored fabric down the street. The smell of roasting lamb drifted across the roofs and Amastan remembered he hadn't eaten since dawn. A child screamed and then laughed. A conversation rose and fell as a group passed by.

"It's not your fault," said Menna.

Amastan kept his gaze averted.

"You're going to have to accept it one day, and it might as well be now," continued Menna. "You couldn't have known. Hell, we still don't know, do we? We're only guessing it's the contracts, but we could be wrong. And if we are—it's *still* not your fault. You didn't kill Usem. You didn't kill Emet. You can't blame yourself for someone else's actions."

Amastan didn't trust himself to respond. His fingers tightened around his knees. Menna sighed and stood up, brushing off her wrap.

"Well, you've got a few hours to feel sorry for yourself," said Menna. "Just get it out of your system before we meet up tonight, okay? Moping's not going to help us find the killer."

She stood for a moment, watching him, but when Amastan didn't move, she shook her head and left. Her footsteps retreated, the scuff of her sandals growing distant until all at once they were gone. He pictured her rolling her eyes at him as she swung over the edge of the roof.

He gave himself another moment, then he stood. Menna was right. He was helping no one by sitting here and beating himself up over things that had already happened. Even if he sat here all night, Usem would never come back. He couldn't undo what had happened, but he could do everything possible to stop what might happen.

He slipped from the alley back onto the road. He didn't have any destination in mind, but his feet dragged him back toward the crypt. He would pay his final respects to Usem in his own way and then he would prepare for tonight.

But he'd only gone one street before he caught sight of a familiar tagel. Silver as moonlight, Yufit's tagel all but glowed in the dying evening sun. Amastan was hit by a heavy mixture of guilt and nerves. He'd promised to meet up with Yufit two days ago and the time had come and gone while Amastan was busy with the rest of the family preparing for the funeral.

Yufit hadn't noticed him yet. Amastan considered turning around and hiding in an alley until Yufit was gone, but he dismissed the thought almost as soon as it occurred. He wanted to see Yufit. Besides, he still needed Yufit. If they didn't catch the killer tonight, then Yufit might have the answers they needed.

Either way, it was too late to turn back. Yufit's steel-cold eyes had passed over him initially, but now they fell on him and widened with surprise.

"Asaf?"

Amastan realized he wasn't at all prepared for this encounter. His tagel was too high and he had no excuse ready for missing their meeting. Belatedly, he wished he'd fled.

"What're you doing out here?" asked Yufit, drawing close. Those eyes swept over him, leaving Amastan feeling naked. "Was there a funeral?"

With a sudden panic, Amastan realized he was still wearing white. "I—uh—yes."

Yufit's expression turned grave. "I'm so sorry. Someone close?"

"No," said Amastan. Not a lie, not exactly—Usem was family, but he was only distantly related. "But I thought I should be there."

Yufit nodded. "May his jaani rest quietly."

"What about you?"

"Oh, just—running an errand," said Yufit, gesturing vaguely. His gaze stayed on Amastan, though, and there was something in his eyes that Amastan couldn't quite place. "You missed our meeting the other night."

"I'm so sorry—the death was sudden, so things were kind of a mess. Menna asked me to help with the funeral preparations. She's a marabi, you know—"

Yufit waved away his excuses. "You don't have to apologize. I'm just glad you're okay. I thought the jaani might have gotten you."

"Oh." *Of course,* thought Amastan, berating himself. How could he have forgotten? He'd disappeared for three days right after Yufit had saved him from the jaani. How callous could he be?

"I mean, I might be a little upset," said Yufit, but his eyes crinkled with a smile. "But I know a way you can make it up to me."

"How?"

"Do you have a few hours to waste? Let's just pretend

it's two nights ago and you didn't miss our meeting." Yu-fit held out his hand. "How about it? We have to leave now, though, otherwise we'll miss the best part."

Amastan hesitated. He'd planned on spending the next hours preparing. Sure, he'd been planning with Menna for the last few days, but it never hurt to take a little extra care, go over everything one more time. Double-check his rope, hone his blades, count his poisons.

Then he thought back to the night of his trial, the time he'd spent on the sands. The missing carriage. He'd tried to prepare for everything, but he hadn't prepared for that. He couldn't prepare for everything that might happen to-night. Maybe it was better if he stepped away from it all and cleared his head. Besides, he still needed Yufit and his knowledge of Yanniq's last days. If they didn't catch the killer tonight, Yufit was his only remaining lead.

Amastan took Yufit's hand.

As Yufit led him through the streets and across plat-forms, Amastan's curiosity expanded with each bridge they crossed. With the sun peeking between the build-ings in occasional flashes of blinding brightness, Yufit headed steadily west until they reached the last platform. He pulled Amastan through the platform's quiet center to an alley that narrowed and ended in a two-tiered railing.

The sunset's light oozed down the alley, turning it red as blood. Amastan hesitated at the mouth, Yufit's hand slip-ping out of his. But the wind hardly stirred and the air stank only of heat and dust. The only sound was the distant cry from a children's game and a subtle thrum near his feet.

Amastan looked down in time to see a gray cat slip between his legs and down the alley. Yufit crouched and scratched beneath its chin. The thrum became a hum: the cat was purring. Yufit gave the cat a final pat, then straightened and gestured toward the railing.

"I thought this might be more your idea of fun."

Amastan forced a smile, unsure if Yufit was serious or

joking. The alley held no secrets or wonders, only flat, sun-bleached stones still hot from the day, empty walls, and a drop on the other side of the railing onto nothing. The sunset's glow lit half of Yufit's face, warming his eyes. He looked hopeful as he waited for Amastan to respond; he wasn't joking.

Without waiting for Amastan, Yufit took a seat on the edge of the platform, slipping his legs beneath the lower railing. Amastan eyed the railing with distrust. Some of the city's metals were impervious to age and heat—a trick the ancients had neglected to pass on—but some, like this railing, showed their age. Brilliant orange rust flecked its length, accumulating at the point where metal railing met the stone wall of the building.

The opening was narrow, barely wide enough for the two of them. Amastan carefully slid between the wall and Yufit, but his arm still brushed Yufit's and their legs dangled over the edge precariously close.

As Amastan settled into place, he finally saw what Yufit meant. At his back, he could still feel the city. But he could no longer see it. He clung to its edge, staring out across a vastness of space toward a horizon impossibly far away. The Wastes. Below: the sands. Beyond: the sands. The sunset turned them red as embers, and as the sun slunk away, for a brief moment it appeared that the whole world was on fire.

Heartbeat by heartbeat, the sun disappeared and the shadows stretched longer and longer, giving the flat emptiness form and shape far beyond its reality. Rocks became boulders and farther west, a dune field grew into mountains. Beyond that, red shimmered like glass across the salt flats.

Out in the Wastes, wild jaan roamed. Out there, guul bided their time until they found their next corpse. And somewhere in the Wastes' vastness, it was said the sajaam still lived.

The Wastes were a place for demons and the dead. Not Ghadid.

The sun disappeared, taking its light with it. The sky faded quickly, turning from a dusty blue to a thin black. Stars peeked out one by one, and the more Amastan looked for them, the more he saw. Their pinpricks of light brightened and formed familiar shapes. The Vulture hung to the north, the brightest star in the sky at the tip of one wing.

Amastan had stood on the edge of Ghadid many times. He'd watched the carriages creak up from the sands, full of merchants. He'd tried to see what was beyond the sands, beyond the curve of the horizon. He'd stared and wondered. He'd looked for storms, for clouds, at the end of season. He'd searched for the caravans he knew occasionally cut into the Wastes. He'd even imagined what the sand would feel like between his toes.

But he'd never paused to take it all in before.

"It's amazing," said Amastan.

"I come here to think," said Yufit, his voice softer and closer than before. He kicked his legs over the edge of the roof. The breeze coming off the Wastes was warm, consistent. Comforting.

For a moment, they sat in silence together, listening to the city as it wound up behind them. For a moment, Amastan didn't think about Usem or Emet or Yanniq or the jaan or the drum chiefs or the family or Tamella or the killer or tonight. He watched as gold faded to orange faded to red faded to black and stars appeared like wavering visions.

But as the night deepened, Amastan's worries returned. He could all but feel time slipping past, slick and quick as sand. In a few hours, he'd be crouched on a rooftop with Menna. In a few hours, he might come face to face with the killer. In a few hours, this could all be over.

Yufit took a breath. Blew it out, fluttering his tagel. "Are you okay, Asaf?"

"Yeah," said Amastan quickly. "I'm okay."

But Yufit shook his head. "It's just, I'm confused by you. You know, when we first met, you seemed inquisitive, interested. Pushy, even. You saved me from a jaani and then you turned that into an opportunity. I mean, I don't mind. Maybe it was just tea. I thought it was something more, but after we last talked, something seems to have changed. If you aren't interested anymore, you can tell me, you know. You don't owe me anything."

The dull glow of a torch reached them from the street and lit half of Yufit's face. His eyebrows were drawn tight, creased with no hint of a smile. Amastan looked at the horizon, unable to meet Yufit's eyes. His stomach felt as if it'd been twisted into knots and his throat was too tight to speak.

He'd been bad at everything, including this. What had Tamella ever seen in him? He couldn't even flirt to save a life. But it was more than that. Even though he barely knew Yufit, he didn't want to lose him. He didn't want to just flirt. The lies he'd told himself and Yufit had twisted with reality until he couldn't tell one from the other.

Was it a lie, though? What he felt now? This increased heart rate, these sweat-slick palms, this burning warmth in his belly? All of it, despite his very real fear of tonight?

Tonight . . .

A hand covered his, pulling Amastan out of his thoughts and back to the edge. Yufit had moved closer. Their wraps brushed against each other.

"I'm . . . interested. I just . . . I'm not . . . I don't think I'm what you're interested in." Amastan carefully extracted his hand, tucking it into his lap.

"What do you think I'm interested in?"

Amastan swallowed. "More than this. More than I can give you."

"I can assure you, what you can give is more than enough," said Yufit. "More than I deserve."

"You don't understand—" started Amastan, suddenly needing Yufit to understand.

Yufit reached out to touch Amastan's fingers, but hesitated. He dropped his hand. "I think I do. I won't push you to do anything you don't want to, Asaf."

"Even if that means I don't want to do anything?"

"Even if." Yufit settled his hands in his own lap. "Tell you what—I'll let you take the lead. That seems to be working so far."

So far. So far in what? What was this? Amastan didn't know but he wanted to find out. He let out the breath he'd been holding and covered Yufit's hand with his own. Yufit started, but didn't move away.

"There's been a lot going on," admitted Amastan. "I mean, beyond the jaani and the funeral and everything else. There're some things I'm supposed to do, that I know are the right things to do—but knowing that they're right doesn't make it any easier to do them. I accepted the responsibility, but I'm afraid I won't be able to see it through. This should never have come to me in the first place. There're others more capable, more willing, but I'm the one who has to do it. Some things aren't fair, I guess." He lifted his head and finally looked at Yufit.

The night had transformed Yufit's dark eyes into liquid metal. Amastan's stomach lurched precariously and he felt just as he had a few nights ago, before this whole mess started, one foot on the edge of the platform, the other stepping onto air, nothing between him and a long, long drop. At least then he'd had the cable to catch him.

"No, a lot of things in life aren't fair. But G-d never gives us more than we can bear. The hardest part is trusting that we are strong enough." He took Amastan's other hand and stared into his eyes. "I may not know you well, Asaf, but anyone who can face a jaani to save a stranger is stronger than he can imagine. If you know you should do this thing, if you believe it's the right thing to do, then it doesn't matter how hard it is. You'll find the strength to do it."

Strong, thought Amastan. No one had ever used that word to describe him.

Yufit let go of his hands. "Do the thing you're afraid of doing. Courage, after all, isn't an absence of fear—it's doing something despite the fear. I know you'll find that courage when you need it. And when you've done it, I expect you to tell me all about it, all right?"

If he caught the killer, Amastan decided, he would tell Yufit everything.

"Agreed."

Yufit's fingers tightened around his and he looked back out over the deepening darkness. "But in the meantime . . . just sit here and watch the stars come out with me."

And they did.

18

This night was thicker than the last, the air laced with just enough moisture to be uncomfortable while still remaining as hot as an ember. The stickiness was a promise: this season would end. But relief from the escalating heat could still be days or weeks away. For the first time since the drum chiefs had dropped this whole mess on him, Amastan hoped for the former. Salt crusted at his elbows and neck where the sweat had dried from the effort of crossing several neighborhoods and a dozen rooftops to arrive here, now.

Here: crouched beside a glasshouse crowded with desiccated stalks on a roof just that much higher than the next.

Now: hours past midnight but still long before dawn, that sliver of time when the markets had finally closed but the caravans—were there any—hadn't yet set out, when Ghadid was at its quietest.

The new glass charms felt reassuringly cool against his neck even as his heart pounded with nerves and anticipation. From here he could see Menna's small form on the adjacent rooftop. She'd only just arrived and was busy setting up for the night. She dropped a bag and rifled through it. She retrieved a length of rope and a piece of telescoping glass. Her fingers glittered as she moved, the moon catching her rings.

Menna tied the rope around her waist, checked the

placement of her knives, and palmed the glass. She slid to the edge of the roof and gazed across, putting the piece of glass up to one eye. The buildings obscured Amastan's view, but he knew what she saw. He'd walked the street below earlier.

A smattering of windows, some open in a desperate attempt to find a breeze, some locked tight, some lit from within, most as dark as a staring eye. Three stories up and five from the right was the mark's window, its glass tinted blue like every other, a dull gray curtain the only distinction.

The mark lived in a bigger, older home with several other families. The contract had been drawn up on behalf of one of those other families. Wasting your own water was a moral offense. Wasting another's was criminal, even if it was accidental. And purposefully, maliciously wasting another's water was a capital offense.

While such crimes were few and far between, the drum chiefs traditionally dealt with water misuse. But sajaam lived in the details, and the details had brought the mark's offense to Kaseem instead.

Detail one: timing. Every end of season was a headlong race between water rationing and shortage. A season could end early or it could linger for weeks. Some years, the water easily lasted until the rain came. Some years, the least fortunate—beggars and slaves and, rarely, free people who'd run into one too many misfortunes—died of thirst or want of healing. When you stole water from one person, you stole from everyone.

This year's season was particularly bad. The previous season's storms had been thin, barely filling the aquifers and leading to a slow market year with a shortage of baats. Now it stretched on and on, more baats disappearing down the pumps every day. A little wasted hurt everyone. A lot . . .

Detail two: amount. The mark had stolen several bobaats worth of water, an amount that could've snatched someone out of death's grip and quenched the thirst of an entire platform for a week.

Detail three: spite. The mark had been spied pouring the water out on the shared rooftop and letting the sun drink it up, probably because she knew the punishment for water hoarding was almost as bad as wasting. But someone had caught the mark nonetheless.

Detail four: the delicate nature of the mark's relations. The mark was Kella Tholemen—the same Tholemen family as Drum Chief Ziri. Kella was Ziri's half sister, younger by a decade but still close. If it came out that Drum Chief Ziri's own family was wasting water, he would have to exact a punishment both severe and public to avoid losing respect and his drum. Moreover, Kella's family would be shunned and her children burdened with an unearned notoriety for a generation or more.

It was kinder, simpler, and cleaner if the mark's punishment was quiet and discreet. Hence, the contract. Hence, Menna across the way, watching the line of windows for any sign of movement.

The details that weren't as important were *why* Kella had done what she'd done, but they interested Amastan. The contract had been silent on this point, but he could see the feud between the lines, one that had escalated between neighbors until Kella had stolen the water—bit by bit, skin by skin, over the course of weeks—and thrown it away. In the end, whatever slight or wrong Kella was using to justify her actions didn't matter. The water was gone.

The night stretched on, Menna watching the mark's window, Amastan watching Menna, and out there, somewhere, if Amastan was right, the killer was watching as well. In his mind's eye, it was still Megar who hid just out of sight, his screwdriver tap-tapping his thigh, even though Amastan knew the gear worker could never have bested Usem. It didn't matter; Amastan would know who the killer was soon enough. No more guessing, no more research. His method had failed. This was how the family handled problems, silent and direct.

Keep it normal, Amastan had insisted while they were planning the contract. Menna had agreed to several nights of surveillance. Dull, but necessary to establish the mark's habits and behavior. They needed to know when the mark went to sleep, when the mark woke up, what the mark did at night—any detail that might make their job easier.

So Amastan wasn't expecting it when Menna disappeared over the edge of the roof.

What was she doing? He scrambled across his roof, pulling out the planks he'd stashed nearby. She was supposed to remain there for the rest of the night, an easy target for their real mark. He slid the planks across the empty space between buildings, waited for the soft *thunk* of connection, then ran across before the wood had stopped trembling.

Was the killer below? Had they lured her away somehow? Was she already dead? Or was it one of the jaan? Amastan choked back the urge to call for her, knowing he couldn't give her away, not yet. He came to the edge of her roof and peered over, searching up and down the street below, but she wasn't there. As he was pushing himself back up, though, he caught a glimpse of movement.

There—Menna appeared all at once as he realized what he was looking for. She clung just below the mark's roof, her dark green wrap disappearing into the shadow of the wall. Tonight she also wore a length of the same fabric around her head like a tagel, knotted so that it left only a scrap of skin around her eyes uncovered. Amastan wore his tagel just as high; they couldn't risk anyone recognizing them.

As he watched, Menna pulled herself up and over and

disappeared from view. Amastan muttered a number of curses under his breath. Then he followed.

She was waiting for him when he rolled over the edge of the roof, only partially out of breath.

When he was close enough, he hissed, "What're you doing?"

Menna gestured toward the metal door set into the roof. "Working the contract."

"This isn't what we planned."

"Isn't it?" Menna locked gazes with him. "We planned to make it look real by actually working it. Sitting on a rooftop for hours isn't real. It's stupid."

"It's what Tamella taught us," said Amastan. "And it's necessary. We have to know every detail of the mark's patterns before we go in. We can't risk being caught."

"Ugh—maybe on any other contract, but this one is so *simple*. The mark's asleep, she's surrounded by family and neighbors so we don't have to worry that no one will find the body, and she has no reason to believe she's been caught. If your theory's correct, then the killer knows that, too. Sitting on a rooftop for hours chewing your cud's going to look more suspicious than actually, you know, working it."

Menna dropped down next to the door and began working the handle. "Besides," she added. "I'm bored."

"Why didn't you bring all that up when we were planning?"

"You were having so much fun," deadpanned Menna. She unlatched the handle and pulled open the door, revealing a square of darkness. "Huh. Not locked. I guess no one expects someone to break in through the roof these days."

"Wait." Amastan grabbed for her before she could slide into the darkness. "You were planning on doing this all along? And you didn't tell me?"

"Of course I wasn't," scoffed Menna, easily ducking

his grasp. She turned and slid herself feetfirst through the door, reaching until her feet found a rung on the ladder, then looked back up at Amastan. The cloth hid her mouth, but he knew she was smirking. "Besides, you were clearly having so much fun fussing about all the little details. I wasn't about to take that away from you."

She jumped to the floor, slipping from sight as she slid her hands along the ladder's sides. Amastan messed with his wrap and belt, silently selecting a dozen curses for Menna. Then he took a deep breath and released it. If they were going to complete this contract, he had to work with her and let go of his resentment. For now.

He glanced around at this rooftop and the other roofs, feeling suddenly exposed. He peered into the opening. A pair of eyes stared back, bright as a cat's in the darkness. Then Menna ducked her head and disappeared completely. Her brass assumption that he'd follow grated on his nerves like sand between teeth. But she was right, of course. Menna was always right.

Amastan found the rungs of the ladder with his bare feet and climbed down after her. The walls closed in around him, unnervingly close after the open rooftops. It was dark and quiet; Amastan could barely see his own hands and hear the patter of his heart. As the moments passed, his eyes adjusted and the darkness gave way. Now he could see the rectangles of doors along this hall, the open darkness that indicated stairs, and a shadow off to one side.

The shadow moved, gained form. Menna stood next to a closed door, one open palm held out to him. Her wrap was knotted tight, allowing her full range of motion. With her other hand, she loosed a dagger from its strap on her bicep. She beckoned with the dagger.

The door was unlocked. But that was no surprise— who locked a door in their own home? The room within was silvery lit, thin shadows cast by the moon through the open window. A breeze twisted the hearth-hot air. Amastan blinked his eyes wet again even as a cold sweat prickled the back of his neck.

A bed filled the center of the room. Two bodies lay across it, one tangled in a thin sheet, the other exposed. Menna moved aside and shut the door without even a whisper. Amastan took in the room's details. The plush rug at the foot of the bed. The basket of folded fabric in the corner. The waste jars beside the bed, one for each occupant. The stringwork suspended from the ceiling near the window, spinning this way and that. The water glass on the side table, with just a few sips left.

Menna caught his eye and Amastan knew in an instant her plan. It was only fair that the mark be killed by the very thing that she'd wasted. Menna touched the ring on her index finger and pointed toward the glass, then began creeping across the room. But Amastan reached out and stopped her, shaking his head.

She frowned her confusion, but Amastan didn't know how to explain without words. He tried a few of the signs Tamella had forced them to memorize, but Menna only looked bewildered. With a grimace, he tugged her toward the door. Menna resisted initially, then pantomimed an exaggerated sigh before following Amastan back out.

Once they were in the hallway and the door was shut, Menna hissed, "What is it?"

"There are two people in the room," said Amastan. "If we poison the water, we can't guarantee that the mark will drink it."

"Of course she will," said Menna. "It was right next to her bed."

"Would you stake your life on it?" pressed Amastan.

Menna started to say yes, then stopped, clearly annoyed. Amastan watched patiently as she came to the same conclusion he had. Finally, she grumbled, "Well, then what?"

"We have to draw him out," said Amastan. "It might still not work—she might go with him, but it's worth a try." He resisted the urge to chastise Menna—they could have known all these details in advance if she'd been patient and waited. But it was too late for that. They were here.

"But we gotta make her drink it, too," said Menna. She poked Amastan in the chest. "And you know what makes someone thirsty?"

"What?"

"Fear."

Amastan frowned, but Menna didn't wait for him to understand. She was already heading for the stairs. Amastan started after her, but Menna held up a hand and made a series of clumsy, but clear, signs.

Stay. Wait. Listen.

A pause as she tried to figure out one more. Then she held her hand over her heart and squeezed it into a fist: *kill.*

Before Amastan could protest, she'd disappeared down the stairs. He tilted his head back, closed his eyes, and bit his tongue until he could taste copper. Then he breathed: *one, two, three.* He relaxed his hands, shoulders, and tried to make sense of her thrown-together plan, his heart hammering too hard in his chest.

Any moment, Menna was going to make a racket to draw out the man. That meant Amastan had to get inside, deliver the poison, and get out before Menna started whatever she was going to start. She hadn't given him a time frame—*of course not*—and he couldn't go after her, not without risking that she'd expose them at any moment. The only way out of this mess was playing along—and fast.

His heart jumped into his throat as he realized what Menna had forced him into. He thought he'd accepted the possibility that he might have to kill the mark, but as he stood outside the door wasting precious seconds, he realized he'd been holding onto a thin thread of hope that Menna would do it. And why not? She'd always wanted to. She'd even offered. At the last moment, she was supposed to swoop in and make the decision for him. But when she'd left, she'd taken that hope with her.

Cold fear blew through him. Could he do it? He tried to push away his fear by remembering that this contract was a mercy. The mark was going to die either way. If it was by his hand, then a lot of unnecessary pain would be avoided. It was necessary and he was the perfect one to do it. He was protecting the city, in a way only the family could.

But the fear didn't leave. It clung to him like cobwebs. He couldn't do it. He was too weak.

You will find the strength to do it.

Amastan was back on the platform's edge, Yufit's warm hand over his own. Yufit believed in him. Amastan opened his eyes, took a shaky breath. If Yufit believed in him, then maybe he should believe in himself. After all, what was a little poison after facing a jaani?

Amastan eyed the door as if it might bite him, then moved despite his fear. And strangely, wonderfully, the fear didn't stop him from moving. The cobwebs stretched and broke and he was able to think clearly again.

He pictured the inside of the room in exquisite detail before his hand touched the door. It would take five steps to reach the water glass. He didn't have Menna's poison rings, but he had a small pouch. Tamella had a wide range of poisons that she'd either cultivated herself or bought off the caravans. The one in his pouch had come from a small, violently colorful creature that could be found in faraway oases. He guessed at the mark's weight and adjusted the standard dose down just a little.

Then he pushed open the door and slid into a room that wasn't his own. Amastan detached the pouch with one hand as he crossed the room. One, three, five steps brought him within reach of the glass, the window at his back. The water had remained flat as he approached. Water that had been carelessly poured and left out for the hungry air. Water that she'd stolen. Water that could save a life.

Water that would take it.

He reassessed the mark's size even as he undid the knot of the pouch, but he only confirmed his earlier calculation. He picked out a tiny, rolled leaf and shook it open over the glass. A sprinkle of powder fell out, heavy as sand. The white grains stuck to the sides of the glass, but instantly dissolved when they hit the water.

He tucked the leaf back into the pouch, picked the glass up, and swirled it, once, twice, and set it silently back down. He stood for a moment, looking down at the poison-laced water. It was done. And it had been so easy.

snak-*clatter-BOOM*

For a terrible moment, Amastan thought that there'd been an explosion. The whole building had shook with the weight of something heavy toppling over. Then both of the bed's occupants were stirring, the man already sitting up, and Amastan *moved*. One second he was beside the glass, the next he'd swung out the open window and was now dangling from the ledge by his fingers, his heart hammering so loud in his ears he couldn't hear anything else.

Then the world caught up with him and he realized *that* must have been Menna's distraction. His toes scrabbled until they found holds, giving his arms a break while his heart calmed down enough so that he could hear the clamor within.

"—by G-d was that?" said a woman's voice.

"I—I have no idea," answered a man, but even without seeing his eyes, Amastan caught the trace of guilt. What had Menna *found*? "I'll go check."

"You can't go down alone." Fabric rustled and feet hit the floor.

A door opened and closed, but it was too far away to be theirs. Menna had probably woken up the entire household.

"It's safer if you stay here."

The mark snorted. "Safer for whom?"

"Just— I'll be right back." The man sounded both frazzled and annoyed.

Feet crossed the floor, and this time when Amastan heard a door, it was theirs. He pressed his toes into the wall and pulled himself up, inch by inch, until he could see into the room. The mark sat on the edge of the bed, her face in profile as she glared at the door. Then she sighed and let herself fall back into the bed. Amastan clung tight to the ledge, his arms beginning to burn.

The mark lay still for a moment before tossing one way, then the other. She wasn't going to drink the water. He'd have to retrieve it somehow or stay hanging here until he could be certain she'd drunk it. If they messed up, if someone else drank it, if she noticed him out here—

The mark groaned. Sat up. Rubbed her eyes. Glanced toward the door. Sighed. Picked up the glass of water. Drank.

Relief blew through Amastan like a gust of wind. He began climbing up the side of the building, back toward the roof. The sound of glass shattering caught up to him before he was even halfway, followed by a choked cry, and then silence. Amastan closed his eyes for a moment in respect. The deed was done.

Now they just had to catch the killer.

19

The reality of what he'd just done caught up to Amastan as he climbed. A body lay in the room below in place of a person. And he'd done it.

It'd been so easy. Almost too easy. There'd been fear, yes. A little bit of residual terror still lingered like an aftertaste. Beneath it lay guilt and the heavy, spreading chill of irrevocability. There was no going back, no way to undo what he'd done. The mark's blood would forever be on his hands. Her children would curse him, never knowing his name, never knowing from what they'd been spared. A hundred arguments would never persuade them, which was fair, as fair as what he'd done.

What *he'd* done. A pinch of poison. A glass of water. No knives, no garrote, no blood. The act itself had passed in a moment, movements too easily separated from their consequence. He felt those consequences unspooling all around him now, and what wasn't quite guilt festered unpleasantly within him.

He could do it, but he hadn't enjoyed it. No, that wasn't entirely truthful. The planning, the debating, the watching, the waiting—he'd enjoyed all of that. He'd put every hour of his training to use in the last few days and it'd been more satisfying than any number of deciphered scrolls.

He hadn't enjoyed actually killing the mark, but that

was just as important. Tamella hadn't chosen him because he'd enjoy killing. She'd picked him because he'd
be good at it. And she'd been right.

Now he only had to worry about whether it had been
enough to draw out the killer.

Menna waited for him on the roof. She leaned against
the glasshouse, tapping her foot. Amastan's guilt came
close on the heels of his relief, when he realized she'd
been up there, alone, for some time. The killer could've
caught her at any moment and Amastan would've been
too far away to help her. He thought about chastising her
for not waiting somewhere safer, but it was done and he
was here and she was fine.

Menna didn't say a word, only pushed herself fully
upright. As she started toward him, a smile brightening
her eyes, something moved behind her. A blur, a shape,
a *person*—

Menna ducked. The blade that'd been meant for her
neck flew over the edge of the roof instead. She spun,
keeping low to the ground, and unsheathed twin daggers from her belt. She swept one through the air in front
of her. A second knife pinged off it at an angle, hit the
ground, and scraped across stone.

The shape had disappeared. Amastan's lungs burned;
he finally remembered to breathe. Menna stayed in a
crouch, still as stone except for her eyes, which flicked
left and right. Then she moved, darting toward the glasshouse as fast as a snake. A moment later, Amastan registered the sound of a sandal scuffing across stone. He
chased after her.

But when he barreled around the corner of the glasshouse, he saw only one shadow. Menna twisted around
and shouted a warning.

"Oil!"

Amastan reached for his belt, but he didn't carry oil.
He had a half second to wonder what else Menna could've

meant, then his leading foot slipped out from under him
and his momentum flung him to the ground.

He could smell it then, the acrid punch of torch oil. For
a moment he was confused, then panic pushed him to his
knees, his palms splayed in a puddle at least a finger's
width deep. He struggled to his feet, the fumes making
his head light and his thoughts as difficult to grasp as
air. One careful step, then another, and he stood on dry
ground again.

But his wrap was now soaked in oil.

Whoosh!

Bright, glaring light flared at his back, followed immediately by a rush of heat. Amastan knew better than
to think. He dropped his belt and tore off his wrap even
as the fire found it by following the thin trail of oil he'd
left behind. Menna yelled something, but he couldn't hear
her over the roar of the flames rushing toward him. He
skipped back on one foot, shaking the rest of his wrap
loose even as fire licked his arm.

The wrap fell off and the fire fell with it. The flames
were smothered briefly between the weight of the fabric and the ground. Then they found air and flared
even brighter. A hot wind caressed his skin, bare but
for his tagel, untouched by oil, and the assortment of
small knives he wore leather-strapped to his arms and
across his chest. The fire had even consumed his belt
and various pouches. He tried not to think about how
many months—*years*—worth of baats had just become
smoke.

The fire lit up the rooftop as bright as day. The shadows gave way to barrels and plants and people: Menna, a
fair distance away, the raised blades of her twin daggers
two mirrors upon which the flames danced; and a second
person, crouched on top of the glasshouse roof.

Their eyes, filled with the flicker of flames, met his. A

tagel concealed the rest of their face—*his* face, Amastan decided, even though a similar tagel covered Menna's. But his shape was lean and his wrap, tied close and tight for optimum mobility and the color of melted shadows, gave no hint of curves. A belt circled his waist, from which dangled several pouches and a sheathed dagger. The toes of his bare feet splayed on the glass, giving him a better grip.

Cousin. He's a cousin, thought Amastan. But that was impossible. Tamella would have known if a cousin had decided to start killing other cousins. Right?

Amastan had enough time to loose a blade, then the man leapt from the roof. A glint of light was Amastan's only warning. Instinctively, he dropped to the ground, catching himself on his palms and knees. Metal *clanged* behind him and a body thumped the roof just ahead. He pushed himself back to his feet and looked up—and into those fire-filled eyes.

They contained more than just fire. Hate, raw and intense, met Amastan's gaze, pushing him back. The blade he'd loosed came up in defense instead of attack as the man lunged. Amastan stumbled back, slipping across the oil-slicked ground. His blade glanced off his attacker's, turning it away before it could meet his bare skin.

Amastan followed through and slammed his fist into the man's side. The man twisted away, a huff the only indication that Amastan's fist had connected. The attacker's momentum carried him a few feet farther, where he pivoted and faced Amastan. His chest rose and fell with rapid breaths, his tagel fluttering.

Amastan didn't let him catch his breath. He threw one knife while loosing another. The man anticipated the attack and easily twisted out of harm's way, dropping his hand to his belt. He came up with a closed fist, which he opened and blew across. A cloud of powdered sand puffed into the air.

Amastan inhaled a lungful. More caught in his eyes. But the powder contained more than just sand, because his eyes began to sting and the world blurred. His lungs felt like they were full of razors, and despite trying to hold it back, he started coughing. He backed away, blinking rapidly as he tried to clear his vision. The fire flared bright to one side, darkness on the other, and between—

A smeared shadow, growing larger.

He closed his eyes and focused on the ground beneath his feet. Amastan hit an oily patch and then bare, rough stone, where he spread his feet and held his head high. He couldn't see his attacker, but he could feel the vibration of approaching footsteps and he remembered every detail of the rooftop around him. He calculated the seconds he'd lost and the number of steps the attacker had taken, waited a heartbeat—then lunged.

His blade hit cloth and flesh, bit through both. A grunt of pain was his reward. The man smelled of fire and ash and sweat and something else, something sweet but sharp like citrus. Then Amastan was spinning away, each step as carefully planned as the next, until the heat of the fire was at his back.

Pain blossomed along his thigh, fine and delicate and sharp. A moment later he felt something warm and wet trickling down his leg. Amastan opened his eyes to a world out of focus. The man pressed a hand against his upper arm, his blade smeared with darkness. He was watching Amastan from only a few feet away, or at least his head was turned that way. Amastan couldn't make out his eyes.

The wet had reached his heel, but it kept pulsing fresh down his thigh. His head spun and his lungs burned and his eyes stung, but Amastan pushed all of that away. He lunged again for the man, this time aiming higher—for his neck.

The man didn't move. Amastan made it two feet before his wounded leg gave out, folding beneath him as if someone had kicked him in the back of the knee. The ground rushed up at him, slammed into his other knee, then his palms when he tried to catch himself.

The man moved. Amastan saw him in the edge of his vision as he pushed himself up. But he couldn't stand. His feet kept slipping across the oil-slick stones, unable to find purchase. The man disappeared. A gust of wind brought the scent of flames and not-quite-citrus from behind. Too late, Amastan tried to turn, but the man had grabbed his tagel and yanked his head back.

Vibrations in the stones. Too many, too confusing. The flash of a knife at the corner of his eye, the delicate press of cool metal against his skin.

"Did you forget about *me*?"

Someone slammed into the man, tearing him away from Amastan. The blade slipped and was gone. Amastan turned, looked, saw.

Menna swung a length of chain over her head, circling with the man just a few feet away. She snapped the chain at him and he jumped back, but not before it caught his arm. He dropped the knife. Menna snapped the chain again and this time he dodged.

The man glanced between Menna and Amastan, who'd finally climbed to one knee. Then he bolted, racing toward the opposite edge of the roof. Menna shouted, dropped the chain and loosed a knife at the same time, one of the small ones strapped to her chest. She threw.

The blade sliced across the man's shoulder. He stumbled, but kept going. Menna cursed, started forward, but then stopped and glanced back at Amastan, who was still struggling to stand. The man was already running across the planks Amastan had left behind. He stopped long enough to kick them down and they clattered in the street below, loud as a drum.

Amastan tried to speak, to urge Menna after the man, but the smoke had stolen his voice and all he could do was cough. He could still *see* him, just a rooftop over, a shadow fleeing like a trace of cloud across the sky. It was still possible to catch the killer, to end all of this, to return to a semblance of a normal life.

Menna rocked onto her toes as if she were about to break into a sprint, but still she hesitated. Then her eyes took on a cold determination. She fell back to her heels and hurried over to Amastan.

No, no, no—Amastan tried to say, but it came out voiceless and rough.

"Are you okay?"

He looked up into Menna's worried face—she'd pulled her tagel down—and saw the real, raw fear there. Before he could respond, she began examining his leg. She hissed through her teeth, then unsnapped another knife. Amastan started to protest, unsure of her intent, but she ignored him, bent, and used the knife to rip a strip of fabric from her wrap.

She took the strip and wrapped it around the top of his thigh, above the cut. She tied it so tight he was sure she'd cut off his circulation. But then that was the point, wasn't it? She was trying to help him.

But all he could think about was that shadow getting away.

He let Menna help him stand. His leg threatened to give out again, and he was forced to lean on her. Menna easily took his weight and guided him toward the edge of the roof.

"Can you climb?" she asked.

There wasn't much choice. They couldn't go through the building, not when Menna had set everyone inside on

edge—and he'd have to remember to ask her what she'd
done—and the attacker had made sure they couldn't cross
to another roof. Over and down was the only option.

Amastan still had one working leg and two hands. He
nodded.

His shoulders were burning as if they'd been drenched
in acid by the time they reached the ground. His searching toes felt solid rock and he eased himself down with a
sigh of relief. Then he had to grab hold of Menna to keep
from collapsing. His head spun and his injured leg was
sticky with blood, despite Menna's makeshift bandage.

He needed a healer.

Menna clearly had the same thought. She helped him
down the alley and into the circle, but passed the first
healer's sign. Even if he was dying, they couldn't get
help in the same neighborhood as the mark. It was too
risky. So Amastan gritted his teeth against the growing
pain and focused on moving forward, step by awkward
step.

At some point, Menna had found him a fresh wrap
and helped him remove all his knives. He was dizzy with
blood loss by the time Menna helped him through the
healers' door. It took him too long to understand why it
was suddenly bright, why more than one pair of hands
were on him, why someone gasped with shock—no not
shock, embarrassment. He was pressed onto a table and
he closed his eyes against the glare.

Words passed over him, incomprehensible. Questions
were asked, but he understood them only after they'd
been answered, and then only in impressions.

*Broken glass—accident—not fatal—loss of blood—end
of season—not enough water—triage only—okay—okay—
okay—*

Someone had covered him with a blanket. Hands
touched and prodded and poked. Mostly his leg, but once
someone pried open an eye. He winced and pulled away

and they seemed satisfied with that. Something cool pressed against his lips.

Drink this.

He did. Then the fuzziness that had been creeping over him bloomed and spread and he sank into the table and away. . . .

20

Voices murmured near his ear, as unintelligible as the wind. Growing louder.

Amastan shot upright, instantly awake, fear closing his throat. But there was no smear of red in the air, no wind whipping around him. He wasn't alone on a rooftop or clinging to a bridge over the sands or trapped in an alley.

No—there were people all around him. Some lying, some standing, some sitting. The voices were theirs, a steady background noise and nothing more. He sat on one of over a dozen beds in a close-packed room. As he took in his surroundings, bits and pieces of memory flashed. He was at the healers. Menna had brought him here. The rooftop—fire—

"Well," said a woman sitting next to him, her voice as familiar as his own hands. "That answers my question of whether you're awake."

"Thiyya?" he said, although her name came out as a croak. "What—?"

His elder sister smiled thinly. "I'm not on duty tonight, but Menna asked me to help keep an eye on you. She's in the other room, resting. You've had a rough time of it. How do you feel?"

Amastan rubbed his forehead. "I'm . . ." he started, then stopped. He'd been about to say *fine*. But instead he felt beat up, wrung out, and sore all over. The single word had scratched his throat and now he coughed. His thigh pounded with pain and the room swam when he turned his head.

He pulled back the blanket covering him and found bandages instead of healed skin. He hid his surprise by pretending to check the dressing. But this was his sister, and he couldn't hide anything from her.

"It's the end of season," said Thiyya. "We're running out of water. Your healer used some to replace the blood you lost, but other than that we've had to let time heal you. Sorry—I think Menna'd hoped I'd be able to do more, and I would've, but there really isn't enough water." She glanced around and dropped her voice. "They would've noticed."

Dread settled heavy in his stomach, but he had to ask. "How long has it been?"

"A few days."

Amastan closed his eyes and breathed deep. So much time. Too much time. And the killer was still loose. Had another cousin died while he was stuck here?

And Yufit—was he okay? Had a jaani attacked him? Or worse—had Yufit given up on Asaf after he'd disappeared for a third time? Amastan felt guilty that he was almost as worried about that possibility as he was about another body.

Thiyya stood. "I'll go get Menna. I promised I'd let her know as soon as you woke up." She weaved her way through the beds to the curtain-covered doorway.

Amastan dropped his head into his hands. He felt sick, but he wasn't sure if it was from his injuries or conscience. He listened to the room, voices mingling with moans and the occasional snore. He'd never seen a recovery room this full before, but he'd also never been in one this near to season's end. The healers were using water sparingly, which meant more people waiting for time to heal them instead.

A few windows lined the back wall, but their glass was covered by thick curtains. All of the light in the room came from several well-placed lanterns and mirrors. It'd been night when he'd arrived here and it was night again, but that told him nothing of how long he'd been with the healers.

A few days—was that two? Three? More?

The curtain parted and Menna entered, Thiyya right behind. Menna wore a fresh wrap and she'd cleaned off the dust and oil and soot from her face, but she looked exhausted. Her eyes lit up when she saw Amastan, though, and she quickened her pace.

"How do you feel?" she asked.

"Fine." This time the word came out less rough, if still hoarse. "How many days?"

Menna's gaze slipped to the side. "Just a few."

"How many?" pressed Amastan.

"Two days, three nights," said Thiyya. She glanced at Menna. "Well, two and a half nights. You haven't missed the end of season, if that's what you're worried about." She put her hand on his arm. "You were lucky. A half inch higher and you would have bled out before Menna could get you here. Whoever attacked you—he meant to kill. People get so desperate at the end of season. Thank G-d he had bad luck." Her voice broke in those last words and Amastan felt a tremble in her fingers.

Menna took Thiyya's other hand. "He's okay now. The watchmen will find the attacker."

Thiyya looked down for a moment. When she looked up again, her expression was calm and still, but there was a wetness to her eyes. "I'll let you two talk. I'll be in the other room."

Thiyya turned to go, but Menna held onto her hand. Thiyya paused, glancing at her, but Menna offered no excuse. Instead, she stepped in close, rose to her tiptoes, and kissed Thiyya's forehead. Only then did she let go of Thiyya's hand. Thiyya closed her eyes for a heartbeat, then left without saying another word. Menna watched her go.

"I told her you'd been attacked on your way home," said Menna quietly. She turned back to Amastan. "That's all she knows."

"Why is she here? This isn't where she heals."

"Because I asked her. I wanted her expert opinion. And . . . I didn't want to be alone." The corner of Menna's mouth quirked up. "Besides, she was worried about you. Thiy' thinks you can't fight your way out of an empty room, you know."

"But . . . why her?" pressed Amastan. "Why not Dihya or Azulay? They would understand. Thiyya doesn't need to know I've been hurt."

"What, you think your own sister wouldn't notice when you didn't return home for several days?" Menna raised an eyebrow. "You might pull one past Guraya, but Thiy' isn't dense, 'Stan. She wanted to help, so I let her. She's a healer, she knows a bit about this stuff. 'Sides, Dihya and Az' would've asked too many questions." Menna rubbed her forehead. "And I don't know about you, but I'm not ready for questions."

Cousin. He's a cousin. "We might not be able to trust them, anyway."

Menna's gaze sharpened. "You don't think—"

"I don't know what I think," admitted Amastan. "But whoever attacked us that night, they had our training."

Menna shook her head. "No, no way. I know our cousins' fighting styles and that wasn't it. I could fight you or Az' or Dihya with my eyes closed and I'd *know* who I was fighting, and I'd still win, too. It wasn't either of them."

"If they're killing cousins, though, maybe it wouldn't be that hard for them to change their style enough to fool you," said Amastan. He'd been so certain that the killer had been a man during their fight, but time had fuzzed the details and now his certainty frayed. Dihya was tall and broad like a man, after all.

"But *why*," said Menna. "What reason could they have to kill Yanniq? And Emet? *And* Usem?"

Amastan stared at his hands. Tamella hung at the center of all three, but she couldn't be the killer. She would never have let a jaani go wild, let alone her own brother's. Could Usem have been retaliation, though? Were there two killers?

"Emet was your uncle," said Amastan slowly. "Was he also related to either Dihya or Azulay?"

Menna started to shake her head but stopped. "No more than he's related to you. I think his sister might've been Dihya's mother—I can check. But 'Stan—you can't seriously suspect that Dihya killed Usem."

"I don't know," admitted Amastan. "But a cousin attacked us that night. Only a cousin could've known about the contracts and only a cousin could've surprised Usem."

"You're wrong," said Menna, but her voice lacked certainty. "We'll talk to Tamella. She'll tell you you're wrong."

"But if Tamella killed Yanniq—" began Amastan.

"Listen to yourself, 'Stan. You can't suspect *everyone*. Who's next, me?"

Amastan started. "No. You were there that night. You saved me."

"But I could've been working with the killer," said Menna. "Maybe I saved you because I chickened out. And what about Azulay? He likes to gamble—maybe he got himself into too much debt."

"You're right. He could have sought out the contracts himself. It's possible he's that desperate."

Menna groaned. "That's *not* what I meant. Look—you gotta trust Tamella. She already laid herself on the line for this city once. Besides, if she was going to kill Emet, it wouldn't have been so messy. She's the Serpent."

Amastan took a deep breath. Menna was right. He was just being paranoid. "All right."

"Good," said Menna, visibly deflating.

"We're no closer," said Amastan.

The despair that'd been lingering on the edge of his awareness closed in. This had been their only chance. And it had *worked*—until it hadn't. The killer had been right there. Yet the killer had gotten away—he'd *let* the killer get away. In all his careful preparations, he'd never planned to fail.

Now who would die because of that failure?

"You should've gone after him."

"And let you die?" asked Menna. "Shards no. Even if I had, I couldn't've caught him. He was already gone."

Amastan's fingernails dug into his palms. Logically, he knew if he'd been in Menna's place, he would've done the same. He could see the distance between Menna and the killer when she'd hesitated, could count the feet and the seconds and knew that, while there had been a *chance* she could've caught him—Menna was fast—that chance was small. But logic didn't make the situation any better.

Menna touched his shoulder. "You need to rest."

"I don't have time to rest." Amastan swung his legs over the side of the bed and instantly regretted it. His thigh sang out in pain and it took him a moment of breathing through his teeth before he could move again.

"What do you think you're doing?"

"Leaving." Amastan shifted his weight to the edge of the bed and then onto his legs. His injured thigh protested, but held. As long as he was careful and slow, he should be able to walk.

Menna stepped in front of him, blocking his way. "The healers said you need a few more days—"

"Did they say I needed to stay here?"

Menna pursed her lips. "No, but—"

"Then I'm going home." Amastan paused and met her

gaze. "My bed might be needed by another." He didn't add *cousin*, even though it was on the tip of his tongue.

Menna frowned but nodded. "Fine. But we're walking you home."

Amastan lifted his hands in mock surrender. With Menna hovering at his side, he tried taking a step. It was easier than he'd expected. Most of the pain had come from stretching the wound as he got out of bed, but once he was on his feet, he could ignore the pain. He took a few limping steps before he found a way to walk without sharp, shooting pain. By the time he'd reached the curtain, he'd figured out how to walk normally—almost.

Thiyya met them on the other side of the curtain. She took his hand and together they left the healers. The night air was laden with moisture; Amastan could taste it as soon as they stepped outside. The street was busier than he'd expected, filled with a thin but constant stream of conversations, exclamations, and people. A market rumbled and cried nearby. It couldn't be long after sunset. The stars were just starting to come out.

As Amastan walked, his despair thickened until it was clogging his throat. He examined the situation from every angle, trying to find a way to go forward, a way to salvage what they had. But the truth was, he'd shattered everything. His one chance, his best chance, and the killer had gotten away. Worse, the killer knew they knew. They wouldn't be able to draw him out again, if at all.

Yufit—he still had Yufit. He had to know something, a connection that Amastan had missed. But even that was tenuous. Amastan had disappeared on him again. Besides, he didn't know where or how to find Yufit. He could be anywhere. Amastan looked up at the sky and traced the stars that made up the Vulture.

I come here to think.

Thiyya tugged on Amastan's hand, concern tightening

her features. Amastan realized he'd slowed down and gave her a reassuring smile. Inside, a different kind of energy set his nerves on edge, a desperate need to do something, now. His failure had left him ragged and raw. He'd been lying unconscious at the healers for the last three days. He could all but taste season's end in the air. He didn't have any time left to lose.

Amastan barely heard Menna's parting words. They'd reached home. Thiyya's grip tightened as she led him inside, promising Menna she'd keep an eye on him. Amastan went through the motions of reassurance, even finding a smile somewhere. Thiyya trailed him upstairs and lingered in his doorway as if he might bolt. Only when their father called from downstairs did Thiyya finally leave him alone.

Amastan didn't wait to see if she'd come back. He retrieved his spare knives from the trunk at the end of his bed and knotted a clean wrap. Then he was climbing out of his window, ignoring the pain in his leg as best he could.

He headed west, following the twilight's lingering glow. He remembered the way exactly, and before long, he reached the last platform. He found the alley that faced due west, a railing the only thing between the edge of the city and the beginning of the Wastes.

But no one sat waiting for him. The alley looked out on darkness, twilight long since faded to night in a splash of stars. The pain in his leg seemed to multiply as Amastan stood and stared. He'd thought, he'd hoped, he'd *known*—

"Asaf?"

Amastan froze for only a heartbeat before spinning around. His leg protested but the familiar sight of those steel-dark eyes was worth it. Yufit stood only a few feet away, head tilted to one side.

"What're you doing here?"

"Looking for you," admitted Amastan.

A smile warmed Yufit's eyes. "Well, here I am."

"Yeah," said Amastan. He searched for the words to say what he'd come here to ask, but none came to him.

"So," said Yufit when the silence stretched too thick. "Did you do it?"

Amastan blinked, panic spiking through him. Yufit couldn't know about the contract, about the killer. But then he remembered what he'd said only a few nights ago, the fears he'd laid bare without any of the details.

He might not have stopped the killer, but he had completed the contract. "Yes."

Yufit waited a moment before prompting, ". . . and?"

". . . and it wasn't as bad as I'd feared," said Amastan. "It was still hard and I hope I never have to do it again, but . . . I could."

Yufit stepped closer and clapped him on the shoulder. "I knew you were strong enough. Now, will you tell me what it was, or are you just going to keep teasing?"

Amastan's ears burned hot. He'd made that promise assuming he would have caught the killer in the same night. He was saved from finding a feeble excuse by the scuff of a sandal across stone behind Yufit, in the platform's center. The platform had become unusually empty and quiet.

Yufit spun around, revealing a figure standing only a dozen feet away. Amastan had expected Menna or the killer, but it was neither. A man in a familiar bronze wrap stepped closer, black embroidery marking him as one of Basil's—*ma* Yanniq's—servants, the silver on his sleeves showing his rank as gear worker. The man wore no tagel at all, which was jarring enough that Amastan didn't at first recognize the servant.

"Megar," said Yufit, but his tone held a warning.

Megar smiled, showing all of his teeth. "Where have you been?" The edges of his words blurred together; he must be drunk.

Yufit placed himself between Megar and Amastan.

Megar took an unsteady step toward them, the light shift-ing across his face. His eyes were red-ringed and watery from drink, but paler than Amastan remembered. The torchlight made them shine. It also glinted off the long metal tool in his hand.

Amastan's pulse picked up. Maybe the answer to his problem had been in the first place he'd looked after all. Two killers—yes, that made sense. Megar could have killed Yanniq alone, but he would've needed help with the cousins. Now Megar must have come to finish what he'd started. Amastan loosed a knife and pushed past Yufit. He wasn't about to let Yufit get hurt because of him.

Megar's smile remained fixed. He closed the distance too fast and grabbed Amastan's wrist as Amastan brought the knife up to strike him. Amastan expected him to reek of wine, but instead all he could smell was dust and oil and hot iron. Amastan tried to pull away. Megar's grip was strong and he held tight. His hand was hot and sweat prickled up Amastan's arm.

"Let him go," said Yufit, reaching for Megar.

"Wait." A chill touched Amastan's spine. Fear. "Don't touch him."

Something was off. Megar should have attacked by now. If he was working with someone else, they should've been ambushed. And his eyes—neither hate nor drink filled them, but something much worse.

Madness.

"Are you sane, sa?" asked Amastan.

"No," said Megar wistfully and Yufit hissed out a breath as if he'd been punched. Megar pulled Amastan close and blew anise-flavored breath into Amastan's face. "Isn't it wonderful?"

Megar radiated heat. But it was more than the heat of a fever; even through the cloth of his wrap, Megar's skin was as hot as embers. His hand on Amastan's arm was growing uncomfortable. Sweat rolled down the back of Amastan's neck even as the chill of fear filled his chest.

But I led the jaani away, thought Amastan uselessly. Amastan's charms had grown as hot as Megar's touch, each glass bead an ember against his skin and he couldn't find any hint of a charm around Megar's neck.

"A-saf," said Megar slowly, relishing the name. But it wasn't Megar anymore—it was the jaani.

"Go. Get help. Get a marabi," ordered Amastan, not looking at Yufit. To Megar he said, "Do you remember who you were?"

"I'm not leaving you with him," said Yufit.

"Then stay back. This might be our only chance to find out where the jaani came from."

Megar's hand tightened, fingers digging into muscle. Amastan winced. The glass beads at his throat flared hotter and one began to let out a high-pitched whistle.

"I am me," said Megar, his breath like the steam from a kettle. "I am he. I am we."

"Then you've got what you wanted, right? Let me go."

Megar hissed and his eyes caught the torchlight, flaring with heat and light. "I want you."

Amastan slammed his fist down onto Megar's fingers. Megar jerked back, but he didn't let go of Amastan's arm. They both stumbled farther into the alley, Yufit thankfully staying clear. The light shifted and a shadow fell across Megar's face, but his eyes didn't dim. They *glowed.*

A wisp of smoke curled out of Megar's left nostril, but he didn't seem to notice. Panic clawed at Amastan like a cat just outside the door, desperate to get in. He started prying Megar's fingers off his arm. He managed to uncurl two and this time when he yanked, he pulled free.

He put a few feet between himself and Megar, feeling Yufit move back as well, and raised his knife. Those too-bright eyes slowly moved from the knife to Amastan's face.

"Why are you like this? Who killed you?" asked Amastan.

Confusion welled in Megar's bare features like blood in a fresh wound, just as raw, just as repugnant. "A man who smelled of blood and water."

He rubbed his hand across his face, then again, pulling at his skin. His movement left a smear of light in Amastan's vision, like a torch waved at night. It was then that he realized that while they'd both moved into the shadows, Megar still looked as if he were standing in torchlight. He was emitting his own light.

Amastan could feel the heat even from a few feet away. He kept the knife between him and Megar like a shield and muttered what prayers he knew under his breath. He was all too aware of how close Yufit was, of how Yufit was still there. Why didn't he leave and find help? Amastan touched his neck, his fingers finding reassurance in the solid glass charms. They were warm—they were *hot*—but they hadn't broken. The jaani couldn't get him.

Unfortunately, Megar could.

He lunged. Yufit shouted. Amastan danced back, slashing with the knife. It caught Megar's arm. He hissed and spit and pulled his arm to himself. But instead of blood, warm light welled in the crack and oozed out.

Megar stared at the crack. It began to spread, splitting apart his arm as if he were made of clay and not flesh. Megar let out a keening wail, his eyes widening. More cracks appeared, branching and spreading like fractures in glass. The light continued to pour, spilling across the alley toward Amastan. He skipped back and away, watching in horror as Megar cracked and fractured.

It was more than light—it was flame, untethered and wild. The fire licked the air and consumed Megar's wrap, his hair, his skin. His mouth widened and flames spilled out. His eyes burst and became twin torches. Amastan saw in that caricature of a face the same eyes and mouth the jaani had formed out of red smoke on the rooftop and in the inn.

Then that face was rushing toward him, Megar's hands outstretched even as his skin crisped and burnt and blackened and crumbled to ash. That didn't stop him from grabbing Amastan's shoulders and shoving his face toward Amastan's, his mouth widening even further as his skin gave way, cheeks caving in toward swirling brightness.

Terror froze Amastan to the spot, unable to tear or even look away. Heat enveloped him, at first no worse than the sun, then as fierce as flame. All he could smell was hot iron and ash and all he could hear was a high-pitched whistle, verging now on a shriek, but he couldn't tell if it was coming from his charms or from Megar—or what was left of Megar.

It didn't matter. At any moment he was going to burn up.

All at once, Amastan became aware of another sound: someone shouting. Hands—real, solid hands—pulled at him and then he was tumbling back, free from the jaani's grip. Those hands pushed him into Yufit's arms who held him as what was once Megar fell apart, burned up from the inside out.

As Amastan's senses returned to him in a rush, he recognized the voice: Menna. She stood between them and the jaani and shouted a string of unrelated prayers while scattering salt on the ground in front of them and waving a piece of burning vellum in the air. The greasy smoke left behind loops and swirls: words. Amastan wasn't sure what she was trying to do, but the jaani didn't try to attack them. It swirled in place, its brilliant light fading to a dim glow fading to nothing but a color, a red smearing the air.

The jaani tried to lash out at Menna, but it collided with an invisible barrier. It reared back and tried again, only to meet with the same barrier. Then, all at once, it shuddered and leaped into the sky, disappearing above the rooftops.

The silence the jaani left behind was deafening. Menna let her arm drop, the smoldering vellum dangling from her fingers. Smoke streaked her face and gray ash had settled in her black hair. Amastan shifted and Yufit let him go.

"G-d," said Yufit.

Then he threw up.

21

Menna headed straight for the back of Idir's inn, picking a table that was not quite, but almost, the farthest away from the door and the torches. She fell into a seat with a shudder and a sigh while Yufit went to find the server. Amastan eased himself down, wincing at the pain in his leg. He wasn't sure, but he might have torn open the wound. It felt damp. He would have to check later.

Menna peered through her fingers at him. "I swear you have a death wish, 'Stan. You owe me. Big."

"How'd you find me?"

"What, you thought I'd just leave you alone after you almost died?" Menna snorted. "I kept watch on your house. I thought the killer might've somehow figured out who we were and come to finish the job. I mean, I would, if it were me. So I saw you sneak out your window. I tried to give you some space when you were talking to your"— Menna cut a glance toward Yufit, a smirk tweaking her lips—"*friend,* which is why I was a little late. I want you to know you deserved whatever I saved you from, by the way. Now—what in G-d's holiest names *was* that?"

"Megar," said Amastan. At her blank look, he added, "He's a servant of Yanniq's. Was."

"I've never seen anything like that." Menna rubbed her face, smearing the soot across her cheeks. "That must've been what Elder Dessin meant when he said the jaan were getting stronger and turning into guul. He'd said that the jaan would burn up the bodies they possessed, but I thought he was being metaphorical. I didn't think—I didn't expect—nothing like *that*." She closed her eyes and let out a long breath. "My G-d."

Yufit appeared over her shoulder and set a jar of viscous amber liquid between them. "I pray G-d had nothing to do with that." He slid into the seat next to Amastan, but his gaze stayed on Menna. "Were you able to speak with your elders?"

Menna poured herself some wine, but her hands were shaking so much that half of it splashed onto the table. She gave up and downed the little she'd poured. "Yes. That's where I got the words and the vellum to quiet the jaani this time. They also taught me how to make a barrier." She stared at the ceiling. "We have . . . some ideas. Unfortunately, the problem lies in scale. There're three elements involved in quieting and guarding against jaan: words, ink, and water. We have plenty of the first two."

"But it's the end of season," said Yufit slowly.

Menna waved her hand at Yufit. "Exactly."

"So we have to wait until the aquifer refills," said Amastan. "Which could be weeks yet."

"We *could* wait that long," said Menna.

Amastan knew that tone all too well. "Or?"

"Water doesn't just come from the pumps. It comes from the skies, too."

Amastan frowned, trying to understand what Menna meant. All of the aquifer's water came from the storms, but most of those storms caught on the mountains in the east, where they dumped their water before dissipating. The aquifer that Ghadid's pumps tapped into stretched all the way from those mountains to the edge of the Wastes. It would take a few weeks for the aquifer to refill. Water came from the skies, but it contained impurities, diseases. The aquifer filtered the rain and made it safe to drink.

People sometimes drank rainwater, but only when they were desperate. Doing so risked illness, death.

But Yufit figured out what Menna meant. He sat up straight. "You think we can use a storm."

"I do," said Menna. "First storm of the season's usually the biggest. That should be plenty."

"But it just comes *down*," said Amastan, still confused. "There's no control. Or do you mean to collect it? I don't know if we can convince the drum chiefs to allow that in time."

"So we go where the drum chiefs don't have any say over water collection. We lure the jaan somewhere that'll also give us lots of room and no chance of a bystander getting hurt."

This time, Amastan knew exactly what she meant. "No."

"Do you have a better idea?"

Yufit looked between them. "Where?"

"The sands," said Amastan, hoping he was wrong.

But Menna nodded. "The sands."

Amastan closed his eyes. He knew it was irrational to fear the sands after all he'd been through. He'd faced jaan four times now and survived, jaan much stronger than anything rumored to haunt the sands, and yet the thought of going down there again filled him with cold terror. It was just so big, so empty, and there was nowhere to hide.

And Menna wanted them down there in the middle of a storm? Storms were violent, dangerous things. Their winds were often strong enough to tear roofs from buildings and to slash apart the landscape. The sands changed drastically from year to year in part because of the storms that ripped across them. It wasn't safe to be outside in the city during a storm. Amastan couldn't imagine what it must be like on the sands.

"Nothing's going to be ideal," said Menna, reading Amastan's silence. "This whole mess isn't ideal. But we've

got to *try*. The jaani is only going to get stronger and we
can't let it kill anyone else. It's one thing to be driven
mad, but that . . . that . . ."

She trailed off but Amastan could still see *that*. The
light breaking through Megar's skin, consuming him, his
face crumbling to ash even as the jaani still tried to get at
Amastan.

He wanted to throw up.

He didn't.

Yufit filled a glass for Amastan, then topped off
Menna's. Amastan cupped his glass between his hands,
but he couldn't drink. The smell of alcohol reminded
him of Megar and churned his stomach.

"Has a jaani ever done that before?" asked Yufit.

Menna tapped her fingers on her glass. "No . . . and
yes. When a jaani does something like that, it's not a
jaani anymore."

Yufit folded his hands in front of him and waited expectantly. Menna lifted her gaze, caught him watching,
and cut Amastan a glance. Amastan nodded: Yufit was a
part of this. He deserved to know.

"This is part of what happens when a jaani's on its way to
becoming a guuli," said Menna, her voice flat. "Normally,
a jaani gets blown about on the sands and grows weak. But
sometimes . . . they don't. For whatever reason. The elders
don't really know, although they have their theories. Elder
Dessin thinks these jaan are able to stay strong by shelter-
ing in bodies, alive or dead. Out on the sands, two or three
people die in a sandstorm, their jaan go unquieted. Those
jaan would get caught in the wind and go wild, but maybe
one stays in a body and lingers there until the next storm,
and the next batch of lost travelers. Fresh bodies, a stronger
jaani. But too strong—this jaani doesn't just possess the living, it tears them apart. Like what happened to your friend.
The next step is for the jaani to figure out how to build a
body that *won't* fall apart. And then you have a guuli."

"But that doesn't explain why it keeps finding me," said Amastan.

"That could be my fault." Yufit turned his glass in his hands. "I don't want to speak ill of the dead, but could this jaani have something to do with Yanniq's death?"

"Why would you say that?" asked Amastan.

Yufit shrugged. "Yanniq died around the same time that the jaani showed up. Yanniq was murdered, so maybe his body wasn't found in time."

Amastan was careful to avoid glancing at Menna. "That's possible. But I don't see how it being Yanniq's jaani would make any difference."

"Can a jaani be angry?"

"If a jaani isn't quieted, it will go wild," said Menna carefully and clearly, as if explaining the concept to a child.

"I know that," said Yufit. He sipped his wine. Put the glass down. Picked it up again. "But if its death was violent, if the jaani knew . . ."

"You think the jaani might seek revenge?" finished Amastan.

"I don't know." Yufit tilted his glass one way, then the other, watching the liquid inside. "Jaan remember their old lives, even if it's not much. After all, that's why they try to possess people, right? Because they remember what it was to be alive. Because they want to be human again."

"They want to be whole," corrected Menna. "A body without its jaani is an empty shell. A jaani without its body is just as empty. They seek an equilibrium they can never achieve again, not until they let go and move on to the next world. But what you're saying . . . might not be wrong. If death left enough of an impression on the jaani, it might remember and specifically seek out its murderer. Or it might be enough to twist the jaani into a guuli."

Hope flashed through Amastan. "So Megar could've been Yanniq's murderer."

Menna pursed her lips. "It went after you, too, remember."

"But I didn't . . ." started Amastan, before trailing off. He'd been about to say, *have anything to do with Yanniq's death*. But that wasn't quite true, was it?

Menna met his gaze and he saw his thoughts reflected there. Maybe it wasn't Yanniq's jaani after all. They'd found Emet's body and trapped his jaani. Maybe that was enough to draw its ire.

"I don't think the jaani knows who killed Yanniq, either," said Amastan.

Yufit nodded and then drained his cup. "I think your friend is correct, Asaf. The jaani isn't just going after the killer. It's going after anyone who's been associated with its death."

"Then why would it go after *you*?" asked Menna pointedly.

"I . . ." Yufit looked down, twisting the empty cup in his hand. "There's something I haven't told you."

Menna and Amastan exchanged a glance. Menna looked bewildered. But Amastan's stomach plunged with sickening speed. He knew what Yufit was going to say, even if it didn't make any sense. In a flash, he saw what would happen next: Yufit admitting that he'd killed Yanniq, Menna rising from her seat, a blade already in hand, Yufit attacking first. Drawing blood. Menna defending herself. Yufit fast, but not fast enough. And himself, frozen in place, unable to act.

Not Yufit, he pleaded silently to any who would listen. G-d, jaan, sajaam—he didn't care. *Just don't let the killer be Yufit.*

"I found Yanniq's body," said Yufit.

Menna dropped her glass, but it only fell a few inches to clatter noisily on the table. She swiped it and set it right again. *"What?"*

Amastan stared. Yufit's words made sense individually, but together they were nonsense. Yufit couldn't have found Yanniq. *They* had.

"He'd been hidden away, as if whoever had killed him didn't want anyone to know. Or to find him." Yufit looked around, but the inn was surprisingly busy and noisy—a saddit tournament had taken up several tables and the crowd whooped as two players hunched over their pieces—and no one paid them any mind. "I think that's why the jaani is so angry. Whoever killed him—they didn't want his jaani to be quieted. The jaani must know that somehow."

Amastan continued to stare. He didn't bother trying to hide his surprise. After all, he wasn't supposed to know the details of Yanniq's death. At the same time, he hoped his surprise hid his blatant relief. Of course Yufit wasn't the killer. He couldn't be. He'd only worked for Yanniq for a month, unlike Megar who'd had years to cultivate his resentment. Besides, he had nothing to do with any of the cousins.

"So that's why you think the jaani has been after you," said Menna carefully.

Yufit poured more wine and swirled the liquid in his glass. "It makes sense. Jaan aren't known for their reasoning. It must've mistook me for whoever murdered Yanniq."

Menna nodded slowly, but Amastan saw the hesitation, the questions. He had the same ones. Had Yufit found the body before or after they had? And if before—why hadn't he told the watchmen? Or had he?

But Amastan couldn't ask those questions, not without revealing that they'd found the body, too. That would bring too many questions that, if answered, would unravel Asaf's whole existence. Although Amastan wanted to tell Yufit who he really was, the time for that wasn't now. They were too close to real answers. He couldn't afford any distractions.

Yufit was still talking. "And the jaani went after Asaf because he saved me from it."

Amastan nodded. "That fits."

"But there's still Megar," pointed out Menna.

"He was in the inn that day the jaani attacked me," said Amastan. "He tried to save me." It could've been the other way around, of course—that the jaani had been after Megar instead of him. But Amastan didn't mention that.

Yufit's eyes widened for an instant, then he dropped his gaze and swirled his wine the other way. He didn't say anything.

Menna sighed and closed her eyes. "Well, whether or not Megar killed Yanniq, we have a wild and very angry jaani on the loose. We've seen what it did to Megar. I have no reason to believe it won't do the same to someone else. And it'll only get worse as the jaani gets stronger." She opened her eyes and looked pointedly at Yufit, then Amastan. "Since it's shown particular interest in the pair of you . . ."

Yufit gestured at her. "Why not you? You've been just as close to the jaani twice now and you fought it both times."

Menna smirked. "And won, remember. The jaani knows better than to tangle with *me*."

Yufit chuckled. "Of course."

Menna abruptly pushed herself back from the table, her glass empty. "Which is all the more reason I need to stop wasting time hanging with *you* lowlifes and go speak with Elder Dessin. *You*"—she leveled a finger at Amastan, her gaze stern—"better not get attacked by a jaani again while I'm gone. And *you*"—she swung her finger around to Yufit, who raised his eyebrows in an amused smile—"better keep an eye on that one and make sure he doesn't get into any more trouble. The jaani should be gone for a good day or two, but . . . walk him home for me, will you?" A sly smile slid across her lips. "Maybe you two can finally confess your undying love and get some real work done."

"We're not—" started Amastan, his ears flaring hot.

Menna laughed, rolled her eyes, and waved as she left them alone at the table. Amastan watched her go instead of meeting Yufit's gaze, the awkwardness she'd left behind stretching thick as storm-filled air between them. The wine in his glass held a sudden, immediate appeal and he downed it. The warmth spread from his ears to his cheeks to his throat to his chest and in a few more moments, he felt a little better.

A hand touched his, warm and rough. Amastan started and looked up into Yufit's steel-cold eyes. Now they held some warmth and a touch of guilt.

"You're okay." His voice was soft, filled with half wonder, half relief. Then Yufit straightened and pulled his hand back, the warmth leaving his eyes while the guilt sharpened. "You almost weren't. I froze, Asaf, and because of me, you almost died. If your friend hadn't come along in time . . ." He shook his head as if trying to dispel the thought.

This time, Amastan put his hand on Yufit's arm. "You heard Menna, jaan don't act like that, not normally. What should you have done?"

"More," said Yufit, the single word heavy with recrimination.

"You still saved me," said Amastan. "And we're both alive. Isn't that enough?"

"Yeah," said Yufit, but his voice was hollow, his gaze distant, his mind still stuck in the alley. "Yeah, it could've been worse."

Amastan turned his glass, the words burning a realization through him. His thigh throbbed, a reminder of several nights before. It had gone horribly wrong, but it could have been worse. He could have messed up the contract. He could be dead. Menna could be hurt. Instead, the killer might still be at large, but so were they. There was still hope.

Yufit looked into his glass, and when he spoke, his voice was thin. "You know, when I didn't see you for a few days, I worried about you." Then he laughed. "I don't know why. I've never worried about someone before." His fingers tapped his glass and he finally looked up. "Do you think what happened to Megar will happen again?"

"I don't know." Amastan's fingers curled around the beads at his throat. "I hope not. But unless we quiet the jaani soon . . ."

"I don't see why this is happening," said Yufit. "Jaan don't act like this. They don't burn people up from the inside. Guul don't either. They just hunt for corpses. This isn't normal. It must be because Yanniq was a bad person. It must be." He reached for the jar of date wine, but hesitated, stopped. He drew his hand back. "Megar didn't kill Yanniq."

Amastan glanced at him, but Yufit was spinning his glass again and the shadow of his tagel hid most of his expression.

"How do you know?"

Yufit turned his glass one way, then the other on the table. "Yanniq might've had a lot of enemies, but Megar wasn't one of them. Besides, he's not—*wasn't*"—Yufit winced—"smart enough. He was a man of passion, as you might've noticed."

"Yeah." Amastan chewed his lip. As much as he'd wanted Megar to be the killer—or one of the killers—Yufit was right. Amastan had nothing that pointed to Megar being the killer aside from a handful of suppositions that didn't quite add up. And the figure on the rooftop couldn't have been Megar.

When Yufit spoke again, his words were careful, measured. "Even though I was only there a month, I still learned a lot about Yanniq's past. Does a man's jaani reflect how he lived his life? That could explain why this jaani is so violent."

Amastan's breath caught in his throat and a slivered edge of hope returned. He was afraid to say anything, though, lest he accidentally discourage Yufit from sharing what he knew. So he only nodded.

"I said before that Yanniq pardoned murderers, but that was only some of the truth," said Yufit. "You study history, right? What do you know about the Serpent of Ghadid?"

Amastan snapped in a breath, too quick. He picked up the half-empty jar of date wine to hide his surprise and give himself a moment to think. What *would* he know, if he wasn't family? "The Serpent is a story told to frighten children."

Yufit leaned across the table, his gaze intent on Amastan. "The Serpent's more than a story. She terrorized this city for years."

"She?" Amastan splashed amber wine into his glass and downed the wine without tasting it. Yufit's unease was infectious.

A smirk twitched at the corner of Yufit's eyes and was gone. "Yes, she. *She* was real. She was caught, eventually. And there were more like her, an entire group of trained killers. They called themselves assassins, but they were glorified murderers. The drum chiefs looked the other way and let them kill without any consequences."

"You're saying the drum chiefs have a secret army of assassins?" asked Amastan, trying desperately to sound amused. "Wouldn't somebody have noticed?"

"Not an army," corrected Yufit. "There aren't that many of them. But yeah—the drum chiefs let them get away with murder. At least, until the Serpent killed one of their own. The drum chiefs should've rounded them all up and had them executed for the safety of Ghadid. Instead, Yanniq convinced the Circle to pardon the Serpent.

The blood of her victims—and the victims of all those assassins—is on his hands. A man like that is the worst kind of evil."

Amastan's breath caught in his throat. "Which drum chief did the Serpent kill?"

"Drum Chief Saman," said Yufit, his voice tight. "Yanniq's worst crime was letting Saman's murderer walk free."

22

The horrors of the night before seemed so far away among bright daylight and dusty scrolls. The sun might have banished the image of Megar's eyes bursting with flame from Amastan's mind, but it did nothing for the pulsing dread and the time hissing past his ears, forever lost. Four dead and what did he have? Nothing.

Nothing—but now everything.

Yufit had given him the slip of string that tied everything together. Or so Amastan hoped. Yufit had also walked him home, or at least as close to home as Amastan had dared. It'd been nice. Quiet. A reprieve. For a few minutes, Amastan could ignore the imminent deadlines and pretend he was normal. But now that reprieve had ended.

Amastan went to the wall of scrolls first, each a tiny piece of Ghadid's history. When he couldn't find what he was looking for there, he scanned through every scroll Barag had given him for the family's history. But that record stopped abruptly over twenty years ago.

He set the last one down and took a small sip of water from his skin. The water softened his mouth but did little to alleviate his thirst. He was running dangerously low and he only had one baat left. The air was as sticky as porridge today, and he thought he'd caught sight of a cloud on the horizon. But one cloud was no guarantee season would end today or tomorrow or the day after. He would just have to lie low and endure his thirst.

But he didn't have time to lie low.

Barag peered at Amastan over the top of his thin glasses. "What're you looking for? Anything I can help with?"

Amastan tapped the box of scrolls. "Where's the rest of the family's history?"

Barag paused, his eyes inscrutable. "Are you done already?"

"No," admitted Amastan. "But it would be easier to put all these pieces together if I knew the whole history."

Another pause. Amastan held his breath, hoping Barag wouldn't press the question. He didn't want to explain about last night, didn't want to tell Barag that a servant of Yanniq's had accused his wife of terrible things. Tamella had certainly done terrible things, would readily admit to them, but Amastan didn't want Barag's version of events. He wanted to read it himself.

"I'm still working on that part," said Barag. "But I've got the original records for the drum chiefs' Circles during that time and the accounts over here. Why don't you wait until I've finished before you add it to your project? It'll only be a few more months."

"It'll help now," said Amastan. "Trust me."

Barag shrugged, then dug around beneath his table. He finally came out with a small box of tightly wound scrolls. Amastan swallowed his immediate disappointment: it didn't look like much. But it would have to do.

He pushed aside the other scrolls on his table and set the box in the middle. Then he picked out a scroll, the biggest he could find. Unrolling it revealed a list of an entire year's imports and exports, item after item squeezed onto the vellum in thin, precise script. Unless he wanted to know exactly how many slabs of salt the caravans had brought in that year, it wasn't going to do him any good. He set it aside.

Three more scrolls led him nowhere. But the fourth—

The fourth had brief accounts of the year's Circles. He scanned them quickly—there were twelve in all. The accounts contained all of the drum chiefs' decisions during their monthly Circles. Disputes between merchants, friends, families. Each neighborhood's annual allocation of baats. A change to the way grains would be taxed.

And there—between a blessing of marriage and a grievance from a gear worker—was a discussion about the Empress's tax collectors and what to do with them. Drum Chief Saman had argued against kicking them out empty-handed. The Circle had decided otherwise.

That had been the last Circle of that year. Amastan picked through the other scrolls until he found the account for the next year's Circles. The first mentioned that several merchants had come before the Circle to express their worry about angering the Mehewret Empire. The same merchants returned several Circles in a row before the drum chiefs officially decreed that Ghadid was not a part of the Empire and therefore owed no taxes.

The merchants disappeared from the record. For a few months, the Circles returned to normal. And then, all at once, the names changed. Two new drum chiefs were part of the discussion. Amastan had to scan them twice before realizing Saman's was one of the two that had disappeared. The other had been Liddas. This was the longest Circle account yet. And for good reason: the drum chiefs had debated the fate of the family.

Amastan's head spun and he realized he was holding his breath. He let it out as he read, taking his time over each word.

The account briefly acknowledged that there'd been traitors among the drum chiefs and that they'd been removed. Then it turned to the matter of Tamella Basbowen:

she'd killed one of those drum chiefs. The debate had been over whether to execute or exile Tamella, and whether to disband or dishonor the family. Whoever had written this account had glossed over the details, leaving behind a dry summary about the final decision—eight for, four against: Tamella would be allowed to not only live, but stay. The family would not be disbanded, but their work was over. Contracts would be banned indefinitely.

The eight who'd voted to pardon Tamella included Yanniq. The four against: Drum Chief Azul, Drum Chief Eken, Drum Chief Hennu, and Drum Chief Yugten. Amastan didn't recognize Azul's name, but he knew the rest. Yugten and Eken were the drum chiefs of the northernmost neighborhoods and Hennu was his own drum chief. Azul and Hennu's names were the two new ones, replacing the names of the traitors.

"You've been reading a long time," said Barag, startling Amastan. "Do you have any questions?"

Amastan looked up from the scroll and met Barag's eyes. If anyone would know . . .

"Why did Tamella kill Drum Chief Saman?"

Barag stared at Amastan until Amastan began to wonder if he'd heard. Then he set down his pen and folded his hands on the desk. "Now why would you want to know that?"

"Please, sa," said Amastan. "It's the only lead I have left. Something ties Tamella and Yanniq together, and I think Saman might be it."

Barag sighed. "I thought you were *working*. Fine. I've already told you some of what happened. Tamella stopped a civil war that would've torn this city apart and handed its shattered shell over to the Mehewret Empire. A few of the conspirators were drum chiefs. One of them was Saman." Barag chuckled darkly. "She was the one who originally took out a contract on *me*, when I started to put together what was happening. You see, history has a way of repeating itself and I'd noticed a particular pattern in their correspondence which turned out to be a code. She didn't much like poets, either. So that was two strikes against me."

Barag shuffled the papers on his desk, but he didn't seem to have any order to his movements. "Saman was their leader. She gathered people sympathetic to the Empire and helped build the conspiracy from the sands up. In fact, it was her idea to cultivate a conflict that would split the drum chiefs and the people. The ensuing chaos would've made it easier for the Empress's conquering force to march right in. She believed that the Empire's control was inevitable and working with them was the only way to avoid being enslaved—as the Empire was rumored to do to any who dared not submit. She sincerely thought she was saving Ghadid from something worse." Barag shook his head, as if Saman had been an ignorant child instead of a drum chief.

"When it all came crashing down, Tamella confronted Saman. It ended badly—Saman died. Tamella said it was self-defense, but that didn't matter. She was an assassin who'd acted outside of a contract."

"But she saved the city," said Amastan. "Saman was a traitor. Wouldn't Saman have been executed anyway?"

Barag shook his head. "That wasn't Tamella's decision to make. You should remember, the family operates on the thinnest line of legality. It isn't up to you to decide who lives and who dies. To put it crudely, the family was the knife that Ghadid used to excise its tumors before they grew too big—too public, if you will. But a knife should never think for itself. The drum chiefs' greatest fear was that their knife would turn on them. And that's exactly what had happened.

"Tamella broke the rules. The drum chiefs called

her before the Circle to answer for herself. She'd saved them—that was never in doubt—but at the same time she'd proven how dangerous the family still was. Some of the drum chiefs argued that the risk of it happening again—of another assassin deciding fate for themselves—was too great. They wanted the family gone completely. Most of them would've been satisfied with some degree of dissolution, like forbidding the training of new assassins or even exile, but one drum chief wanted the family executed. Every trained member of the family. Especially Tamella.

"Of course, that drum chief was outnumbered, otherwise we wouldn't be having this conversation. Yanniq was the one who argued for Tamella's life the loudest, and rightly so—without her, the Circle wouldn't even have been able to meet. The other drum chiefs came around, but Tamella was barred from ever acting again, let alone taking a contract. Honestly, even the drum chiefs realized this was an empty gesture—too many people knew Tamella and the myth of the Serpent of Ghadid was already spreading. It was no longer safe for her. But they had to make it official, and in a way that stung worse than anything else they'd dealt her."

"But they didn't exile or execute her," pointed out Amastan.

"True," said Barag, spreading his hands. "But they might as well have. Being an assassin was her life and she lost everything. All because she tried to do the right thing in the wrong way."

Barag paused to catch his breath. He smiled at Amastan, but the smile lacked warmth. "All that to say: yes. Tamella killed Drum Chief Saman. It's a bit of a sore subject." He picked his glasses back up, signifying that the conversation was over. "Now, don't you have some scrolls to transcribe? Everybody needs to work for their water."

"It's the end of season," said Amastan. "There isn't any water."

"But there will be." Barag turned back to his work. "The storms always come."

Amastan nodded, but he wasn't thinking about the storms. He stared at the scroll in front of him, seeing the fight play out between the drum chiefs as if he'd been there. Yanniq was one of the eight that had voted to pardon Tamella. Azul, Eken, Hennu, and Yugten—against. They'd all wanted Tamella gone, the family disbanded. One of them had even wanted to have Tamella executed.

But which one? He needed to know more about Drum Chief Saman.

Amastan put his pen down and glanced at Barag, but the older historian was already engrossed in his work. He didn't even look over when Amastan stood and headed for the shelves. He tapped the stacks as he passed them, marking each year and counting back twelve. Then he scanned the labels until he found what he was looking for: a record of the year's deaths.

He picked through the scrolls until he found the appropriate one, then, keeping his back to Barag, unrolled it. Names filled the vellum, each marked by dates and a few sentences about the deceased. He found Saman's with ease; like Yanniq's, hers had more than a few sentences.

Saman Uzbamen ma Anaz, Drum Chief of Seraf Neighborhood

Took up the drum from Anaz Inesolen, may his jaani rest with G-d in peace, in the year 352. Ruled with fairness and faith for 12 years. Maintained the peace and prosperity of the Seraf Neighborhood. Negotiated . . .

Amastan started skimming. It was in the same formulaic style as the one that had been written about Yanniq. Saman had done her job and she'd done it well—up until she'd betrayed Ghadid. But Amastan found no mention of that particular history in this account. Instead, he came across a peculiar section, which made little sense out of context.

Died from severe blood loss.

Amastan could only imagine. But the next line was what caught his interest.

Survived by three sons and Hennu ma Saman, who has been named drum chief on behalf of the eldest son, until he comes of age.

Hennu. The one and same who was still drum chief of their neighborhood over a decade later. If Drum Chief Hennu was the deceased Saman's wife, then she had reason enough to dislike Yanniq and Tamella both, as well as every other assassin.

Amastan carefully rolled the scroll back up and returned it to the shelf. His thoughts buzzed with the new information, fitting it into its place. Everything was beginning to make a terrible sense. Hennu had a very good reason to hate Yanniq and want him dead. She'd argued for Tamella's execution. She'd wanted the whole family disbanded. And she'd gotten none of it. Instead, she'd been forced to watch her wife's killer continue walking Ghadid, free and alive. It must've felt like a slap to the face.

The only problem was: why now? Why wait so long?

The other thing that didn't make sense was *how*. That couldn't have been Hennu on the rooftop. For one, she was shorter. For another, unless she was a very good actor, there was no way she could be that strong or fast. Which meant he hadn't found the killer, not yet.

But Amastan had found who'd hired him.

Now he needed proof.

Sunset was nearing when Amastan knocked on the wall beside Kaseem's doorway. He waited with his hands behind his back. It wasn't until his neck began to itch with sweat that he realized several minutes had passed. He was about to knock again when the curtain swished to one side and two glittering eyes peered back at him.

"If you're here for your baats, you'll have to wait until the rains," said Kaseem. "I'm afraid even I'm out for this season."

"Sorry, sa, but that's not why I'm here," said Amastan. "May I come in?"

Kaseem looked him over, then disappeared into the gloom of his home, leaving the curtain pulled aside. Amastan took that for a *yes* and entered.

The room was largely unchanged from his last visit. Kaseem waited next to the hearth, leaning on his cane. Amastan joined him, his thigh protesting more now than last night. But Amastan refused to limp.

"I have a simple question, sa," said Amastan carefully, picking a spot near the middle of the room to stand.

"Then ask it and be gone. You're interrupting my evening tea."

Amastan glanced toward the cool hearth, which held nothing but ash. The kettle hung above it, for all the good that would do. He decided it was better not to say anything.

"Twelve years ago, the drum chiefs put a halt to the contract system. When did it start again?"

"Recently, as I'm sure you've figured out already," said Kaseem. He placed both hands on top of his cane and peered at Amastan with those watery eyes. "How did your contract go? I heard it was successful—the mark's funeral was today. But usually I hear about this success from *you*."

"We've been busy, sa," said Amastan. But then he saw no way around it. "It was a trap. Like we'd expected. The killer was there. I was with the healers for several days. Then there was a jaani and work and—I've only been able to come see you now."

Kaseem rotated the cane beneath his palm, but his gaze remained fixed on Amastan. "Somehow I don't think you're about to tell me that you caught this killer."

Amastan winced and shook his head. "No, sa. Even though we were prepared, he still caught us by surprise. But he wasn't ready for two of us. I doubt he'll use your contracts again, now that we've figured out his scheme."

"Which is good for me, but bad for you," said Kaseem. "Now how will you capture him?"

"That's why I'm here today," said Amastan.

"Not so good for me, then." Kaseem sighed and took a seat next to the hearth, folding in on himself like a thick sheet.

"Please, sa—" began Amastan, but Kaseem waved him to silence.

"You needn't beg. I'll answer your questions." He raised a finger. "Within reason. You've already done me a service by exposing a flaw in my system and excising it. I'll take the appropriate steps to patch it, I owe you that much. As an untested assassin, you have performed well. So yes, the contracts started recently. Within a month, if my memory still serves me—and it does. And yes, there've only been the three, which came quite close together. Perhaps I should have been more suspicious, but a decade had passed and clearly there was want for your family's services."

Amastan swallowed the urge to point out that two men had died because Kaseem hadn't been suspicious. Instead, he asked the question he was there for. "The contracts were halted by the drum chiefs. So how did they start again, sa?"

"By the drum chiefs," answered Kaseem.

"How?" pressed Amastan. "Did they call you before them? Did they come to you? How did you know the ban had been lifted?"

Kaseem thumped his cane on the floor and scowled. "Nothing so obvious. The drum chiefs would never allow themselves to be seen with or near me, even if they knew who I was. No, my network brought me notice from the last Circle that our activities would be ignored again."

"Notice? Like a letter?"

"Yes, a letter," said Kaseem, annoyed. "What else would you expect? A singing mule?"

"How could you be certain it was from the drum chiefs, sa?"

"Saying 'sa' doesn't make that question less insulting."

"It's still an important question."

Kaseem snorted, then used his cane to leverage himself up. He went to the table and lifted the top, revealing a hidden compartment within. He slipped out a small, rolled scroll and shut the table, his fingers briefly moving beneath it. He was too quick for Amastan to catch a glimpse of what was inside.

He untied the scroll's string and flicked the scroll open. He scanned its contents, then held the piece of thin papyrus out to Amastan, who took it with great care. The scroll held only one line, beneath which was a black wax seal.

By order of the Circle and by G-d's will, the ban restricting and limiting contracts of a necessary nature is no longer in effect.

The words were written in a standard, boxy script, the kind perfected by scribes throughout Ghadid. It could have been written by anyone, even Amastan. The seal bore more information, if not much. It was the official seal of the position of drum chief—an intricately carved drum with a circle around it—and nothing more. Each drum chief had two seals: one for their position, which was identical for every drum chief, and one for their particular neighborhood.

But the wax bore only the one seal.

It made sense. If the order came from the Circle as a whole, then there was no need for a neighborhood seal, because the order would apply to all of Ghadid. Still, Amastan was disappointed. He'd hoped that whichever drum chief had fabricated this order would have slipped up and put their own seal on it. He'd wanted to see the seal for Seraf on that slip of fragile paper, because then he'd know for certain that Drum Chief Hennu was behind the murders.

Instead, it could've been any of the twelve drum chiefs. Or none at all, if this order was real. His suspicion was only that—a suspicion.

"Are you satisfied?" asked Kaseem, holding out his hand for the paper.

Amastan wanted to stomp his feet in frustration like Menna. Instead, he settled on gritting his teeth. He started to hand the paper back to Kaseem, but another idea crossed his mind. He jerked his hand back before Kaseem could grasp the order and rubbed his thumb across the seal.

Twelve identical seals. But they couldn't be perfectly identical, could they? There had to be differences, even slight. If he could find the exact seal that had been used on this order, he'd have his answer.

"Can I borrow this, sa?"

Kaseem frowned, his hand still extended. "I'm not sure I can do that."

"Just for a few days," said Amastan. "Then I'll bring it back. But let me see if I can find its match, sa."

"Need I point out that there're twelve possible matches?" asked Kaseem. "Need I also point out that you're treading a very fine line if you use that order to condemn a drum chief?"

"I'm aware, sa," said Amastan.

Kaseem hesitated a moment longer, his eyes examining Amastan anew. Then his hand dropped, and with it his shoulders. "I'll leave it in G-d's hands, then—you have until season's end."

23

The drum chief's order burned in Amastan's pocket as he wove through the streets toward home. He hardly noticed the crowd blowing past him as he walked, head down, thoughts too loud. Unless someone had stolen or forged the seal, a drum chief had lifted the ban. Now he just needed to know which one.

Hennu ma Saman, now Drum Chief Hennu, had more than enough reason to want revenge against both Drum Chief Yanniq and the family.

But. Yet. And.

But—it had been over a decade. Why now? What had changed?

Yet—the killer couldn't have been Hennu herself. Amastan knew her height and build and it didn't match that of the figure on the rooftop.

And—the killer moved with a precision and grace that could only have come from years of training. The kind of training he and his cousins had received.

But—the killer had the kind of knowledge only those fully trained as assassins had. Why else would the contracts have specified only *one* cousin? How else could the killer have taken Usem and Emet by surprise?

Yet—if the killer had been a cousin, surely Tamella would have known.

And—a cousin wouldn't have killed other cousins. A cousin wouldn't have let jaan go wild.

But—if the killer had been *trained* as a cousin, that didn't guarantee they would pass their test and become one. *You wouldn't be the first to leave the family. . . .*

Yet—

"Asaf!"

Amastan started, realizing all at once that that hadn't been the first time someone had shouted his assumed name in the past few minutes. His path home from Kaseem's had brought him through the Aeser neighborhood. By choice or by chance? He didn't know for sure. He turned just as a hand found his shoulder. Yufit stood there, sweat glistening faintly above his eyebrows. He was breathing in quick little bursts, as if he'd just been running.

"I've been calling to you since the last platform," said Yufit. He dropped his hand from Amastan's shoulder. "Are you okay?" Then worry flashed across his eyes. "Are you sane?"

"I am," said Amastan. "Both. Sane and okay. I mean, I'm fine." His ears only burned hotter as he stumbled over his words. He felt vaguely queasy, as if he'd eaten too many fermented fruit.

Yufit's worry dispersed, replaced by relief. "Oh thank G-d. I'll live a calmer life when your marabi friend quiets the jaani. I've been trying to find you because I wanted to ask: have you had a chance to talk to her? Has she said anything else?"

"I haven't seen her since last night."

A frown briefly creased Yufit's eyebrows. "She's fine. She can handle herself."

"Right."

Amastan resisted the urge to reach up and pat Yufit's shoulder reassuringly. Yufit shifted from foot to foot, darting glances up and down the street. Night spread through the city and watchmen chased it, lighting torches along the main roads. Amastan knew what Yufit was looking for. He'd been looking for it, too—that telltale swirl of red. But whatever Menna had done last night— only last night?—had forced the jaani away.

Of course, there were still two more. But Yufit didn't need to know that.

"I think we're safe," said Amastan.

Yufit didn't relax. His hand touched his neck, found the charm there, and dropped again. "Will it happen again? We know nothing about this jaani. If it attacks someone else . . ."

Megar's crumbling face, eyes burning too bright— Amastan shut his eyes, as if he could rid himself of the image that easily. A hand slipped into his and Amastan opened his eyes to see Yufit; too close. Too earnest.

"Are you busy?"

Amastan shook his head: a lie. But also a partial truth. There wasn't much he could do right now, not until he'd had some time to think. To plan.

He also needed a break.

"Walk with me," said Yufit.

His hand was warm, his grip strong. Yet Amastan knew Yufit would let him go if he tried. Amastan didn't try.

It felt easier to just be with Yufit this time, as if something had changed. Maybe it had. Yufit certainly seemed different after last night. Watching Megar die had clearly rattled him. And for once, Amastan didn't feel the pressing need to find out more about Yanniq. He had his answers. He didn't *need* to spend time with Yufit. Instead, he wanted to.

The night settled around them as they walked. More and more people peppered the street as the day's heat faded to a background warmth. Stars sprinkled the darkening sky, but so did clouds, softly glowing with the city's light. There were only a few of them, but their presence energized the crowd. Amastan overheard more than one conversation about when, exactly, the season would end. His back was sticky with sweat that refused to immediately evaporate.

"How much longer do you think it'll be?" asked Yufit.

"Until what?" *Until the next murder, until the next jaani, until the drum chiefs demand an answer, until—until—until—*

"Until the rains."

"Oh." Amastan mentally shook himself. He needed to stay here, now. But he wasn't sure he had the luxury of time. "Maybe a week?"

"I'd say a few days, at most," said Yufit. He tilted his head back, sniffing the wind. "The storms this year will be amazing," he added, sounding wistful. He squeezed Amastan's hand. "Promise you'll enjoy it for me."

Amastan blinked, confused at the odd request. "The celebrations will be pretty big, at least, since season has gone on for so long."

"Drum Chief Eken's going to throw a party," said Yufit. "But then, he does that every year. Maybe I'll go this year. If I do, you should come, too."

"Eken doesn't usually invite people like me to his parties."

"He will this time," said Yufit. "I'll make sure of it. You should have fun for once."

"I have fun," protested Amastan.

Yufit laughed. "You wouldn't know fun if it bit your nose. You're always so serious."

"Am not."

Yufit let go of his hand and poked him in the chest. "Prove me wrong. What should we do tonight?"

Amastan frowned. "I . . . well, I was just on my way home. . . ."

"Exactly."

They had come to a bridge, but Yufit stopped short of it. Instead, he turned toward the nearest alley and gestured to Amastan. "Come on."

Yufit led him down the alley and around the corner, where he pulled out a barrel and shoved it against the brick wall. He climbed onto it and offered his hand to Amastan. The barrel was barely big enough for the both of them, but they huddled close as Yufit ran his hand along the wall.

"This is going to be a bit of a climb," said Yufit apologetically. "But I'll help you up."

Amastan bit his tongue and swallowed his remark. Instead he watched Yufit find the handholds that he'd already picked out, then begin climbing. This building was just over a story tall and so Yufit didn't have far to go. When he reached the top, Amastan took his offered hand and let Yufit help him climb. When his thigh started to throb, he was thankful for the help.

The roof wasn't much to look at. Why had Yufit brought him here? Then Yufit pointed to the next building: a multistory glasshouse rose from the roof, its blue-tinted glass transforming its contents into vague shadows.

Yufit led Amastan across a board between the buildings, then up to the glasshouse itself, which seemed to hum as it let off the accumulated heat of the day. Flaps fluttered on the sides, letting out too-hot air while keeping in what precious moisture remained at this time of year.

Yufit approached with confidence, although the door must be locked. Even when all the plants were dead or dormant for want of water, the glasshouse keepers still had to safeguard their soil. Good soil was difficult to maintain and expensive to buy and vital to have when the rains arrived. Caravans brought bags of soil to trade, but since they didn't travel at the end of season, good soil was scarce when it was needed most.

So Amastan wasn't surprised when the door refused to budge. But he was surprised when Yufit fished out two thin pieces of metal and began messing with the lock. In another moment, it had clicked and the door opened, if only by a few inches.

Yufit replaced his lock picks and grinned at Amastan. "I don't show off that trick to just anyone."

He pushed the door open farther and gestured for Amastan to go ahead. Amastan stepped into the relative darkness of the glasshouse, a flicker of unease unfurling in his chest. For a moment, he was back in another glasshouse, blood smeared on the ground and a body in front of him. But this glasshouse was clean, immaculate even, without a drop of blood in sight. The beds ran on either side of him at waist level, filled with nothing but coarse dark soil. A hint of moisture suffused the air, just enough to fill the glasshouse with the heady scent of loam.

"Go on."

Amastan had stopped halfway down the path, but now he noticed the ladder at the end of the row, leading to the next story. Most of Ghadid's numerous glasshouses were one story, owing to the weight of the glass and the plants' hunger for light. Over the years, a few keepers had experimented with taller structures and even fewer had succeeded. This had been one of them.

The metal ladder was still hot, but not painfully so. Likewise, the crisscrossing metal that made up the second floor warmed his feet, even through his sandals. More dirt lined the walk up here, but these beds were shallower. Tall glass rods stuck out of the dirt at regular intervals, string tied taut between them. Old vines and dried leaves still curled around some of the strings, dormant for now.

The glass roof was so close Amastan could touch it, if he

just reached up. Condensation fogged the glass, turning the sky and its spread of stars beyond into an indistinguishable smear of pale light. At the end of the row was another door. Amastan moved forward, drawn to it.

The door was unlocked, but for good reason: it opened onto nothing. Not even a cousin could climb sheer glass. Another ladder hung off the roof of the glasshouse, its bottom rung just within grasp. With Yufit silent behind him, Amastan reached and grabbed and began to climb.

The glasshouse roof was sloped, but not precariously so. Someone'd had the foresight to put sand in the glass before it had cooled, giving it a non-slick surface. At the roof's far end sat a thick roll of shade cloth, ready and waiting for the end of season. Amastan walked carefully across the roof, testing each step before he committed, in case the glass was in any way compromised. But it held and within moments he stood in the center of the roof, gazing out across the city.

He realized then why Yufit had brought him here. This was easily the highest point in Ghadid. The city spiraled away all around them. They were close to Ghadid's center, so all Amastan could see were buildings and platforms and neighborhoods. The sands were tucked safely out of sight. From here, Amastan could imagine Ghadid went on forever.

"This is the other place I like to go." Yufit's voice came from directly behind him. "When season ends, you can watch the first storms roll in from here. They're visible even while they're still hours away. And at night, the clouds are lit up inside with lightning. It's a spectacular sight." He paused for a beat, then added, "I'd watch it with you if I could."

Amastan turned to Yufit and was surprised by the wistful look in his eyes, the narrow swath of his features lit from beneath by the city's warm glow. The wistfulness was immediately replaced by a sly smile.

"Or I could teach you how to pick locks and you could come up here yourself."

"Where did you learn to do that?"

"Oh, you'd be surprised what you pick up from hanging around servants," said Yufit, still smiling.

Servants. A distant part of Amastan noted that Yufit didn't include himself as part of them. But Amastan brushed it away. Yufit was a scribe. He probably thought himself above servants.

Yufit looked out over the city. "Do you know the neighborhoods?"

By heart, Amastan wanted to say, but he shook his head instead. "Not well enough to tell you which platform belongs where."

Yufit pointed. "That's Seraf there, where the blue light is." He turned. "And that's Telem, just beyond it. Telem's darker than the others because Drum Chief Yugten doesn't bother replacing torches. He thinks no one should be out at night in the first place—it's 'amoral.' So his people go to the other neighborhoods for markets instead. But his allocation is fair, so he gets to stay."

"You know a lot about the city."

"I worked with other drum chiefs before Yanniq." Yufit stared for several heartbeats out at the city, silent and still. When he shifted his weight and turned toward Amastan, his steel-cold eyes no longer held a smile. "Look, Asaf . . . I'm not any good at this. But I've enjoyed spending time with you. I've never really done that with anyone before. I didn't think I had the time, but you've made me see otherwise. You've also given me a run for my money as the most serious person in Ghadid." He snorted a laugh, then let out a whoosh of air and clasped his hands behind his back. "But you're more

than that. You make me laugh. You listen. For once, I
feel heard."

Amastan forced himself to meet Yufit's eyes, even
though his heart was beating much too fast and his palms
had become inexplicably sweaty. Guilt lay beneath the
rising tide of breathlessness, tied to the repeating thought:
I'm not Asaf.

He wanted to say it. He needed to say it. There was
no reason to hide behind that assumed name any longer.
He'd gotten what information he needed from Yufit, he
knew—or at least seriously suspected—that Hennu was
behind the murders. In another day or two he'd be able to
prove his suspicions and stop the killer. He no longer had
a pretense to keep seeing Yufit.

No pretense except—

"I have something I need to do," continued Yufit. "It's
important. I don't know how long it will take and I don't
know if I'll see you again. It's . . ." He paused and Amastan heard him lick his lips, "dangerous." He laughed
softly and shook his head. "That word doesn't seem ad-
equate. But I had to see you again. To tell you: I'm glad I
met you, Asaf."

I'm not Asaf. But the words stuck in his throat like day-
old bread. Instead, he said, "It's not the jaani, is it? We
just have to wait for season's end."

"It's not the jaani." Yufit gave another soft laugh. "I
know you and your friend—Menna?—will take care
of that particular threat. No, it's something that's been
around a lot longer than the jaani, something I've been
working toward for as long as I can remember. I'd call it
my destiny, if I believed in such a thing. If I pull it off, the
city will be safer. You'll be safer. We'll all be safer. But
it's risky and sometimes I don't even want to think about
it. Days I've wondered if it's even worth it. But then I met
you, Asaf, and I realized I wasn't just protecting Ghadid.
I was protecting you."

Yufit fully turned toward Amastan and the distance between them became insignificant. Amastan could smell the anise on Yufit's breath, could see the slight flutter of his tagel as he breathed in and out.

"It's only fair," continued Yufit. "You saved me. Now I'll save you."

"But what're you saving me from?" asked Amastan, worry vying with dread.

Yufit reached out, strong fingers curling back as he hesitated, not quite touching Amastan. "It's better if you don't know."

He started to drop his hand, but Amastan caught it in his own. For a moment, he held it there, suspended in the air. He hadn't thought any further than that. He hadn't thought at all. And he continued not to think as he brought Yufit's hand to his cheek, guiding those fingers up beneath his tagel.

They stayed like that, an arm's width apart, for another heartbeat. For the first time in days—*weeks*—the constant swirl of Amastan's thoughts had slowed, quieted. He was only aware of the hand against his skin and Yufit, standing stock-still in front of him.

Then Yufit moved. His free hand went to his own tagel and his fingers found the knots. Undid one. The bottom of his tagel fell away, revealing a cheek, a nose, lips. Amastan stared into a face that he'd only imagined before and, even though it didn't quite meet up with his mental image, it still fit those steel-cold eyes perfectly.

A hundred warning drums boomed in his head like cracks of thunder as he reached up and undid a knot on his tagel. He shouldn't do this. Tamella wouldn't just chastise him if she found out, she'd skin him and tan his hide and use the leather for sandals. Yufit didn't even know his real name.

Then I'll tell him.

Amastan's tagel fell and his face felt strange, bare. His

cheeks and ears warmed, but Amastan didn't turn his gaze away.

Tell him.

"I'm not—"

But Yufit stepped close and cut him off with a kiss.

24

Clouds lined the horizon, thick as foam. Season's end was here.

They hung on through the morning. Both Amastan and Barag took turns peering out the door and checking on the clouds throughout the day. Despite the despair that clung to him like webbing, Amastan couldn't help but be heartened by the excitement that pulsed through the city. Heat that normally wilted even the most stubborn grandfather couldn't keep the streets clear today.

In the afternoon, the clouds bubbled and boiled. Far out past the horizon, past sight, stood the mountains that caught the moisture in the air and baked it into clouds. Most of the moisture would linger over the mountains, raining for days and weeks and filling the vast underground aquifer that fed Ghadid from afar. But at the end of season, when the wind and the moisture and the heat aligned, the clouds boiled over and spilled across the sands, coming for Ghadid.

If not tonight, then tomorrow. If not tomorrow, the day after. If not the day after, soon. Very soon.

Amastan was running out of time.

But when he dropped the last scroll into its basket, done with the bare minimum for the day, his thoughts weren't strictly on his task. They dipped instead into the night before and he felt again the warm brush of Yufit's lips, the heat of his breath, the press of his fingers. The moment had only lasted seconds, but it held the weight of days. Yufit had left without another word and Amastan had lingered, hesitant to return to a world where that moment wasn't the most important thing.

Now, as quickly as he delved into the memory, he returned. *Focus,* he reminded himself as worry twisted through him along familiar paths. He glanced up, but Barag was still busy with his own work. Holding his breath, he retrieved the scrap of paper Kaseem had given him from his wrap and spread it out on the table. He scrutinized the seal for the tenth or twelfth time, but it gave up no new secrets. He needed to find the original.

"What's that?"

Amastan started, tried to cover the scrap with his hand, then gave up. Thana peered over his shoulder, lips pressed into a thin line. Her eyes scanned the words and then her nostrils flared and her breath hitched as she registered what it meant.

She looked up. "Does Tamella know about this?"

Amastan started to nod, then stopped. Did she? She knew her brother had been on a contract, but beyond that, she didn't know the ban had been officially lifted. Didn't know about Hennu or any of the rest of it. Which was probably for the best. If Tamella thought Hennu was behind Usem's death, she might go after the drum chief herself. Amastan wouldn't blame her, but the rest of the drum chiefs would. She'd scraped by with a pardon once when the city had been at stake. That wouldn't happen again. This time, the family needed to act within the law or risk being disbanded permanently.

"Don't tell her," said Amastan.

Thana's expression was as inscrutable as if she'd been wearing a tagel. But she nodded. "What does it mean?"

"That's what I'm trying to puzzle out."

"Oh."

She dropped her gaze back to the piece of paper. Amastan studied her. She looked so much like her mother. Even her hair had been divided into several thick braids. But instead of tied back into a knot, they hung heavy around her face, sharpening her cheeks even further.

Like her mother. He couldn't tell Tamella, but maybe—

"I need to match this to its seal." He tapped the wax indentation. "How would you do that?"

Thana tossed one of her braids over her shoulder. She touched the seal with the tips of her fingers. "You need the original seal. Who has it?"

"I'm not sure," said Amastan.

Thana's gaze sharpened. "Who do you *think* has it?" When Amastan didn't respond, she pulled back from the table. "It's so simple, Amastan. You already know what you need to do. Why're you asking me?"

Amastan blinked, started a reply, then stopped. It was true. He did know what he needed to do. He'd just wanted someone else to confirm it. The last time he'd stolen into someone's home, it'd gone so disastrously wrong. He was afraid of messing up again.

The door opened, interrupting his thoughts. A woman entered, her wrap the undyed cream of mourning: Rema, Usem's widow. Without a word, Thana slipped from Amastan's table and crossed to her.

"G-d bless," greeted Rema.

Barag pushed back from his table and stood. "How're you doing?"

Rema's gaze flicked down, not meeting Barag's. "Well enough."

Barag nodded. "You'll have her back by sunset?"

"Of course," said Rema. "It shouldn't take too long to find a wedding gift for her cousin." She leveled her gaze at Barag. "But girls her age also need time out of the house."

Barag waved a hand. "I'm all right with that. Just have her back before dark, unless you want to risk her mother's anger."

This elicited a quirk of Rema's lips. "I wouldn't dare."

Thana crossed her arms. "I'm not a child—don't talk about me like I'm not here."

"Is that the wind?" teased Barag, looking around the room. "I swear I heard someone just now."

Thana sighed, rolled her eyes, and pushed the door open. She disappeared into the afternoon sun. The other side of Rema's lips quirked up, but her smile vanished almost as soon as it had come. "It shouldn't take long."

She bowed her head, then followed Thana outside. The door closed, leaving Amastan a little nearer to his answer. He pulled a spare scrap of vellum close and began to write, sketching out the beginnings of a plan. He worked best when he could sound off against someone, but Menna was working with Elder Dessin today to finalize their modified quieting ritual. The storms would be here any day now and they needed to be ready for them.

For a while, the only sound in the room was the scratch of pens on skin and the occasional rustle of a scroll. Amastan lost track of time as he tried to consider his problem from every angle. He needed Hennu's ring. It became increasingly clear to him that the only way he would get it in time was by breaking into her room. To do that—safely and properly—he needed to know more about Hennu. But he didn't have the time for surveillance. He needed another way to get that information.

Maybe . . .

He stood and stretched and approached the shelves of scrolls. The record of deaths wouldn't be of any use here; she wasn't dead, not yet. Neither would the Circle records. But certain details of the drum chiefs' lives were made public by necessity. Their wealth, their debts, their influences. Their husbands and wives. Their children. Any of that might give him more insight into the woman herself.

Here, a thick scroll of fine vellum, its edges embossed

with gold. He unrolled it slowly, his fingers gripping the edges tight. When he'd fully unrolled it, he realized it was several sheets instead of a single one. Thick black ink unfurled across the first sheet, but just beneath he traced the indistinct echoes of old words, long since scraped away. This record was in constant flux, scraped clean and rewritten as the drum chiefs and their lives changed.

He found Hennu on the third sheet, the ink of her entry sharper than the ones above and below. From scanning the other entries, he'd already lowered and lowered again his expectations. The number of slaves in her household wouldn't tell him anything useful, not when all of the drum chiefs owned a similar number of the lowest class, and neither would the age of her drum. But he read her entry anyway, hopeful despite himself. And then his breath caught.

The last line listed the names of Saman's children with Anaz, three in all. Names Amastan didn't recognize. After those three came one more, Hennu's only child. But Amastan couldn't read it: the name had been scratched out with midnight-black ink.

The door opened and closed. Amastan rerolled the scrolls and slid them back into their place on the shelf, thoughts thrumming. It could mean nothing. It could mean everything. He turned just as Menna reached his desk. She wore her marabi wrap, gray as stone, and a wide smile. She held up a thin, bone-white scroll.

"Guess what I have," she sang.

Amastan crossed his arms and looked at her, waiting. Menna laughed, then dropped the scroll on his desk. Amastan settled back into his chair and picked up the scroll. He unrolled it and stared at the looping letters curling around a sketch. It took him a moment to parse what he was seeing: the letters formed several prayers and the sketch appeared to be a diagram of connected circles.

"It's a seal." Menna leaned farther over the desk and

pointed to the center. "Once the jaan go in, they can't come out. Then all we have to do is set the prayers and wait for the rain."

"And this will quiet the jaan?"

Menna's smile dissipated. "No," she admitted. "It'll bind them to the sand. Elder Dessin thinks they're too strong to quiet. The binding will hold them for long enough. He hopes that in seven years, he'll be able to perform the crossing ceremony and finally put them at rest. It's not ideal, but it'll stop the jaan from hurting anyone else."

Amastan nodded even as he felt sick. He didn't want to go down to the sands and confront the jaan, let alone in the middle of a storm. But Menna was right. They couldn't let anyone else die.

"When?" he asked.

"First storm," said Menna. "Everyone thinks that'll be tonight or tomorrow, so you better be ready. Let your friend know, too. We might need him to draw the jaan."

"The seal won't do that?"

Menna shrugged. "It should. But we can't take any chances. This'll be our best and maybe only chance."

"Okay. I'll find him." Amastan couldn't help but feel a little glad for an excuse to talk to Yufit again, even though he needed to spend the rest of his evening on Hennu's ring. After all, he also only had until the first storm to match the seal and deliver Hennu to the drum chiefs. Yufit could wait.

"Y'know," said Menna, sliding into the chair across from him. "Things might just be okay."

A bubble of hope rose inside Amastan. "Do you have a way to find the killer?"

Menna blinked. "What? Oh—no. Not yet, but I'm sure you'll think of something." She patted the table reassuringly and the bubble popped. "I just meant, not having contracts. I have to admit, I resented the wild jaan at first because I'd always dragged my feet about being a marabi and the jaani made me focus on it. But I've discovered I actually kind of like it. At least, the jaan part. You saw me quiet that jaani. That was amazing. *I* was amazing. That's what I want to be doing, not overseeing funerals or living in stale crypts. And, to be honest, that contract we worked on together? A little too dull." She straightened in her seat. "Anyway, Elder Dessin agreed. He wants me to research and develop new rituals to quiet wild jaan. I actually came up with most of this." She tapped her finger against the scroll.

Amastan's stomach dropped. "So it's completely untested?"

"You have so little faith in me," said Menna. "Of course it's untested, but the principles are sound. We don't *need* to test it. It'll work, 'Stan. Trust me."

Amastan swallowed. Technically, Menna had never broken his trust, even if she'd sometimes bent it. And she had the help of the elders. "Okay."

Menna watched him expectantly. Amastan sighed. "What?"

"Aren't you going? I thought you left at evening bell."

Amastan frowned; he hadn't heard the bell yet. But it was possible he'd missed it as he worked. The light was thin enough for evening. Just how long had he been sitting here, scribbling on this piece of vellum?

As if in answer, the evening bells began to ring, first farther off, then in their own neighborhood. Amastan carefully rolled up the vellum he'd been writing on and tied it with a scrap of string. As he gathered his things, the door opened and the last peal struck the room like thunder. Rema stood in the doorway, framed by the fading light. Although Amastan couldn't see her face, he knew something was wrong. Menna stiffened next to him.

Rema was shaking. Her wrap was smudged with dirt and dust all the way up one side. As if she'd fallen, or been lying on the ground. Her hands were dirty, too, and one of them was curled around a scrap of white. Barag skirted his desk, closing the distance between them with quick strides.

"Rema?" said Barag as he reached her. He took her hand between his. "What is it? What's wrong?" He glanced around, looked behind her. His voice took on a sharp edge. "Where's Thana?"

Amastan's throat closed up. He approached Rema, guilt and fear twisting together into a heavy knot. Had he failed another cousin? Who was dead this time?

Menna reached behind Rema and closed the door. Now Amastan could see her face: pale and drawn, eyes wide with shock. Her cheek was smudged with dirt. Wordlessly, Rema shoved her fist and the scrap clutched in it at Barag.

Barag slipped the paper from her fingers and unfolded it. The room held its breath as he held the paper up and read. Then he cursed and turned, took in a breath as if to yell—but let it all out when he noticed Tamella at the foot of the stairs.

She crossed the room in an instant. She snatched the paper from Barag's hand and gave it a cursory glance. Then she crumpled it and threw it across the room. She rounded on Rema.

"What. Happened?"

Under the force of Tamella's will, Rema finally spoke. "I don't—I don't know. We were coming back. She was right next to me. I had her hand so she wouldn't get lost in the crowd. But there wasn't any crowd. It was just us. And then—and then—it wasn't just us. I didn't get a look at who. They were too fast. Next thing, I woke up on the ground and she was gone. They left that note."

Dazed, Amastan walked over to where the scrap of paper had landed. He picked it up. Read it.

The roof of Drum Chief Yanniq. When the moon is

overhead. Surrender yourself, Serpent, and she will not be harmed.

It was the killer. Had to be. The coincidence was otherwise too much. In a flash, Amastan understood. This was his fault. He'd let the killer get away. Now the killer knew they were after him, knew they knew. He'd panicked and gone after Thana, but he really wanted Tamella. He'd always wanted Tamella. Yanniq, Usem, Emet—their deaths had been revenge. Megar's, an accident. Tamella's would be justice.

Amastan realized Tamella was staring at him. He still held the piece of paper. She stalked toward him, her whole body tense as if ready to strike. He wanted to shrink away, but he resisted the impulse.

"What do you know?" she hissed.

"Nothing," said Amastan. "I don't—"

"Is it him?" asked Tamella.

Amastan met her gaze and saw she knew, too. She wouldn't accept a half answer. "Yes."

Tamella made a gargled noise, then whirled on the room at large. Her gaze found and pinned Menna. "Go get Dihya and Azulay. This is a family matter now, and we're going to settle it our way."

"Do you think that's really the best course of action?" asked Barag. "The drum chiefs—"

"This is our *daughter*," snarled Tamella. "I don't give a damn about the drum chiefs." She glared at Menna. "What're you waiting for, girl? *Go.*"

Menna started. Nodded. Took off. The door slammed behind her, leaving them in silence. Rema let out a faint sniff. Her cheeks glistened with tears. How long had she been crying?

Tamella turned to her. "Rema—you're welcome to stay here tonight. In fact, I insist. There's an extra bed upstairs on the right. You'll be safest here."

Rema's eyes widened; she hadn't considered her own

safety. She nodded, dabbed at her eyes with her sleeve, then trudged up the stairs. Tamella watched her. Once Rema had disappeared from sight, Tamella's gaze fell on Amastan like a hammer.

"I tried playing the drum chief's way," said Tamella. "Even after Emet. Even after Usem. But no longer. The drum chiefs will either understand or they won't. I don't care."

As she talked, she moved, crossing to the hearth. She picked up the edge of a carpet and yanked it to the side, revealing nothing but smooth stones beneath. She knelt, felt around for a moment, then dug her fingers around the edge of one stone. It lifted easily. She set the stone to one side and pulled out a square metal box, several hands wide and deep.

Tamella brought the box to Barag's table and set it there with a thump. Her fingers played along its sides until there was an audible *click*. She opened the box.

Barag stood a few feet away, his eyes closed as if in pain. But Amastan drew closer. Dark green fabric pillowed on top. Tamella drew this out with a flourish and the fabric swirled around her. She undid the knots of her wrap with one hand while holding the new wrap in the other. Amastan looked away when she let her wrap fall.

When he looked back a few seconds later, Tamella had just finished knotting the new wrap in place. The green was as dark as her skin, turning her into a living shadow. She drew out a leather belt next and secured it around her waist. Then: leather straps around her upper arms, her wrists, her chest, her thighs. Then: knives for each of those straps, some as small as Amastan's pinky, some as long as his hand.

Tamella looped a fine wire garrote through her belt before drawing out the last item: a smaller, leather box. This she handled with great care, setting it on the table first before opening it. Nestled into the underside of its lid were four large rings. Beneath the rings and secured with a thin loop of leather, was an assortment of small glass vials: poison.

"Tamella . . ." said Barag, her name a warning.

But Tamella ignored him. She ran her fingers across the vials—most filled with a fine, white powder, but some filled with clear liquid—and selected the last one. She picked up one of the rings and twisted it. The top popped open, revealing a small cavity within. Her hands as still as stone, Tamella tapped some of the vial's contents into the ring. Then she carefully stoppered the vial and closed the ring, returning one to its box with reverence and the other to her finger.

Tamella straightened, her hands running across her wrap, checking the knots, the knives. As she adjusted her belt, the door opened, closed. Menna led Dihya and Azulay into the room. At least now Amastan could safely discard any lingering suspicions he had about his cousins. Neither of them would've laid a finger on Thana in a thousand years. Which made him wonder: did the killer understand what he'd done?

Azulay looked bewildered, but Dihya saw Tamella and she immediately straightened. A smile ghosted her lips and was gone.

"What's going on?" asked Azulay, taking in Barag, Amastan, and the room.

Tamella finished her check and turned to her audience. "Thana's gone. And we're going to get her back."

25

Amastan poked his head over the edge of the roof, scanned the area, then swung up and over. Ignoring the rush of pain in his leg had become almost second nature by now. Menna followed a heartbeat behind, silent as a cloud. The moon hung in the east halfway to its zenith, a half-lidded eye that watched the events unfolding below with neither sympathy nor care. They had hours yet until the appointed time.

On a nearby rooftop, Dihya and Azulay would be hunting for any sign of Thana or her kidnapper. While they secured the perimeter, Menna and Amastan would hide in plain sight. When the killer arrived, Tamella would approach alone.

Five cousins against one. The killer had no chance.

Despite the overwhelming odds, unease stuck in Amastan's throat. He knew what Tamella would do when they finally cornered the killer. If Thana was all right, Tamella might just show mercy. But if Thana was hurt at all, well—

Would it be considered murder just because it was outside of a contract? Any other citizen would be excused such violence when their own family had been threatened, but as assassins, cousins walked a thin and fragile line. They served a purpose. They were a tool. And tools weren't supposed to seek revenge.

The killer had to stand trial. That was the only way forward. But Tamella clearly wasn't so inclined and Amastan wasn't sure he could stop her. If he *would* stop her.

But that didn't matter just yet: they had to find and save Thana first.

Amastan's wrap was sticky with sweat. The air hung heavy and hot, as unpleasant as it was unwieldy. He'd had to dip into his pouch of fine sand to keep from losing purchase on the wall as he'd climbed. He dabbed his forehead with his tagel to stop the sweat from trickling into his eyes.

The clouds on the horizon had grown with the evening. Now they flickered bright and spat lightning. Every so often, a far-off growl of thunder would reach them, so low that Amastan felt its vibrations in his bones. The wind tasted of wet dust and metal.

Yanniq's glasshouse loomed before them, large and quiet. Tamella's plan required that he and Menna hide in there among the dirt and dried stalks. Amastan couldn't see anything but vague, motionless shadows inside. Menna reached the glasshouse first, twin metal picks already between her fingers. Amastan scanned the roofline as Menna worked the lock. After only a moment the lock clicked and gave way.

They slid into the glasshouse. Inside, it reeked of stale dirt, hot metal, and something viscously astringent which Amastan couldn't quite place. The vents must have been locked for the season. Above, someone had begun to roll a reflective mat out across the glasshouse roof that would cut the sun's excessive heat. He closed the door behind him. Then he followed Menna between the dark rows of dirt down the center of the glasshouse.

Menna, just a step ahead of him, gasped. She hurried forward, toward a figure slumped on the floor of the glasshouse. A girl, bound with rope and gagged with cloth, eyes closed and skin ashen. Thana. She'd been left sitting up, leaning back against a bed wall. Her black braids blended in with the soil. No wonder they hadn't seen her from outside.

Menna slid to the ground next to Thana and sawed at the thick rope with one of her knives. The rope frayed and snapped, releasing the girl from its grip. Thana slumped farther forward and almost fell, but her eyes snapped open and her hands jerked up and she caught herself. Menna grabbed her arm and helped Thana sit up.

"Are you all right?"

Thana's throat worked as she swallowed, but she didn't say anything. She nodded even as she glanced around. She took in the glasshouse and Amastan and then her fingers felt her arms, her wrists. She frowned, turned up the edges of her wrap, but there was nothing beneath but bare skin. Amastan understood: she was looking for her weapons. The killer must have taken them.

"We're going to get you home," said Menna.

Amastan freed a knife from his belt and handed it hilt-first to Thana. The girl took it with relief and tucked it into her boot. Then she nodded and let Menna help her to her feet. Yet she kept glancing around and her unease was contagious.

"This is too easy," said Amastan.

Menna glared at him. That's when Amastan noticed that the dirt in the bed near the door was shifting. Shuddering. Erupting.

Amastan didn't think. He pushed forward and shoved Menna back, putting himself between whatever was clawing its way out of the dirt and Thana. A hand first, followed by an arm, then a head, then—too quickly—a body. A man stood and stepped out of the bed, dirt cascading from his shadow-dark wrap and spattering the ground.

Cold, hate-filled eyes locked onto his.

The killer.

Amastan drew the daggers at his hips, holding one

curved blade in each hand. But the killer didn't attack. Instead, he stepped back toward the door and, without looking, reached behind him and opened it. His gaze still on Amastan, he took another step into the doorway. Then he reached, carefully and deliberately, making certain they saw what he was doing, into the folds of his wrap and drew out a bent piece of metal. As he slowly lifted it over his head, Amastan realized it was a striker.

Suddenly, the *something else* Amastan had noticed in the air when they'd entered the glasshouse had a name: *oil*. The air was tinged with the acrid taste of oil, but he'd been so intent on the figure in the walkway, and it hadn't made *sense*—

Amastan grabbed for Thana and Menna as the man struck a spark. Amastan shoved them both to the ground. For a heartbeat, nothing. Then: the air roared and heat, as intense as the sun's, rushed at and struck them. Even with his eyes closed, Amastan could see the flames.

They died down almost as quickly as they'd flared, but smoldering fires lingered and smoke filled the glasshouse. Amastan crawled toward the glasshouse door: shut. On the other side, a dark figure waited and watched. The figure didn't move as Amastan grabbed the door handle and turned, wincing at the burning metal. Amastan wasn't surprised when the handle resisted.

He *was* surprised that, upon further examination of the handle, there was no way to unlock it from this side.

They were trapped inside the glasshouse. And, while the fire had mostly subsided, the smoke was growing thicker. The vents were closed. There was nowhere for the smoke to go.

"Stay down!" said Amastan, dropping to the ground himself.

The smoke burned his throat and lungs and, even though he couldn't have breathed that much in already, made his head swim. There was something in the air that tasted different from normal smoke. Regardless of whether or not something had been added to the oil, the smoke would suffocate them if they didn't get out, and soon.

Amastan sheathed his daggers and crawled to Menna and Thana, both sprawled on the ground. Menna helped Thana pull her wrap up and around her mouth, but already they were coughing.

"The glass," said Menna between coughs. "Break it."

Amastan freed a small blade. He sucked in a lungful of relatively clean air from near the ground, then jumped to his feet and lunged over the bed. The tip of his blade *ping*ed off the glass, ineffective as a mouse. Lungs burning, he stepped into the soil to get closer, leaned forward even as his leg protested, and tried again, but the glass resisted. It wasn't even scratched.

He threw himself back down to the ground and gasped for air, but even this air was growing too heavy. The world tilted and whirled around him, his thoughts harder and harder to piece together.

He could do this. He had to do this. No glass was unbreakable. He just had to apply the right kind of force.

A hand grabbed his and Thana met his eyes. "Ceiling. Thinner."

Thana pulled the knife free from her boot, then rolled onto her back and sighted along the blade through the smoke. Then she breathed deep, sat up, sighted again—and threw.

Glass cracked, broke, shattered. Sharp, crystalline shards rained down around them. A gust of air swirled the smoke, thinning it. The smoke rolled up and out and the next breath Amastan took didn't burn as much. He got to his knees, then to his feet, following the smoke as it was sucked upward. Around the glasshouse, fires still smoldered and burned, but the initial burst of smoke was gone. In another moment, he could think clearly again.

Thana pushed past him, running at the door full tilt. Amastan started to cry out, but Thana pulled back her arm and he saw something small and sharp and metallic in her hand. Then she slammed into the door and cracks spider-webbed out from the impact. She struck again and the glass gave way, falling outward.

Amastan and Menna caught up to her as she stepped out of the glasshouse. Thana froze. They all did.

The killer had his back to them. Across from him stood another: Tamella. Her gaze flicked past the killer to the three of them and she smiled. "Took you long enough."

The killer didn't move. He stood, hands empty, in the middle of the rooftop. He was surrounded. He was trapped. His plan had failed. In another moment, Dihya and Azulay would join them and it would be five cousins—six if he included Thana, and clearly he should—against one. It was already over.

So why did he still feel uneasy?

Twin thumps signaled the arrival of Dihya and Azulay. They approached from opposite ends of the roof, Dihya sauntering, her ax swung casually over her shoulder, Azulay advancing with his machete at the ready. They took up positions on either side of the killer, their postures expectant. But all that time, the killer's gaze never wavered from Tamella.

The killer spoke. "Kneel."

It was one word, one single word which rang out across the rooftop. Tamella smirked and drew her sword slowly, letting the metal sing out. Amastan felt ill, as if all the heat in his body had been left behind in the glasshouse. He was mistaken. His ears were still ringing from the explosion. He hadn't heard right. One word wasn't enough to know, that voice couldn't be familiar—

Tamella laughed. "Have you looked around yet, friend? You're surrounded. Your captive is free. Your plan is in ruins. How you could be the same man who killed my cousin and brother, I don't know. If you surrender, I can make this quick."

"I poisoned her."

This time, Amastan couldn't deny what he'd heard. He recognized that voice. He'd heard it two weeks ago in Idir's inn. He'd heard that voice conversing over date wine and he'd heard that voice yelling for help. He'd heard it whisper and he'd heard it grumble and he'd heard it laugh.

And now, he heard that voice tear apart everything he thought he'd known.

26

Yufit.

"It's not true," said Thana, but she sounded uncertain.

"I have the antidote, but it's not here," said Yufit. "If you attack me—if *any* of you attack me—then the location of the antidote dies with me. Or with her, I should say. If you kill me, I can promise that you won't have enough time to discover which poison I used before she dies. But I'll go ahead and give you a hint, Serpent—it's not one of yours."

Thana grabbed Menna's arm and didn't let go. From where Amastan was standing, Thana appeared fine. But poisons deceived, a fact Tamella had hammered into them time and again.

But Yufit couldn't—Yufit wouldn't—Amastan's thoughts stuttered and stopped and started again as he tried to understand what was right in front of him.

"You're lying," said Tamella. But her gaze flicked to Thana.

"The poison's been working for several hours already," said Yufit. "She should be feeling lightheaded and dizzy, with a tightening in her chest."

This time when Tamella looked to Thana, the girl nodded. Dihya let out a hiss and held her ax at the ready, but didn't step any closer.

"Do you understand?" asked Yufit. "One life in exchange for another. It's more than a fair trade—hers must be worth a hundred of yours, as bloody as your hands are."

. . . something I've been working toward for as long as I can remember. I'd call it my destiny, if I believed in such a thing. If I pull it off, the city will be safer. You'll be safer. We'll all be safer . . . You came along, Asaf, and I realized I wasn't just protecting Ghadid.

I was protecting you.

"Yufit," said Amastan, but the name was little more than a breath that passed between his lips. Yufit didn't hear him.

Menna heard. She glanced at him, eyes wide. She'd recognized Yufit's voice, too. The glimmer of hope he hadn't even known he'd been harboring vanished. It wasn't a delusion.

"How do I know you won't withhold the antidote?" asked Tamella.

"Unlike you, I'm not a monster," said Yufit. "I don't kill the innocent. Only the guilty. If your friends let me go, the girl will have the antidote within the hour. Do you understand?"

A tense silence swallowed the rooftop. Amastan and the rest of his cousins might as well not have been there, for Yufit had eyes only for Tamella. Menna held tight to Thana, as if the girl might try to run. Waning moonlight thinned shadows and flattened faces as the moon reached its zenith. The horizon flashed and Amastan felt thunder shudder through the rooftop and the soles of his feet. Dihya and Azulay stood tight as bows, ready to be fired at Tamella's slightest command. But blades couldn't stop a poison.

Tamella dropped her head. Her shoulders sagged. "I do."

"Drop the sword. Kneel."

Tamella let her sword drop to the rooftop with a clatter and knelt. Thana cried out, started forward, but Menna held her back. Yufit approached Tamella, a knife already in his hand. Amastan knew he should say something, reveal he was Asaf, rush and stop Yufit, but his body was paralyzed with indecision. Surely Tamella wouldn't let Yufit do this, surely she wouldn't just stay kneeling, surely she would fight back—

Surely Yufit hadn't actually poisoned Thana—

Surely—

"Tell me one thing, though," said Tamella, speaking to the ground. "Why? Why Yanniq? Why Emet? Why Usem?"

"You're a plague on this city," said Yufit. "A tumor that the drum chiefs were too weak to remove. You killed Saman and now you're finally facing the consequences."

"But *why*?" Now Tamella did look up, and her face held no fear, only confusion. "Drum Chief Saman has been dead for years. You're not one of her children. What could you possibly have to do with her?"

"I am Yufit Uzbamen, son of Hennu ma Saman."

"Huh," said Tamella. "I never knew Hennu had a son."

A name, scratched out. No—

"Few did."

Yufit's knife caught the moonlight as he stepped close to Tamella. He wound his fingers into Tamella's braids and pulled her head back. He brought his knife to her exposed throat and—

THUD

Tamella jerked her head back, slamming her skull into Yufit's chin. Yufit staggered back, his knife slicing skin, but not deep enough. Tamella rose to her feet, as smooth as a snake. Her hands twitched and knives slid from hidden sheaths at her wrists and into her waiting hands. She didn't wait for Yufit to gather himself.

The Serpent struck.

Her blades bit deep, sliding up beneath his ribcage. She drew her blades out and Yufit crumpled, wheezing for air. Dihya and Azulay started forward, but Tamella raised a hand. They stopped.

"Both of your lungs are punctured," said Tamella. "You've got one, maybe two hours to live if you stay still and calm. That should be more than enough time to tell me where the antidote is. I wouldn't recommend trying to crawl to a healer by yourself. Trust me—you won't make it."

"I won't . . . tell you . . . ," gasped Yufit.

"Fine." Tamella wiped her blades clean on her wrap and sheathed them. She freed a much smaller knife from her belt, this one thin as a razor and not much longer. "We can do this the hard way. I don't really care." She turned partially toward Menna and Amastan. "Take Thana home. She doesn't need to see this." She beckoned to the other two cousins. "Help me hold him down."

"See what?" asked Amastan, the words as hollow as his chest.

Thana tried to step toward her mother, but Menna held her back. Thana's expression was clouded with worry. "Please—don't—"

"Go. Home." The force of Tamella's words were enough to send Thana stumbling back.

Dihya grabbed Yufit's left arm and Azulay his right. They wrestled him to the rooftop as Tamella loomed over Yufit like her namesake. Menna steered Thana toward the roof's edge, but Amastan was frozen in place.

Yufit had killed Yanniq. Yufit had saved him from the jaani. Yufit had killed Emet. Yufit had sat with him and watched the stars come out. Yufit had killed Usem. Yufit had drawn back his tagel—

Tamella struck. Yufit grunted in pain. A line sliced through his eyebrow and welled red. He struggled against the cousins' grip, but they were much stronger. His breathing was quickly becoming ragged and wet. Tamella considered him, pressing the point of her blade against her fingertip.

"Tell me where the antidote is," said Tamella.

But Yufit only glared.

Amastan could see what would happen next. Yufit wasn't going to fight back and he wasn't going to give up the antidote. He'd make Tamella kill him first. He'd still get his revenge when Tamella was forced to watch her daughter die.

And that would only be the beginning of his revenge. Once Drum Chief Hennu found out her son was dead— and she would—Tamella would face the Circle again. A second death, a second time Tamella had acted without a contract. This time, there would be no clemency. Not for her and not for the family.

If Yufit died here on the rooftop tonight, then so did any chance of proving to the drum chiefs that he was behind Yanniq's death. They wouldn't listen to Tamella when she had blood on her hands. Amastan would fail and the family would be disbanded, if not worse.

Unless he stopped her.

As Menna and Thana disappeared over the roof's edge, Amastan cautiously approached Tamella, feeling renewed pain in his leg with each step. Dihya had her back to him, but Azulay lifted his head and watched, curious. Tamella put her knee on Yufit's chest and leaned in, slowly increasing the pressure. She reached up and slid her knife behind his ear.

"Let's start here, shall we?"

Yufit glared his silent defiance.

"There's another way." Amastan crossed the last few feet so that he stood within striking distance of Yufit— and Tamella. "Let me talk to him."

Tamella's eyes narrowed. Her knife stayed tucked behind Yufit's ear. But Amastan was watching Yufit. Had he recognized Amastan's voice? Was that a flicker of recognition, or of annoyance? Yufit met his gaze with his steel-cold eyes. Why hadn't Amastan recognized those eyes before? But this Yufit blazed with hatred and anger and a violence that the Yufit he'd known had never expressed.

Never . . . except for when he'd spoken of the Serpent.

"You know what's at stake," said Tamella. "It's too late for talk. Stay back."

"I'm not Asaf."

Those weren't the words Amastan had meant to say, but those were the ones that came tumbling out. For a heartbeat, nothing moved. Then Yufit's calm cracked. Pain and hurt flashed across his eyes, but they were quickly crowded out by hot anger. Worse than the anger, though, was Yufit's continued silence.

Tamella's gaze flicked to Amastan. "You two know each other?"

Amastan knelt next to Dihya at Yufit's shoulder. He felt her stiffen, but she didn't move or let go. "Please," said Amastan. "It doesn't have to end this way. The Circle made their decision. Let the past be the past."

"You're one of *them*."

The venom in Yufit's tone cut Amastan deep. Then Yufit twisted the knife by turning his head away. Tamella's hand tracked with his ear, but otherwise she didn't move. Despite her protests, she was giving Amastan a chance to make his case. Amastan just had to make the best of it.

"I'm sorry about what happened to Saman," continued Amastan. He felt both of his cousins' gazes heavy on him. Shame crept up his neck, warm as a fever, but he kept going. "But she conspired to start a civil war. If she hadn't been stopped, a lot of people would've been hurt. Killed, even. Her hands weren't clean."

Yufit stayed silent. Tamella moved her blade from his ear to his throat. The gesture communicated enough— she was done with threats. It was up to Amastan to convince Yufit with words. Otherwise . . .

"I'm not Asaf," repeated Amastan, quieter now. "My name is Amastan."

Tamella stiffened and she shot him a warning look.

Yufit kept his gaze on Azulay's leg, ignoring him. The wind picked up, tugging at Amastan's tagel.

"Killing an innocent girl won't bring back Saman," said Amastan. "Neither will killing the Serpent. Please."

"None of you are innocent."

Tamella hissed through her teeth. Her blade bit into his neck and blood welled up in the thin cut, trickled, fell. Yufit closed his eyes, accepting his fate. His breathing was becoming labored and there was a distinctly wet rattle to it. Dully, Amastan realized that this is what Yufit had meant when he'd talked about not coming back. On the glasshouse just last night, Yufit had told him that he planned on confronting the Serpent. He'd never intended to survive this confrontation. If only Amastan had listened.

"Ghadid won't be safer without Thana in it," pressed Amastan. "Nor will it be safer without the Serpent. We keep the balance. We're a lot like you, I think—we want Ghadid to be safe."

"You're nothing like me," spat Yufit.

Amastan licked his lips. He felt like he was losing with every second that passed. He wasn't good with words, he'd never tried to convince anyone before, especially not of something so important, something he'd struggled with himself. His fingers found the knot of his tagel behind his ear. He remembered the feel of Yufit's hand there, on his skin. Warm as air. And then lips, like an inhalation before a storm.

His fingers loosened the knot, pulled it free. His tagel dropped. Dihya jerked back as if stung. Azulay let out an audible gasp and looked away. Yufit's gaze was dragged to his and for a moment, that hate cracked. Dissipated. Amastan no longer stared at a stranger.

For a moment, it was going to be okay.

Then the hate returned. Yufit squeezed his eyes shut.

"I'd rather go through all the seven hells than be anything like you."

Tamella sighed. "You can't reason with hate."

"Please," begged Amastan, at a loss of what else to do. "Yufit—where's the antidote?"

Yufit didn't open his eyes. His breathing had become even, if wetter than before. He'd accepted his fate.

"The healers will save her," said Tamella. She tensed and shifted her weight and Amastan knew that he was out of time.

"Stop!" he cried. "You can't—he's Hennu's *son*. If you kill him, the drum chiefs won't forgive you. They won't forgive us. It'll be the end of the family."

"Maybe it's time for the family to end," said Tamella, her voice as cold as a winter wind.

Amastan stared at her, unbelieving. Azulay looked uncertain, but he didn't let go of Yufit. Dihya kept her face down, her expression hidden. Amastan couldn't let this happen.

He wouldn't let this happen.

Amastan stood. He carefully knotted his tagel back behind his ear. Then he drew his own twin blades. "No."

Tamella turned toward him, nothing but disdain in her posture and tone. "Go home, Amastan."

"No."

"Your part in this is done," said Tamella. "You did your best. But sometimes your best is still not good enough. This man killed Usem. He would kill my daughter. I can't let him live."

Yufit's breath caught and his eyes opened. "Daughter?"

And Amastan saw it, all at once. Yufit outside at the funeral. Yufit there by chance. But no—he'd been watching who'd come to Usem's funeral. He'd seen Rema walking with Thana. Had thought Thana was her daughter. Therefore: Tamella's niece.

Yufit had gravely miscalculated.

"This ends tonight," continued Tamella. "If the Circle had acted when it was in their power to do so, we'd never be here. So no, I don't trust them to handle this. I'd rather let things fall the way they will than allow my brother's murderer to go free."

"No," repeated Amastan. He shifted his stance, brought up his blades. "You're wrong. Killing him won't help anything, it'll only make things worse. I won't let you kill Yufit."

"Don't be a fool," said Tamella. "You can't fight me."

Amastan pressed his lips tight, letting his silence be his answer.

Tamella rolled her eyes. Then she struck. Not at Amastan—her knife cut toward Yufit's throat. But Amastan had been waiting for this and he acted as soon as he saw her shoulders tense. He blocked her knife with his blade, turned it aside, and used the moment of her surprise and unbalance to push her away. His leg protested, but held. He put himself between her and Yufit. Now he just had two more cousins to contend with.

Dihya was quicker. She let go of Yufit and drew her ax, then swung the flat of it at Amastan's head. Amastan caught the head of her ax between his blades, the force of her blow making his teeth ache. He cut down, throwing Dihya off balance, then spun and forced Azulay to jump back, letting go of Yufit. Azulay unslung his machete and eyed Amastan. Between them, Yufit slumped on the ground, his breathing harsh and uneven.

His cousins fell back, flanking him but no longer attacking. Amastan turned to find Tamella considering him. She'd picked up her sword and now held it at the ready, its tip aimed at Amastan's heart.

"This is your last warning," she said. "Step aside."

Amastan set his feet. Ignored the pulsing pain in his thigh. Raised his weapons. "No."

For a moment, it felt like every other practice session

they'd had. But this time when Tamella attacked, she held nothing back. Her sword swung as fast as a viper's strike. But Amastan knew her moves, knew them well enough to dance with. So dance he did.

He didn't think. He moved. He sidestepped her swing, felt the breath of sliced air as her sword missed him by a finger's width. He brought up his blades, caught the underside of her sword as she shifted, recovered. He heaved up with all of his strength, sending her stumbling back. Giving him a breath of room.

Dihya came for him next. His cousins were still acting out their play on the rooftops, waiting their turn and fighting clean. It was more than enough against a mark. But Amastan wasn't a mark.

He ducked her ax and swung his shoulder into her stomach. Dihya *oofed* and doubled over. Amastan smacked her wrist with the butt of his blade and her fingers sprang open, dropping her ax. He kicked it across the roof, then spun, catching Azulay's machete and deflecting it. He stepped into Azulay's space, came so close he could smell Azulay's clove-spiced breath.

"Sorry," he said, then stomped on Azulay's bare foot with all of his weight.

Azulay screamed, fell back. Amastan turned to face Tamella again. She'd drawn near, only to hesitate when he got too close to Azulay. Her expression was calm fury. She swung.

Amastan dropped, rolled away. As Tamella recovered from her swing, Amastan got back to his feet. Tamella didn't wait for him to recover. She charged. Amastan danced to the side, but his leg crumbled beneath him and then Dihya was there, her fists full of knives. One hand sliced across his fingers and he dropped a blade. Another hand grabbed his tagel and yanked his head down to meet her knee.

His vision erupted with stars. Amastan gasped, sagged.

Hands grabbed his, yanked his arms behind his back, his other blade from his hand. Amastan didn't struggle; he knew when it was over.

Tamella loomed before him, her eyes twin pits of rage. The corner of her lip curled up in a snarl, but Amastan's gaze was drawn past her. Behind, to the rooftop beyond.

The *empty* rooftop beyond.

"Too late," said Amastan, voice rough. "He's gone."

Tamella whirled around. Let out a snarl of disbelief. She threw her sword on the ground. Then she turned and struck Amastan across the face. Amastan fell, hitting his head so hard against the rooftop his ears sang. A fuzziness burst and swelled and expanded, black as ink across his vision, cold as frost across his skin. The last thing Amastan remembered seeing was the moon.

27

Rough hands hauled him up until he was sitting. Amastan's eyes flew open and he stared into the face of fury. His disorientation was doubled by the fact that he was still on the rooftop, still surrounded by his cousins. Yufit was gone. How long had he been out? Seconds? Minutes? Hours?

"Tell me why I shouldn't kill you," said Tamella.

Amastan blinked, his thoughts fuzzy and vague. He registered that Dihya and Azulay were still there, each armed again, waiting. Piecemeal, he remembered what had happened. Why he was on a roof. Why his head pounded. Why his thigh felt as if it were on fire.

Thana—Tamella—*Yufit*. Bile rose in his throat, acrid and sharp, but he swallowed it.

"I know who Yufit is," said Amastan. "And I know Drum Chief Hennu is involved. I almost have the evidence to condemn her. I can bring them both to justice."

"Hennu," snarled Tamella. "Of course. I should've realized. You can never quit the family, no matter how hard you try."

Amastan shook his head, uncertain if he'd heard correctly. "Hennu has something to do with our family?"

"Hennu's a cousin," spat Tamella. "*Was* a cousin. When she married a drum chief, she had to give up that title."

"Why . . . why didn't you tell me?"

"Why did it matter?" asked Tamella, opening one hand.

"Cousins leave. A lifetime of training will never guarantee a lifetime of service. There might've been a time when leaving the family meant death, but that time is long past."

"But Saman . . ."

Some of the rage left Tamella and she sat back on her heels. "Drum Chief Saman was one of many people caught up in the conspiracy and not the only one to die. Besides, that was over a decade ago. Hennu was in the generation before me." Tamella shook her head. "She could've killed Yanniq, but she's too old to have bested Usem or Emet. Clearly she taught her son a few things, but do you really expect me to have known, or even thought, she'd do this? Family doesn't hurt family."

"You killed Saman."

"Saman wasn't family," said Tamella, voice sharp. "Saman was a traitor. If Hennu was a true cousin, she would've accepted that and moved on."

"She didn't."

"No." Tamella briefly closed her eyes. The moon picked out the silver in her hair and dug deep pits beneath her eyes, aging her by decades. "She didn't."

Tamella rose slowly, her sword limp at her side. "You should leave. I'll give you this chance to find Yufit and expose Hennu. Maybe you're right. Maybe it's wrong for me to repeat my mistakes." Her gaze sharpened and her lips thinned. "But if you fail to bring them to justice or if Thana doesn't return from the healers, then I'll do it my way." She sheathed her sword. "And I'll make sure you suffer the consequences."

Menna found Amastan hunched over a cup of cold and bitter tea next to an empty hearth. She dropped a few pillows next to him and took a seat. Amastan acknowledged her with a nod. He drank the tea slowly, savoring every sip. It was the last of his water. He was out of baats and time. If season didn't end tonight, he'd be in trouble.

He was already in trouble.

After a few moments, Menna cleared her throat. "Thana's all right. We had enough water to stop the poison. She'll need to rest for a few days, but no lasting damage."

Amastan closed his eyes and felt some of the tension he'd been holding release. "Thank G-d."

"Indeed," said Menna. Then her calm cracked. "What were you *thinking*? Tamella has promised to have your head if you don't deliver Yufit. I can't believe you *fought* her. For a murderer."

"She was going to kill him," said Amastan.

Menna threw up her hands. "You should have let her! I'm astounded she didn't kill *you*."

"She didn't have a contract."

"For all that's holy and whole, 'Stan, that man killed her brother. She doesn't *need* a contract."

Amastan shook his head. "It still would've been murder. The drum chiefs—"

"The drum chiefs would never have known," said Menna. "Tamella would've made it look like he fell off the roof or something."

"No." Amastan could still clearly see the murderous intent in Tamella's eyes. "She wouldn't have. She would've killed him first and decided what to do later, after it was too late. The drum chiefs wouldn't have just punished her, Menna. They would've punished all of us. It would've been the end of the family." He paused and added glumly, "It might still be."

"There was a time when you would've welcomed the end of the family," said Menna, a little too sharply.

"Not its end," said Amastan. "The family has its place. We do things that are hard but necessary." If Amastan closed his eyes, he knew he'd see white powder dissolving in a glass. *None of you are innocent.* He didn't close his eyes. "But Yufit was right—there's a line and we've crossed it in the past. I didn't want to see Tamella cross it again."

Menna pressed her palm against her forehead and breathed in deep through her nose. Then she let it all out in a sigh. "*Fine*. You are damn lucky to be alive. Tam' must've been just as surprised as the rest of us. And, my G-d, *Yufit*. He was in my home. How many cousins had he murdered by then?"

Amastan had already done those calculations. "Two."

Menna dropped her hands and looked at him, really looked at him for the first time since she'd arrived. "G-d, 'Stan, you're a mess."

Amastan had changed out of the shadow-colored wrap and into one that was clean, if bland and colorless, but he hadn't bothered to wash the streaks of dust and dirt and sweat from his face and hands. He'd tied his tagel low, not wanting to deal with the stifling fabric tonight and assuming he'd only be around his sisters. He hadn't bothered to adjust it when Menna arrived; she might as well be a sister.

"You really didn't know," said Menna quietly.

Amastan snorted, but didn't bother replying.

Menna shook her head. "For all of your cleverness, you're really stupid, you know? He was right there, the entire time, and you never once wondered who in the sands-blasted Wastes he was. What did you even know about him? Anything?"

"I knew he was Yanniq's scribe," said Amastan. "I just never thought . . ." He didn't bother finishing his sentence. He hadn't thought. He hadn't even considered. Yufit had never lied to him because Amastan had never asked. He hadn't wanted to ask.

But now that he stopped to think about it, he could see the bits and pieces that might've led him in the right direction had he only looked. Yufit's disdain for Yanniq.

The short time he'd spent in Yanniq's household. His too-clean hands only days after he'd left. His easy use of baats, too easy for a servant. His self-confidence. His fluid grace. A name, scratched out.

A dozen small things that simply didn't add up. A dozen small things that, when taken together, were more than suspicious. Even Megar's insistence on accompanying him to speak with Yufit took on a new light. Had Megar suspected?

But Amastan hadn't wanted to see.

"I know," said Amastan, his voice hollow. "Did you only come here to berate me?"

Menna's expression clouded with something else, something unexpected: sympathy. "I did, yeah. But I think I'm done with that. You spent so much time with that man and you *really* didn't know. That seems like enough punishment to me." She paused, shook her head again. Amastan wanted to reach out and stop her. That repetitive motion was beginning to annoy him.

"I was only teasing when I called you lovers, you know," she continued in a softer tone. "But you cared about him, didn't you?"

Amastan couldn't look at her, so he opted for his hands instead. "That wasn't supposed to happen."

Menna's laugh was a light, musical sound, like a glass-caster's beads hitting the bottom of a bucket. She leaned forward and took Amastan's hand. "Oh, 'Stan. It never is."

His cheeks and ears warmed. He turned the cup around and around in his other hand, even though it was empty. Menna let go of his hand after too long a moment and sat back, some of the mirth gone.

"I didn't *just* come here to scold you." She tugged at her belt and pulled free a large pouch. She dumped a ball of tinder into one hand and held it up. "We're ready for the quieting ritual. Dessin and the elders are making the rest of these today. This is what we're going to use to build the seal."

Amastan set his cup down and took the object in his hands. It was a tightly rolled ball of dried plant fibers and camel dung. It smelled faintly of oil.

"There's going to be fifty-seven of them," said Menna. "And every single one of them has a scrap of prayer inside. We set it up according to that design I showed you, lure the jaan in, and poof"—Menna splayed her fingers—"light it. The prayers burn and, if we time it right, the rain turns the prayers to steam and we quiet the jaan."

"How do we lure the jaan in?" asked Amastan.

Menna shifted in her pillow pile. "Well, they've come for you and Yufit before . . ."

Amastan lifted his eyebrows. "I'm your lure?"

"I'd've liked to have both of you down there, just in case, but seeing as how that's not going to happen, it should still work with just you."

"Okay." Amastan held the tinder out and Menna took it back, tucking it into the pouch. Not for the first time, he wondered what had happened to Yufit. If he'd made it to the healers. If he'd survived Tamella's bite. He'd had enough strength to get off the roof while Amastan fought his cousins. He hoped that meant Yufit'd had enough strength to find a healer.

"It looks like season will end tonight," said Menna. "That's what all the stormsayers are claiming, anyway. Of course, anybody with one eye and a nose would say the same. Those clouds are close. They'll break this afternoon and come our way."

Amastan closed his eyes. "Season's end," he said, feeling a strange sort of relief. No matter what happened today and tonight, it would soon be over. He owed Kaseem, he owed the drum chiefs, he owed Tamella, and all those debts came due tonight. He couldn't pay them all.

But at least he could pay one.

"What do you need from me?"

"I was hoping you'd ask," said Menna, the ghost of a smile on her lips. "We could use an extra pair of hands."

Dusk fell like dust, coating the world in a darkness that accumulated in one continuous, ever-thickening layer. The clouds hadn't broken yet, but they were denser now, billowing and dark. They hunched on the horizon like a brooding crow, flashes of light briefly illuminating their depths. Soon, they would head toward Ghadid, filling the sands with wind and rain and thunder.

Season was finally at an end.

Tomorrow, the celebrations would begin. A weeklong period of festivity marked the return of rain and the refilling of the aquifers. Baats would be given out again, distributed by each drum chief to their neighborhood. The rationing would be lifted and healers would be able to do more than stabilize and stave off death. In another week, the glasshouses would fill with shoots of fresh green. It was a time worth celebrating.

Amastan didn't feel like celebrating.

Fifty-seven balls of tinder waited in waterproof leather sacks next to a carriage a neighborhood over. Fifty-seven balls that had taken all day to assemble. First, he'd had to copy the quieting prayer onto a scrap of papyrus with the right kind of ink. Then, he'd had to fold camel dung around it. Another layer of plant fibers, which had been soaked in oil. And last, more dung. His fingernails had never been dirtier and the smell clung to him like a bad dream.

Each tinder ball had to be the right size and each had to be handled carefully lest it fall apart. A few marab had assisted him and Menna, but they'd only made a handful before some other duty called them away. All of the other marab were preoccupied with end-of-season preparations, but Menna had assured him that the fewer were involved, the less likely it was someone else would get hurt. He and Menna had been stuck with the bulk of the work, which had taken most of the day.

Even when he'd realized how tedious and time-consuming making each ball was, Amastan had still held out hope that he might have time at the end of the day to look for Yufit or find a match for the seal. Time to meet his other obligations. But that time had passed and so had any remaining hope.

He'd helped Menna carry the sacks full of tinder over to the nearest carriage and then she'd sent him home. To prepare and to rest. The stormsayers predicted rain by midnight. Amastan and Menna would have to go down to the sands an hour or two before to set up and lure the jaan. But until then, he could relax. Secure his windows against the storm. Pretend to enjoy the festivities.

Amastan opened the door to a hearth full of flames and a room full of laughter. His sisters sat with his uncle and father and aunts on the rugs and cushions, sharing tea. A few other familiar faces were there, cousins and neighbors, all joining in to celebrate the end of season.

"'Stan!" called Thiyya, waving him over. "Come join us. Have a cup and sit."

Suddenly all Amastan wanted was the complete opposite: to be alone in his room with nothing but the quiet. He shook his head and kept on going toward the stairs.

"You might not have noticed, since you keep your nose in a stack of scrolls, but it's season's end," teased Guraya.

Thiyya lifted a jar of wine. "Come on, loosen up!"

Amastan raised a hand as his only answer, then began climbing the stairs. Behind, Guraya sighed loudly, then said in a mock-whisper, "Poor 'Stan must be in love and wants to be alone with his thoughts. We'd better let him."

If only she knew.

The second story was blissfully empty and silent. All Amastan wanted was to scrape the dirt and dung out from under his fingernails, peel off his sweaty wrap and tagel, and crawl into his bed and sleep until morning. He didn't care if he missed the first thunder or the first rain. There was always next season. He just wanted this one to finally, finally be over.

But it wasn't over, not yet, and Menna would be waiting for him in two hours. He'd have enough time to change, gather his things, and maybe close his eyes for a minute.

He opened the door to his room. Inside, all was dark and still. Welcoming. His fingers found the knots of his tagel and began undoing them as he walked to his bed. His sisters had thoughtfully left him a glass of water on his desk. He gulped one, two, three sips before he even tasted it. The elders had shared some of their water with him, but that had been hours ago and the sticky heat had leached him dry.

He set the glass down. A breeze circled the room like a snake from his open window.

His window shouldn't have been open.

A knife met his throat.

"G-d's greeting, Asaf," said Yufit in his ear. "Or should I say: Amastan Basbowen."

28

Amastan didn't let himself think. He snapped his arm up, hand sliding between his chest and Yufit. He pushed Yufit's arm away, hard, and the blade left his throat. Amastan twisted out of his grip and reach, a dagger already in hand. In another heartbeat, he faced Yufit, their weapons widening the distance between them even farther.

Lightning flickered through the window, briefly filling the room with cold, uncaring light. Yufit's fingers tightened around his knife. Those same fingers had touched his face only two nights ago. The dissonance rang in Amastan's head like a bell.

But Yufit was alive. His breathing, although strained, held none of the wet gurgle it had on the roof. He must have found a healer in time. Relief flashed through Amastan, quick as lightning.

Yufit's gaze fell on him and filled with hate, which burned through Amastan's brief relief. "You're one of *them*. And I thought—I wanted . . . how much of it was a lie?"

"I'm not a server," said Amastan. "And my name isn't Asaf. That's it. The rest—"

But Yufit wasn't listening. "You used me. How long did you know? How *long*?"

"I didn't know. Not until last night. I never suspected."

"You're lying." Yufit's hand was shaking, even as he pointed the tip of his knife at Amastan. "Here I'd thought you were so naïve and innocent, someone I could actually trust." His laugh was brittle and broken. "And the entire time you were playing with me. I thought you cared. I was so stupid."

"I did care."

"Stop lying!"

Yufit struck, his blade aiming for Amastan's eyes. Amastan deflected it with ease, then stepped forward into the opening Yufit had left and slammed the hilt of his blade against the side of Yufit's head. Yufit let out a grunt as he stumbled away. He flailed with his knife, caught Amastan's arm by chance. Amastan ignored the flash of pain, grabbed Yufit's shoulders, and drove his knee into Yufit's stomach.

Yufit folded, the wind knocked out of him. He gasped and Amastan heard a deep rattle; Yufit wasn't so cured after all. It wouldn't take much more to undo whatever healing he'd received.

But Amastan held back. He let Yufit catch his breath. Amastan's knife dangled at his side and he felt only cold, empty. As if someone had hollowed out his chest and filled it with brittle glass. He told himself that he was lucky that Yufit had come to him. He knew that next, he had to bring Yufit to the watchmen, yet all he could do was watch Yufit straighten and stand. He wasn't worried about Yufit getting away. Not this time.

"I could say the same about you," said Amastan. "You murdered Yanniq and Emet and Usem. Worse—you let their jaan go wild. You committed blasphemy."

Yufit met his gaze. The hatred Amastan had seen in Yufit on the roof came and went, there and gone again like a guttering candle. But when it was gone, disgust took its place. Amastan forced himself to watch.

"They deserved it," said Yufit, voice falling flat, quiet. "And I never lied to you. Not once. You couldn't even use your real name. What does that say about your intent?"

"I was hunting a killer."

"As was I," said Yufit with a sneer in his voice. "But I didn't go around pretending I was someone else. Even though I was risking my life and ridding this city of its infestation. And for what—the Serpent's still alive. How many more will she kill? How many more lives will she destroy?"

"None," said Amastan. "She's done with all that. The drum chiefs made her retire."

"You saw her last night. She would've killed me."

"You kidnapped her *daughter*. You pushed her to it. If I hadn't—" Amastan cut himself off and shook his head.

"Yes." Yufit's voice was quieter now. "If you hadn't. Why did you?"

"It wasn't right. It's not our role to decide justice."

"Says the assassin."

"I am an assassin, that's true." Amastan spread his hands. "But we're not an infestation. We work for Ghadid. Look—on the night you tried to set me on fire, I killed a woman who had been stealing water."

"I know who she was." Yufit's fingers tightened around the hilt of his knife, but some of the bite was gone from his voice.

"You knew about the contract." Amastan nodded. "Then you knew that it was better for her to die by our hands than to face a public trial. Her family would've been ruined. We spared them that. But we didn't *decide* justice. That had already been decided. We carried it out." Amastan swallowed. "I carried it out."

Yufit closed his eyes. "You weren't supposed to." When he opened them again, they glistened. "You were too fast. I should've stopped you."

"How did you know about the contract?"

Yufit laughed, but there was no mirth to the sound. "I found some who had grievances. I encouraged them to talk to the right person and ask the right questions.

From there, it was only a matter of keeping an eye on the marks' homes. Three a night became two a night became one. It wasn't *hard*. Your kind are predictable. You haven't changed at all since Hennu left. You watch. You wait. And you never expect someone else to be watching and waiting."

"If I hadn't killed her," said Amastan, "she would've been tried publicly and her family would've suffered. Some justice is better done quietly."

"Maybe," admitted Yufit, turning the blade of his knife. "But that doesn't mean the drum chiefs should allow assassins in our city."

"We're more than assassins, though," said Amastan earnestly. "We protect Ghadid in ways the drum chiefs can't. The contract system allows for justice when it would otherwise be impossible or unfair. The family has been around for centuries. I'm not saying it's perfect—far from it. Tamella was wrong to kill Saman outside of a contract, but you were just as wrong to kill Yanniq in revenge."

Yufit snorted. "I never pretended to be anything else by hiding behind a contract. You're a perversion, nothing more than a den of vipers the drum chiefs've been too craven to eradicate." Yufit widened his stance, his body tensing. "Yet even after your pit was uncovered, drum chiefs like Yanniq thought it was okay to let you keep terrorizing the city. Even though you'd already proven publicly that you had nothing but disdain for the law. You act like your will is G-d's will. But you're a tumor slowly strangling our city." Yufit raised his blade. "And I'm the knife."

Yufit led with his right foot, telegraphing his move. Amastan easily blocked his attack, turning away his knife. He twisted, and was ready to follow through and slam his elbow into Yufit's face when pain blossomed in his gut as if he'd been punched. But Yufit was too far away. Amastan doubled over. The pain was gone as quickly as it had come, but it was too late. Yufit slammed the hilt of his knife into Amastan's hand. Amastan dropped his dagger and Yufit kicked it away.

"Yanniq deserved what he got," said Yufit, hate filling his voice, thick as venom. He loomed over Amastan, but he didn't attack.

"And the others? You let their jaan go wild. Did they deserve that?"

Yufit touched the glass charms at his neck. *Amastan's* charms.

"They did. And worse. They don't deserve to have their jaan pass over. Better if they go mad instead and tear themselves apart."

"And terrorize the city," said Amastan. "And kill Megar. What crime did he commit that he deserved to die like that?"

The hatred in Yufit's eyes faded, only to flare again. "His blood is on *your* hands. You never stay behind to deal with the consequences of your actions, and this was a consequence. You killed Saman, but you weren't around for the consequences. Well, here they are."

"Drum Chief Saman was a traitor," said Amastan. "She would've torn apart Ghadid if she hadn't been stopped."

"Would she?" Yufit spun the knife between his fingers. "Was she? You mimic what your elders say, but you weren't there. You aren't G-d. You don't know what happened."

"Neither do you. You couldn't have been more than a child—"

"I was old enough." Yufit stopped fidgeting with the knife and clutched it tight. "You don't know what they did to her. My mother was torn apart. She loved Saman. And you took that away from her as if it was your right.

When you murdered Saman, you murdered my mother. You took her future away. What crime did she commit to earn that punishment? How can you call yourselves good and not consider the harm you inflict with your actions? You ruined her life and in turn you ruined mine. It's only fair that I ruin yours.

"Every day Hennu takes up the drum, she's reminded of what she lost," continued Yufit, his voice lower now, almost a whisper. "When Drum Chief Anaz died, Saman took up his drum. When you murdered Saman, Hennu took her place, because none of Saman's children were old enough. Now when Saman's eldest reaches age, Hennu will step aside. She never wanted to be a drum chief. She's only a drum chief because of what you did."

Yufit stepped closer, the dim light from the window catching on his blade. Thunder rolled, still distant. The wind tasted of rain. Pain pulsed in Amastan's stomach again, there and gone like a bad memory.

"What you do is wrong," continued Yufit. "You ask how I can be so angry with something that happened long ago, but it has never felt longer than yesterday to me. I knew Saman. She treated me like a son. I didn't understand what had happened when she died, but my mother helped me understand. It's up to me to correct this wrong. She taught me everything I know and hid me from you."

Amastan fidgeted with the edge of his wrap, riding out another stab of pain. It was beginning to worry him. He would need to end this, soon. But he wasn't ready yet. Instead, he said, "This isn't your fight, Yufit. She's using you. You said so yourself—she trained you for revenge against us—*her* enemies. You're her weapon. But she knew who we were, where we were. She could've come for us herself. As a drum chief she even had the power to call us out. Why didn't she?"

"You answered your own question—she's a drum chief. You would've seen her coming. You never expected me."

"Maybe. Maybe not. I'm sorry about your mother, I'm sorry about what she went through. But this"—Amastan gestured broadly—"this won't change the past. This doesn't have to be your future. You can still walk away."

"And what?" pressed Yufit. "The Serpent will leave me alone? My mother will forgive me? The drum chiefs will show me clemency? This *is* my future. It's too late for me. And it's too late for you."

The pain hit again, sharp as a knife. Amastan doubled over with a gasp. This time the pain receded slowly, leaving a stinging sensation in its wake. Yufit glanced toward the desk. Amastan followed his gaze to the half-empty water glass.

A cold certainty filled Amastan. He stood, or at least tried to. He made it to his feet, but the world spun away into darkness for a heartbeat and the next thing he knew, he was kneeling on the floor, awash in a cold sweat. His heart was beating too fast and his head began to pound.

Tamella had made them memorize the symptoms of poisoning.

His heartbeat was increasingly erratic, at times thundering ahead as if he were sprinting, at times skipping a beat here and there, sluggish as midday. Idly, he catalogued the symptoms and came up with a possible culprit: a poison derived from the rock-like pits of fleshy fruit. He even had the antidote in his chest.

If he could reach it within the next few minutes, he might be all right. He might live.

If not . . .

Yufit was watching him closely, the knife now still. Amastan stood, more carefully this time. The world swam, darkened, then steadied. He sucked down air, but it wasn't enough. The pain stabbed again and this time when he doubled over, he threw up a thin stream of burning yellow liquid and the stale bread he'd remembered to eat hours before.

When he straightened, Yufit struck him across the jaw. Amastan stumbled back, his knees hitting the edge of his bed. He sat down with a thump. When Yufit came at him again, Amastan tried to stand, tried to bring his arm up to defend himself, but he was too slow. His nose blossomed with fresh pain and blood trickled over his lips.

Yufit stepped back, satisfied. Amastan understood.

"You had to poison me." He breathed a weak *hah*. "You're not good enough to best me without cheating. Did you poison the others?"

"No. They died quickly, as is fair for vermin." Yufit's anger sharpened and he pointed the tip of his knife at Amastan. "You used me."

"No," said Amastan. "Never. I talked to you because I wanted to know about Yanniq, true, but after that—I cared. I listened. I wanted to help you. Save you from the jaan and watch the stars come out and see the whole of Ghadid with you."

The words slipped out before he could stop them, but he didn't have the strength to care. It was true. All of it. He'd cared.

Yufit's brow tightened. "Stop lying."

"I'm not," said Amastan. "Believe me or not if you will, but I'm not lying." He closed his eyes, felt his pulse heavy and fast in his fingers and his wrists and his feet.

He lunged for the end of the bed just as his stomach knotted in fresh pain. He fell short by a foot, slamming his knees on the floor. Yufit had moved for the door, throwing out his arms, expecting Amastan to make a run for it. He dropped his arms and stared at Amastan with fresh confusion. Amastan used the moment to haul his body the last foot to the chest and heaved its lid open. It seemed heavier than he remembered.

Yufit rushed him, but Amastan was already tossing out the chest's contents, scattering knives and bags and rope across the floor. Amastan reached the floor of the chest and his fingernails found the edges of the bottom panel and he pried it up, revealing a hidden space and a black box beneath.

Yufit snatched the box from his hands. "No."

Amastan curled around another stab of pain. When he could breathe again, he gasped, "Please."

Too late, too late, it was going to be too late—

"I'm not going to enjoy watching you die," said Yufit. He sat down on the edge of Amastan's bed, his expression grave and the box on his lap. "You brought this on yourself."

Amastan pushed his fingers into the floor, riding out another wave of pain. When it passed, he said, all in one breath, "What will you do about the jaan?"

"The elders will take care of them," said Yufit.

"Will they?"

"Of course." But Yufit didn't sound so certain.

"And how many more will die like Megar?"

Yufit looked away.

"We can stop the jaan," pressed Amastan, even as pain stabbed fresh. He gritted his teeth. "The elders figured it out. Today I helped Menna put together what we'll need for the ceremony. It's all ready and waiting for me—for us. I was going to meet her soon. We have to do it tonight, when the first storm arrives. If we work together, the jaan will take no more victims."

Yufit laughed, dry and humorless. "Work together?"

"The ceremony requires at least two people," said Amastan. "You need to be one of those people. The jaan"—pain cut him off and all Amastan could do for the next few heartbeats was breathe. When the pain dulled, he continued—"they're drawn to you. You're the reason they're wild. They'll come if you're there."

"Then I'll go see your marabi friend after this is done."

It was Amastan's turn to laugh, although it came out more like a wheeze. "Menna won't help you. She's a cousin."

"A *marabi*—?"

"She was there last night. She took Thana to the healers."

"You both lied to me."

"We tried to *help* you," said Amastan. He closed his eyes. The floor felt more and more comfortable and his thoughts were growing harder to parse. His thin window of hope was drawing closed. "The jaan . . . if I had been lying to you all along . . . would I have saved you from the jaan?"

Amastan felt Yufit's stare on him. He didn't look up.

"We all think we're right," said Amastan, slowly and carefully. "Even the monsters. But how do you know when you're the monster?"

Silence. Amastan's heartbeat pounded in his ears. His stomach was a mass of pain. He knew what would come next. Convulsions. Loss of consciousness. Death.

A hand touched his, warm and real. Then he felt the smoothness of old wood. He opened his eyes to find the box in his hands. Yufit watched him, twisting his knife between his fingers. The box opened at the precise touch of thumb and forefinger on opposite sides of its lid. Inside: over a dozen glass vials, unlabeled. They held various powders, most white, some gray, one a lurid green. The second to last vial held a clear liquid. Amastan grabbed this one. Prayed he was right.

His fingers fumbled the cork. He was shaking now, and he had to set the box on the floor to avoid dropping it. He closed his eyes and took several steadying breaths, but it didn't help.

The vial was plucked from his hands. Amastan reached

for it as it left him, his stomach dropping. Yufit had been playing with him. Of course.

Yufit popped the cork from the glass, then held it out to Amastan, who stared in disbelief. Then he grabbed the vial as relief flooded him. The antidote tasted like soap and iron. It was the sweetest thing he'd ever drank.

Together, they waited in silence. Amastan was too weak to do anything but sit on the floor, hoping, praying. After what felt like hours, the pain in his gut started to loosen. At first he wasn't sure if it was real, but then the sweat began to dry on his forehead and his pulse evened out. Distantly, he knew it'd take several days of rest before he felt anything close to normal. Being poisoned, Tamella had once told them, was a lot like being run over by a camel. The camel might no longer be in the process of running him over, but he was still left sore, battered, and bruised.

And he wasn't out of range of the camel's hooves yet.

He raised his gaze to Yufit, who stood frozen in the center of the room. He'd stepped back and away from Amastan, unwilling or unable to help any further. Already his brow creased with doubt. Whatever agreement they'd arrived at was tenuous.

One deep breath, then another. Amastan leaned back against the side of his bed, the urge to crawl into it, even with a killer in his room, still overwhelming.

"We don't have much time," he said. "I'm supposed to meet Menna soon. If you're going to help us quiet the jaan, I'll need to trust you."

"I don't think that's possible anymore," answered Yufit.

"No," admitted Amastan. "Not really. But I'll take your word for now."

Yufit shifted uncomfortably. "That's it? You'll take my word? After I tried to poison you?"

"What else is there?"

Yufit considered, then nodded. He offered Amastan his hand. "You have my word I won't kill you while we're working together."

Amastan took his hand. "Good enough. Let's quiet some jaan. For Megar."

"For Megar."

29

Menna's lips formed a thin line as she watched Amastan and Yufit approach. She leaned against the carriage pole, arms crossed and eyes narrowed. The carriage floor was covered in precariously stacked leather bags. Although the carriage was locked in place, the wind was so strong that it rocked the carriage back and forth, the metal cable creaking.

Menna straightened and pulled a dagger from her belt, which she held loose at her side: a promise, not a threat. "What's *he* doing here?"

Yufit eyed her with equal wariness. "I promised I'd help."

Amastan held up his hands. "We need him."

Menna frowned. "No. We don't. We've got the two of us—"

"And we need someone to stay up here," said Amastan, realizing it was true as he said it. "Otherwise we'll be trapped on the sands during the storm."

Menna held up her hands. "If you think I'm going to trust *him* to get us back up, you must be touched."

"Not him. You."

Menna blinked. Dropped her hands. "But—that means just you and him down there. You trust him enough to be alone on the sands with him? 'Stan, he poisoned Thana. He killed Emet. Tamella wants his head. And honestly, I don't really know what's stopping me from calling the watchmen."

"I trust him," said Amastan. "Do you trust me?"

Menna chewed her lip. He could see that she was thinking of last night, of his fight with Tamella. Not for the first time, he was glad she hadn't been there to watch.

She sighed. Sheathed her dagger. "I do, even if I'm not sure I should."

"Right now, we all want the same thing," said Amastan. "We want to stop the jaan before they claim another victim."

"Yeah, now. But—what about after?" Menna's gaze flicked to Yufit and back again. "Have you thought about that?"

Amastan looked into Yufit's steel-cold eyes, but Yufit gave nothing away. Amastan knew what *he* planned to do—turn Yufit in. But he also knew Yufit wouldn't go quietly.

"I have." Amastan turned back to Menna. "I'll cross that bridge when I reach it."

Lightning lit the area with too-bright light and was gone just as quickly. Thunder followed, shaking the stones beneath Amastan's feet. One of the bags started to roll off the side, but Menna reached out without looking and snatched it out of the air. She nestled it between two other bags.

"We're running out of time." Amastan gestured to Yufit. "Get on."

"Do you have the diagram?" asked Menna.

As Yufit stepped onto the carriage, Amastan shook out the scroll. He turned it around and showed it to Menna. She checked it, counting under her breath, then nodded.

"Good. You know what to do?"

"Set the tinder in the right places, light them before the rain gets here, and pray to G-d that the jaan come."

Menna clapped him on the back. "Exactly. Remember, the one marked with red has your blood—set it in the middle. That should be enough to draw them, but if not . . . you have your knife."

Amastan nodded. Then he climbed onto the carriage, taking care not to step on any of the bags. He found a spot near the rail and held on tight. Yufit stood on the opposite side of the carriage, staring at the oncoming storm, his back to Amastan. That suited Amastan just fine.

"Three hard yanks on the cable," said Menna. "Make sure you give yourself enough time to get back up before the storm hits. It's going to be a narrow window, but I know you of all people can do that. And, by the way," she pitched her voice to carry to the back of the carriage, "if you don't come back alive, I'll kill Yufit myself." Yufit twitched, but didn't turn. Menna smiled a smile that was all teeth, then sang out, "Ready?"

She didn't wait for an answer. Menna unlocked the carriage and it swayed and dipped. Amastan tightened his grip as his leg protested. Then they were moving, sliding, and occasionally jerking down the cable, over the edge of the platform, and out into nothing.

As if in a bad dream, Amastan descended for a second time to the sands. But instead of the momentary, exhilarating flight down the cable, he was stuck on a carriage with a killer. He wished idly that he could take up a chain again and leave both the carriage and Yufit behind.

He should be grateful for the time. He needed to focus on the quieting ceremony. They only had one chance to get it right, but a hundred things could go wrong. And if everything did go right, what then? What would Yufit do after they quieted the jaan? What would *he* do?

Amastan lifted his gaze from the sacks of tinder to find Yufit watching him. Caught, Yufit looked away. But not so fast that Amastan hadn't seen the cold calculation there, the same thoughts circling behind his eyes. One of them wouldn't return from the sands tonight.

Ghadid was only a smear of the palest orange behind them, little more than an afterimage. The darkness consumed their carriage bit by bit, taking its edges first, then the sacks, then Yufit, then himself. Amastan's world grew very close and dear, little more than his breath and the wind and the storm's wet balm. Then,

Flash.

His world expanded infinitely. An endless stretch of sand. Clouds boiling overhead. Yufit just out of arm's reach. All of that in an instant that lingered and faltered and faded and died and became afterimage. Until the next lightning strike.

During one flash, Amastan noticed that the ground was closer. In the next moment, he was tossed forward as the carriage clanged hard against the pole. He grabbed for the rail but instead caught cloth, flesh. Then rail. He'd pinned Yufit to the railing. His heart raced and his ears burned hot as he pushed away.

He hastily checked himself as he swayed with the carriage. No wounds. Yufit hadn't taken the opportunity to stab him. As he finished checking, he felt silly. Yufit had promised to help. Despite his betrayal, Amastan still trusted Yufit's word.

Lightning flashed, revealing the ground only a few feet below. Trusting what he'd just seen, Amastan swung over the side. His stomach, however, didn't have such trust, and twisted into a tight knot as he fell. Amastan miscalculated just how far away the sands were and stumbled when his feet hit. He straightened and steadied himself with one hand on the carriage's edge.

He grabbed blindly for the sacks on the carriage floor and began offloading them. He felt more than heard Yufit land beside him, the sand and the wind sucking up sound. Then a light flared, but unlike the lightning, this one lingered and strengthened. Amastan squinted against the glare, just as blind as before. He kept moving the sacks as his sight adjusted.

Yufit had lit a lantern and set it on the edge of the carriage. Its single, small flame stood impossibly straight within the glass despite the gale growing around them and provided more than enough light to work by.

Within minutes, they had all the sacks on the ground. Amastan thought he felt a drop of rain on his face and hoped otherwise. They were running out of time.

Yufit looked from the sacks to Amastan. "Now what?"

"We build the seal," said Amastan. He retrieved the instructions from his pocket, unrolled the thin paper, and held it up so Yufit could see the diagram at its center. "I'll mark the paces around the perimeter and lay the fuse and you can start placing the tinder behind me."

Yufit nodded and grabbed a sack, spilling one of the balls of tinder into his hand. It took some effort for Amastan to turn his back on Yufit and walk away, but he did. The darkness rushed at him, then steadied and even receded somewhat. Yufit had grabbed the lantern and was following.

They worked quickly and efficiently. Amastan walked the outer circle of the seal, laying the long coil of fuse and digging his heel into the sand at every place Menna had marked on the diagram. Yufit came behind and set a tinder into each shallow hole. Thunder growled overhead and lightning turned the darkness into a cast of silver glass.

The seal started out simple, but soon became intricate. The lines were easy, but the whorls and loops stopped Amastan several times. He backtracked once and another time stood for almost a whole minute, terrified that he'd messed up and would have to start again. He could almost hear time hissing past his ears. But then he counted his steps a fifth time and realized that he was right after all.

The sacks dwindled and disappeared, becoming a small mound of empty leather skins that Yufit piled on the carriage. Finally, Yufit set the last tinder in the center of the seal, the vivid red paint Menna had used now little more than a flat black. It was the only tinder unconnected by the circles and swirls of fuse wire.

Amastan held his breath, expecting . . . what? The jaan to suddenly arrive? The rain to start? To feel something, anything, that would rid him of the growing fear that this was a fool's errand. Menna hadn't had a chance to test this ceremony and the elders had never done anything like this before. How could they be so sure it would work? What if it didn't?

"What now?" asked Yufit, his voice barely audible over the wind.

Amastan reached up and tightened a knot in his ta-gel. It had almost come free several times now, the wind snatching and dragging at it. Rain spat intermittently, thin as a mist. They had time yet, but not much.

"We have to lure the jaan into the seal."

"How?"

"By lighting the red one." Amastan unhooked the striker from his belt. "When they're all in the seal, we'll light the outside and the rest of the seal should catch fire, trapping the jaan. It's fairly simple. The difficulty is in the timing."

Amastan squeezed the striker. Sparks flashed and fell onto the red tinder, which caught and flared. Heat struck his face and pushed him back. Whether or not it was the right decision, it was done. They silently returned to the carriage and waited, the lantern perched among the empty bags, giving off just enough light.

The wind howled, first one way, then the other. Rain spat and blustered, dark dots appearing and disappearing on the sand. The small fire in the center of the seal flick-ered and danced, a bright beacon that Amastan imag-ined could be seen for miles. Yet it looked so small and weak in the crushing darkness of the oncoming storm. Had Menna calculated correctly? Would it bring the jaan? And would the jaan come before the storm broke?

Then the glass charms at his neck grew warm. The sound of the wind changed subtly. Now it carried whispers under its breath. Despite the heat and the wet, the back of his neck prickled. And despite having faced these creatures half a dozen times, despite having walked alone across the sands, despite having fought the Serpent herself, despite sharing space with a man who had all but outright vowed to kill him—

Amastan was afraid.

Thunder crashed, bringing with it the roar of wind and rain. The flicker of flame seemed even smaller than before. Then lightning lit the area silver-white and Amastan saw them.

Three smears of red. Three jaan. And all of them coming straight for him.

30

Amastan's charms sang, a thin piercing whistle that cut through the crash and boom of the storm. The wind had turned impossibly hot and dry. As the jaan flew at them, they darkened and thickened. No longer smears of red, they were almost corporeal. Smoke given form and strength.

"Why're they coming this way?" asked Yufit, his voice oddly high. "Why aren't they going into the seal?"

"I don't know." Without looking, Amastan reached for Yufit's hand and grabbed tight. In that moment, it didn't matter that Yufit had promised to kill him. "The blood should draw them in."

"Oh," sighed Yufit.

Amastan glanced at him, but only briefly, too afraid to take his eyes off the jaan. "What?"

"How much blood did you use?"

"A few drops. Why?"

"And how much blood is in you?"

The realization hit like a fist. "Oh. But—the tinder must have more to it, to draw them. The marab wouldn't have made such an oversight."

"Isn't that why they wanted us both down here?"

"It was just a precaution . . ." Amastan trailed off, the rest of his thought only confirming Yufit's concern. Besides, while the marab wouldn't have made such an oversight, Menna could have.

"Too late now," said Yufit, grim. "We've got to get them in the seal. Do you think . . . ?"

Amastan nodded. "They'll follow us in."

Yufit ran for the seal, Amastan only paces behind. The jaan changed their course to meet them, two coming from one side, the third from behind. Something brushed Amastan's back and he stumbled, but caught himself.

You won't make it, he thought. But no—that thought wasn't his. His charms burned, hot as molten glass. He expected to feel them dripping down his chest at any moment. *They hurt. Take them off.*

Amastan gritted his teeth. He stepped into the seal, headed for its center.

This won't work. Nothing can stop jaan. Let go. Give in.

It was easier to ignore the intrusive thoughts now that he recognized them as the jaan. But the charms hurt, their heat exquisitely sharp and painful. He'd be surprised if he survived this without burns.

Yufit had reached the center. Around him swirled a mass of red, no longer opaque. His steel-dark eyes watched Amastan, lit beneath by a dim glow. From the fire, but also from his own charms, which were bright enough that they could be seen through his wrap. He was protected, they were both protected, as long as they kept the charms on.

He'll kill you.

Amastan halted suddenly, still a few feet from the center of the seal. He swallowed hard. Yufit's eyes were cold. The flame's flicker reflected in them and for a moment, Amastan was back on the mark's rooftop, the acrid taste of oil in his mouth, a killer watching him with hatred and fury.

Amastan shook his head. He was on the sands, not the roofs. Yufit had promised.

And when you're done? What then? Better to finish this now, when he least expects it.

His fingers twitched toward his belt and the dagger

sheathed there. Yufit's gaze followed. Yufit already held a knife, gripped carefully between thumb and forefinger. How had Amastan not noticed before?

Amastan stepped back, his heart hammering in his throat. But something struck him from behind, hard as a camel's angry hoof. His surprised cry stuck in his throat and he stumbled forward one foot, two. Yufit's eyes widened and he broadened his stance, brought up his knife. Amastan caught himself and dug in his feet. But he'd seen Yufit's reaction. The jaan were right.

You won't make it back alive.

Amastan gritted his teeth. Yufit had said as much himself. *I won't kill you while we're working together.* But after was another thing.

Kill him now, before he can fulfill his promise. Kill him and avenge us.

Amastan could see it: Yufit's body at the center of the seal, the sand drinking up his blood. The perfect sacrifice to placate the horrors Yufit himself had created.

Yufit shook his head. He stepped back, raised one hand to his forehead. That hand dropped to his neck, dug beneath the folds of his wrap. He yanked, hard, and pulled out a fistful of glowing charms. The red around him that Amastan hadn't been able to see mere moments before drew back, repulsed. Yufit turned to Amastan, took a step forward, pushing the red back further.

Something around Amastan shifted and he felt lighter. His senses cleared and he could smell the rain, hear the storm. He hadn't even noticed that everything had grown muted. Panic spiked through him: they were almost out of time.

Yufit held out his charm-laced hand to Amastan, who took it. The charms burned his skin as if he'd stuck his hand into a fire, but Amastan welcomed the pain. It cleared his thoughts—or rather, he realized, the jaan's words.

"Run," said Yufit.

They ran. The sand ate at their momentum, slowed them down, and the wind tugged them back. With their backs to the tiny flame, the lines of the seal became increasingly difficult to see. They couldn't risk breaking or smudging the lines. If they did, they'd break the seal and it would no longer hold the jaan. Yufit slowed as the same thought occurred to him. But Amastan closed his eyes and tugged him onward.

He didn't need to see where the lines were, now. He remembered where he'd placed them and in his mind's eye the seal spiraled around him. He led Yufit through the seal, turning here and rounding there. The wind brushed hot as fire across his exposed skin and, at one point, the air became thick as porridge. He pressed on regardless.

Finally, Amastan placed his palm against Yufit's chest, stopping him. "We're at the edge. Take a big step and then run for the carriage."

His eyes still closed, he could only feel Yufit's head duck in a nod. He let go of Yufit's hand and stepped out of the seal, his toes brushing neither tinder nor fuse. Then he turned until he was facing the carriage, opened his eyes, and ran.

The carriage's metal glinted in the darkness, the fire's dim light revealing only its contours. The wind must have snuffed the lantern out. The carriage was dead ahead, exactly where Amastan had expected it to be. He reached it a second before Yufit. He spun to take in the seal as Yufit gasped for breath behind him.

The tiny flame of the lit tinder was barely visible through the seething red of the jaan. One swirled thick in the middle, tight as a dust twister. A second ran along the edge of the seal, occasionally slamming against something invisible, unable to get through. And the third . . . where was the third?

Lightning flashed. Amastan could see the seal, spiraling away from them. The two jaan trapped within became red smears in the air, as if the wind had been stained with blood. To the north, the sands abruptly ended in a wall of darkness. Amastan felt a spray of rain. They were running out of time.

Amastan's only warning was the heat from his charms. They flared hot as fire. Amastan grabbed at them, batting them away from his skin as he spun around. The third jaani was feet away, eyes and mouth gaping holes that flew at him. Amastan yelled, which didn't stop the jaani, but alerted Yufit.

Then the jaani barreled into him, its sudden weight like a kick to the chest. Amastan hit the ground hard, the breath slammed out of him. He started to suck in air, but then all the air around him was jaani. He choked and sputtered. All he could see was red. His charms shrieked, burning his skin, *through* his skin. Despite the pain, he tried not to panic. As long as he had the charms, he should be fine—

The first charm shattered, spilling hot glass down the front of his chest. Panic spiked through him, his chest tightening with need for breath. He still had four left. He just had to get up, get out—

The second and third charms broke at the same time. That left two, both of which were giving off a high-pitched shriek like a kettle left too long. The jaani closed in tight, the dark holes of its eyes staring at him. Waiting.

Amastan tried to scramble backward, but the jaani moved with him. Beyond the jaani, he could just make out Yufit. He stood still as stone, watching. Those eyes, cold as steel, dark as the storm, were as merciless as both.

He'll kill you.

This time, the thought was his own. The jaani didn't need to convince him. All Yufit needed to do was nothing at all. Watch and wait and let the jaani do what he couldn't.

The fourth charm gave up in a burst of hot glass. One

left. Amastan couldn't hold his breath forever. In a moment or less, he'd be at the mercy of the jaani. It would infiltrate his mind and break him, shattering his thoughts and memory, erasing who he was. He remembered Menna's real horror in the crypt when Tamella had asked her what would happen if a jaani possessed someone. Those had been weaker jaan—what would happen with this one? Would he burn up like Megar had? Or worse?

He'd been foolish to trust Yufit. Foolish to save him from Tamella. Foolish to care about him at all. Yufit had only ever known hatred and vengeance. Of course that was all Yufit could give him. To think that he had once sat with Yufit and watched stars come out, blissfully ignorant to the darkness eating him up inside. The darkness that would now abandon him to a jaani, that would rather watch him die than save him.

Amastan had failed. Two jaan might be trapped, but a third would still be free. Tamella would damn the entire family to find Yufit and kill him. She might even go after Drum Chief Hennu. The family would be exiled, if not worse. Their history at an end.

Maybe it's time for the family to end.

Amastan closed his eyes and counted down, trying to extend what little air he had left in his lungs. It burned, everything burned, but he clung desperately to life. This wasn't over, not yet, not *yet*—

A shadow passed across his eyes. Amastan opened them. Yufit was close—too close. Lightning caught the edge of Yufit's knife. Amastan didn't have a chance to defend himself. Pain sang up his arm and Amastan gasped, breathed deep dust and too-hot air.

Blood ran down Yufit's blade, dark as the sky. He turned it, considering. The jaani weighed Amastan down, pinned him to the spot. This was it—it was over.

Yufit struck. But this time, his knife bit into his own flesh. Right above the crook of his arm. Blood ran down the blade's tip, mingled with Amastan's. Startled, Amastan could only watch as Yufit raised the knife over his head and ran toward the seal.

Amastan's last charm stopped shrieking and a pressure he hadn't even noticed was lifted from his skin. At Yufit's heels came a whirl of red.

Yufit was luring the jaan into the seal.

Amastan sucked in breath after breath as he struggled to his feet. His thigh, sore only moments before, sang in agony. He yelled, or tried to yell, but no sound came out. Only a heartbeat earlier, he'd silently damned Yufit, but now he watched with a different kind of distress as Yufit leapt over the outer edge of the seal, heading straight for its center.

Rain spattered the sand in thick, dark circles. Behind Amastan, just over the sound of the wind, came a rushing roar. They were out of time. The season was at an end. The rain was here.

The jaani followed close on Yufit's heels, a red darkness that swirled and pulsed. Yufit reached the center of the seal. He spun. His gaze searched for, found, Amastan. Even from this distance, Amastan could see the smile in those eyes. Yufit raised his striker.

"No," said Amastan, but the word refused to pass his lips. He took a deep breath and yelled, "Don't!"

All that came out was a silent breath of air. Vividly, he recalled the way the jaani had struck his chest, remembered how Megar had fallen in the inn, his lips moving soundlessly. Like Megar, the jaani had stolen his voice. Amastan couldn't stop Yufit.

Yufit struck a spark.

The spark fell, unhindered by rain or wind. It hit a tinder. Caught. Flared. Fire fled down the fuse and caught the next tinder, and the next, and the next. Flames jumped from tinder to tinder in a cascade of light until the whole seal was ablaze. Yufit disappeared behind a haze of fire and smoke and jaan.

The jaan whirled angrily. One tried to escape, coming straight at Amastan, but it ran into an invisible wall. The red of the jaani spread across the air only feet away, but came no closer. Then it was abruptly sucked back toward the center. A moment later, Amastan heard Yufit screaming.

The rain hit. A sudden rush of cool, wet wind was the only warning before a wall of water crashed over Amastan and rolled across the seal. The flames went out in a great puff of steam, taking the light with them. Suddenly, it was darker than midnight. All Amastan could hear was the rain, roaring and raging all around him.

His tagel soaked through first, stuck quick to his head. Then his wrap became sodden and heavy. He tried to take a step, but the fabric stuck fast to his limbs like weights. He undid his wrap's knots and tossed it onto the carriage, leaving him naked but for his tagel and his weapons.

Rain ran cool across his bare skin. Lightning flashed, revealing the scene before him for a split second. Then it was dark again, darker than an unlit crypt. But a split second was all Amastan had needed.

He could see the carriage, waiting only for his signal to begin the ascent back up. He could see the lightning-lit seal, steam still rising from the burnt tinder. No sign of the jaan. But there was a body huddled at the seal's center, unmoving.

Yufit. The murderer. The killer. The man who hated Amastan for everything he represented, for a crime Amastan didn't commit.

Yufit might be dead already. And if he wasn't dead, the storm would kill him. All Amastan needed to do was climb onto the carriage and signal Menna. He could go up and know Yufit had no way of following until morning, until well after the storm had passed.

It would be so easy to leave Yufit. After all, Yufit had tried to poison him. Yufit had kidnapped Thana, angered Tamella, murdered cousins, killed a drum chief, dishonored and disrespected the dead. Yufit had promised only to help until the jaan were quieted. Well, the jaan were quieted.

He'll kill you.

All Yufit had known was death. Hennu had raised him on hatred and vengeance. But Amastan had glimpsed a different Yufit on the rooftop and in the inn. A Yufit without anger and revenge foremost in his mind. Who could Yufit have been if he'd had half a chance at his own life?

It's too late for me, Yufit had said.

Amastan didn't go for the carriage. He walked into the seal. Each time lightning flashed, it cut through the rain and showed him more. *Flash.* The tinder balls were little more than dark smears in the sand. *Flash.* As he neared the center of the seal, he felt the sand beneath his feet growing warm. *Flash.* In some places, the sand had turned to pockets of glass, red as blood.

Amastan didn't touch them. The sands would bury the glass. Already one was half submerged.

Flash.

Yufit was curled into a ball, his hands over his head. Blood ran bright red between his fingers, but whether it was stained rainwater or fresh, Amastan couldn't tell.

Flash.

Yufit hadn't moved. Amastan couldn't see if he was breathing. But this time, he did see the wound in his shoulder, the blood staining his wrap.

Flash.

The rain was coming too fast. It pooled around him, filled previously invisible trenches and runs in the sands. The area he stood in was turning into a river, and fast. He had to get out.

Flash.

He wouldn't leave Yufit. He didn't bother checking Yufit's pulse; if he was dead, then he still deserved the dignity of having his jaani quieted. Besides, Amastan didn't want to have to fight any more jaan. And if he was alive . . .

Yufit was heavier than Amastan had expected. Or maybe Amastan was just weaker. He paused, his arms around Yufit's ribcage, wondering if he should try picking Yufit up a different way. He'd started by assuming Yufit was alive, but a dead weight should be carried over the shoulder.

Then Yufit shifted. Relief rushed through Amastan, as cool as the rain. The relief brought energy, which helped him get Yufit to his feet. Yufit was barely conscious, but, leaning on Amastan, he was able to put one foot in front of the other.

One foot. Then the next. *Flash.* The carriage a little closer. The water a little higher.

The growing river was ankle deep now and tugging at their feet. Worse, it was pulling away the sand beneath, turning normally tricky footing treacherous.

Flash. A few more feet. *Flash.* A few more. *Flash—*

Amastan grabbed onto the carriage railing. The river ran right beneath it, inches away. Amastan helped Yufit onto the carriage first. The river swelled, lapped over the edge of the carriage. It pulled at him. His feet slipped.

But Yufit reached out and held onto him. Amastan kicked against the water and the sand and hauled himself onto the carriage. He lay there for a moment, gasping for breath, rain beating against his face. Staring up into Yufit's eyes.

He gave himself the luxury of that moment.

Then it passed. He hauled himself to his feet. Hit the wire three times. The storm muted its *clang,* but the vibrations would travel. He fell to the floor of the carriage and pulled his sodden wrap over himself, exhausted beyond belief.

"Is it done? Are they gone?" asked Yufit.

"They're gone," said Amastan, surprised to hear his own voice again.

Yufit smiled. Then his eyes rolled up in his head and he slumped. A moment later, the carriage jerked, jolted, and began to move.

31

Amastan kicked open the door to the healers. He'd meant to nudge it with his foot, but Yufit's unconscious, rain-soaked body had started to slip off his shoulder and he'd overcompensated mid-nudge. The wind hadn't helped. The result was a loud *thwack* as the door hit the inside wall. Two wide-eyed healers stared at him. One scrambled to help as Amastan maneuvered his awkward burden into the room while the other disappeared through a curtain. The door closed on its own behind him, abruptly cutting off the sound of pouring rain and rushing wind.

"What happened?" asked the healer, guiding Amastan toward a table. She was an older woman, her eyes marked by crow's claws and her braids thick with colorful salas.

Amastan slid Yufit onto the table. Water dripped from his forehead onto Yufit. "I'm not sure," he said. "I found him in an alley. There was blood on his head, but the rain washed it away. His shoulder, though . . ." He glanced around the small, empty room, noticing the wet trail he'd made on his way from the door to the table. "I don't have any baats, but . . . bring me a bowl."

Without taking her eyes off him, the healer grabbed a bowl from beneath the table and set it in front of him. Amastan hiked up the corner of his wrap and squeezed rainwater into the bowl. He worked his way around the edge of the fabric until the bowl was full.

"Is that enough?"

The healer pulled the bowl to herself. "Until we know what the problem is."

"Bring me another."

Amastan filled two more bowls, twisting and squeezing out every last drop of water from his sodden clothing. It'd taken the entire carriage ride up, but he'd managed to knot the wrap back on. Menna had met them at the top, then disappeared into the night to alert the elders of their success, trusting him to handle Yufit. The fewer cousins who visited the healers, the better.

Amastan took off his tagel and wrung it out over the bowl while the healer averted her eyes. He tied his tagel back on, damp but no longer dripping.

"If that's not enough, I'll step outside again," said Amastan. "The drum chiefs only prohibited collection."

"Technically, that's collection." But the healer settled her hands over the bowl as she spoke.

"Does it count if I go down to the sands? That should be far enough out of the drum chiefs' authority?"

"You're doing a lot for a stranger."

Amastan bit his lip. "Just . . . see what's wrong with him. Please."

The healer had already closed her eyes. Tendrils of blue wound out of the bowl and up her arms like snakes. Then the tendrils unfurled and spread across Yufit's body until he was covered in a thin blue shroud. The blue gently settled on him, like a layer of dust. Then it disappeared beneath his skin.

The water level in the bowl dropped imperceptibly but inevitably. Seconds passed. Outside, the wind howled and somewhere too close metal tore in a long, ear-piercing screech. Amastan watched Yufit's chest rise and fall and rise again, twisting his damp wrap between his fingers.

Then the healer let out a breath and opened her eyes. The blue broke and was gone. The healer placed a hand on Yufit's chest. "He's suffered some trauma to his head. A particularly bad blow. He has a concussion and a nose-bleed. That's where the blood came from. That—and his shoulder had a superficial wound. I've already healed it. The water you brought should be enough. He'll be fine after a few days' rest."

Amastan sagged with relief. "Thank G-d."

"He's lucky you found him." The healer poured the remaining water into another bowl. "If he'd been left alone, he might never have woken up."

Amastan stared at Yufit, whose eyes occasionally darted beneath his closed lids. What did he see? What did he dream? Amastan hoped he would have a chance for better dreams, although he doubted it. Amastan may have spared his life, but the drum chiefs wouldn't. Yufit was a murderer. The very laws that had stayed Amastan's hand, that had made him confront Tamella, were the laws that would see Yufit executed.

Amastan couldn't deny that Yufit had murdered Yanniq and Emet and Usem. He wouldn't try. But was Yufit's conviction that he was doing the right thing, however misguided, any different than Amastan's own? Hennu had taught Yufit that Saman needed to be avenged. She'd raised him with the sole purpose of bringing her revenge against Tamella. She'd sowed the seeds of hatred in him.

The scratched-out name in the record—had she done that? She must have known what would happen, after her revenge had been carried out. As a drum chief herself, she couldn't be ignorant of that fact.

Yet Amastan could see her argument. How was what she'd done any different from what Tamella did when she trained the next generation of assassins? They were both raised to a single purpose: to kill. But Yufit's purpose had been selfish. From its very beginning, the Basbowen family had protected Ghadid. Yufit had protected nothing.

Tamella had given Amastan and his cousins a choice. At any point in their training, they could have dropped out, taken up another craft. Even after they'd passed their tests, they could have still left the family. Tamella might not have understood, might've even been disappointed, but she would've let them. And Amastan knew, now, that having that choice was one reason he'd decided to become an assassin, to continue being an assassin. He'd needed that space to understand and accept his role.

Yufit hadn't had a choice. Not when his own mother had set him this task. Not when everything he'd learned had been filtered through layers of anger, resentment, and revenge.

Yanniq's blood wasn't just on Yufit's hands. It was also on Hennu's.

Drum Chief Hennu. He could see her as she was on the day she announced Yanniq's death. The brilliant, sky-blue wrap. The glittering rings. One of those, he was sure, bore the same seal that had allowed the contracts to resume.

He could understand the pain of losing someone you loved. He'd been young when his mother had died, but that didn't erase the sting. But that was no reason to twist the life of your child into a weapon. She'd wielded the knife through Yufit, had murdered the drum chief and the cousins from afar. And yet, if Amastan brought the evidence of her collusion before the Circle, what would they do?

Would they see her guilt as plain as Amastan did and spare Yufit? Or would they only see that she was marginally complicit? Little more than an unfortunate association.

Amastan didn't know. It wasn't up to him to decide. The drum chiefs had asked him to deliver Yanniq's killer—and he would.

The downpour had thinned to a drizzle. Amastan walked slick streets, his wrap growing sodden and heavy once more. Torches glowed like lonely outposts in the gloom, their light dimmed by haze, their glass smeared with condensation. The streets were empty, save for bits of roof and broken glass, but he could hear laughter and loud conversations bursting from homes as he walked by. Occasionally, a child darted out from a door, screaming in delight at the illicit sensation of wet skin, hair, clothes.

But it wasn't safe to be out in a storm, even its tail end, and so inevitably an adult would run after the child and drag them back inside. Lightning could still strike. A gust of wind could finish the job of tearing a roof apart that the storm had started.

So Amastan walked alone.

The rain stopped all at once, there one moment, gone the next. The stars blinked through a gap in the thick blanket of clouds. A gentle breeze cooled his skin and closed the opening. For the first time in months, the city didn't smell like dust. Instead, it smelled alive.

Amastan squeezed the water from his wrap as he walked, but it was still dripping damp when he arrived at his destination. He stepped into the narrow alley and eyed the wall. He didn't know which window he needed. He didn't have all of his tools and weapons. He knew nothing about his mark's habits or tendencies. He didn't even really know what he planned to do once he found the right room.

He was as unprepared as he could be. And he didn't care.

Amastan tied up the bottom of his wrap so it wouldn't

tangle in his legs and knotted his tagel higher. Then he started to climb.

Almost every window had been left cracked open to let in the cool, wet air, so it was easy for Amastan to peer in and give each room a cursory glance. The room he was looking for wouldn't be on the first floor and it wasn't on the second. He paused at the end of the row and crouched in a windowsill to let his muscles rest. He was tired, so tired, but he dismissed the possibility of giving up and going home as soon as it crossed his mind.

He found what he was looking for on the third floor. A large bedroom with a desk in one corner, a rich, thick rug across half the floor, and a wide bed in its center. The drum next to the desk only confirmed it: he'd found Drum Chief Hennu's room.

The room was empty. Of course it was. Hennu would be downstairs or at Eken's home, publicly celebrating the end of the season. Amastan took his time searching the room. He caught himself hoping that Hennu would walk in on him and give him an excuse to hurt her. A fire had caught in his chest as he'd crossed the city and Amastan wanted to destroy something, anything—anyone.

But she didn't walk in on him. Amastan finished searching at his own pace. He didn't find the ring. Hennu must have worn it to show her station, even for something so trivial as a party. He'd have to wait for her to return. He wasn't going anywhere until he had that ring.

The room offered little in the way of hiding places. He took up a spot next to the door, opposite the handle. When it opened, the door would hide him from view. Beyond that, he didn't plan. He knew so little about her that he couldn't plan. Things could go wrong. He might have to kill her.

He didn't shy away from the possibility.

So he stood. And he waited. Minutes passed. Hours. Amastan counted his breaths, lost count, started again.

His eyes itched with exhaustion. He considered lying down in her bed.

Not for the first time, footsteps approached outside. He waited for them to pass. They didn't. The door opened.

Drum Chief Hennu entered her room.

32

Hennu wore the same sky-blue wrap she had on the day she'd announced Yanniq's death. The hem was darkened by water, but the rest of it was pristine, the color as clear and vibrant as the sky itself on a cool winter day. She moved to her desk, letting the door close on its own behind her. She shed her gold bracelets and necklace, leaving them in a glass bowl that she set on a high shelf.

Amastan moved as she moved, his bare feet silent on the stones. When she turned toward her bed, he was no longer next to the door. Hennu slid off her sandals, then began to undo the knots of her wrap. As she did, she stepped in one of the damp spots Amastan had left behind. She stopped. Glanced down. Her head turned as she followed the wet footprints around the room.

Then her body turned with them, from the door to the bed to the open window. She went to the window, closed it, and turned back to the room. She gave a start when she saw Amastan leaning against her door.

"How did you get in here?" she demanded. Then she shook her head and took a step back. "Contracts aren't allowed. You shouldn't be here."

"You should know better," said Amastan, not moving from the door. "You lifted the ban."

Hennu's eyes widened, then narrowed. "You can't know that."

Amastan spread his hands, empty and open. "Does it matter? I'm here."

"Who took out the contract? Was it Eken? That scorpion, I bet it was. He's always been jealous of my neighborhood."

"There's no contract," admitted Amastan. "If there was, you'd be dead by now."

"Then why are you here?"

"Because you and the other drum chiefs asked me to find Yanniq's killer."

This caught Hennu by surprise. She frowned. "*I* didn't kill Yanniq."

"I know." Amastan straightened. "Your son did."

Hennu stepped back, her mouth opening slightly. She hesitated and her dilemma played across her bare face. To deny or not? Finally, she decided. "Is he dead?"

Amastan felt a weight on his chest. Then he reminded himself that Yufit was fine, the healers would take care of him. But how long before his execution?

How long before Amastan turned him in?

"Yes," said Amastan, the single word both a lie and not.

Hennu let out a breath and closed her eyes. When she opened them again a heartbeat later, though, there was no trace of tears. "You didn't come here to tell me my son is dead."

"No." He twisted his wrist just so, loosening the strap there so that a small dagger slid free, its hilt fitting perfectly into his palm. The flame burning in him had flared at Hennu's lack of remorse. He wasn't sure what he was going to do next, but the uncertainty didn't terrify him; it thrilled him. "I came here because you lifted the ban and because you're the reason why Yufit is dead."

Hennu's gaze tracked the blade. "Am I now?"

"If you wanted to kill the Serpent, you should've done

it yourself. I have proof that you lifted the ban. The other drum chiefs don't know you did it. What will they do once they find out?"

The edge of Hennu's lips turned up in a sneer. "Where's your proof?"

Amastan danced forward, tucking the knife beneath Hennu's throat. With his other hand, he grabbed her fingers and felt along them until he found her rings. This close, he could smell her vanilla-perfumed breath, cloying and rank. His fingertips passed over two, then slid off the third. Amastan stepped back, the knife between them as he fumbled the ring and confirmed that it was the drum chief seal. He held it up.

"This."

Hennu laughed. "That won't get you far. Each drum chief wears an identical ring."

"They're not identical," said Amastan. Keeping Hennu in his line of sight, he examined the ring. He didn't need to see Kaseem's order to know it was an exact match.

"Prove it."

Amastan pocketed the ring. "I will."

"Is that it? Is that your threat?" pressed Hennu. "You know I'll tell them that you stole the ring and forged the order yourself, right?"

"Why?"

Hennu shrugged. "How should I know? Your family is bloodthirsty. That should be answer enough."

"You would know," said Amastan quietly. "You're family."

That made Hennu freeze. Then anger spilled out of her, hot and fast. "I haven't been family since Tamella murdered my wife. Don't you dare say that again."

"Your fight with Tamella should've stayed between the two of you," said Amastan. "You should never have brought Yufit into it."

"What, and hide it from him? Yufit deserved to know what happened to his mother."

"He did. But he didn't deserve for that to define his life." He sighed, exhaustion eating away at his resolve. What was he doing? He'd never get through to Hennu. "What will the Circle do when they find out you lifted the ban without consulting them?"

"They'll never believe an assassin."

"I wouldn't be so certain about that." Amastan slid his dagger back into the sheath at his wrist. He didn't want to be here in this room anymore. He wanted to leave, to check on Yufit, make sure he was all right. He had what he'd come for, after all. He turned toward the window.

"That's it?" asked Hennu, sounding skeptical. "You're just going to take the ring?"

The fire in Amastan flared suddenly, as bright and hot as the fire on the sands, as the fire that had consumed Megar, as the fire on the rooftop when he'd first fought Yufit. In an instant, he had a blade in each hand and he'd crossed the space between him and Hennu. But this time Hennu wasn't as passive.

She sidestepped and reached under the desk. Her fingers played for a moment and Amastan heard a click. Before he could trap her against the desk, she'd slipped away again. Now she held a short sword between them, her eyes glittering with anger.

"You forget," she said. "I was trained, too."

She swung. Amastan danced back. Hennu anticipated his reaction and cut her swing short, throwing her weight into a stab. Amastan twisted to the side and out of the way, but just barely: her blade sliced through his wrap, already sticky from the rain, to skin beneath. Hot pain followed moments later, as Hennu had recovered and pressed her attack.

Amastan gave ground foot by foot. Hennu was surprisingly quick for her age and she attacked with a chaotic

ferocity. More used to his cousins' measured and practiced moves, Amastan was hard-pressed just to defend.
He deflected blow after blow as Hennu hacked at him like
a butcher trying to dismember a goat.

His foot touched the wall first, then his shoulders. He
was trapped. A triumphant gleam glinted in Hennu's
eyes. She drew her sword back and stabbed as if it were
a spear.

Amastan dropped his daggers and grabbed her sword
by the blade with his bare hands, stopping it a hairs-
breadth from his wrap. Hennu's blade was sharp as glass
and cut into his palms. His blood pulsed in ribbons down
the metal. In another moment the blade would be too slippery to hold. Amastan pushed the blade aside with all of
his strength and stepped away.

Hennu's blade clanged against the wall. She pivoted
but Amastan was there, his bloody hands over her eyes.
She flailed blindly. Amastan grabbed her wrists just
as she started to raise her sword and his fingers dug in
deep. She hissed in pain and then let go, the sword clattering to the ground. Amastan shoved her back against
the wall, picked up the sword, then stepped in close.

Breathing heavily, he settled the point of the sword at
the base of her throat. Despite the exertion, the sword did
not waver.

He met her eyes, finally wide with fear. One twitch and
he could bleed her dry. One cut and he could end this.
He wouldn't have to rely on the Circle's whim for judgment. He could avenge Yanniq and Usem and Emet and
Yufit in one swift movement. He could even claim it was
self-defense. The Circle would understand. They couldn't
have hired assassins to find a killer and not expected a
body in return.

He pictured it. Leaving her body to cool on the floor
of her bedroom. Not bothering to alert anyone to her

death. Someone would find her before it was too late, but if not, wasn't it right for her jaani to go wild? Wasn't it just?

Tamella would tell the Circle that they had found the killer. The Circle would believe her or they wouldn't. The family would end or it wouldn't. Amastan wasn't sure he cared.

But in the same instant he saw more hatred and more bloodshed. Hennu had other sons, other daughters through Saman. People she loved and who loved her. Which of them might want revenge if Hennu died as her wife had, at the hand of an assassin? The Circle might have expected blood when they demanded the family to act, but blood didn't have to be the answer. It wasn't up to him to decide.

Amastan didn't have to make the same mistakes Tamella had. He didn't have to repeat the past. No matter how much he wanted to in that moment.

He let the sword drop and stepped back. "You will admit to lifting the ban without consulting the Circle, to inciting your son to violence on your behalf, to causing, if indirectly, Drum Chief Yanniq's death. You will take whatever punishment the Circle sees fit to give. You will retire and pass on the drum. And you will be done with your vengeance. If you don't, I will be back. If not me, another cousin. Even if we're rounded up or exiled, I promise you it will be the first and last thing that we do. Let the past be the past."

Drum Chief Hennu swallowed. In that moment, Amastan hoped he'd judged her correctly. He started to raise her sword again, but then she nodded.

Amastan let the sword drop to the ground with a loud clang, final as a drum. He kicked it away, then picked up his daggers. Hennu stayed where she was, only her eyes moving as he walked to the window. He pushed open the glass, letting a breath of wet air in. He climbed out, but paused while he was still in the window frame.

His gaze met hers one last time. "I'm sorry for your loss."

Then he dropped out of the window and was gone.

33

"The drum chiefs accepted your evidence."

Amastan raised bleary eyes to Tamella, standing before him in a wrap the shade of evening purple. It brought out the warmer tones of her dark skin, making her look vibrant and alive. Tamella had no smile for him. Amastan held up his cup of tea in a silent offer, but Tamella shook her head. She stayed where she was. Her gaze drifted toward the hearth, and the glow of the embers reflected in her eyes.

"I wouldn't have let her live," said Tamella. "She's a danger to herself and the city. She's already demonstrated she can't let the past go. And now she'll be stripped of her drum. She has so much more to resent. What were you thinking?"

"I didn't want to repeat your mistake, ma."

Tamella winced. "What do you know about mistakes?" she asked, but her tone made it clear she didn't want an answer.

Finally, she sat. She perched on the edge of the hearth, her back to the embers. "I can find a hundred different ways to fault how you went about your task. I wouldn't have done what you did, not even close. But maybe that's the point. You found the killer. You turned in Drum Chief Hennu. You stopped what could easily have become another cycle of murder and revenge." She sighed. "And on top of all that, you convinced the drum chiefs to officially lift the ban."

That caught Amastan's attention.

Now Tamella smiled, if only thinly. "Not your intent, was it? But you showed them the value of the family. You also showed restraint. You would have been in your right to kill Hennu. She attacked you. You defended yourself. But you didn't kill her." She shook her head. "Whether or not that makes you exceptional or stupid, I still can't decide, but the Circle was impressed. So." She met his gaze and placed her fist over her heart. "Congratulations, sa."

It was Amastan's turn to wince. "Please don't use 'sa.'"

"Why not?" asked Tamella, her smile thin and humorless. "You earned it."

The streets were full of people talking, laughing, smiling. An air of celebration suffused every platform Amastan crossed, every neighborhood. Doors and windows were thrown wide open, feet were bare, and children zigzagged around clusters of chatting adults, screaming with delight. Girls wore red ribbons in their hair, boys wore red strings around their wrists.

The day season ended was a holy day—for all the classes, including slaves. It was one of the few days a year that slaves were allowed off. Bare-faced men and clean-shorn women gathered in small clumps, carefully ignored by all. They, too, wore red on their wrists like children.

Amastan walked through clashing smells of bitter tea, savory lamb, sweet date syrup, and pungent spices. It seemed as if the whole of Ghadid had been shaken out onto its streets. Yet Amastan might as well have been walking the streets at midday during season. He felt distant, ungrounded, and alone.

But he walked with purpose. He knew exactly where he was going, even if he didn't know what he would do when he got there. He'd left Yufit with healers in the Aeser neighborhood last night. He should be stable now, resting. The healers would keep him asleep if he asked. At least long enough for the watchmen to arrive.

Tamella had told the drum chiefs that Yufit was barely holding on to life. She hadn't told them where he was, because Amastan hadn't told her. The drum chiefs wanted Yufit turned over to face trial as soon as he could walk. After all, why waste water healing a condemned man?

Amastan knew what he had to do. Yet his feet dragged along the stones the closer he got to his destination. He could have alerted the watchmen from a distance. He didn't have to go himself to the healers. But he knew he'd regret it if he didn't see Yufit one last time.

Too soon, he came to the door he'd kicked open last night. This time he pushed it open with the palm of his hand before he could hesitate or turn away. Inside was much the same as he'd last found it. Quiet. Beds empty. The air as clear and damp as outside. All the windows thrown open. Two healers, one older, one younger. This time, the younger one didn't disappear into the back when he entered.

Amastan stopped two steps inside. *Beds empty.* He scanned the room again, but it was small and had nothing to hide.

"Where is he?" he asked. Then, with increasing panic, "You said he would *live*."

The older healer held up her hands. That's when Amastan picked out a new salas in her braids, this one silver. "Your friend is fine."

Amastan let out a puff of relief. He glanced toward the curtain in the back. "Then where is he?"

The older healer met his gaze and clasped her hands before her. "He left."

"But—he couldn't have left. He was unconscious. You said he'd be out for a while."

The healer shrugged, a small, ineffectual gesture. "I was wrong."

Amastan thought he'd be angry. He thought he'd be frustrated. But instead, all he felt was relief.

He let out all the breath he'd been holding and he sat on the edge of an empty table. "Did he say where he was going?"

"No." The healer rustled around in her wrap and pulled out a folded scrap of vellum. "But he left a note. He said to give it to you when you returned. And he also said . . ." Here she hesitated, her gaze briefly dropping to the floor before meeting his again. "He said he was sorry."

Amastan accepted the vellum. The healer waited, clearly curious about its contents. But Amastan couldn't bring himself to read it. Not yet.

"Thank you, mai." He pressed his closed fist to his heart. "You did everything you could." He started to go, but then paused and drew out a few of the baats the drum chiefs had given him. He set them on the table before leaving, their metallic clink the only sound.

The note burned in his fist. Amastan left the healers. He went south, crossed two platforms, and came to a familiar wall. The barrel was gone, but a rusty ladder lay in the rain-stirred dust, one of its rungs broken clean through. But Amastan didn't need a ladder. There were more than enough handholds in the old stone.

The glasshouse looked different with daylight. Its lock gave easily under his picks and in another moment, he stood on its roof. Sunset was creeping closer, but there was still plenty of bright, hot light, now weighed down by humidity. Yet Amastan could see the same patterns he'd picked out before, the circles of platforms, neighborhoods, and city.

A knot in his throat made it difficult to swallow. A cloud dimmed the sun and Amastan blinked at the sudden change in light. Overnight, the world had changed. Clouds rolled lazy across the sky, thin and puffy. Another storm brewed in the east, but whether or not it would break free and come for them, not even the stormsayers knew. Either way, it would still rain over the mountains and that rain would feed the aquifer and the pumps would run again.

In a few weeks, the first of the iluk caravans would return. The markets would spill through the streets, bursting with fresh spices, new fabric, and expensive wood. Vibrant green life would fill the glasshouses and the heady smell of plants and flowers would suffuse the city like tea. The drum chiefs would allocate baats and new work would be commissioned, debts repaid. The city's life cycle would start anew, revitalized for another year. Another season.

Overnight, everything had changed.

It was a time to celebrate. But Amastan felt none of that.

He sat down on the edge of the roof, his legs dangling over the side. Then he unclenched his fist and opened the note.

Asaf—

I recognize that's not your true name, but you will always be Asaf to me—the overly earnest server, not the murderer. Yet how much of a murderer can you be when you saved me from the jaan, not just when you thought I was innocent, but when you knew I had killed family of yours?

Your adherence to the law is admirable, but it does not erase the blood on your family's hands. What you are is wrong; what you do is wrong, and no amount of recasting your role or your name will change that.

But perhaps you are right in one respect: it's time to let the past go. I did what I could, and while I failed to stop the Serpent, further action on my part would be foolish. I choose to believe that your strong sense of justice will prevail among your kind and that you will emerge as their natural leader, even if I cannot believe in what you do.

By the time you receive this note, I will be gone from Ghadid. I don't see a life for me here anymore. Don't look for me. I couldn't tell you all of this in my own voice because I feared I would not be able to leave. If G-d is kind, we will meet again in another future and another existence. If G-d is kind, we won't meet again as we are now. I fear I would not withstand it.

You said once that even monsters think they're right. Perhaps we are both right.

Perhaps we are both monsters.

May G-d light your darkness,
Yufit

EPILOGUE

"There's a man at the door asking to see you."

Amastan looked up from the wrap he'd been mending to find Thiyya standing in his doorway, wearing healer's blue. Thiyya glanced around his room, her brow furrowing with concern.

"You know, you can always bring your work downstairs," she said gently. "We won't bother you. It's not good for you to sit alone up here."

"I'm fine," said Amastan.

Thiyya looked as if she wanted to contradict him, but then just shook her head and left. Amastan folded the wrap and set it on the end of his bed. Then he surveyed his room, wondering what Thiyya had seen. Everything was neat and in order. His scrolls were stacked in a perfect pile on his desk, his pens laid out in a line next to them. His sheets were clean and folded and even the curtains drawn over his window hung straight.

He pushed the curtains back and was surprised to find that the sun had already set. He cracked open the window and took a breath of the night air. It almost tasted sweet compared with his room. Maybe it was a little stuffy in there.

He didn't think too much about who was here to see him. Barag stopped by sometimes to pick up his work and drop off more. Barag had been more than understanding these last few weeks. Amastan wasn't ready to see Tamella or Thana or the city just yet. He needed more time.

But it wasn't Barag waiting for him at the top of the staircase. Kaseem leaned on his cane, wearing the same green tagel and wrap Amastan had last seen him in. The sight was so jarring that Amastan stopped in his doorway. But Kaseem didn't disappear or leave; he waited patiently, his watery gaze fixed on Amastan.

Slowly, Amastan stepped out of the doorway and into the upper living area, stopping a few feet shy of the old man. "Why are you here, sa?" he asked in a low whisper, even though they were alone.

"You proved yourself more than capable over the course of the past few weeks," said Kaseem. "Despite your inexperience, you successfully completed a contract and found justice for your cousins. You impressed the drum chiefs, who are themselves very difficult to impress. I'm aware that they didn't expect you to actually achieve the task they set you. Yet, you did."

Amastan passed a hand in front of his eyes, disbelieving. "I don't know what you mean. It was a mess."

"Perhaps," said Kaseem with the smallest of shrugs. "There are always things that we could've done differently. But what matters is your success. I'm confident that you have the skills, patience, and knowledge to perform admirably. Which is why I have chosen you for the first legal contract in over twelve years." He held up a finger. "Technically, the other contracts were legal as well, given that the order was sealed by a drum chief, but we'll just go from here."

Amastan reached out a hand to steady himself against something, but found nothing. Kaseem was watching him with the slightest of smiles, waiting for acceptance, appreciation, something. Clearly, this was an honor. Clearly, Amastan should be grateful.

Instead, he was numb.

A contract. After everything, was that to be his reward? More death?

But as his initial reaction subsided, Amastan realized that he felt differently about contracts. They were necessary, and if not him, then who? Dihya and Azulay had been ready to break the law to help Tamella kill Yufit. Tamella herself had shown a dangerous lack of judgment multiple times, and not only in the past.

The family was here to protect Ghadid, against outsiders and against itself. Amastan was a part of that and he could choose either to fade away or step up. Yufit had wanted him to step up. Yufit believed he could keep the family perfectly balanced on the thinnest of lines.

Amastan still didn't like to kill, but Tamella had been right about that: an assassin who enjoyed killing shouldn't be an assassin.

Amastan would be the perfect assassin. He met Kaseem's eyes.

"I'll do it."

ACKNOWLEDGMENTS

Many of us hold the romanticized notion that writing a novel is a solitary affair, that a book grows solely from a singular human dreaming up words before the rest of the world stirs. But step back and you'll see all the people around that human, supporting them and believing in them and actively working with them to not only create those words, but to give them form and transport them all the way to here, to now, to you.

Thank you to the whole Tor team and your unrelenting enthusiasm and professionalism. Thank you, especially, to my editor, Diana M. Pho, who first asked: *What about Amastan's story?*

Thank you to my agent, Kurestin Armada, who maintained calm and clarity when I couldn't and also explained exactly why Amastan deserves a happy ending. I'm so sorry.

Thank you to my beta readers—Eldridge Wisely, Anya Vostinar, and Sarah Doore—who helped me beat a draft into a manuscript in an exceptionally short amount of time.

Thank you to my parents, Barbara and Daniel, who kept the bookshelves stocked with Anne McCaffrey, Edgar Allan Poe, and K. A. Applegate when I was the most impressionable, and who, decades later, held a sleeping newborn so my hands were free to type.

Thank you to Grandma McDaniel and Grandmum

Paterson, who always wanted to know what I was working on and never once laughed when it was unicorns and dolphins.

Thank you to my daughter, who entered this world only a few weeks before this book, who occasionally slept long enough for me to complete it, and who reminds me of what's most important in life: giggles, snuggles, and unrepentant exuberance.

But most of all—thank you to my wife, Sarah, who has been with me through this story and many others, who read every draft, who listens to me prattle on about plot and character and story arcs, who understands that there are highs, yes, but there are lows, and people are confusing, complex confluences of events, and who always believed I'd get here, even when I couldn't.

Read on for a preview of

THE IMPOSSIBLE CONTRACT

K. A. DOORE

Available now from Tom Doherty Associates

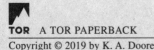
TOR A TOR PAPERBACK

1

Drum Chief Eken's end of season party was unflinchingly raucous. The unfettered flow of date wine and the thunder's erratic interruptions only encouraged the partygoers to an ever-greater volume. The wind puffed the sound and smell of rain through open windows and doors. A storm was coming; it was season's end. All of Ghadid was celebrating tonight, safely indoors and away from the strong winds and violent rains. A mixture of excitement and relief pulsed beneath the too-loud conversation.

But Thana felt neither. Instead, she ground her teeth against the crowd's onslaught, thrumming with a nervous anticipation that had nothing to do with the storm or the party. Balancing a tray of wine-filled glasses on one hand and holding a pitcher in the other, she threaded her way through the bodies, attuned only to the tone, not the content, of the words blowing past.

For this event, she'd borrowed a dull purple wrap that sucked away the warm undertones in her brown skin. It served its purpose in transforming her into just another background blur, as unexceptional as the other slaves. She'd even done her hair up in a common slave style, all tight black knots in uniform rows across her scalp.

Her gaze tracked the crowd and snagged on a figure in green conversing with one of the drum chief's wives, his wrap cinched tight with a silver belt: her cousin Amastan. He wore his tagel higher than usual tonight, covering even his nose, but Thana would know her cousin's build and stance anywhere.

She let out a breath of relief. He'd made it.

Not that she'd ever doubted he would. But there was always a chance, however small, that he could've been delayed, or worse, barred from entering the party. Then they would've had to scrap their plan, wasting the months of preparation and planning it'd taken to get them this close to Eken.

After all, this conveniently public spectacle afforded them their best—and only—chance to kill the drum chief.

It wasn't personal. Not for Thana, anyway. The contract had sealed Eken's fate. But it *was* personal for their employer, whose daughter the drum chief had dishonored—one among many, if the rumors were true. If Eken had been anyone but a drum chief, their employer would've approached the Circle for justice. But, although a drum chief wasn't technically above the law, going the traditional route would've allowed Eken to turn the trial into a public spectacle and bring shame upon the girl's whole family, while incurring little more than a small fine himself. The girl had suffered enough already.

Instead, a network of sympathetic ears had brought their employer to Kaseem, the broker of so many bloody deals, who in turn selected Amastan out of all the cousins. Only Amastan had previously demonstrated the precision and subtlety necessary to kill a drum chief. While the family's contracts were now sanctioned—if unofficially—by the Circle, they'd still be exiled or even executed if they were caught killing one of the Circle's own. Drum chiefs were fickle like that. Hence: months spent carefully assembling the pieces of their plan until each was exactly where it needed to be and nothing could go wrong.

Thana averted her gaze as she served the guests, only

occasionally sneaking a glance to check Amastan's progress. As she circled the room, she picked out other drum chiefs, their wraps rich and vibrant, their fingers glittering with rings. Ghadid had twelve drum chiefs for its twelve neighborhoods. Half of them were here tonight.

But one was still missing. The night was no longer new and Drum Chief Eken had yet to make an appearance at his own party. Where was he?

A sudden quiet settled on one corner of the room and oozed outward like spilled oil. Heads tracked its spread. A moment later, the crowd near Thana parted and two men passed by, one wearing a wine-red wrap and the other, bone white. The first was broad-shouldered but stout. His extravagant wrap hid most of his peculiar shape, its embroidery and hem of tiny bells pulling the gaze away from a bulging paunch. His equally lush tagel concealed his entire face but for a thin swath of dark brown skin around a pair of even darker eyes.

Thana had worked in his household for three weeks already. She would've known Drum Chief Eken's wide-legged stride and shape anywhere. The other man, though, was a mystery. White was inappropriate for a celebration and Thana doubted he was in mourning. Everything about him yelled *foreigner*, from his loosely wrapped tagel, to his lighter, almost golden eyes and sand-pale skin. He ignored the greetings flung his way as the drum chief led him through the room, all the while trying to engage Eken himself.

Mutters nipped their heels but sputtered out when Drum Chief Eken signaled for the party to continue. The conversations started and stopped and started again, like a tired mule failing to pull its load. Thana caught snatches of worry and confusion as she resumed circling the room.

"—audacity to be seen in public with—"

"—was always saying Eken's a shards-cursed imperialist—"

"—of the Empire doing here?"

Thana kept her expression blank even as worry tightened her chest. Rumors had circulated in the few days about the Empress's man who had arrived along with the year's first caravan. Who was he? And why had he come all this way from Na Tay Khet to their city on the edge of the Wastes?

Now he was here, at Eken's party, in the company of the drum chief himself. The implications were unsettling, but they had nothing to do with her contract. Thana wouldn't let his presence distract her.

"It's true, then."

The voice came from beside her. Thana smoothed over her jerk of surprise with a smile and offered the speaker a glass from her tray. A tall man stood at her elbow, thin but strong like a palm, his dark red tagel almost as loose as the foreigner's. His eyes, though, were as dark as midnight. As he studied Thana, she realized he'd spoken to her. He raised his hand, refusing the wine.

"Sa?" prompted Thana.

The man turned his gaze back to Eken and folded his arms. "The fool has finally arrived."

As much as she might want to, Thana couldn't respond. Legally, the fool was her master and agreeing with the man could see her whipped. So she kept silent and moved away to fill an empty glass. When she glanced back, the tall man was gone.

Meanwhile, Eken had shed the man in white and joined his wife. Amastan greeted the drum chief and pressed his closed fist to his chest. Eken mirrored the gesture, then laughed at something Amastan said, his whole body heaving with the motion.

Keeping one eye on their exchange, Thana weaved

through the crowd. She handed out glasses of wine and topped off empty ones as she went, smiling blandly at each passing thanks. Soon, her tray was half-empty. She paused long enough to rearrange the glasses.

Amastan was explaining the history of glasswork to Eken as Thana approached. She twisted the top of one of her rings beneath the tray, then offered her tray to the drum chief. Fully engrossed in Amastan's words, Eken reached for a glass. Thana turned the fuller side toward him and, as she brought her hand back, tipped her ring over the glass that'd soon be nearest him. Fine white powder fluttered into the date wine, dissolving instantly.

With the smallest metallic *clink*, barely audible even to Thana, the ring's cap settled back into place. Thana gave the drum chief her blandest smile, but he took the poisoned glass without even a glance her way. Then she continued on, offering wine to the next guest. She didn't dare linger to see if the mark drank the poison. That was Amastan's job.

Thana glided across the room, her thin smile belying none of the thrumming nerves beneath. This may have been her third contract with Amastan, but it was by far her most important. No one was beyond the family's reach, but killing a drum chief wouldn't come without consequences if they screwed up. Over two decades ago, her mother had killed a drum chief and almost ended the family. But her mother hadn't been under contract and they were. As long as she and Amastan stayed within the confines of the contract, everything would be fine. They'd be fine.

Thana welcomed the nerves. They were a part of the work. *That's what keeps you alive,* her mother had said time and time again. Nerves and anxiety were encouraged. It was the calm you had to be afraid of. Complacency got you killed.

The nerves were well-earned: in the next few moments, all their work would come to fruition. Thana had spent months living among the slaves, while Amastan had spent that time gathering facts and rumors. In the next few moments, they'd either become legends in her family's history or cautionary tales of failure.

Despite the tension of the moment, she couldn't help but feel a spark of jealousy. If they succeeded—and they would, they had to—all the credit would go to Amastan. This was his contract, after all, even if she'd put in half the work. More, if she was being honest with herself, since she'd been the one playing a slave. Amastan would be the one remembered for killing a drum chief, not her. And he didn't even want the prestige.

Thana took a breath and pushed away her jealousy. In its absence, the nerves came roaring back. It was out of her hands now. She had to trust they'd chosen the right kind of poison, that Amastan had calculated the correct dose, that she'd ground it fine enough, that the mark had drank all of it, that the timing had been right, that no one had seen, that Amastan kept their mark engaged, that—

The storm broke, rain pounding against the roof and drowning out the crowd, the air suddenly laden with it. For a moment, Thana couldn't hear anything but the rush of rain. That moment soon passed, but the din worsened as people shouted to be heard above the roar. Slaves rushed from window to window, closing the shutters before the spray could dampen the drum chief's guests. As each window was closed, the storm was further muffled, until its rage was only a distant scream.

Then the shouting started.

Thana turned, her face a mask of surprise as she fought a surge of panic. *We've been found out, someone noticed the ring, the chief can taste poison, it was the wrong poison, Amastan slipped up—*

Drum Chief Eken clutched at his own throat, his eyes

so wide that the whites showed all the way across the room. His tagel had been yanked down and his lips were moving, but Thana couldn't hear him over the crowd. Amastan waved one of the drum chief's wives over. No one else was responding to the crisis; the other slaves stood frozen in place, confusion and terror on their uncovered faces. Past the growing chaos, the man in white leaned against a wall, eyebrows furrowed as if this were a mere annoyance.

Froth spilled from the mark's lips. Thana's panic spiked, became paralysis. It wasn't supposed to happen this fast. The mark was supposed to survive the evening, only to complain about stomach pains and die later that night. Even to the healers, it would've seemed as if he'd eaten spoiled meat. The contract required a quiet, inconspicuous death. But this—*what was this?*

Whatever it was, she wouldn't let it ruin their contract. Thana shoved her tray into the hands of another slave and all but dropped the pitcher on a table as she rushed to Amastan's side. Now was not the time to disappear. No one would notice the slaves who rushed to help, but they'd notice any who ran away. She couldn't risk breaking her cover, not when the contract wasn't done.

The mark's wife helped Amastan guide him out of the room. Thana ducked under Eken's other arm, spreading out his bulky weight and using her body to shield his features from the wall of staring guests. Even if the mark was dying, it was still disrespectful to let so many see his bare face, most of whom belonged to a lower class.

Once they were out of sight and in the hallway, the wife pulled over a chair and they guided the drum chief into it. He slumped, his shoulders heaving with each pained breath. He wheezed and hacked as he fought for air and he kept shaking his head like a stunned dog.

His wife turned on Amastan. "What in G-d's name happened?"

"I don't know, ma." Amastan echoed her worry. "One minute he was fine, the next—" He waved at Eken.

A second woman joined them, the gold chain at her waist marking her as Eken's senior wife. She went straight to her husband, her fingers finding first his wrist, then his neck. She tilted his head back and peered into his eyes before prying open his mouth and staring down his throat. She did all of this in the same perfunctory manner as an Azali examining his camel.

She stepped back, shaking her head. "He's having an acute reaction to something he ate. Girl"—she snapped her fingers at Thana, who stiffened—"did you see him take any nuts of any kind?"

Thana kept her gaze averted but shook her head. "No, ma. Just the date wine that was served to every guest."

"Then there must have been some pit in the wine." The senior wife pinched the bridge of her nose, irritated. "The fool should've known better. The cores of some fruits make him very ill. Quick, girl—fetch a healer. We have little time."

"Yes, ma."

As Thana left the room, she made a circle with her thumb and forefinger on her hand nearest Amastan. He grunted and said something, but the noise from the crowd was too loud. She could only hope he'd seen her signal and knew to look for her coded note outside the slaves' quarters later. They hadn't been exposed yet, but the situation was getting away from them.

Thana grappled with what had happened as she slipped outside and down a side street, running through the pouring rain for the nearest healer. The possibility of dragging her feet crossed her mind, but it was just as quickly dismissed: if Eken died because she was too slow, all the blame would fall on her. No, their original plan was shattered. But Thana was still a slave in the drum chief's household for a few more days. There was still a chance they could salvage this contract. Still a chance *she* could fix things.

When Thana returned with a healer, three of Eken's wives waited outside his room. They let the healer through, but one of the wives blocked Thana from following. Thana caught only a glimpse of the senior wife and Eken inside, still alive. She retreated to the slaves' quarters and wrote Amastan the promised note. Then she scrubbed the floor—and planned.

Only one course of action remained. They'd never get those months of preparation back, but Thana was still here, a part of the drum chief's household. Just because the poison would be cleaned from his body didn't mean he couldn't still die quietly tonight. If anything, it'd be less suspicious than before. Eken was old and the reaction had weakened him. It wouldn't be surprising if his heart gave out. Thana just had to make sure that it did.

It'd be risky, acting on her own. For generations, assassins in her family had traditionally worked in pairs. When a murderer had caught several of her cousins alone and unawares, that tradition had become a rule. Of course, her mother had been known to work on her own, but Tamella was a legend. Even forced into retirement, her name was still a whispered warning. Someday, Thana would reach the same level of notoriety.

But aspiration was one thing; action was another. Thana couldn't wait for Amastan. She had to act tonight. If her mother could get away with working a contract alone, than so could she.

While the decision set part of her at ease, it set the rest of her on edge. She was on her own. If she failed, all of Ghadid would learn her name and she'd be hunted. Her family and cousins were tolerated as a necessary evil, a vanguard against corruption and injustice, but only if Ghadid could pretend they didn't exist. G-d did not condone murder, even when it was for the greater good.

With only a few hours left to act, Thana got to work.